MIRRORWORLD

MIRRORWORLD

JEREMY ROBINSON

Thomas Dunne Books   St. Martin's Press   ≋   New York

THOMAS DUNNE BOOKS.
An imprint of St. Martin's Press.

MIRRORWORLD. Copyright © 2015 by Jeremy Robinson. All rights reserved.
Printed in the United States of America. For information, address
St. Martin's Press, 175 Fifth Avenue, New York, N.Y. 10010.

www.thomasdunnebooks.com
www.stmartins.com

The Library of Congress Cataloging-in-Publication Data
is available upon request.

ISBN 978-1-250-05410-4 (hardcover)
ISBN 978-1-4668-5705-6 (e-book)

St. Martin's Press books may be purchased for educational, business, or
promotional use. For information on bulk purchases, please contact the
Macmillan Corporate and Premium Sales Department at 1-800-221-7945,
extension 5442, or write to specialmarkets@macmillan.com.

First Edition: April 2015

10 9 8 7 6 5 4 3 2 1

For all you readers who have taken the time to write and post a review for one of my books. Every one helps, and I truly appreciate the effort!

ACKNOWLEDGMENTS

With every book, I find writing acknowledgments more difficult. Not because I have no one to thank. Nothing could be further from the truth. It's that, every year, I have the exact same group of people to thank. In a constantly shifting industry, I've been blessed to work with the same core team for the past eight years. But since my job is ultimately to entertain, I fear my repeating thanks to them is becoming redundant for any readers taking the time to peruse these acknowledgments. That said, these are the people who help make my books shine, and like my marriage, which is twenty years strong this year, each new year hones the relationships and improves the end result. So if the following acknowledgments sound familiar to long-term fans, know that these are the people who helped make all these crazy books possible.

Scott Miller at Trident Media Group, my agent and defender, who discovered my first self-published book ten years ago, we're still just getting started. Peter Wolverton, my editor at Thomas Dunne Books, your honest edits and keen sense of story continue to act as this writer's forge, refining my stories into something better. Mary Willems, it's always a delight to work with you, and the critiques you provided for *MirrorWorld* were spot on and supremely helpful. Also always, thanks to Rafal Gibek and the production team at Thomas Dunne Books for copy edits and critique that make me look like a better writer than I am. Once again, I must thank the art department at Thomas Dunne Books, for supporting this author's efforts to illustrate and design his own cover. It's a rare treat. Kane Gilmour, editor of my solo projects and sometimes coauthor, thanks for your unwavering support, time, and energy. And as always, thanks to Roger Brodeur for awesome proofreading. Your attention to detail helps balance my blindness to typos.

Just as my publishing family has remained dedicated, I must also thank my real family, whose unwavering support and excitement about all my projects makes all of this even more fun. My children, Aquila, Solomon, and Norah, your creative energy reminds me of my own childhood and inspires me to keep my imagination young and flexible. And Hilaree, seriously, by the time our coauthored hardcover (*The Distance*) comes out next fall, we'll have been married twenty years! Not only have you supported me all that time, you are now launching your own creative career as an author, poet, and artist (on top of homeschooling All. Three. Kids.) I couldn't be more proud of you, and I look forward to watching your creative path evolve.

MIRRORWORLD

PROLOGUE

Perfect.

That's how Bob Alford, vacationing widower-retiree, described his day by the pool, watching the scantily clad women, drinking mai tais, and admiring the sun's lazy track through the sky. *Perfect.* Right up until the moment a man of equal age and better physical shape slapped against the concrete beside Alford's lounge chair. The sharp, wet snap of a body hitting the solid ground opened Alford's eyes, hidden behind a pair of boxy fit-over sunglasses. Annoyed by the interruption, he glanced at the man, whose wetness suggested he'd just come from the pool.

He closed his eyes again, but the image began to resolve like a photo in a darkroom displayed on the inside of his eyelids. The man wasn't dressed for the pool. He was dressed for dinner. And the wetness on the pavement . . . was red. Dark red.

His eyes snapped open just as the first screams rang out. He turned toward the man again, this time noting that he looked flatter than he should, and broken. A pool of blood had formed around him. Definitely dead.

Knowing the man had not simply tripped, Alford turned his eyes up. He didn't expect to see anything other than empty balconies. Maybe a few people looking down.

But there was something there. Something moving.

Oh my God—something falling. *Someone!* A woman plummeted from high above, her dinner dress fluttering like a flag caught by a stiff wind. As Alford's horrified cry joined the chorus, the body sailed past, plunging into the pool. There was a moment of collective stunned silence as the poolside vacationers seemed to be waiting for the woman to surface. Even the lifeguard's mind had shut down. Alford was the first to snap free from the strange trance.

He ran to the edge, feeling momentary hope that the chlorine-scented pool could have saved the woman from the same fate as the man, but the water was already turning red.

While the pool emptied of screaming youth, Alford dove straight in. The water tore his sunglasses away, and the sudden crisp coolness stung his recently burnt skin like lit fireworks, but he didn't give his discomfort a second thought as his body arced down through the water to the unconscious, maybe dead woman. He wrapped an arm around her chest, shoved off the bottom, and rose up to find a lifeguard reaching down. While Alford fought against creaking joints to lift himself over the pool's edge, the lifeguard hoisted the woman onto the concrete and went to work, performing rapid CPR.

Exhausted by fear and effort, Alford gasped for breath while he stood over the lifeguard. People all around began snapping photos and tapping out messages on their phones. Then, hope blossomed. The woman breathed, deeply. Just once. With her final exhalation, she said, "The darkness came for us," and then departed the world, lying in a puddle of water, ten feet away from the man lying in his own blood.

LONDON, ENGLAND

"What do you think?" Kelly Allenby said, striking a pose while wearing a gaudy, feathery cap. It barely held her wild salt-and-pepper hair down, and in the small shop's elegant surroundings, it looked as ridiculous as she hoped it would. "Am I posh?"

"Fit for a royal wedding, you are," her husband, Hugh, replied, failing miserably at matching his wife's natural British accent.

She swatted his arm. "Bollocks, they won't let me within a block of the palace. And, please, no more accent."

"Is it really that bad?"

She placed the hat back on the mannequin's head. "I just like your natural accent better."

"That's right," Hugh said, reverting back to his natural Hebrew accent, exaggerating the rough *h* sound. "Hhhow do you like my Hhhebrew?" Hugh was born and raised by Jewish parents who immigrated to the United States. His Hebrew accent emerged when surrounded by family, but otherwise he had a bland American accent, which to an American meant he had no telltale accent at all.

"Hhhilarious," she replied, patting his face. She glanced at the shopkeeper and saw he was far from enthused by their antics. When they'd entered the shop, he'd greeted them kindly, no doubt sensing a sale. But it quickly became clear they were simply amused by his wares. "Time to go."

She took Hugh by the arm and dragged him to the door.

"But I still need to try on the hat," he said.

"You need to buy me lunch."

The bell above the door chimed as Hugh opened it and poured on his horrible British accent. "What'll it be then, love? Jellied eels, cockles in vinegar, or some soggy tripe?"

Allenby laughed hard, but the sound of her voice was cut short. At once, the pair fell to their knees. A fear unlike anything Allenby had ever felt suddenly twisted inside her gut. Something was behind her!

Hugh took her hand. "Kel, what—"

His eyes suddenly went wide. She watched the hairs on his neck stand straight like the most disciplined beefeater. He felt it, too.

And then he felt it more.

With a scream of pure fright, Hugh spun around. He scrambled away from something unseen, but felt. He climbed to his feet, screaming, out of his mind, and then in a flash of unforgiving violence, he was removed from his body. He had run into the busy street, directly into the path of one of London's hallmark double-decker buses. The swift-moving, seven-ton vehicle struck him hard and carried him from view.

While the bus's brakes squealed and its occupants shouted, Allenby sprung to her feet, pursued by something unseen, her need to race to her husband's aid replaced by the uncontrollable urge to run in another direction. As she scrambled forward, she failed to hear the shop bell ring behind her. Oblivious to the still-moving traffic in the lanes beyond the bus, Allenby charged ahead, destined to meet the same fate as her beloved.

Unlike Hugh, she never made it into the traffic. The shopkeeper had seen everything, alerted by a sudden and fleeting spike of fear. He didn't react in time to save Hugh, but he tackled Allenby to the pavement, holding her in place for five minutes while she screamed in unhinged terror. And then, all at once, the strange mania wore off. She wept for her husband, but only for a moment. Clarity slammed into her with a gasp and she took out her phone, scrolling through her contacts with a shaking hand.

NORTHWOOD, NEW HAMPSHIRE

The creak of the staircase sounded like the high-pitched whir of a dentist's drill, making Maya Shiloh cringe. It wasn't because she feared the dentist or that the sound would wake her son, it was because the creak came from three steps above and behind her.

She spun around with a gasp. The stairs were empty.

She paused halfway down the old wooden steps as a shiver ran through her body. Her arms shook, the nervous energy working its way out through her fingers. She clenched her fists. Reined in control. She'd never been one to scare easily, but the dream that had woken her . . .

Images of her drowning son, just out of reach, flashed back into her mind. She squeezed her eyes shut and calmed herself with a deep breath. She'd been crying when she woke. Sobbing. The tears had faded when she realized it had been a nightmare, though the white, salty streaks crisscrossing her cheeks remained.

She'd checked on Simon immediately. He slept soundly, his stuffed triceratops clutched in his arms. His eight-year-old chest rose and fell with each gentle breath. This was his last night in this house, at least for a while. They'd already moved into their furnished apartment across town, but he'd requested one last night, nearly in tears. How could she say "no"? Seeing him sound asleep and peaceful had calmed her, but a sense of dread, that time was short, increased with each downward step.

There were three clocks in the house: an antique grandfather clock in the foyer, six steps below her; a designer clock hung in the kitchen, the numbers centered above '50s-style bathing-suit-clad women; and a cheap plastic number in her husband's rarely used office. Their out-of-sync ticking filled the home with a sense of haste.

She descended into the foyer, opened the grandfather clock, and caught its pendulum, stopping its operation. She glanced through the living room to her husband's office, where the second offender ticked away. As was often the case, her husband wasn't home. Working late. Again. She didn't mind. They'd soon be together more often, and his work was important. But she longed for his strong, calming presence. He would be able to unravel the fear twisting around her.

So can wine, she thought.

Ignoring the office clock, which she wouldn't be able to hear from the kitchen, she entered the dining room and skirted the table, feeling her way through the dark. As her fingers slid over the top of the hutch's faux weathered surface, goose bumps sprang to life on her arms. She couldn't see anything, but the fine hairs standing on end tickled her skin.

She hadn't heard or seen anything other than the kitchen's ticking clock, but she sensed something . . . horrible. *Someone is in the room,* she thought, and said, "Hello?" She immediately felt foolish. If a malicious burglar lay in wait, he wouldn't reply.

After three silent steps back, she slid her hand across the canvas-textured wallpaper and stopped when she found the round plastic dimmer switch. She twisted the small knob clockwise until it stopped. It clicked when she pushed it in.

The eight-bulb chandelier hanging over the table, seven if you didn't count the blown bulb, illuminated the room with a suddenness that made Maya squint. She fought against closing her eyes, scouring the room for danger that did not exist. The only aberration in the room was the stacks of empty moving boxes, waiting to be filled and moved to the new apartment.

A warm breeze, like breath, on the nape of her neck spun her around. She screamed and swung out with hooked fingers, some primal part of her rising to the surface to defend the modern woman.

But she was alone. Still.

"Dammit." She stood for a moment, hands on the hutch. Her heart beat hard in her chest, the flow of blood through her body carrying unnecessary and uncomfortable adrenaline. Her stomach muscles quivered.

She searched the room again, confirming her paranoia.

Maya continued toward the kitchen, peeking through the doorway before entering. The sensation of being followed chewed at the base of her skull, commanding her to turn around. The room stood empty. She had no doubt, though her instincts disagreed.

She flicked on the kitchen light, revealing nothing more horrifying than a collection of dirty dishes. While her husband liked things neat and tidy, she let messes pile up before giving them any attention.

Twelve conservatively dressed bathing beauties looked down at her from the ticking designer clock. The gentle click of each passing second felt like a hammer striking an anvil. She looked at the clock and then toward the cupboard above the stove, where she kept the wine.

Wine first, she thought, *then the clock*.

The Pinot Noir, about the only wine she had a marginal palate for, opened with a loud pop. The tangy scent made her nose scrunch. She wasn't a fan of how wine tasted. She rated the various types by degrees of nasty. Her interest in the drink had nothing to do with taste or the rustic flavor of oak, hints of boysenberry, or whatever bullshit they put on the label. It simply put her to sleep. Fast. And that was exactly what she needed.

Failing to find a clean glass, she opted for a mug. Filled it to the top. She stared down at the chipped pottery. A gift from her husband. Her reflection in the deep purple liquid looked distorted and ugly, despite her bright blue eyes, high cheekbones, and lips framed by dimples. As a strong sense of fear crept back into her gut, she lifted the mug to her lips, sneering at the flavor the way her son did with cold medicine. Squeezing her cheeks together to prevent the bitter liquid from striking the sides of her tongue, she swallowed a mouthful. Then another. After taking a deep breath, she downed half the mug.

It was all she could handle. She shook her head in disgust, put the mug down, and turned to the clock.

Tick, tick, tick.

As the alcohol warmed her stomach, she felt her limbs relax.

"Your turn," she said to the clock.

She dragged her black rocking chair beneath the clock, which was mounted just beyond her short reach. Simon would be taller than her in the next year or two. By the time he was a teen, he would tower over her. Unsteady on her tiptoes, she caught the clock and lifted it away from the wall. Back on her heels, she turned the clock around, unclipped the plastic battery case, and removed a single AA battery.

"There." She reached up, lifting the clock back to its high perch.

A shiver ran through her legs, traveled through her abdomen, and settled in her chest. She gasped for breath as her skin went cold and goose bumps returned. To her arms. Her legs. Her long, wavy black hair shifted as the follicles tensed. With adrenaline rushing alcohol through her veins, she saw movement in the clock's glass front. Someone *was* in the house! Her eyes flicked toward the dark shape as the rest of her body reacted with panic.

She spun around to face the intruder, but the rocking chair, wine, and her own limbs conspired against her. With a shout, she fell. The glass clock front shattered on the hard tile floor, a kaleidoscope of curved shards spreading out around her.

Footsteps to the right. From the dining room.

Her throat clasped shut. Each breath came as a gasp.

Glass crunched under the intruder's feet. Her mind shouted at her, *Defend yourself! Defend your son!* Images filled her mind. Her drowning son. Her murdered son.

She moved quickly, half aware, lost in a frantic mental slideshow displaying images of Simon's death. Fear consumed her, deforming her perception of the world around her, and she fought against it and her attacker with blind rage. She opened her eyes, just once, and saw four angry red eyes staring back. The pitch of her screaming grew painful to her own ears, but she kept attacking, fighting for her life.

For her son's life.

A vague awareness of being struck began her journey back to lucidity. She felt claws scratching at her, pulling at her cheeks. She fought against the attacker, striking again and again, too afraid of those eyes to look again. The sound of her screaming voice drowned out the high-pitched shriek of the monster attacking her, the *thing* she'd seen in the clock's reflection.

It wasn't until her enemy, now beneath her, stopped struggling that she dared to look at it. What she saw made no sense—a nightmare invading reality.

She saw her son, lying beneath her, still drowning, but this time in blood. His own. It seeped from a number of wounds covering his body. His hand, resting against her cheek, fell away. His eyes shifted up, widened, and then changed. The energy behind them faded.

He was dead.

Reality collided with her, knocking her back. She slammed into the fridge. Sharp pain drew her eyes to her hand. A long shard of glass, covered in blood, poked her palm. She loosened her grip and glanced from the clear triangular dagger to her son's punctured body.

The phone rang. It rang and rang and rang, playing backup to her anguished screams.

Her insides quivered, fear returning, gently molding her actions. She lifted the glass still in her hand. Placed it against her wrist. And pulled.

Somewhere, a door slammed open. A voice shouted her name. And then, it too joined the pained chorus of despair and parental loss.

1.

I want to tell you a joke. The punch line might elude me for a time, but we'll get there. I tend to ramble. Details make humor more robust, I think, though some would prefer I skip right to the end. Too bad for them; I don't give a fuck.

A guy and a girl walk into a bar. He's a philistine. The build suggests ex–football player. The high-and-tight haircut screams military, but the cocksure way he carries himself tells me he was too chickenshit to handle war and is boosting his ego by intimidating the folks of this small town.

I don't know the name of the town. It was dark when I strolled past the WELCOME TO sign. The bar's sign was well lit, though, THE HUNGRY HORSE. I'm not sure if that's some kind of reference to something. Maybe there are a lot of horses in the fields around town. I don't know. Like I said, it was dark. Maybe the bar's owner just likes horses? I'm not sure if I do. Can't remember if I've ever been on one.

Can't remember much beyond an hour ago, which should concern me, but it doesn't.

I think I'll remember the girl hanging on the philistine's arm, though. Just a quick glance is enough to etch the curves of her body in the permanent record of my short memory. It's not that she's beautiful. She's caked in so much makeup that her true self, and worth, are impossible to see. Anyone with that much to hide is either the victim of unfortunate parentage or concealing their guilty conscience.

I never wear makeup. At least, I don't think I would.

The woman's voluptuousness is as artificial as her face, and thrice-dyed hair. Something tight hugs her waist. Probably her thighs, too. She's a too-full sausage, ready to burst. And while her breasts are prodigious, they're held aloft by an underwire bra capable of holding a child. Nothing about her is honest, except for her eyes—desperate and pleading for attention.

I don't give it to her.

Anyone who does is a fool.

And there is a fool in every bar.

The man sitting across the room from me, on the far side of the worn pool table, beneath a neon-pink Budweiser sign and a mounted largemouth bass, watches the giggly entrance with wide-eyed fascination. She might as well be a peacock, strutting about, flashing her wares, entrancing the susceptible. That's a poor metaphor. She's not a male peacock, and she's not simply entrancing.

She's luring. Like an anglerfish, she dangles her quick meal, summoning her prey. Much better.

The fool hasn't looked away yet. He's hooked. And he's been spotted. While the bait takes a barstool, the philistine glares at the fool until noticed. Then he grins, whispers to the woman, and heads for the fool, who is now staring down into his amber drink, wishing he wasn't himself, or perhaps that he was just someone stronger.

The philistine stands above the fool, reading from a script everyone knows. "You looking at my girl?"

The fool shakes his head and offers a polite, "No, sir."

The big man chuckles. He knows how easy this is going to be. He glances back at the woman, making sure she's watching. And smiling. This is for her as much as him. Bruised egos seeking validation through the pain of idiots.

"You don't think she's worth looking at?" The philistine has him trapped now. To say she isn't worth looking at is to call her ugly, but the opposite confirms that he *was* looking, and the lie will be enough.

The establishment is mostly empty. There's the tender behind the bar, who just looks annoyed by the proceedings. No doubt, he's seen this charade before and knows how it ends. He confirms this by saying, "Charley. Outside, please."

Then there is the man sitting at the bar. He's at least ten years my senior. Maybe fifty or an early gray late forties. Like me, he's no fool, not even now that the target has been chosen. He just sips his beer, ignoring, which is ironic because out of everyone here, it's his job to step in. The bulge beneath the man's sport coat reveals a holstered gun. While a lot of people in this neck of the woods—New Hampshire—might carry weapons, the piece strapped to his ankle, which I can see clear as day, thanks to his too-short pants, says he's a cop. Off-duty but, still, an officer of the law.

And then there is the fool, who is damn near to weeping. He's scrawny and physically weak but has nice clothes, shiny shoes, and a laptop bag. He probably makes four times as much money as the philistine, has a 401(k); stock options, and a hedge fund, details that fuel the philistine's insecure rage. The fool's just passing through. On his way to Boston. Or New York. Maybe visiting family. Just happened to stop for a drink, like me.

Well, not exactly like me. I'm here because I had nowhere else to go and hoped a little alcohol might help my lost memory return. I've got fifty dollars in my pocket. No ID. No keys. No clue about who I am other than the clothes I'm wearing and a name that isn't a name.

The fool says nothing. It's the first right thing he's done since the bimbo opened the door. But it's too little too late.

"Answer me, or I swear to God, I will—"

"She's worth looking at," the fool says, biting hard on the hook, believing incorrectly that insulting the woman would be worse than admiring her body, which is now bouncing like an inflatable fun house full of sugar-doped kids. She's getting off on this, smiling broadly, nearly clapping.

The cop does nothing. The bar man sighs.

The philistine, lost in anger, has nothing more to say. He lifts the fool by his expensive, salmon-colored shirt, cocks back his fist, and grins. The fight—if you can call it that—will be over in one punch.

Except, it won't be.

The philistine's fist never reaches the fool's face. It finds my hand instead. Without fully realizing it, I've crossed the room. Part of me feels confused, like I'm not sure how my proximity to the philistine changed, but the rest of me understands that everything about this situation is wrong. And that is something I cannot abide.

The punch stings my hand, but the pain only serves to focus me. And in that moment of clarity, I realize I've picked up a pool stick, which I swing with gusto. I'm no fool. Nor do I believe in a fair fight.

The pool stick breaks over the man's broad back, pitching him forward with an embarrassingly loud, high-pitched shout. Despite the man's penchant for drama on the scale of an injury-faking soccer player, he's far from out of the fight. I have about a second before he swings one of his meaty arms at me. He'll miss, but the time it takes me to dodge the blow will allow him to recover, and then this could drag on. None of that happens, of course. The cue ball is now in my right hand. I drive it into the man's forehead. He crumples to the floor, upturning the fool's table as he descends. Beer and peanuts mix with the blood flowing from his forehead.

The fool looks up at me with the same wide-eyed admiration he'd given the bimbo, who, I might add, is no longer bouncing or giggling. Her barbarian king has been dethroned by a transient with a two-week beard, messy hair, and a worn leather jacket.

"Th-thank you," the fool says.

I respond to his gratitude by slapping him hard across the face. The resounding clap of his clean-shaven skin sounds like a snapping carrot. I lean in close while the man rubs his reddening cheek, tears in his eyes. "It is better to keep your mouth closed and let people think you are a fool than to open it and remove all doubt."

The man's brow furrows. "Mark Twain?"

I have no idea whom I'm quoting, but I don't let him know that. I stand up and turn away.

The police officer has spun around in his chair, watching the scene with indifference. I head back to my table, chug what's left of my beer, and walk toward the bar with my empty glass.

I stop in front of the woman, a condescending eyebrow lifted. My eyes tell her that it is she who is ultimately responsible for this mess. She brought the trap. She set the bait. Without her, the philistine would be home watching television. The fool would be finishing his drink and on his way. And I . . . well, I'm not sure what I'd be doing beyond sitting alone at a table.

She gets the message, loud and clear, and responds with vehemence, reading from the same script the philistine had been reciting since high school. "Fuck you, pri—"

Her words are silenced by the sound of breaking glass. She falls to the floor, wrapped around her stool, as unconscious as her boyfriend, or whatever he is. As I put the remnants of my beer stein on the bar, the officer takes action. Apparently, striking a woman is an actionable offense, whereas assaulting a philistine or fool is acceptable behavior.

Before the gun is fully raised, I clasp my hand atop it, twist, and free it from the officer's grasp. He's had a few drinks but is still pretty quick. Just not quick enough. He tries to lift his foot, going for the weapon on his ankle, but I've already stepped on his shoe.

I turn the gun around on him.

He stops moving but stands his ground, hiding his fear. I respect that, but his inaction offends me. I motion to the philistine and then to the woman. "You should have stopped them."

"I couldn't," the officer says.

"You had two guns." The point can't be argued.

"You don't know who he is."

"I know exactly who he is," I say, speaking of his character rather than his name, which confuses the policeman. "You're a shame to your profession." I spin the gun around in my hand, prepared to coldcock the man and be on my way. But a roar interrupts.

The philistine is awake.

I turn toward the mountain of a man, his arms spread wide, re-uniting with Violence, his long-lost lover. His face is covered in blood. Peanuts cling to the viscous red fluid. He looks like something I can't quite remember.

Dodging the attack is easy enough. A quick duck and sidestep is all it takes. The man careens into the bar, but it's not enough. I consider the weapon in my hand but decide against it. The man deserves a lesson, not execution. But a harsh lesson. I tuck the gun into my jeans as he turns around, coming at me again.

I meet his rush with a quick jab to his face. He's stunned by the force of it, but also because he never saw it coming. As he staggers back, I sweep his legs, knocking him onto his back. Before he can recover, I drop to one knee beside him and lift his arm.

"Don't!" the officer shouts. He's got his small ankle revolver leveled at my chest.

"He needs to learn," I tell him, then slam the philistine's arm down on my leg, snapping it like a branch.

The big man screams anew, his high-pitched wail waking the unconscious woman, who begins to weep.

"Get up!" the officer shouts.

I raise my hands and obey. "You could have prevented this."

The bartender is on the phone. No doubt with the police.

"Turn around! Hands on the wall!"

I obey.

"What's your name?" the officer asks.

This is a tough question, mostly because I don't know the an-swer. I have a name. I'm as sure of that as I am that at one point in my past, I had a mother and a father. I can't remember them either, but the fact that I exist is biological evidence that a man and woman, at some point in the past, copulated and gave birth to a boy. I'd like to think those same people would have given me a name. "I'm Crazy."

"You're bat-shit crazy," the officer says.

I look back, over my shoulder. "With a capital *C*."

The officer inches closer. With his revolver pointed at my back, he reaches around my waist, fumbling for the gun I stole. "Don't move."

But I do. Slowly and subtly. I twist away from his reaching hand, drawing him in closer. When he's all but hugging me, I reach back with my left hand. The bartender shouts a warning, but it's too late. I twist the revolver away from my back and keep on twisting until the officer shouts in pain and releases the weapon. I spin around, draw the sidearm from my waist, and level both weapons at the police officer.

"Don't kill me," he says, hands raised.

"I don't kill people for being incompetent," I tell him.

Do I kill people at all? I wonder. I certainly have the ability. I'm fast, and strong, and know how to fight with brutal efficiency. I *could* kill him, with these guns, with my bare hands, or with a peanut from the philistine's face. When the officer had first come into the bar, he'd waited for the tender to remove the bowl before sitting down, and then he wiped the bar down with a wet wipe. The man feared peanuts. Allergic, no doubt.

But I don't want to kill him, merely educate him. I raise the revolver, aiming for the man's arm, debating the severity of his lesson. Should I wound him or simply scare him? He's already scared. But he's an officer of the law. He failed to serve and protect the fool. He didn't care about the man's fate. Didn't care about his job. Didn't care about his life.

"Eat a peanut," I tell him.

His eyes widen. "What? Why?"

"Eat a peanut, or I'll shoot you."

"N-no," he says. "You can't. I won't."

"Why not?"

"I'm allergic. I'll die."

"You have a reason to live?" I ask.

To his credit, the officer thinks on this. "My kid."

He's not sad, like a father who desperately loves his children would be. He's regretful. "You've wronged your child?"

The officer nods.

"Bullet it is," I say, my finger squeezing the trigger.

Before the round can be fired, I'm struck from behind. I fall to the bar's hardwood floor, lying beside the writhing philistine and crying bimbo, looking up. The fool stands above me, a pool stick in his hands.

I grin at the man. "Good for you."

The officer recovers his weapons and points them at me as backup storms through the door.

Turns out, the joke is on me. The philistine is the mayor's boy. The bimbo is the sheriff's daughter. And the fool . . . he's a clinical psychologist. By morning, I'm committed. And while I believe everyone in the bar needed to learn a lesson, I can't fault them for the straitjacket or the padded room. I am Crazy, after all.

2.

"Hey, Crazy."

Three of us turn around. We're sitting along the back of an old plaid couch. Red, orange, and brown stripes. Ugly as crap from a crayon-eating dog, but it's become our triple throne from which we can watch TV, which is currently showing *The Price Is Right*. No volume. All the screaming gets our lower-functioning friends riled up. And since there are twenty-three of them sitting around the room, bouncing back and forth, talking to gods or plotting the world's end, silence is a good thing. It lets us hear them coming. But really, I just don't want to get them in trouble or hurt them. After all, they don't know what they're doing. They're crazy.

Like me.

Like everyone in this place. Not counting Chubs, the other orderlies, doctors, nurses, guards, and janitorial staff, though some of them are suspect.

"Which one of us are you referring to, Chubs?" Shotgun Jones asks the orderly, whom we have deemed Chubs on account of his prodigious love handles. Shotgun is Chubs's antithesis, a skinny man with equally thin glasses and hair.

"The only one of you who goes by Crazy," Chubs says.

Seymour, the craziest of us, claps his hands frantically. "Crazy to the principal's office! Ohh, you're in trouble!"

"Actually," Chubs says, "he's got a visitor, and I needed to know you guys were going to play nice before I brought her in."

"Her!" Seymour wiggles his fingers in front of his mouth. His big teeth and wide eyes complete the illusion that the man is an oversized chipmunk.

"Seymour," I say. He stops. I look back to Chubs. "They'll behave. But why does she want to come in here?"

He shrugs. "Some kind of specialist. Feels comfortable around nut . . . you guys."

"Close one," I say.

Chubs smiles nervously. "I'll go get her."

When the orderly is out of earshot, Shotgun taps my shoulder. "You ever get in trouble for . . . you know?"

"Breaking his finger?"

"Crack!" Seymour says a little too loudly, acting out breaking a branch over his knee. Some of our fellow "nutjobs"—the word Chubs is forbidden from saying—look up but don't move from their positions around the room.

I shake my head. "No one ever said anything. He's been a perfect gentleman since." I slide down from the couch. "I'm going to take a walk. Let me know if she wins the dinette set."

The large space is pristine. The white floors glow with a near-magical shine. When I first arrived at the SafeHaven, one word, I wondered why they kept the floor so clean. My first theory was that they wanted to impress visiting relatives. While some people are here for doing violent things, others are committed by loved ones before they get the chance. But I realized the truth after the first fight. Just a drop of blood on the gleaming floor stands out like a stop sign in the snow. Between that, the fourteen cameras, and several sets of watching eyes, committing a violent act inside this space, while not impossible, is hard to cover up. Unless you're good at it, which, apparently, I am. Broken fingers don't bleed.

The large, barred windows draw me toward the light of day. The outer wall is covered with tall windows, allowing those of us trapped inside a view of what we're missing. I appreciate the ample sunlight, but it's really just a tease. I can't smell the rain, or the fresh-cut lawn, or anything else other than the scent of mold-tinged air-conditioning. I've considered leaving. I think I could manage it. But if this is where the law and society say I need to be, who am I to argue? I certainly don't have anywhere else to go.

At least the people here understand me . . . not that they understand much of anything. But they accept me as one of them, even though I know, at my core, that I don't belong here. Of course, most everyone here, save for Seymour, thinks the world would be better with them flailing through it.

The view today is mostly primary and secondary colors. Blue sky. Green grass and trees. White clouds. Black pavement—they redid it a week ago. Couldn't even smell that. Looking down at the parking lot, I see far fewer cars than usual. It looks like half the regular staff are missing. Also interesting is an orange car. *That's new*, I think. I can't tell the make or model, but it sticks out among the various shades of gray preferred by SafeHaven's staff.

"See anything interesting?" The voice is feminine. Quiet. My visitor has arrived.

"Your car," I say. "I like the color." I turn around. My visitor is attractive. Blond hair, tied back tight. High eyebrows that imply a good nature. And a kind smile. But her outfit . . . "You look like a pumpkin."

Her smile broadens as she looks down at herself. "I do, don't I?" She lifts her arms and the sides come up, like Batman's cape, only neon. It's a poncho. A bright orange hunter's poncho.

"They wouldn't let me in if I wasn't wearing it. At least it matches the car." She lowers her arms, revealing Shotgun and Seymour standing behind her, one to a side. She senses their presence and flinches, stepping closer to me. A few eyes around the room glance up, and then turn back down.

"She's a doctor," Seymour says, his fingers twitching madly in front of his mouth. "No, a specialist!"

"Ex-girlfriend," Shotgun says with a smirk and a confident nod.

"An expert!" Seymour says. He's getting a little too excited.

"Can you give us some privacy?" I ask the pair.

"Ex-girlfriend it is!" Shotgun says, pumping an imaginary shotgun, "Chick, chick," and firing it into the air. "Boom!"

As the duo retreats back to the couch-throne, the woman turns to me again, looking a little less sure of herself.

"That's why we call him Shotgun Jones," I explain.

"Right," she says, straightening her pumpkin suit. Her smile disappears. The eyebrows descend. "Do you want to be here?"

"I want to smell the new pavement," I tell her.

A mix of confusion and disappointment contorts her pretty face. "You know I'm crazy, right?"

"With a capital *C*," she says. "I've been told. But you're not crazy."

"You know my real name?"

"Lowercase *c*."

"Oh. Then what am I?"

"I'll let your doctor explain it to you. Later. Right now, I need a very plain yes or no answer. Do you want to leave this place? Or do you want to spend the rest of your life waiting to see who replaces Drew Carey on the *Price Is Right*?"

"He's funny," I say.

"Bob was better."

"I don't really remember Bob."

"You don't remember anything past a year ago." She makes sure I'm looking in her eyes. "All but two days of your remembered life have been in this place. Before that was two days in a jail cell and an hour at a bar. Am I wrong?"

"No."

My eyes turn to the floor and then back out at the view. "Would I be leaving today?"

I see the motion of her nod in my periphery.

"Yes," I say. "I want to leave."

"First," she says. "I need proof."

"Of what?"

"Step one. What do you think of me?"

I look her up and down, appraising her. I stop on her eyes. "You're intelligent. Driven. Brave. You're also hiding something, but who isn't?"

"Is that all?"

"I'd also like to sleep with you, but you already knew that."

"What makes you say that?" she asks.

"Have you looked in a mirror? Who wouldn't want to sleep with you?"

She looks down at the bright orange poncho. "Most of me is covered."

"Your face would more than make up for any flaws beneath it, and not everything is hidden." I glance down at her chest, from which the loose poncho hangs, and am only slightly surprised to find my right hand cupping her left breast. A complete lack of fear means that I sometimes act without thought. Fear acts as a social buffer, giving most people time to contemplate their actions and the ramifications. Not only do I lack that buffer, the potential negative effects of my actions don't faze me. Only my strong moral code keeps me in check, but on occasions like this, it's all hindsight.

"Very good," she says, like I've passed a test.

I withdraw my hand and apologize, but she waves the words away like they're some kind of stink. "Step two." She reaches up and slides her fingers beneath the collar of my shirt. For a moment, I think she's going to repay the fondle with one of her own, but she takes hold of something that she shouldn't know is there. The chain slides out from under my shirt. Having it is technically against the rules, but the few times they've tried to take it, I've gone actual crazy. I don't know what it is, where it's from, or why I cling to it, but I know I can't live without it. And that I would kill to retrieve it.

The pendant at the end of the chain falls free, hanging on the metal links. It's a colorful mash-up of melted plastics formed into a crude circle.

"Are you afraid?" she asks.

"I'm resisting the urge to break your hand."

She turns the pendant around, reading the single word etched into the flat backside. "Evidence." She frowns for a moment but covers it up quickly. "Do you know what this is?"

It feels like my soul, but I know that's ridiculous, so I shake my head. "It's the craziest thing about me, so you better put it back."

She does, slipping it inside my collar and letting it drop.

"Now, step three." The vinyl of her poncho makes a shhh sound as her arm rises. Her hand emerges holding a ceramic three-inch blade. "Stab yourself."

"Why?"

She squints at me. "Are you afraid?"

"I'm not stupid, if that's what you're trying to figure out."

She looks out the window to the long driveway that ends a quarter mile away, the gates blocked from view by lush oaks. "There is an ambulance waiting at the end of the drive. They'll be here within minutes. You'll be rushed to the hospital."

"Only it won't be a hospital," I say. "Where *will* it be?"

She smiles; this time it's forced. "Won't be here."

I reach out and take the blade from her. "Run."

She looks horrified for a moment, hearing a threat where there was none intended.

"This isn't going to go over well." I look around the room.

Understanding widens her eyes. She backs away slowly, turns around, and hurries for the metal chain-link gate, which Chubs opens from the other side.

Knife in hand, I look out the window. It's a beautiful day. I bet it smells wonderful.

A scream tears my eyes away from the window. "Dollar ninety-five! Dollar ninety-five!" It's Seymour, repeating what he'd just seen on TV. Both hands flail in my direction. At my stomach. "Help! Help! Help! Dollar ninety-five."

"Chick, chick, boom!" Shotgun says, shooting his imaginary weapon straight at me, his face twisted up in horror. "Chick, chick, boom!"

As the large room explodes with activity, I look down. Two inches of the knife's blade are currently buried in my torso. *Someone's going to have to clean this floor tonight,* I think, and fall to my knees.

3.

"Do you know what you did?" the paramedic asks me, her thick British accent distracting me from the question. Her face is hidden by a surgical mask and thick glasses. An explosion of hair frames her nonface. Graying. Maybe fifty-five. Despite the accent, I hear the bewilderment in her voice and replay the question in my mind.

A full twenty seconds later, I lean up and look down. My shirt is missing, but the plastic pendant still hangs from my neck. Which is good for everyone in this ambulance. I turn my gaze lower. The knife handle sticks out of my gut like the first skyscraper built in Dubai. "I stabbed myself."

"More accurately?" she asks.

"I stabbed myself in my right kidney."

She presses on my torso with her gloved fingers, feeling all around the wound. "Actually, you missed it. Nothing but muscle and fat. Mostly muscle."

"Even better," I say.

"But why?"

"Because I wanted to leave."

"What I meant," she says, "is why did you choose to stab yourself in the kidney?"

"You mean, why did I choose to stab myself *next* to my kidney?"

"Right."

I shrug. I don't recall making the decision, but I understand the logic of my subconscious. "If I missed and struck my kidney, who cares? I have two of them. If you ever need to stab yourself, keep that in mind." I lean back. "I can't feel the wound."

"I've given you a local anesthetic so we can take care of this."

I look around the ambulance's interior. It's what you'd expect, except I'm alone in the back with this woman. I think there are usually two people in the back. But what do I know? Aside from where my kidneys are and what Dubai is like. While I don't remember the events of my own life, I know a lot about the world. "Aren't you a paramedic?"

She pulls out a hooked needle and thread. "I'm your doctor."

"My doctor?"

"For now." She threads the needle, ties a knot, and cuts the remainder. "Not afraid of needles, are you?"

I motion to the knife in my gut. "I *stabbed* myself."

"I was joking." She places the needle on a tray as the moving ambulance bounces over something in the road. My doctor leans toward the front and raps on the door. It opens a crack. "We're starting now, so do try to avoid any more bumps for a few."

"Trying," says a man. "But it's hard to with all this—"

She shoves the door shut. "Right. Enough of him."

"Who is he?"

"Your driver," she says. "Try to hold still." Before I realize it, she's dousing the knife with alcohol. "Still nothing?"

"Fine."

"Wonderful." She takes hold of the knife and slips it out of my gut. The ceramic blade clangs against the tray, and she scoops up the needle and thread. She leans over my exposed stomach and starts sewing. Her hands move quickly and efficiently. She's done this before. Not just stitching a wound, but while on the move.

"You were in the military," I say.

"Handsome, fearless, *and* perceptive," she says without looking up. "My, my."

She's clearly not going to say anything more, so I don't bother digging. There's something else I'd rather know. "Why am I fearless? The woman I met told me my doctor could explain it."

"The woman?"

"Who told me to stab myself."

She gives the needle a few tugs, cinching my skin together. "You trusted a woman, whose name you didn't know, who asked you to stab yourself?"

"I don't know my *own* name," I tell her. "Or yours."

She pauses, turns to me, and offers me a bloody gloved hand. "Doctor Kelly Allenby, at your service."

I shake her hand. "I'm Crazy."

"With a capital *C*," she says, the phrase old hat.

My mind freezes up for a moment. How did she know? Before

I can ask, she turns to me and says, "Winters filled me in. She's the woman you met. Jessica Winters."

"Who is she?" I ask.

"Not my place to say."

"You're avoiding my question," I tell her.

"Winters will brief you later," she says.

Brief me. Definitely military.

The ambulance sways from side to side for a moment. I hear the engine revving loudly. We're moving fast. But the siren isn't wailing.

"I wasn't talking about Winters," I say.

She smiles at me. I can't see her lips behind the mask, but her eyes crinkle on the sides. "Short-term memory seems to be fine."

"Please."

She turns back to stitching. "Do you know what the amygdala is?"

"A region of the brain," I say, though I have no idea how or why I know the answer to this question.

"Two regions," she says. "On either side. The size of almonds. Part of the limbic system. Not very big, but they regulate a few functions that are applicable to your situation. Memory and fear. Typically, a condition like yours is the result of Urbach-Wiethe disease, which destroys the amygdala. The result is a complete lack of social, emotional, and physical fear. But you're not like a sociopath. You still feel other emotions, like empathy, sadness, and joy, and you understand concepts of right and wrong, though in your case that sense of moral judgment is a bit exaggerated." She glances my way. "I read your file."

"You said 'typically.' Are there other ways to destroy the amygdala?"

She pulls the line tight and ties a knot. Scissors appear in her hand and she cuts the line. She turns away from me to put the needle and thread beside the discarded knife. "Brain trauma could do it, but it would have to be one hell of a coincidence to destroy both amygdala on either side of the head without turning you into a vegetable."

"But it's possible?"

"Anything is possible," she replies, taking her bloody gloves off and tossing them atop the tray. The mask and glasses follow. "But that's not what happened to you."

"How do you know?"

"Because you're sitting here having a conversation with me instead of watching *The Price Is Right* every day, or just plain dead."

"My file is pretty detailed," I say.

She turns back around and gives me a tight-lipped smile, the kind a mother might when her child is being naughty while simultaneously adorable.

"I'm not adorable," I point out.

She laughs. "Far from it. It's just . . . it's good to—"

The ambulance sways hard to the side. Tires squeal.

Allenby leans forward and opens the door a crack. She gasps. "What's happening?"

"They're everywhere," says the man behind the wheel. "I don't know if I can find a way around them."

"Can we stay here?" she asks. "Wait for them to pass?"

"I don't think they're going anywhere anytime soon."

"What's happening?" I ask. I turn my head back, but the upside-down slice of the world beyond the ambulance is just blue sky.

"Just relax," Allenby says, patting my shoulder. "We're fine."

I push myself up, inspect the expert stitching on my abdomen. "I wasn't worried."

Allenby is so entranced by what's happening outside, she doesn't notice me moving. I slide up behind her, angling for a view.

"We should be okay," the man says, "unless they get hungry for ice cream."

Ice cream? "What is it, a Little League parade?"

Allenby jumps, placing a hand to her chest. "Bloody hell. You shouldn't be up. I still need to cover that."

I push past her. The man in the front seat is short but fit. The kind of guy who's got energy to spare and can eat entire pizzas. But he's not young. Despite the full head of dark hair, the crow's-feet framing his eyes and flecks of white in his goatee give away his age.

When the driver swerves again, I look up.

The street is filled with angry people. Some carry picket signs with slogans like: RAISE MINIMUM WAGE, NO MORE PROPERTY TAXES, and my favorite, NO MONEY, LESS PROBLEMS. Some carry bricks. Others wield guns. Their voices rise and fall, repeating some kind of chant, muffled by the vehicle's thick walls. On the surface, they're protestors, but they feel more like a mob. The violent tension brewing outside is almost explosive, a powder keg just waiting for the fuse to be lit.

We pull to the side of the road and stop. It's a downtown area. Tall brick buildings line both sides of the street. Looks familiar. *Manchester, New Hampshire*, I think. The driver raises his palms to the people outside the vehicle, mouthing the word, "Sorry," over and over until they're placated and move on. But there are more where they came from. Many more. All of them angry. Afraid.

"We're in an ambulance," I say. "They won't move if you hit the siren?"

The driver just shakes his head.

Allenby puts a hand on my shoulder. "It's best to—"

People move for ambulances. It's a universal fact. I'm not sure why I believe this so soundly, but I do. If staying here is a risk, then we should use the tools at our disposal.

"No, don't!" the driver shouts.

My finger is already resting on the switch for the siren. I flip it.

The siren blares to life.

But it's not a siren.

It's a song. "Do Your Ears Hang Low?"

The plucky tune puts words in my head. "Do they waggle to and fro?" I look at Allenby. "We're in an *ice cream* truck?"

But she doesn't respond. Her eyes are locked straight ahead on the frozen mob of more than a hundred people, all staring at us with hateful eyes. The signs lower. The chanting stops. These people have no real cause. They're just afraid and angry, expressing it as a hot-button issue bandwagon. But the violence in their eyes is different from the eyes of people with a cause. There is nothing righteous in these people's eyes. Instead, I see a kind of vacant mania that was commonplace in SafeHaven. These people just lacked an outlet for their pent-up violence. But now I've given them direction. The jingle of the ice cream truck, its jovial blare like a mocking voice, has lit the fuse. All of this comes clear to me in a moment. Only one mystery remains. "Why are we in an ice cream truck?"

4.

The crowd outside shouts at us. There are so many commingling voices that understanding the individual messages would require a supercomputer. And yet I clearly understand the communal meaning of their words: hate. But why? Who hates an ice cream truck, other than protective, corn-syrup-fearing parents?

"What are they so afraid of?" I ask, not because I'm concerned for their well-being, but because I know there could be a subtle danger that I'm not seeing simply because I wouldn't fear it.

"How do you know they're afraid?" Allenby asks.

"People only act like this when they're afraid." It's not a memory. It's simple knowledge. "I don't feel what they're feeling, but I've learned to recognize it in other people and understand the kinds of things it can lead to. There is no short supply of fear in a mental institution."

"Things . . . are not good," Allenby says. "Anywhere. People are afraid. And angry. *Because* they're afraid. It's boiling over into the streets. Major cities—New York, Los Angeles, Boston—are a mess. Rural areas, like most of New Hampshire, have been calm, but that appears to be changing. At first, they take to the streets, like this, latching on to whatever hot-button issue affects a certain area. Here it's all about money. Wages. Taxes. The working-class money struggle. But things eventually take a turn for the worse. Violence. Looting. Vast destruction. People are dying."

The driver turns off the ice cream truck music and rolls down the window a crack. "Sorry! Sorry! It was an accident."

"Asshole!" someone shouts back. "You think what we're doing is funny? That this is some kind of joke?"

Others join in, shaking their fists at one of America's most beloved summertime-fun icons. The images of Bomb Pops, orange Dream Bars, and ice cream sandwiches no doubt plastered to the side of this ambulance in disguise somehow appear as a threat to these people. Something to be dealt with harshly.

The driver rolls up the window and turns to me and Allenby. "I think we should force our way through. This isn't going to end well."

"We can't just run them over," Allenby says.

"I could," I say.

The driver shakes his head. "Of all the people to be stuck in this mess with . . ."

Allenby silences him with a gentle touch to his arm.

He looks back at me. "Sorry."

Hands slap against the truck's hood. And the sides. There's a *click* all around us as the driver locks the doors. The vehicle's interior rumbles as the people outside start pounding, venting their fear.

"Shit," the driver says. "Shit!" The fear outside the vehicle seeps inside, taking hold of him.

I take hold of his prickly chin and turn his face toward mine. "What's your name?" My voice is as calm as always. My pulse is rock-solid, like a metronome. Luckily, calm can be as infectious as fear.

"Blair," he says. "Ed Blair."

"Does whoever you work for have a helicopter?" I ask.

He nods.

"Are they far?"

"A few minutes to prep and a five-minute flight."

I look up through the windshield. The buildings lining the downtown street are six stories tall, tops. "Call them," I say. "Tell them where we are and to pick us up on a rooftop."

"I'm not getting out of this truck," he says.

I pat his arm. "Just call them." Then, to Allenby, who is watching the crowd swarm toward the truck, "Finish your job."

"W—What?" She seems dazed. There were times at SafeHaven when my lack of fear put me in physical danger, causing me to later wonder about a cure for my condition. But in situations like this, where fear cripples people, I'm happy to be who I am.

"My stitches," I say. "You said you weren't done."

"But the crowd. We have—"

"Time."

With Blair now dialing his cell phone, I move back into the ice creambulance's rear and take a seat on the gurney I'd been lying on. The vehicle shakes back and forth. Feels like we're on a boat.

Have I been on a boat? Muffled voices and slamming fists reverberate, thunderlike, through the small space.

Allenby, focused on her task, opens a medical kit. She removes a tube of antibiotic, some gauze and a roll of medical tape.

The vehicle rocks harder, knocking her off-balance. I catch her by the arms. "Just focus. Ignore them."

"Easy for you to say," she grumbles. "Lean back."

I lie down on the gurney while she quickly smears the ointment over the wound and tapes down the gauze. Just as she finishes, the door to the front opens. Rather than just looking back, Blair slides out of his seat and joins us in the rear. "Helicopter is on its way. ETA seven minutes. But we're not going to make it out of here."

I look around Blair's head as something red and rectangular spirals through the air. A brick slams into the windshield, creating a spiderweb break in the laminated—and oddly tinted—safety glass.

Allenby moves toward the back door. "We should go. Now."

"Not yet," I say. "Can I have a shirt?"

She points to a hook behind Blair, where my torn and blood-soaked olive-drab T-shirt hangs. The shirt, along with my blue jeans, have pretty much been my uniform for the past year. While many of the patients at SafeHaven wear hospital gowns, the higher-functioning patients were allowed the dignity of real clothing. The brown shoes on my feet are new, though. We wore slippers back at SafeHaven. I slip into the shirt, knowing the gory appearance will help back people away, and look back out through the windshield.

"What are we waiting for?" Blair asks. He follows my eyes, looking ahead. "The longer we wait, the—oh, no!"

I watch the green bottle's arc through the air. It was a good throw from about forty feet away. The bright orange flame trailing the improvised weapon helps it stand out from the throng. The Molotov cocktail strikes the windshield. Flames burst in all directions, obscuring our view, but I don't need to see.

The pounding stops.

The vehicle settles.

The crowd has been repulsed by a splash of mankind's original tool of mass destruction. In minutes, the truck will be an inferno, the crowd pushed back fifty feet by the heat. But we don't need to wait that long.

"Do either of you have a weapon?"

"We're a medical team," Allenby says while Blair shakes his head, nervously eyeing the rear door.

I take the bloody ceramic blade from the metal tray. "Okay, just—"

A thump and the sound of shattering glass against the rear of our vehicle interrupts me. Flames cover the two small windows.

"Oh, God," Allenby says.

"We're going to jump through," I tell them. "It's just like running your finger through a candle. Move fast enough, and the heat won't touch you."

"I—I can't," Blair says.

I shrug, indifferent. "You can risk a minor burn, and the crowd, or you can cook alive in your very own ice creambulance turned urn."

He looks at me like I'm insane while he debates possible death against certain death. Without another word, I unlock the door and leap through the flames.

5.

"You're on fire," someone says, explaining why I wasn't immediately greeted with violence upon flinging myself from the back of the ice creambulance.

I don't need to ask where. I can feel the heat upon my head. During my time at SafeHaven, I let my hair get a little out of control. As the stench of burnt hair wafts around me, I reach up and calmly pat the top of my head until the smoldering brown mane is extinguished.

While playing fireman with my scalp, I take in the crowd surrounding us. A circle of humanity stands twenty feet away, pushed back by the flames behind me. Some look a little stunned by my emergence from the blaze, but most still look angry and capable of violence. They're just waiting for a new trigger to push them past the fear of this fire and the bloodied man that emerged.

One man, a particularly burly specimen, is the first to break ranks and step toward me, menace in his eyes. And for what? Because I was in a vehicle that had the audacity to play a plucky tune during a protest? While I was in an asylum, the world seems to have gone nuts. I relax my body, prepared to deal with the man in a way that will keep others from making the same mistake. But he stops short and looks a bit surprised.

Allenby emerges from the inferno with a shout of fear. Her explosive hair, like mine, smolders. I shake my hand through her hair, cutting the stands of bright orange away before her head looks like a fiery troll doll.

Blair exits next, falling to the ground and rolling. "Shit, shit, shit!" But he's not on fire.

"Get up," Allenby says, and kicks Blair's foot. She understands that of the two dangers surrounding us, the crowd surrounding us is worse. To them, we've become the antagonizers. They don't want their pound of flesh from the government or the man, they want it from the ice cream truck. And now that it's on fire—judgment meted out—they're weighing the fates of the people who exited the offending vehicle. I consider pretending to be one of them, shaking my fist against injustice, but I can see it's too late for that. These people might not be thinking straight, pumped full of fear, but they're not stupid, either.

With a subtle movement of my hand, I tap Allenby's hip. She glances up at me. Makes eye contact, until I glance away, looking at the shop door to our left. Only three people stand on the sidewalk between us and the door, which will hopefully provide access to a staircase.

I pull Blair to his feet. "Follow her." Then to Allenby. "Slowly."

Allenby does her best to ignore the cold stares of the people surrounding us and steps up onto the sidewalk. Blair, far more shaken up, manages to stay silent and follow her. But his hands are shaking. Watching the crowd, without making eye contact, I bring up the rear. The people in front of the store—two twenty-something women and a young man—instinctively part for their elders. They're either not worked up enough to be violent or have correctly assessed my capabilities: afraid, not stupid afraid. Not yet, anyway.

The door remains shut when Allenby tugs on the handle. A man appears in the window, his thinning gray hair combed back tight, his light blue eyes wide with fear. I see Allenby's lips moving, mouthing the words, "Help us," without letting the crowd hear. She's smart. Understands people.

I pause on the edge of the sidewalk, unsure if we're going to make it off the street or if I'm going to reenact the battle of Thermopylae, by myself, while Allenby and Blair make a futile run for it.

For a moment, the old man doesn't move, but the way Allenby is able to plead for her life, just with her eyes, is impressive. The man nods and unlocks the door.

The heavy, painted green door opens, its well-oiled hinges slipping silently, until—*jing jing*. A bell at the top of the door clangs loudly. The crowd starts, bouncing back like someone has just fired a gun.

The old man pushes the door open wide, allowing Allenby and Blair to hurry inside. I make a step to follow, but am stopped by movement at the fringe of my vision. The large man, whose build, crooked nose, and response to the ringing bell suggests a pugilistic history, strides toward me. I could get inside without facing him, but a man of his bulk would make short work of the door.

"You the jackass who switched on the music?" the pugilist asks as he wipes his nose with both thumbs, makes twin sledgehammer fists, and starts bobbing.

"Yes," I tell him.

The crowd around us buzzes with excitement, eager for the violence to begin.

"I thought it was an ambulance," I add. The statement makes the man pause for a moment, long enough for him to notice that I'm not backing away, nor have I taken up a fighting stance.

"Ain't you afraid?" he asks.

I jab. The fast strike slips past his defenses, crushes his nose, and staggers him back. Before he has a chance to realize I've broken his nose, I kick him square in the nuts. The great thing about having no social fear is that I can fight dirty and not feel bad about it later. The pugilist howls and drops to his knees. I finish him off with a roundhouse kick that knocks him unconscious and spills him into the road. He'll live, but he might not be able to reproduce, which is my little gift to the world today.

I glance at the crowd, which is stunned by the sudden and extreme violence. It's more than they bargained for and didn't go the way they expected. But it won't hold them back forever, and now that I've hurt one of their own, they'll be out for blood.

Moving casually, I step toward the shop and slip through the door, carefully closing and locking it behind me.

The shop is full of eclectic antiques. There's a tall 1950s radio, glowing with power. A stained-glass lamp. A medieval helmet opened to reveal a secret decanter and shot glasses. I feel like there is someone I would like to tell about all this, but there isn't anyone. My only friends are Shotgun Jones and Seymour, and their tastes run a little closer to the crap given away on *The Price Is Right*.

"Crazy," Allenby says. She takes my wrist and pulls me away from the door. "This is Matt Williams."

The old man nods at me.

"How can we get to the roof?" I ask.

He points up. "I live on the second floor. Fire escape goes to the roof. Stairs are around back." He starts leading the way but isn't going anywhere fast.

I snap my fingers at Blair. "Get to the roof. Make sure the chopper knows where we are."

Blair runs for the back of the store. I hear his feet thundering up the staircase a moment later.

"Help Mr. Williams to the roof," I say to Allenby. "I'll try to slow them down."

When Allenby reaches out to take Williams's arm, he shrugs away. "I'm not going anywhere. This is my store, and I'll be damned if I let them hooligans make a mess of things." He hobbles behind the counter and retrieves a shotgun. He struggles with the pump action for a moment but manages to chamber a shell. "I've seen war before."

War?

"And I'm not afraid to shoot the first of those bastards to come through my door."

I pat his shoulder, say, "Thank you," and head for the back of the store.

Allenby rushes up behind me and says, "We can't just leave him! They'll kill him."

"Do you want to stay because you think it will change his fate? Or is it because you fear being ridiculed later on for leaving an old man to die? If it's the latter, I won't say a word. If it's the former, you're a fool. He chose his path. Respect it." I start up the rugged stairs without looking back.

One of the shopwindows shatters. Allenby starts up the stairs, revealing her personal truth—her life is worth more than her honor. There is no help we can provide for Williams that will avoid his death. But ours . . . we still have some control over how our lives come to a close. At least for a few more minutes.

The apartment above the store smells like history—dust and mold hidden within the folds of countless overfull bookshelves. If the fire outside reaches this building, the apartment will all but explode. This much brittle, dry paper will ignite like gasoline.

"Here!" Blair shouts from the back.

We hurry through the living room to the kitchen, which is equally packed with old books. A pile of them has been spilled on the floor, apparently shoved away by Blair, who is peering back in through an open window above the spilled books. He waves us on. "This way!"

Blair's feet clang on the fire escape as he runs toward the roof.

A second window breaks beneath us. It's followed by a shotgun blast, a scream, and then the sound of thunder as countless people stream into the shop. If Williams screamed, the sound was blocked out by the rumbling, which I can now feel in the floorboards beneath my feet.

Allenby crawls through the window, but not nearly fast enough. My hand hits her ass and shoves. She spills forward with a shout of surprise. I dive through, spin around, and close the window. As Allenby starts to protest about her rough treatment, I lie down on top of her, which fills her with enough fear to close her mouth.

"If you stand, they'll see you," I whisper. "Crawl away before standing, but quickly. It won't take long for them to figure out why the books have spilled."

She nods and slides forward. I hold my weight off of her and follow, but our stealth is a wasted effort. The window behind us shatters as a book—an old leather-bound Bible—careens through, strikes the black metal railing, and explodes into a flurry of ancient pages. A baseball bat begins clearing away the remaining glass shards.

"Go!" I shout as the distant chop of a helicopter reaches my ears. "I'll hold them here."

"But . . ." she says, clearly confused about why I would stand my ground here but not downstairs.

"They can't overwhelm me here," I say.

She understands, and runs up the stairs to the second story. I glance up and see Blair climbing a ladder to the roof. The helicopter sounds about a minute out. It will take nearly that long for Allenby to reach the roof. *One minute,* I tell myself and then turn to face the first person through the window, which is actually a pair of people, one holding a knife, the other a Louisville Slugger.

6.

The pair pauses for a moment. That I'm standing my ground has them wary, no doubt recalling the pugilist's crumpled form.

"You're going to have to get close to use those," I say, pointing at their weapons.

For a brief moment, my logic seems to seep through. Both men look unsure, confused, and ready for a beer. But then the hairs on their arms rise up. The man with the knife shivers. With the suddenness of a fired bullet, they're both back on task, refueled by fear of something greater than me, and ready to kill.

The man with the bat steps forward. The muscles of his tattooed forearm twitch as he twists his hands around the grip. "Not that close."

I shrug. "Your funeral." And I mean it. These men would kill me. I have no qualms about returning the favor. Even if I could feel fear, a jail sentence or return to SafeHaven wouldn't be on my list. Not in this situation. I'm not only defending myself, I'm defending two other people.

Bat-man steps closer. He's got the Slugger cocked back, twisting around in tight circles. A real Jose Canseco.

I wait patiently.

He steps into his swing, grunting his power into the weapon. But his aim is off. I don't even need to duck. Clearly, he's never killed anyone before, which begs the question: *Why does he want to kill me?* I'm never going to get a chance to ask him. The powerful missed swing overextends him. I close the short distance between us, catch his arms, and spin him around.

The man shouts in fear, but not because of me. His overeager friend has lunged with the knife and is plunging it toward where I was supposed to be. If the knife continues its arc, it will plunge into bat-man's heart.

Only it doesn't.

I'm struck by something as heavy as a cartoon anvil—mercy.

Back when these people were an angry mob, I could have driven through them without a second thought, but I can see now that they're out of their minds. Not themselves, and not really deserving of my wrath. Not all of it, anyway.

I twist the bat in front of the knife. The blade bounces off the wooden barrel. A quick shove knocks the bat into the man's forehead. He drops the knife and stumbles back against the railing as a third person—a girl-next-door type—crawls out the window.

The hell is going on?

These people seem like they need to be in SafeHaven more than Seymour. They're out of their heads. Terrified to the point of rage.

With a quick twist, bat-man's wrists overextend, and he relinquishes the bat. I spin him around and pull back my fist to slug him, but he's done. The man raises his hands, finally more afraid of me than whatever brought him to this point. "Who are you?" he asks.

I pick up the knife. "I have no idea."

Shattering glass turns my gaze upward, but back down just as quickly. Glass rains down from above, breaking into smaller pieces as it strikes the grated metal stairs. When I'm finally able to look up again, girl next door is charging, fingers hooked, a scream building in her throat. Above me, a man leaps through the window and starts up after Allenby. He's fast.

I sidestep the girl, tripping her with my foot and elbowing her in the back. She spills forward, introducing her forehead to the railing behind me. She slumps down to the fire escape floor, blood running down her face.

As more people pour through the window, I start up the stairs, armed with a bat and two knives—one ceramic, one stainless steel. For a moment, I feel good about my chances for surviving this mess. Allenby's life is still at risk, but I can do a lot of damage to a lot of people with a knife and bat. My positive outlook changes when I reach the third story and bullets start flying. Someone inside the apartment fires three times. Only two of the bullets make it through the window, each of them sending sparks into the air as they strike the fire escape's metal framework.

I run past without slowing or flinching. The missed bullets have as little effect on me as a shift in the breeze or a degree change in the temperature. I'm two flights higher when the shooter makes it to the window and starts firing up. But there are two levels of metal between us, and the rounds don't make it far.

At the top story, I quickly take stock of the situation. Loud chopping and billowing dust, both the results of a helicopter's rotor blades, mean our ride has arrived. But Allenby and her pursuer are nowhere in sight.

I discard the bat, slip one blade beneath my belt, pop the second sideways in my mouth, and leap onto the ladder like a pirate boarding a merchant's vessel. I bound up the rungs, jump the wall at the top, and take in the scene. Allenby is on the tar-paper roof, crawling away from her attacker, a spindly man with a pipe. I don't think she's been struck yet, but the man is just seconds from delivering his first blow. Beyond them is the helicopter, a black number with no identifying marks, hovering a few feet above the roof. Blair sits inside looking paralyzed with fear. I see no weapons, meaning I'm the only hope Allenby has.

As I climb over the roof's short wall, I shout, "Hey!" but the man doesn't turn. He's locked on target.

I run at him, taking aim with the ceramic knife. It's a nice blade. Sharp. Well balanced. But it's not a throwing knife. The odds of hitting the man with the blade are fifty-fifty. But I only need to hit him hard enough to get his attention.

The pipe comes up in sync with Allenby raising her arms. The defensive posture will save her life from the first blow, but she'll have two broken arms for the effort. Twenty feet from the man, I throw the ceramic knife. The man doesn't see it coming but twists just right as he steps over Allenby, and the blade sails past. The second knife is in the air a fraction of a second later.

The pipe descends.

The butt of the knife strikes the man's right shoulder, knocking his strike off center, but the pipe will still connect with one of Allenby's arms.

Except it doesn't.

She surprises the attacker and me by rolling to the side at the last moment and kicking the man's knee. He yelps in pain and jumps back but isn't deterred. He raises the pipe for another strike but never gets the chance.

My shoulder strikes the man, midspine, as I ram him, lift him off the ground, and then slam him to the roof. There's a loud crack as all my weight is transferred to the man's spine via my shoulder. He screams in pain, still alive, but when I stand up, he's not moving anything below the neck.

I turn to Allenby, who is now on her feet. "I knew you were military."

She turns for the chopper. "Once upon a time."

"Better hurry," I say, pushing her along. "The next person has a gun."

The helicopter lowers as we approach, allowing us to board by stepping on the skid and climbing in through the side door. Blair helps Allenby inside but leaves me to climb in by myself. As I find my seat and slide the side door shut, bullets punch into the metal where my head had been a moment before.

The pilot takes us up and away, blinding the gunman with a cloud of dust and roof grime. As we ascend, I lean to the window and look down. It's Manchester, New Hampshire, all right, but I've never seen it like this. The streets are alive with people. Vehicles and some buildings are burning. The mob rushes forward. Ahead of them, a line of riot police, each holding a clear bullet-resistant shield, wait.

Molotov cocktails sail through the air, accompanied by rocks, and then bullets. The police respond with tear gas, water cannons, and then bullets of their own. *War indeed.*

"Hard to believe," Allenby says.

Not really, I think, except for one detail. While scenes like this have played out all around the world for one reason or another, this is New Hampshire. It's 90 percent forested, has a culture of holding people accountable for their actions, and the lowest murder rate in the country. How could this level of violence seep into one of the nation's quietest states? Even more pressing, how can a city I don't remember visiting be so familiar, and why the hell do I know so much about New Hampshire?

7.

The helicopter races toward the roof of what appears to be a black Mayan pyramid. As we descend, I can see the faint outlines of the tinted windows that make up the building's flat, forty-five-degree angled walls. At the center of two sides of the building, the smooth slope is divided by what looks like giant staircases, each "step" a story tall, completing the Mayan feel. I count nine levels. The top level is three hundred feet across. Maybe more. The bottom is at least three times that. The building is surrounded by tall pines, and the roof is just below the tree line. Despite its size, the megalithic building would be invisible to anyone on the ground. Not exactly covert since anyone in the air can look down and see it, but the single access road winding through the woods is blocked by a gate. And while I can't see it, I have no doubt that the entire facility is surrounded by a fence. Anyone interested in the building is going to have a hard time reaching it.

Which begs the question, why am *I* here?

"You're not going to assimilate me?" I ask. The pilot, Blair, and Allenby can all hear me over the thunderous rotors thanks to the headsets we're wearing.

"What?" Blair asks. He's still shaken up by our experience in Manchester. "I don't—"

"Resistance is futile," Allenby says. She slides up next to me and looks out the window. "It does smack of the Borg, doesn't it? But no worries, the collective isn't interested in the likes of you."

I smile at her. "If you were younger and prettier—" I stop as my logical mind puts the brakes on the statement my lack of fear let slip.

Allenby gets a good laugh out of it, though. Slaps my shoulder. "Oh, you." Her demeanor is casual. Comfortable. I find this strange, but perhaps it's just a result of being institutionalized in a place where most everyone is afraid of me.

The helicopter touches down on a black landing pad at the center of the roof. As the rotor slows, Allenby slides the door open and hops out. There is no greeting party, just a flat black surface and a halo of pine-tree tops surrounding us. The scent of the deep woods is invigorating. I breathe deeply and step out.

"Follow me," Allenby says, almost shouting to be heard over the still-slowing rotor blades. I fall in line behind her as we walk across the roof. "Some ground rules. Don't talk to anyone who doesn't first talk to you."

"That's a strange rule," I point out. "Kind of old-world parental discipline."

"It's just that most people here are working on something, in their heads, even when they don't appear to be working at all."

"I see," I say, but I really don't. I stop walking.

After a few steps, Allenby notices I've stopped. She turns back. "What?"

"Why am I here?"

"To not be *there*," she says, and I get her meaning.

"Anywhere is better than SafeHaven?" I say. "I'm not sure I believe that. From what it looks like, once I set foot inside this building, no one will know I'm here."

Allenby grins. "And if I don't tell you?"

"I'm going to run."

"And get caught."

I shake my head. "I think you know that's not what will happen. You have five seconds to tell me why I'm here. Five . . . four . . ."

Allenby grunts and stomps her foot. "You're infuriating. Fine."

I grin, but also note she didn't wait until I got to one, or until I started running. She believed me. Trusted what I said. I haven't been given that kind of respect in a long time, and I appreciate it despite the circumstances.

"It's a drug trial." She waves her hand at her head. "For your condition."

"What if I don't want to be cured?" I ask. "I've seen what fear does to people, and I'm not sure I—"

"Not that condition," she says. "The other one."

I'm confused for a moment until I realize she's talking about my memory. "What if I don't want to remember?"

She turns away and starts walking. "You do."

"You're calling my bluff?" I ask.

"We both know you have a horrible hand," she says, stopping.

A square of rooftop before her comes to life, rising up. A black rectangle, ten feet tall, six wide, emerges from below and stops, looking like a futuristic megalith. And then it opens, revealing an elevator. Allenby steps inside and turns around. With a single raised eyebrow and a matching grin, she says, "Coming?"

Stepping out of the elevator, we enter a hallway that defies all of my expectations. Given the stark feel of the building's obsidian surface, I expected something similar to the SafeHaven floor—stark, gleaming white, and brightly lit. Instead, it's . . . homey. Warm hardwood floors. A thick, oriental runner down the middle of the hall. End tables with a variety of lamps. "This doesn't look like a laboratory."

"It isn't," Allenby says. "It's the residential level." She starts down the hall. She stops three doors down on the right. "This is your room."

I feel like I'm in some sort of strange dream, and peek into the room, which is more than a room. It's an apartment. From the doorway, I can see a kitchenette, living room, and dining area. The furnishing is comfortable. The brushed metal appliances are modern. The décor is casual, almost primitive, with wooden carvings and emotionally charged, modern oil paintings.

I step inside.

I'm *drawn* inside.

Immediate comfort washes over me. My muscles relax. "How did you do it?"

"What?" she asks.

I motion to the apartment. "*This.* I don't think I could have told you what I would like in an apartment, but . . . this is it. Every detail feels . . . right. Like home."

"I'm not an interior decorator," she says.

A painting in the living room attracts my attention. It's a two-foot square of color—thick dabs of red radiate out from the middle to orange, yellow, and a hint of green around the fringe.

"How does it make you feel?" Allenby asks.

"I thought you were a medical doctor."

She steps up beside me, eyes on the painting. "I'm not evaluating you."

"Yes you are," I say. "How does it make *you* feel?"

"Melancholy." She turns away and heads back toward the door.

"Well, it makes me hungry." I turn toward the kitchen, which is separated from the living room by an island. I open the fridge and find it fully stocked. Most of it looks healthy, but hiding in the door, among the brand-new bottles of condiments and cups of chocolate pudding, is a Snickers bar and a can of Cherry Pepsi.

My mouth salivates and both hands reach out, claiming the prizes. The wrapper comes off faster than a male stripper's pants. I take a bite and moan with pleasure. I haven't had something this sweet since . . . well, I can't remember. While taking a second bite, I pop the soda top with one hand and, before swallowing the mash of chocolate, caramel, peanuts, and nougat in my mouth, drain half the can.

"You clearly don't fear diabetes, either," Allenby says.

I raise the can as though giving a toast. "Or sugar lows." Three more bites, two drinks, and sixty-five grams of sugar later, my meal is done.

"Ready to go?" Allenby asks.

I take a step to follow her. "Actually . . ." I look around the room and realize that I'm not turning my head. The room is spinning. I grip the island to keep from falling over.

"Whoa there," Allenby says. I feel her holding my arms, steadying me. "Let's get you to the couch."

I let her guide me. The couch is just fifteen feet away, but it feels like I'm walking through knee-deep mud to reach it.

"Okay," she says, guiding me down. "Slowly. Slowly."

I fall from her grasp, but the couch catches me. I try to open my eyes but lack the strength. Allenby places her fingers against my neck, checking my pulse. With a sigh, she stands back up and says, "He's out."

A door opens and a new voice, deep and masculine, asks, "What did it, the candy or soda?"

"Both, actually," Allenby says. "He's going to be unconscious for a long time."

And then, I am.

8.

I'm paralyzed.

But I can hear. And smell. And feel.

The soft cotton against my skin reveals a sheet. The weight of a blanket rests atop it. I can feel the sheet on my chest, my stomach, and legs, but not my midsection. I'm dressed in boxers. There is a tightness around my wrists. Restraints.

Poor Allenby. I had begun to like her.

A heart monitor beeping out a steady beat echoes sharply. I'm in a small room, full of hard objects. I picture it in my mind. Some kind of examination/hospital room. Cabinets along the walls. A sink maybe. No chairs. Nothing soft aside from the blankets. The temperature on my skin is even, so there are no windows. Or the shades are pulled. Or it's night.

The smell is antiseptic. Sterile. Like SafeHaven, but with less bleach and more . . . what is that? Thyme and clove? Strange. But there's something else in the air. Old Spice. Rose soap. A man and a woman. The man smells new, but the woman is Allenby. The rose scent was fainter on her before, but she must have taken a shower.

I can hear them breathing now that I know they're there. But what are they doing?

Watching me, I decide. Or listening to the heart monitor. Trying to decide if I'm awake. Too bad for them: my heart rate, at rest, is rock-solid. Anyone else waking up to this situation would panic. A spike in the heart rate would reveal consciousness.

"He's still out," Allenby eventually says.

"He did consume both sedatives," the man says. He sounds older. Sixties, maybe.

"Will he be okay?" Allenby's earnest-sounding concern for my welfare is intriguing.

"The drugs will wear off soon enough," the man says. "He'll be fine. You know he's tough."

"It's not his body I'm worried about. Did the MRI reveal anything? Is the damage reversible?"

"His memories are not our primary concern. Honestly, I think we'll all be better if he doesn't remember."

"He might not comply without them," Allenby says. "He might run again." *Again?* "He already threatened as much."

The man's voice is louder when he speaks again. Leaning over me. "Then let's hope he realizes the perilous nature of his situation."

Whatever he intends to do with me, it doesn't hold my attention nearly as much as the revelation that this isn't my first visit to . . . wherever this is. Allenby seemed comfortable around me earlier. Like she knew me. They certainly knew I'd go for the candy and soda, even though I couldn't have told you that about myself. But is she a friend or the architect of my amnesia? Just because she knows me doesn't mean we're pals. I can't conceive of how she'd be both a friend and responsible for my lack of memory. Despite her apparent concern for my well-being, mounting evidence suggests the direr of the two relationships. What experimental scientist doesn't hope for a positive outcome? Doesn't mean they're not willing to have a few patients die—or forget their lives.

A tingling sensation moves through my body, starting in my feet and ending at my head. That's when I notice the chill atop my head. They've shaven off my ratty hair. But why? Have they already performed some kind of surgery, or did my dirty hair disgust them?

The tingling becomes pins and needles. I wiggle a toe beneath the blankets. Mobility is returning.

The man, who is apparently quite observant, takes note. "He's coming out of it."

With the ruse up, I open my eyes. It's harder than I expected, like fighting against the effects of too much alcohol. But the heavy feeling fades fast. A few blinks later, my eyes are open. The room looks pretty much like I expected it to. Mostly white, hard surfaces.

Allenby leans into view, her lion's mane of gray hair swaying like great pine trees in a strong wind. "How are you feeling?"

I glance toward the man. He's older than I thought. Perhaps in his seventies, with bright white hair, an equally white beard, and spectacles over his blue eyes. He's overweight and slightly hunched but carries himself in a way that says, *I'm in charge.*

I look back to Allenby. "Betrayed." While she's focused on my serious gaze, I slowly clench my fists and bend my wrists in, pressing them against the restraints.

"I'm sorry about this," she says. "I really am."

"Uh-huh." I turn to the old man, who's still watching me. "Nice to meet you, Mr. Hitchcock."

"Hitchcock?" Allenby asks, looking back at the man.

The man stares at me in a way I can't read. Is he amused or about to torture me? I can't tell. "Because I'm old and fat and up to no good, is that it?"

I nod.

He dips his head to me in greeting. "My name is Doctor Stephen Lyons. I'm the head of Neuro Inc. You're currently in our headquarters."

"I didn't see a sign," I say.

"And you won't. We're not a public corporation."

"A black organization funded by the government, then," I say, watching his eyebrows rise, "which would explain why some of your employees have military histories, though if Blair is military, he needs a refresher."

"I'll take that under advisement," Lyons says. "But not everyone has your special set of skills."

"Unless a dangerous lack of fear and amnesia have become desirable traits, I'd say he's better off than me."

Lyons points a finger at me and winks. "A debate for another time, I'm afraid." He steps toward the door. "I'm retiring for the evening."

"What time is it?" I ask.

"Midnight," he says. "You've been asleep for eight hours."

"And you expect me to sleep now?" I lift my arms. The restraints snap taut. "In these?"

Allenby looks at my hands and gasps. The purple mottled skin caused by my cutting off the circulation looks horrible and has the desired effect. She takes one of the restraints in her hands and looks at Lyons, who nods. She looks at me. "Please don't try anything. There's a guard right outside."

"I saved your life today," I tell her. "We fought side by side. For now, we're comrades. You'd rather that not change."

She nods slowly and loosens the strap, not enough to free me, but enough to ease my phony discomfort. "Can't argue with that."

I make a fist as she refastens the buckle. The flexed muscles and swelling caused by the buildup of blood increase the thickness of my arm by a few millimeters, but that should be enough.

She moves to the other side and repeats the process.

"Don't do anything stupid," she whispers, leaning in close. Her voice seems loud enough that Lyons should be able to hear, but he shows no indication of having heard her warning.

Allenby makes unflinching eye contact while she works the second strap. Is she trying to tell me something beyond, *don't be stupid*, or am I being played? They knew I'd go for the sweets. Maybe she knows what I intend to do next? Could I really be that predictable? Up until this moment, I've always seen myself as unpredictable. Not even I know what I might do or say, moment to moment.

Finished, she stands back.

"Now sedate him," Lyons says.

I lift the leather manacles holding me in place. "I'm not going anywhere."

"Do it," he says. Despite his elderly appearance, he's not senile enough to underestimate me.

Allenby opens one of the white cupboards and retrieves a preloaded syringe of who knows what. She jabs my shoulder and shoves the plunger down. As my consciousness begins drifting back toward darkness, I watch Allenby and Lyons leave. She gives me an apologetic glance and then switches off the lights.

Lyons speaks before the door closes fully. "I want him prepped in the morning. I don't see the point in waiting any longer."

"I'm not sure he's ready," Allenby says.

The man sighs. "I'm not interested in giving him a choice."

The door clicks shut.

9.

Despite the all-encompassing darkness, my return to wakeful-
ness is sudden. There's no tingling. No pins and needles. Whatever Allenby gave me, it wasn't the same substance they put in
the food.

Other than the distant hum of the building's air-conditioning,
the room is silent. Even the heart monitor has gone mute. Or has
it been turned off? I lay still for a moment, gathering my thoughts.

I'm held captive—restrained and sedated—in a secret facility.
The doctor, Lyons, intends to perform some kind of test, or surgery, on me in the morning. For all I know, the sun has already
risen. Everyone here is lying to me. Playing me. Controlling me.
And because of that, I can't believe a single thing I'm told. Two
courses of action emerge. I can escape, plain and simple. Or I can
find out who these people are, what Neuro Inc. is after, and possibly get some answers about myself, since it seems I've been here
before.

The second option is clearly the riskier of the two, but since I
don't worry about risk, it's also the only acceptable option.

I lift my arms up, fold my thumbs down and pull hard on the
restraints. They're still fairly tight, but there is just enough wiggle
room to pull my hands free. It's an uncomfortable process, but
within three minutes of squirming, I'm free.

Cool air raises goose bumps all over my body as I pull the blankets away. As I thought, I'm dressed in boxers. I feel the elastic waist.
It's tight. New. Someone undressed me. My hand goes to my chest
next, feeling that the pendant is still there, somehow keeping me
grounded.

With my hands outstretched, I step toward where I remember
the door being. I find it in five strides. After gently running my fingers over the door's surface to confirm there is no window, I feel
for the light switch. I squint at the bright light but notice a second
door just to the left of the bed. Without a thought, I open the door

and find a small bathroom. New toilet paper is on the roll, its band of glue still intact. The whole space is so pristine I'd guess it's never been used. But the strangest aspect of the bathroom is the clothing that's folded up atop the closed toilet.

An olive-drab T-shirt. Blue jeans. Black ankle socks. Brown sneakers. All brand new. All my size. Even the extrawide 4E shoe size. I take the apparel as a positive sign that Neuro Inc. expects me to live long enough to need clothing.

I break in the toilet and get dressed. After splashing some water on my face and toweling off, I step back into the mock hospital room and freeze.

"Mrs. Winters," I say to the blond woman who freed me from SafeHaven by giving me a knife, knowing I'd use it. She's seated on the far side of the small room.

"Ms." She stands. "Going somewhere?"

"Yes."

She crosses her arms, drawing my attention lower. She's dressed in a black power suit that makes her blond hair appear brighter. "That's probably not a good idea."

"Coming here wasn't a good idea."

"You don't know that yet," she says.

"I'll know, one way or the other, soon enough."

She smiles. "That confidence of yours . . . I wish I knew if it was real or just the lack of fear talking. Maybe we could find out?" She doesn't quite lick her lips, but I see seductive possibilities in her eyes.

I grin, not because the suggested invitation intrigues me—though it does—but because I know she's trying to distract me from noticing her left hand, folded under her right arm, sliding beneath the jacket of her suit. She's after something. Pepper spray. A Taser. Maybe even a gun.

"We can do this two ways," I tell her. "You can draw whatever weapon you've got and I can knock you unconscious—"

The hand beneath her jacket stops moving.

"—or you can get in bed, let me sedate you, and you wake up feeling refreshed."

She's thinking about it. Not a good sign.

"You've read my file," I tell her. "You know I'm willing and capable."

"But you don't know anything about me, do you?" Her expectant eyes irritate me. She's digging for an answer, maybe even hoping for one, but I have nothing to offer.

She makes her move, kicking suddenly so I have to lean away from the tip of her solid-looking shoe. By the time I've righted myself, I hear the telltale crackling of a Taser. She thrusts the bright-blue arc of electricity at my midsection. Fear or not, if she connects, I'm done.

But I react quickly, or rather my body does. Acting on some kind of body memory, using techniques I have no memory of learning, I catch her wrist with my right hand, squeezing a pressure point. A painful, cold sensation is rushing up her arm. She hisses in pain and drops the Taser, but I'm not done.

With my left hand, I squeeze a second pressure point at her elbow joint. It's like completing a circuit, doubling the pain and eliciting a shout. But her voice is cut off a moment later, when I release her wrist and give her a backhand slap behind her right ear, striking a third pressure point and once again completing the circuit, overloading her neurology. She drops into my arms, unconscious, just as the door swings open.

"What's going—"

I lift Winters and shove her toward the security guard. He instinctively moves to catch the woman. As his arms wrap around her, I punch the defenseless man in the temple. The pair drops together, limbs tangled.

It takes three minutes to lift Winters and the guard into the bed, gag them, and shackle them with the restraints, which they'll be able to remove once the sedatives I've given them wear off. I check them for cell phones but find nothing. No IDs, either. Winters has a blank, red keycard around her neck, which I transfer to mine. I take a set of car keys from her pants pocket and recover the Taser from the floor. The security guard carries a pair of plastic zip cuffs, a stun gun, and a radio. I pillage the nonlethal armaments, clip the radio to my belt (after turning it off), and pocket the cuffs.

I take one last look at the unconscious pair and slip out the door into an empty hallway. I'm at the end of a hundred-foot-long, straight-as-an-arrow corridor. The floor is checkered linoleum, a far cry from the oriental rug on the living-quarters level. The tan walls are barren save for the occasional room label and utilitarian sconce. An EXIT sign glows red from the far end of the hallway.

Stun gun in hand, I stalk down the corridor. The first three doors I try are locked. The fourth opens smoothly. I flick on the light. The room is identical to mine with two exceptions: there is a vase of roses decorating a countertop, filling the air with their scent, and a woman asleep in bed. She's not restrained, but she's not waking from the light, either, so she must be sedated.

I step inside and close the door behind me.

A heart monitor beeps slowly and steadily. An IV hangs by her bed, the needle strapped to her wrist. She's thin. Gaunt. Hasn't eaten anything substantial in a very long time. But I can see her beauty beyond the malnourishment. I lean in close to her face, inspecting the details. "Who are you?" I whisper.

A splotch of purple on her arms draws my eyes away from her face. I turn the limb over and find it pocked with deep purple bruising and long, thin scars, some of them blazing with red freshness. *What the hell are they doing to this woman?* A chart hanging from the end of her bed catches my attention. I read the name. "M. Shiloh."

Muffled voices, just outside the door, spin me around. The door handle turns. I'm in motion before I can develop a course of action, but my body moves like fluid, bending around obstacles as they emerge and striking with force. The first man, dressed in a long white doctor's coat, is on the floor by the time my consciousness catches up. Clear fluid from a burst IV bag pools around him. The second, a security guard, twitches madly as the two metal prongs buried in his chest deliver a hundred thousand volts into his nervous system. Before he falls to the ground, I drop him with a punch. It's a low blow, hitting a guy who's being shocked, but I need him unconscious, and the stun gun won't do that.

His twitching body slides along the wall and collapses. Moving quickly, I drag both men inside the room and shove them in the bathroom. I don't find any sedatives in the cupboards, so I bind and gag them with spare sheets, take the guard's radio, and wedge a chair beneath the bathroom door's handle.

With so many people around, it must be morning, which means my time is short. I leave the room and move quickly down the hallway. Assuming all the unlabeled doors lead to more examination rooms, I jog down the hall, reading labels as I go. None sound interesting until I get to a set of double doors labeled DOCUMENTUM.

It's Latin.

What the hell? I know Latin?

Documentum means "proof" or, more loosely, "evidence," which is the same word etched on my plastic pendant; I don't think they're related, but it sounds like what I'm looking for.

I shove the doors and find them locked. I swipe Winters's keycard across the panel next to the door. It turns green, and I hear the lock click back. I shove the doors open, rush into the space beyond, and stop in my tracks.

For the first time in my one-year memory, I'm shocked into silence.

10.

Dead eyes stare at me. Hundreds of them.

The vast room is split in two. Both sides contain large numbers of ten-foot-tall, four-foot-diameter glass tubes full of green fluid. The tubes are lit from above and below, exposing the contents while leaving the rest of the room, which is black from floor to ceiling, in darkness. Serial numbers and bar codes are etched into the glass of each tube.

I step inside the macabre space and let the doors swing shut behind me. On the right side of the room, the hundred or so specimen tubes are empty. But on the left . . . The remains of tortured men, women, and children are suspended in the green liquid. While I know they feel no shame in death, their naked display is repulsive. But their nudity isn't the worst of it. Each and every person met with a violent and untimely end. Some have multiple stab wounds. Others were shot. A few were eviscerated. I see broken bones, some protruding from the skin, and caved-in skulls. It's a menagerie of violent ends.

That woman I found. Shiloh. Will she end up here, too?

Will I?

I shake my head. *Not likely.*

The sound of voices pulls me deeper into the room. A rectangle of white light glows, revealing a door on the back wall. Lit by lime-green gore, I walk toward the door, Taser in hand.

I look at the dead faces as I pass, my anger growing like a supervolcano. Who were these people? Mothers. Fathers. Innocent children with long lives ahead of them. I see different ages, from babies to gray-haired grandmothers. A variety of nationalities are represented. It seems like a perfect sampling of the entire human race, and since we're in New Hampshire, where only 7 percent of the population isn't gleaming white, many of these people must have been collected from around the country, if not the world.

While in SafeHaven, I heard stories from some of the older,

higher-functioning patients who'd spent time at the New Hampshire State Hospital, which was basically an asylum for the "insane
and feeble-minded"—like SafeHaven, but with a deplorable moral
fiber. One of my many counselors, a young woman with high hopes,
told me the lurid details, which was against all sorts of rules, but
she, like most people there, could see I was "normal," aside from
a complete lack of fear.

Hundreds of "patients" were sterilized as part of a statewide
eugenics program. The hospital carried out lobotomies, electro-
shock, and insulin-shock therapies. A horror show, it was closed
in 1983. Rampant abuse left patients worse off than when they
entered. Those who died as a result of their abuse were buried in
the hospital's cemetery and forgotten.

This . . . is worse.

Not only were these people likely tortured and brutally slain,
their corpses are on display. Objects of necro-admiration. At
least the patients at the state hospital were put in the ground.
Even if these bodies are still being studied, I don't see why they
should be staged in a gallery.

I turn my eyes to the right. Given the number of empty chambers, Neuro Inc.'s collection still has room to grow.

The bright glow of the small door's window beckons me. The
voices grow louder. Sliding up beside the door, I peek through the
window. The room is some kind of large laboratory. Where *Documentum* is black and green, the space on the other side of the door
is almost pure white, save for the table and countertops, which are
black. Cabinets and refrigeration units, all with glass fronts, line
the walls. Inside each is a collection of liquids and powders kept
in vials, test tubes, beakers, and vessels for which I have no name.
I see petri dishes, computer stations, and various scientific equipment. The only one of which I recognize is a centrifuge. At the far
end is an operating table and a collection of surgical tools.

How many of the bodies behind me once lay upon that table?

Lyons is inside, as is Allenby and a third man I haven't met.
While the two doctors are dressed in long white coats, the stranger
is dressed in black battle-dress uniform, otherwise known as
BDUs. His hair is cut close—I run a hand over my prickly head—
like mine is now. A gun is holstered on his hip. This man isn't a
security guard. He's something else.

I look back at the roomful of green glowing bodies.

He's the collector, I think, part of some kind of abduction unit, taking these people out of the world and bringing them here. But for what purpose?

I suspect the answers lie on the other side of the door. If not physically, then inside Lyons's brain. After what I've seen, I have no doubt I can get him to reveal everything. But first, a little recon.

I grip the doorknob and twist it slowly. It's unlocked and well-constructed. When the latch disengages, the door opens an inch without sound. Lyons's voice is no longer muffled. "We're moving forward."

"He's a wild card," the stranger says. "He's dangerous. Unpredictable. You should have told me before bringing him here."

"You know why we need him," Lyons says, his face turning red.

"And if he doesn't cooperate?" the man asks. "If he gets violent? Refuses the treatment?" He makes air quotes with his fingers when saying, "treatment." "How long are you going to let this go, and will you allow me to do what I need to if he becomes a problem?"

Lyons waves the man off and opens a refrigeration unit. "We will all do what we must." He reaches inside and pulls out a syringe with a rubber stopper over the needle. It's full of translucent, yellow-tinged liquid. He holds the syringe with both hands, like it's the most precious thing in the world, like other people hold newborns. The fridge holds at least a dozen more prepped syringes. Whatever it is, it's important and rare. He places the syringe into a protective foam holder on the countertop. "It's taken years and a good number of lives to get this far. If we must resort to force, then we will."

"Stephen," Allenby says, admonishing. "You know that won't work. He's—"

"Someone upon whom subtlety is lost," Lyons interjects.

Allenby shakes her head. "People could get hurt."

The military man plants his fists on the countertop and leans toward Lyons. "This isn't just business, it's war, and people are already getting hurt. If a second augmentation makes him even crazier"—he looks at Allenby—"we'll do what's needed, whatever that might be."

They're talking about me.

I'm the one who might get violent.

He's right about that, I think. Also about being dangerous and unpredictable, as they'll soon discover.

"Katzman, *please.* Just stop." Allenby paces, eyes on the ceiling, head shaking back and forth. Lyons has a cold streak beneath that grandfatherly exterior, but from what I know of Allenby so far, she doesn't belong in a place like this. *What are you doing here?* As I watch Allenby, her head lowers, and her eyes track toward me. She freezes when we make eye contact through the glass, but then she just looks annoyed. "You just couldn't stop yourself, could you?"

Katzman is fast, but he's also the closest to the door. As he spins around, gun rising into position, I kick the door as hard as I can. The metal door strikes the gun barrel, twisting the weapon out of the man's grasp. I'm on him in a flash, but this isn't like knocking out Winters or assaulting the security guards. This man is a skilled fighter, and he blocks my first three blows, all of which would have ended the fight before it began.

The problem for my opponent is that I'm equally skilled—somehow—but nothing is holding me back. When he begins his counterattack, I dodge the first two punches, but when he launches into a spinning kick, I block it—with Allenby. I take her by the shoulders and rotate her into my position. Katzman's kick connects with Allenby's head with all the force intended for me. She slams into the door and falls to the linoleum.

When the soldier sees what he's done, he reels back in shock. "Shit!" He looks at me. "You motherfu—"

My fist on the side of his jaw cuts him off. Even the most seasoned warrior can be slowed by the sudden realization that they've just injured a friend. He spills back onto the counter, knocking the syringe to the floor. The foam case fails to do its duty.

Glass shatters.

Liquid spills.

Lyons shouts, "No!"

I pull my fist back to pummel Katzman into submission, but the first blow did its job. He slides across the counter, pulling a computer keyboard and mouse with him, and falls to the floor.

"What are you doing?" Lyons shouts. He should be backing away from me. He's not a threat, but he's standing his ground.

I rub my foot through the spilled liquid. "This is important to you?"

"Yes." The word comes out as a gasp. He's clutching his chest, falling back. He slides down against the counter, suddenly out of breath.

I recognize the signs of a heart attack but make no move to help the man. Instead, I open the refrigerator and take out the remaining vials, shattering them on the floor.

Lyons fumbles to open a pill case, which I'm assuming contains medication that could save his life. He stops when I lift up the very last syringe. His eyes go wide. Desperate. Revealing its worth. "Don't." I lower the syringe, looking at the liquid within. This is my insurance policy.

When I put the syringe in a protective plastic case and slip it in my pocket, he starts digging for his pills again. He's not going anywhere fast—maybe nowhere ever again if he can't get his pills—so I leave him there on the floor. I recover Katzman's gun and head back into the *Documentum* room, mentally planning for how I'll retrieve the Shiloh woman and get us both out.

That's when the alarm sounds.

11.

The Shiloh woman is still out, despite the blaring, high-pitched shriek of the building's security alarm. She looks frail. I consider leaving her behind, but it would be like abandoning a wounded bird in the clutches of a house cat—death would only come after drawn-out torture. The bruising and fresh scars on the woman's arms suggest that she's been tormented long enough already.

But can I keep her safe during my escape? It seems unlikely, but I picture her floating in green liquid, just another face in the death gallery, and know I can't leave her behind.

I lean over her, tapping her face. "Hey. Wake up."

No reaction. Whatever they've been lacing her IVs with, it's powerful stuff.

With time running short, I slip the IV needle from her arm, undo her restraints, and pull the blankets away. She's dressed in a loose hospital johnny. I lean her up. Her head lulls, but I catch it against my chest. "I got you." Moving carefully, I scoop her up behind her back and under the knees. She's light. Maybe a hundred pounds.

I head for the door, leading with Katzman's gun, which is poking out from under the woman's knees. The hallway is empty. I head for the distant exit sign, passing the *Documentum* room. There are voices within—shouting. Sounds like Allenby and Lyons. Katzman is either still unconscious or heading my way. I look down at the woman's face, soft and peaceful. She doesn't know it, but she's depending on me to save her.

Just beyond the *Documentum* room, on the opposite side of the hall, are the elevator doors. Red numbers above the doors scroll higher. Someone is already on the way up, most likely security of some kind.

I move on, toward the exit sign at the end of the hall, which ends at a T junction and a row of windows, slanted at a forty-five-degree angle. Turning left, I see the exit door ahead. I try the knob with my left hand, balancing Shiloh's weight on my forearm. It's locked. A key-card terminal is mounted next to the door.

I gently place the woman on the floor and swipe Winters's card across the flat card reader, but the light flashes red. I try again with the same results. The security alarm triggered by Lyons must have put the building in a lockdown. But there might be a way to override it. I sprint back to the T junction. Halfway between the end of the hall and the elevators, I had spotted a bright red fire alarm.

I round the corner and run for the alarm. It's encased in a plastic dome to prevent it from behind triggered accidentally, but it lifts up easily enough. I wrap my fingers around the small white handle and pull. The alarm ripping through the hallway becomes a whooping siren. Strobe lights flash.

It's all enough to keep me from noticing the opening elevator doors—that is, until someone yells, "Don't move!"

But I move.

And the guard, who probably has no idea what kind of situation he's just run into, doesn't see it coming. Because he's a low-level employee and probably doesn't know the full extent of what goes on here, I'm merciful. I fire two shots. The first strikes his hand and knocks his weapon—a stun gun—to the floor. The second hits his thigh, far from the femoral artery. With a shout, he drops to the floor, clutching his good hand over his wounded hand over the hole in his leg.

The attack took just over a second.

Geez, I have good aim.

"Switch to lethal response!" shouts a strong-sounding woman still inside the elevator. "This is Alpha Unit. Target is armed. All units switch to lethal response." Through the wailing siren, I hear various teams confirming the news. I also hear the sound of readying weapons. I have successfully roused the hornet's nest.

Running backward, I retreat—not out of fear, but the desire to free Shiloh. A shadow inside the elevator shifts, and I squeeze off a single round.

Someone yelps and ducks back inside.

I keep the security force at bay with two more equally spaced rounds. They saw how fast their man went down. When I reach the T junction, they finally get up the nerve to return fire. A barrage of bullets scorches the air where I stood a moment ago. The rounds punch into the slanted, tinted glass window, which spider-webs but doesn't shatter.

While the security team continues to fire blindly, I swipe the key card. The light shines green. Whatever lockdown was put in place by the first alarm has been undone by the fire alarm. The door is unlocked. I whip it open to find a stairwell. But it's not empty. A team of five security guards turn their heads, and guns, in my direction. I duck back as bullets punch into the backside of the metal door.

The blind fire from the elevator continues until magazines run dry.

In the moment of silence that follows, I heft Shiloh over one shoulder so I can run and fire at the same time. Holding her is a risk. She could get shot. But I'm willing to bet both our lives that the security guards won't shoot at an unconscious woman. Me? I might. No, I *would*. But they're not me.

I lean against the corner wall of the T junction, poke my head around the corner, and fire two more missed shots into the elevator. A moment later, a second barrage tears up the hallway and the window at the end. When the firing stops, I step out into plain view, weapon raised, ready to charge into the elevator and finish things. But before I can, a door at the far end of the hall bursts open.

Five soldiers in black armor, complete with helmets and face masks, storm into the hallway. They're armed with laser-sighted MP5 submachine guns. I can't beat them. Not now. But my gambit has paid off. They haven't opened fire.

Yet.

That changes when the *Documentum* doors swing open and Katzman steps out. He points at me and shouts, "Kill him!"

I turn and run.

Bullets chase me, punching into the window ahead as they buzz past. Despite the order to kill me, the soldiers are obviously trying not to hit Shiloh. There's a good chance she's going to die anyway, but they haven't left me with much choice. I put a few more holes in the now loose and sagging window, lower my shoulder, and slam into it like a hockey player against the boards.

The abused pane bends outward, resists for a fraction of a second, and then gives way. Instead of punching through the glass, as planned, the window lifts up and falls beneath me as I leap out of the window. I land hard on my ass, feet forward, like a kid on the world's biggest slide.

Startled shouts pursue me but fade quickly as I begin my glass-on-glass carpet ride down a several-hundred-foot-long, forty-five-degree slope. The windows beneath shriek as we etch a path of scratches in our wake. Our escape is going to cost Neuro Inc. a lot of money, though I suspect the damage is a negligible expense compared to losing the contents of the syringe in my pocket.

I lean forward, watching the ground quickly approach. Looks like a five-foot drop at the bottom, but the building is surrounded by a carpet of thick grass that should cushion our fall. Shiloh's the lucky one. She's as limp as a rag doll in my arms. Of course, I have no trouble staying loose, either. A lack of fear means that I'm free of the thirtysomething hormones dumped into the body when afraid. My muscles are relaxed. My heart rate is regular. There's no tunnel vision, meaning I'm still able to focus on the larger picture, planning moves in advance, rather than just reacting.

With five stories to go, an explosion blows out the third-floor window directly below us. I glance up. Katzman is above us, shouting into a two-way radio, no doubt directing the unit waiting for us below.

When we reach the fourth-floor window, with just a moment to spare, I roll hard to the left, throwing myself over Shiloh and then yanking her back on top of me. We whip past the open window and the startled faces of the team waiting to put a bullet in my head.

Our descent slows thanks to the friction created by my jeans and the soles of my feet. When we reach the bottom, I have time to sit up, get Shiloh into my arms, and inch over the edge. I land on the grass, bending at the knees to keep Shiloh from being jolted too hard—again. If she wakes up anytime soon, she's going to hurt.

Better than being held prisoner or kept in a tube.

With the woman over my shoulder again, I glance up. No one in sight. Not a single man is willing to follow my escape route. I dig into my pocket, remove Winters's keys, and push the lock button. A distant horn beacons me onward.

12.

The horn guides me like the returning sound waves of a sonar ping, but I try not to cram the car's lock button too many times lest I advertise my destination. I doubt anyone inside can hear the horn over the two alarms reverberating through Neuro Inc. Even outside, I can hear the blaring sirens. Hell, I can see the windows vibrating with each shrill whoop.

I round the corner to the front of the building. A massive parking lot stretches out before me. It's full, but not just with cars. A steady stream of confused Neuro employees hurries out the front doors, filtering into the parking lot. They're a blessing and a curse. They'll help me disappear, but they'll also slow me down, giving the security teams time to reach the parking lot. I slow my stride, shift Shiloh into both arms, and do my very best to look afraid.

The first person who sees me looks at Shiloh first, then at me. She reels back upon making eye contact and hurries away. She either recognized me or my attempt at fear went horribly awry. I give up trying to look afraid and calmly strut into the parking lot, which is swirling with more people than a football tailgate party.

Walking calmly with the woman in my arms while showing no fear garners far less attention. A few people look my way, concern in their eyes, until they see my rock-solid confidence. It's like some voice in their heads is saying, "Don't worry. He's got it under control." And they go right back to chatting about what could have caused the double alarms. It's a far greater mystery to them than the fate of the unconscious stranger dressed in a johnny. It's also possible that Shiloh isn't the only unconscious patient being brought out of the building. I didn't get a look in the other rooms. They might have all been occupied for all I know.

I push the lock button. The horn responds, pulling my eyes to the right. Winters's orange SUV is easy to see. Unfortunately, so is the woman my worried face sent running. She's got a man in tow, but a quick assessment of the man reveals he's not a threat. For starters, he's pudgy and soft. But it's the medical kit he's holding, along with the red cross on his white polo shirt, that reveals he's a medic, which, if I'm honest—and I always am—could come in handy.

"There he is!" the woman shouts, pointing at me.

The people around us turn and stare, but my continuing calm and the medic's arrival make us a nonevent compared to the continuing evacuation. It probably helps that no one seems to recognize Shiloh. Or me.

"What's wrong with her?" the medic asks me. He's out of breath. Hands on knees.

I motion to the back of the SUV and click the unlock button. The rear lights flash yellow. "Get the hatch so I can lay her down."

He nods quickly and opens the hatch. "Good idea." He climbs inside the SUV and puts down the back seats. He turns to me and waves me in.

This is going to be easier than I thought.

I gently place Shiloh into the back of the SUV and the medic, supporting her head in one hand, helps guide her inside. Once she's settled, he puts his fingers on her wrist and stares at his watch, checking her heart rate.

A hand on my arm turns me around. I'm ready to deliver a number of attacks, but it's the concerned young woman. "What happened to her?"

"I rescued her," I say.

She turns to the Neuro building. "Is there really a fire?"

A quick glance around reveals that no one is watching us. In reply to the woman's question, I quickly squeeze, tap, and slap the same three pressure points that knocked Winters out cold. But here's the thing: a very small number of people are resistant to the technique. This woman is one of those people. Instead of falling unconscious into my arms, she reels around and says, "Oww! What the hell was that—"

The butt of my empty handgun against the side of her head does a much better job. I catch her in my left arm and lay her down in the empty space beside Winters's SUV. When I stand back up, the medic is staring at me with wide eyes. Eyebrows turned up in the middle. Lips pulled tight to the sides.

Now *that's* what fear looks like.

I point the gun at him. "She's your patient now. You take care of her and you'll be just fine. Understood?"

He nods furiously.

With one last look around to confirm we've gone unnoticed, I close the SUV's hatch.

That's when a gunshot rips through the air.

"Everybody down!" The amplified voice is followed by a loud three-round burst. "On the ground! Now!"

All around the parking lot, people drop in fear.

All but one.

Dammit.

I need to start watching people's fear-based social cues and mimic them when appropriate. It's too late now. Being the only person still standing in the parking lot, in front of a bright-orange SUV, has made me stick out like a—well, like a bright-orange SUV.

I duck down a fraction of a second before the first bullet comes my way. I dive to the unforgiving pavement along the driver's-side door. The gunfire stops as I disappear from sight. They want to stop me something fierce, but they've got a lot of bystanders to worry about, too. I roll back to my feet, staying low, and open the driver's door.

The tall seats hide me from view when I climb inside, but that won't be much help when the security teams flank the vehicle. If they're even remotely competent, they have two teams already moving up the sides of the lot. I've got just a few seconds.

"Who are you?" the medic asks.

I glance back, reassessing the man. Most people would have bolted when I came under fire, but he stayed by Shiloh's side. He's got a blanket over her and a blood pressure cuff on her arm.

"And what happened to this woman?" He lifts her arm, revealing the string of bruises.

"Wish I knew," I tell him, answering both questions. "Better hold on tight."

He nods and lies down, draping an arm, a leg, and a portion of his torso over Shiloh's body. It's as secure as they're going to get.

The engine growls to life. I yank the gear shift into drive and crush the gas pedal. Tires screech as I punch forward, shoving aside the small hybrid car parked in front of us. People run for cover as the SUV roars through the parking lot, hitting thirty miles per hour. I hammer the brakes at the end of the row, twisting the wheel. All four tires squeal as we spin. A gray cloud of burning rubber billows around the vehicle. When our turn hits the ninety-degree mark, I hit the gas again and race toward the back of the lot.

Rows flash by. Five to go, then it's an empty lot and a clear shot to the long winding drive through the woods.

"Look out!" the medic shouts. He's still lying down, but he's leaning up, looking out the passenger's-side window. I follow his line of sight and see what has him concerned—a black Humvee complete with a mounted machine gun races up the parking lot's center aisle.

The big gun turns toward us and opens fire.

A row of cars flash between us, absorbing the high-caliber ammunition that would have shredded the SUV.

I hit the brakes and turn hard to the right, into the next row. The Humvee races ahead into the empty lot, turning in a wide circle. The SUV's throaty engine shakes my seat as the big vehicle accelerates to fifty miles per hour. We quickly reach the center aisle, and I turn hard to the left, just missing a car but careening over a concrete wheel stop at the end of an empty parking space. The right side of the SUV bounces into the air and slams back down with a jolt.

"I've got her!" the medic shouts, reassuring me that he's doing his job.

While the Humvee rounds toward us, I aim for the drive at the back of the lot and keep the gas pedal pegged.

Asphalt explodes from the parking lot ahead of us as a line of heavy machine-gun fire, lit by bright-orange tracer rounds, cuts across. Chunks of tar bounce off the windshield, but the gunfire stops as the gunner adjusts his aim.

A second volley of bullets shatters the rear side window, but we're quickly beyond the line of fire. Whoever is shooting at us hasn't had a lot of practice with a moving target. Even if the security team is ex-military with real-world experience, a lack of practice can dull reaction times.

Not for me, though. All of this seems to just come naturally.

The empty lot around us morphs into a wall of trees. Tall pines line the road, their scent washing through the shattered window and overwhelming the stench of burnt rubber.

Gunfire erupts behind us, but the trees get the worst of it, and continue to as the Humvee gunner spews lead. The winding path through the woods slows our flight, but it also keeps the Humvee from getting more than a brief glimpse of the SUV.

We round the final bend and race toward the security gate. A public road is just twenty feet beyond the solid-looking guard-house. Four men in security uniforms stand in front of the gate, handguns raised. One of them shakes an open palm at me. These men have clearly not been warned yet. If they had been, they wouldn't have wasted time trying to request me to stop; they would have simply opened fire.

They get the idea when I accelerate toward them. The bravest of the four squeezes off two rounds. Both miss. Probably because the man was already running when he fired. They dive away, two to a side, narrowly missing being added to the long list of New Hampshire's daily roadkill. The gate, however, doesn't move for me. But it's not nearly as robust as it looks. The metal pole bends with a shriek and allows us passage.

I glance in the rearview.

The Humvee skids to a stop. The guards pick themselves up.

No one pursues us.

The chase, it seems, ended at the gate.

I turn onto the road and tear away from Neuro Inc. I'd like to say it's the last time I'll see the place, but I know it's not. Once Shiloh is safe, I'll be back. What they're doing is wrong, and that's something I can't let go. Not because I'm a bleeding-heart vigilante, but because they thought they could add me to their collection of tortured souls, and I take that personally.

I look back at my passenger. He looks shaken. Frightened. But he's still tending to Shiloh. "How is she?"

"Hell if I know," the medic says. "What happened to her? Is she in a coma?"

Hadn't considered that. "I assumed she'd been sedated, but I honestly don't know."

"Was this done to her at Neuro?" he asks.

I nod. "I'm guessing your security clearance is pretty low."

"I started a month ago." He looks back at Shiloh, then to me. He extends his hand toward me. "I'm Jim. Jim Cobb."

I twist my hand back and give his a firm shake. "I'm Crazy."

He gives a lopsided nervous smile. "I noticed."

13.

I turn into the driveway after my third pass. The home, a tan cape with an attached three-car garage, is definitely unoccupied. Though the mailbox is empty—likely being held at the owner's request—three plastic-wrapped newspapers rest on the front porch steps. Even if the homeowner had lackluster feelings about reading a paper in the digital age, someone would have, at the very least, kicked the staircase obstacles aside.

I stop the SUV in front of the garage and turn it off, pocketing the keys. I glance back at Cobb, still monitoring Shiloh's condition. "Any change?"

He shakes his head.

"You gonna run if I have a look around?"

He frowns. Pats his soft belly. "I'm not a very fast runner."

"And you don't want to leave her alone with me, right?"

His frown deepens. He avoids eye contact. "That a bad thing?"

"I'd call it admirable." I open the door and slide out into the morning heat. Winters's vehicle has all the bells and whistles, including a frigid air-conditioning system and cooled seats. My ass is downright chilly.

I take a quick look around. The house is in the woods, trees on three sides and across the street. The nearest neighbors are a hundred yards away. I jump up the front stairs and try the door. As expected, it's locked. On my way back down the steps, I notice a fist-sized rock sitting amidst the brown wood chips surrounding the neatly clipped bushes. I stop, eyes on the rock, and sigh.

What kind of moron puts a key in a fake rock and then leaves that rock in a place it doesn't belong?

I pick up the rock and give it a shake. A metallic clanging from inside confirms my suspicions.

Looks like I'm about to find out what kind of moron.

Key in hand, I discard the rock and unlock the front door. Hot, humid air that smells faintly like dog washes out of the home. But there's no barking. Definitely on vacation. With one last glance back at the SUV, I move into the house. It's spotless, despite the scent of dog. Ignoring the staircase leading up, I step into the small dining room, through the kitchen, and down the hall to the garage. I open the door and whistle. A black 1969 Boss 429 Mustang is parked on the far side. I take back every bad thought I had about the home's owner. While he had bad taste in security, his taste in cars is impeccable, though I'm now absolutely certain he's a moron, leaving this vehicle so poorly protected.

The garage itself is the pinnacle of organization. Pegboards hold a variety of tools. A wall of shelving holds an array of plastic bins with labels like WINTER, YARD GAMES, and GARDEN. A generator, snow blower, and riding lawn mower are parked along the back wall. All red. And above everything, arranged along a pair of two-by-fours hung from the ceiling is an assortment of skis.

I slap the middle of three large white buttons and the center garage door grinds up. I run outside, pull the SUV into the garage, and close the garage door. We're only a thirty-minute drive from Neuro Inc., but we'll be a hell of a lot harder to find inside the house than driving around in Winters's bright-orange beacon. It's a small miracle they didn't already locate us by helicopter, but they must have been relying on the vehicle's GPS unit to track us. Unfortunately for them, I stopped and removed the device's antenna the moment I realized we weren't being pursued on the ground.

I open the vehicle's rear door. Cobb is waiting for me, one hand supporting Shiloh's head, the other holding her hands over her stomach. "Take her under the knees. We'll carry her together."

"You in charge now?" I ask him.

"Do you have a medical degree?" he asks.

"I don't know."

"Let's just agree that you don't," he says.

Cobb is afraid. Probably terrified. But he's controlling it better than most, focusing on his job. I don't know anything else about him, but he's still earning my respect. I hook my hands around the back of Shiloh's knees and pull. Working together, we slide her out of the SUV and carry her into the house, depositing her on the first-floor bedroom's king-sized Posturepedic. Her lithe body sinks into the plush down comforter. Still immobile, but still breathing.

Cobb stands back and clears his throat. His nervous eyes glance at the handgun tucked into the waist of my pants.

I decide he's earned my honesty. "It's not loaded."

He clearly doesn't believe me, so I point the weapon at the floor and pull the trigger several times. "But, just so we're clear, I was just released from a mental institution. I don't feel fear. And I don't need a gun to kill you."

"Thanks," he says. "I feel much better."

His sarcasm brings a smile to my face. I motion toward the living room with my head. "Let's go have a chat."

The living room is typical Americana retiree with plaid couches, a collection of Hummel figurines, an unused exercise bike, and a massive flat-screen TV. I pat the recliner with my hand and wait for Cobb to sit in it. While he's sitting, I head for the kitchen and check the fridge. There's nothing inside that could spoil in less than a month, but there are four bottles of beer and a stick of pepperoni. After removing two beers and the pepperoni, I search the cabinets until I find a jar of peanut butter. I return to the couch with my booty and hand Cobb a beer. He takes it with a nod, digs out a jackknife from his pocket, and pops the top. He hands the knife to me.

I pop my beer top and then extend the two-inch knife. I rub the blade sideways across my thumb. It's razor sharp. "You could have slit my throat."

Cobb takes a swig. "Taking lives isn't my job."

I fold the knife back down. His initials are engraved on the side, beneath the white cross. "Was it a gift?"

"From my aunt," he says.

I hold the potential weapon out to Cobb. He stares at it. "Seriously?"

"If you were going to kill me, you would have done it before we reached the front gate."

He takes the jackknife, pockets it, and takes a long drink. When he's done, he breathes deep and lets out a long sigh. "Are there any more of these?"

"Two."

"I'm going to need them, I think."

"They're all yours."

Cobb stands, walks to the fridge. While he's gone, I open the peanut butter and disrobe the pepperoni. On some level, I know this snack is disgusting, but I'm craving protein, salt, and fluids. I dip the pepperoni into the peanut butter, scoop up a thick glob, and take a bite. The supernova of powerful flavors is nearly overwhelming. The food at SafeHaven was mass-produced, preservative-filled, cheap slop. This is a feast in comparison. All that time I was missing the scents of the world, I never realized I also missed flavor.

Cobb returns with his beers while I chew. I can see the revulsion in his face when he looks at my snack, but he doesn't say anything. Before sitting, he turns on a window-mounted air conditioner.

I tip my head in thanks, chase my food down with a swig of beer, and say, "So, you've worked for Neuro for one month?"

"Yeah," he says, and there's not a trace of hesitation.

"And before that?"

"I was a paramedic for Portsmouth Regional."

"Why the switch?"

"There was a fire. I saved a few people. A wild day—less wild than today, though. But it was front-page news, and two days later I got a call. A recruiter for Neuro. He said they wanted people like me, who could handle a crisis if one ever developed. I thought it was strange that a private company would want a paramedic on staff, but he offered double what I was making, and I thought it would be a quieter job." He forces a grin. "Until today, it was."

I believe him. He'd be acting squirrelly if he was lying to me. That's good for him, but bad for me. Some intel would go a long way right now.

"What about you?" he asks. "Were you really . . . you know?" He twirls his index finger around an ear.

"Yup. SafeHaven. North of Concord."

"I've heard of it. For what?"

"I don't feel fear," I say.

"Like at all?"

"Not even a little."

"So, if I pulled a gun on you?" he asks.

"That would be a bad idea," I tell him. "But, no."

Cobb pops open his second beer. "So, no dreams about being naked in public places or late for a college test?"

"I'm . . . not sure if I dream, but no. And I don't remember college."

"Must have had a lot of fun," Cobb says.

I shake my head. "I don't remember anything beyond a year."

"Geez . . ." Cobb leans forward, elbows on his knees. "What happened a year ago?"

"Hell if I know."

"So, amnesia then?"

"That's the diagnosis."

Cobb scratches his chin. "But you remember *some* things, right? Like, you can speak English. You can drive—very well, by the way. What else?"

"I know how to hurt people," I say. "And I've played this game. I don't think you're going to like where it leads."

That kills his curiosity. He leans back, wiping dew drops from the beer bottle. "Whoever you were before . . . that's not who you are now?"

"I don't know." I shake my head. "This isn't helpful."

He takes a drink while I turn my thoughts inward. I don't need to know who I am. Not right now, anyway. But what *do* I need? To get Shiloh someplace she'll be cared for. And then what? Go back to Neuro and shut them down. I know I should just run. It's what most people would do. They have a security force, some kind of black ops team, heavy weapons, and who knows what else. Definitely government-funded. But fleeing requires fear and the ability to look past what is right and wrong. I'm incapable of both.

"You worked at a hospital?" I ask.

"Portsmouth Regional."

"How far?"

"Forty-minute drive."

"Still know people there?"

He nods.

"Then that's where we're headed."

"Now?" he asks, surprised.

"We'll wait until Shiloh wakes up. See what she has to say." I tilt my beer back. Polish it off. "If Neuro is out looking for us, they'll have widened the search far beyond this place in just a few hours, and they won't be looking for that sweet number out in the garage. If we take back roads and avoid tolls, we shouldn't have any trouble getting to the hospital."

"So we go to the hospital, and then what?"

I smile the kind of smile that also serves as an apology. "You're going to help me get back inside Neuro."

He groans, no doubt hoping that wouldn't be the answer I gave. "And *then*?"

I dip the pepperoni in the peanut butter, take a bite, and, with a full mouth, say, "You should probably . . . start looking . . . for a new job."

"And what if they just kill you?" he asks.

"They won't."

"'Cause you're sooo good at hurting people?"

I smile, genuinely, and dig the plastic case containing the syringe out of my pocket. "Because I have this."

He leans forward, looking at the syringe behind the clear plastic cover. "And that is?"

"I have no idea."

"What *do* you know?"

"That they've killed a lot people to create this." I tap the plastic case. "And that they will kill me to retrieve it. I'm just never going to give them the chance."

14.

Full of pepperoni and peanut butter, I lounge back on the couch, lost in thought. About Neuro, the things I saw there, and Shiloh. It all made some kind of twisted sense when I first saw everything. But now, in retrospect, it's a mess. Too many questions remain unanswered, but doubt has begun weakening my resolve. It wouldn't be the first time my lack of fear has caused me to act without thinking beyond immediate circumstances.

It's not that the horrible things I saw no longer seem horrible, it's that Allenby was downright likable. And I don't think it was an act. She struck me as a good person, and I'm a fairly good, and quick, judge of character. So how could she abide such lethal human experimentation?

Part of me says she couldn't. That's where the doubt comes from.

And here's the thing about doubt. It changes nothing. While I may not be 100 percent certain in my verdict about Neuro, I have no fear of discovering I'm wrong, even if I've already reduced the building to a pile of rubble. I should probably still be locked up. I recognize the flaw. But it doesn't change anything.

The large-screen TV blinks on.

"Do you mind?" Cobb asks, remote in hand.

I shake my head. "What time is it?"

Cobb looks at his watch. "Eleven in the A.M."

"*Price Is Right* is on," I say. "Channel seven."

Instead of punching in the number, Cobb surfs through the channels, one digit at a time, counting down from 347. Around 300 he starts hitting the cable news networks. The images I see on each are very similar.

And familiar.

"Wait," I say. He stops two channels past the news networks. "Go back."

The TV blinks twice and then displays an aerial view of New York City. The streets are full of people, swarming about. I can't tell if it's a protest or a riot, but if things turned violent in Manchester, New Hampshire, the atmosphere in New York must be worse. "What's happening?"

"What, the riots?" Cobb looks confused. "You don't know?"

"I've been in an institution," I remind him.

"Right." He turns back to the screen.

People swirl through the streets, entering and leaving shattered storefronts, taking part in or cheering on several brawls. Safe-Haven now seems like an asylum for the sane compared to the scene unfolding in New York.

"It started in the largest cities with the highest violent crime rates. Detroit. Memphis. St. Louis. They were small protests at first, but there was no unified theme. People just seemed to be protesting whatever made them afraid. The government. Wall Street. GMO foods. The protests grew in size and spread to the larger cities. Los Angeles. New York. Washington, D.C. For a week, this is how it went. Until Portland."

"Maine?" I ask.

"Oregon—which, by the way, is basically the world capital for nice people. A parade of atheists protesting an Easter egg hunt on government property turned violent. Killed a guy in a bunny suit. The whole thing was live on TV. It acted as a catalyst. In response to the bunny murder, a religious group torched an abortion clinic. One act of violence led to another, spreading across the country's most densely populated areas. But things really got bad when riot police began pushing back. Some cities are like war zones."

"Is anyone instigating the attacks?" I ask. "Foreign countries? Terror organizations?"

"That's just the thing," Cobb says. "The protests didn't stop at the U.S. border. They're now worldwide. And you're not the first person to wonder if fear had somehow been weaponized. Tension between nations is building the same way it is with people on the street. And that's only making things worse. It seemed like New England, north of Boston, was a safe zone, like there was a buffer of calm logic holding the fear back, but yesterday . . ."

"What happened?"

"A riot in Manchester. It was quelled faster than most. The population is fairly small compared to places like New York. But people died. Some in a gunfight with police before the tear gas broke things up, and two others in a—"

"The owner of an antique store and a man with a broken back," I say.

He turns toward me slowly. "I thought you said you hadn't seen the news?"

"I was there," I say. "In Manchester."

His eyes widen. The look in his eyes shifts from amazement to abject fear. He stands and steps away from me, hands over his mouth. "Oh my God, you're him!"

"Him?"

"The guy from the roof! *You* broke the man's back!"

"Didn't mean to kill him." He's about to argue the point. "Did you see the woman?"

He blinks. "What?"

"The woman about to get her arms broken and head bashed in, did you see her?"

He blinks twice more. He nods slowly. "You saved her."

I snap my fingers and point at him. "Now you're getting it. Her name was Allenby. Know her?"

"Should I?"

"She works for—"

A scream, feminine and primal, cuts me off. I'm on my feet and racing from the room before Cobb even reacts.

I'm down the hall.

Doorknob in hand.

Inside the room.

Shiloh.

She's sitting up, eyes open nearly as wide as her mouth. The scream is high-pitched, like some invisible torturer is conjuring a nightmare only she can see. Despite her open eyes. She doesn't see me. Even when I get in front of her. I'm invisible.

Until I speak. "Hey!"

Her eyes flick to mine. A switch is flipping. Her mouth snaps closed. Her eyes remain wide.

"You're okay," I tell her.

"I'm okay," she says, her voice almost trancelike.

Her wide eyes flick back and forth. "Where?"

"A house," I tell her.

"Whose?"

"I don't know."

"How long?" she asks.

"What?"

She reaches up. Touches the side of my head where the hair has started to salt and pepper. "Gray."

I smile at her and the expression is returned. The weight of that grin nearly breaks my heart. But then it's gone.

"Thirsty."

I turn toward the door, where Cobb is standing. "Get her some water."

Cobb leaves. I turn to the woman. "Look, Ms. Shiloh, I need to know what—"

"Miss?" she asks.

"Mrs.?"

I see the first signs of fresh fear emerge as tiny wrinkles at the center of her forehead. She's looking back and forth again, reassessing her surroundings.

She points a shaky finger at me. "Are you real? Who are you?"

I don't think telling her my name is Crazy will help much, so I tell her the truth, which isn't perfect, but far less intimidating. "I don't remember."

She leans forward, glaring into my eyes. The intensity of her stare churns up emotions that are new and uncomfortable.

Is this fear?

"You're a liar," she says.

"I am?"

"You lied to me!" She grips my forearm. Her nails dig into the skin. I barely notice.

"I did?" I take hold of her free arm, interlocking us in a circle of desperation. "When? What did I say?"

"That I was safe," she says.

"You're safe now."

She melts from the inside out, folding in on her frail self. "Too late." I can barely hear the whispered words. "Never safe. Not there. Not here."

"Shiloh," I say, putting my hand beneath her chin. I lift her head up. Her intense gaze is now vacant. Tears slide down her cheeks. She's shaking.

Cobb slides into the doorway. I see him out of the corner of my eye but don't look. This woman has answers about me. She knows me. Who I am. Who I was. And, apparently, how I failed her. Maybe this isn't my first attempt to rescue her? Maybe that's what happened a year ago?

Cobb clears his throat. "Hey."

I turn toward him. He's not holding a glass of water. Instead, he's rubbing his pants with his palms. Nervous sweat. His pupils are dilated. His skin is paler than I remember. He's afraid, and not because of me. "What?"

He licks his lips and with a shaky voice, says, "They're here."

15.

"Who's here?" Shiloh asks, looking confused. She starts whipping her head back and forth, like people might slip into the room through the solid walls. "Is it them? They've come back!"

The fear building inside this woman is like nothing I've seen before. Her face contorts to impossible angles, twisting her beautiful face into some macabre visage of a medieval gargoyle. She hooks her fingers and rakes her nails up her legs, scratching the skin. As she lifts the johnny, revealing her thighs, I see long scars that match the new scratches. She's done this before, and harder.

"No, no, no, no," she repeats the word over and over as she tears at her legs.

I take her face hard in both hands. She gasps and stops. "Listen to me," I tell her. "I *will* keep you safe."

She seems to weigh the validity of this statement and comes to a verdict. With a sneer, she growls out the word, "Liar," and then screams and flails until I let her go. "Liar!"

A shadow outside the bedroom window returns my thoughts to the impending intrusion. I would like to know how they found us, but there isn't time for questions that neither I nor Cobb will have the answer to.

"Stay with her," I tell Cobb. "If she hurts herself, throw the blankets over her and restrain her."

"And if they come in?" he asks.

"They won't be looking for you." I pat the plastic encased syringe in my pocket.

"Right. What are you going to do?"

I give him a smile that reflects my unnatural inner calm. "Probably something crazy."

I leave the room, lock the door, and close it behind me. Shiloh's screams fade as I run back to the garage. I have just seconds, maybe a minute tops, before the house is infiltrated. I have no idea exactly what I'm up against, but I have little doubt they're going to start the attack with gas, and / or flash bangs. They know what I can do. They won't risk a fair fight.

Neither will I.

I quickly find the plastic bin labeled WINTER and tear it open. A few seconds of rummaging provides what I need: a ski mask, ski goggles, and a scarf. I run across the garage, where a pristinely maintained riding mower is parked. On the seat is a pair of noise-canceling headphones. I snatch them up and run back the way I came.

On my way to the living room, I don the ski mask, goggles and headphones. I make a pit stop at the kitchen sink. The tap runs fast and cold, quickly soaking the scarf, which I then wrap around my face three times. Movement outside the kitchen window turns my attention outside. The yard is empty, but shadows in the surrounding woods shift unnaturally.

I head into the living room, which has windows on three sides. They'll note the movement and know I'm here, but it's bright outside. They won't see my alien-looking headgear.

Waiting for the action to begin, I look down at my hands, relaxed and open.

And empty.

Damn. I didn't get a weapon. My mind picks through the garage, remembering a baseball bat, garden tools, and a number of chemicals that could have been used as improvised weapons. There are also knives in the kitchen, which is closer.

But I don't move.

Instead, I make fists.

"I *am* crazy," I whisper, and the first window shatters.

A canister punches through the kitchen window, filling the sink with shards of glass. It looks loud, but I can't hear a thing. White smoke quickly fills the kitchen and dining room. When I see smoke swirl around me, I turn around and find a second canister behind me. It came through a living room window, and I didn't hear it. I could pick it up and hurl it back out, but I embrace the shroud of white, protected from the chemicals now filling the home.

Breathing steadily, I wait for the second phase of the assault to start.

Windows shake. Somewhere in the house, a door has been beat down.

The floor beneath my feet shakes. Someone heavy is running through the home. Before I see him, a small object the size of a pill bottle shatters another window. I clutch my eyes shut, cover them with an arm and open my mouth. The force of the explosion slaps against my body, but it's not enough to harm me. With my mouth open, the pressure against my lungs has minimal effect. But flash-bang grenades aren't supposed to cause bodily harm. They attack the senses, primarily hearing and eyesight, both of which I've managed to shield.

I pull my arm away from my eyes just in time to see a goliath of a man set upon me. He's dressed in all black, covered in tactical armor, and wears a gas mask over his face. I could pummel his body all day long and not do him any real harm. Curiously, he's not carrying a weapon.

Smart, I think, and sidestep the man's open arms. If they'd sent him in with a weapon, they would have basically been arming me. Whoever is in charge of this operation must know that.

One thing is for sure: the big man is not the brains of this outfit. Pulled past me by momentum, he careens into the heavy coffee table and snaps downward, face-planting against the couch. The cushions and armor absorb most of the impact, but he's dazed and confused. While rumbling feet approach from behind, I casually reach down, unclip and yank the man's headgear away. He snaps rigid, flips over, and claws at his face and throat. Whatever is in the air, it isn't fun. He closes his eyes and falls unconscious. Not dead.

A second black shape slips out of the fog. Then a third and fourth. They come at me without hesitation, working as a group. Each is a skilled fighter, but they've opted to go without armor, giving them greater range of motion and superior speed while sacrificing protection, which they could use.

The first man attacks with a chop. It's directed at my neck and would have put me down if I didn't see it coming. I duck, but not enough to avoid impact. His hand strikes the side of my head, near the top. It's some of the thickest, strongest bone in the human body. His fingers snap. I can't hear his scream of pain, but he reels back, clutching the hand.

The second man leads with a punch. The fist slips past my head and leaves his midsection open. A quick knee to his gut stumbles him back.

Attacker number three stops in his tracks. At first, I think he's taking stock of the situation or waiting for his injured teammates to collect themselves and rejoin the fight. He's either smart or chicken. When he puts two fingers to his ears, I realize there is a third scenario. He's receiving orders.

I have no intention of allowing him to fulfill those orders. A quick leap back plants my feet atop the coffee table. The backward motion confuses the man just long enough for me to jump forward and up. He tries to defend himself, but it's not only too little too late, it's a really bad idea, because I'm not throwing a punch. I'm kicking. Hard. The forearm he's blocking with snaps. I don't hear the sound, but I can feel it in my foot—resistance and then not. The man topples back into the haze.

His partner, the one I struck in the gut, takes his place. Punches and kicks come with brazen ferocity. But like his comrade with the broken fingers, I don't always avoid the blows. After his seventh swing, I appear to be on the ropes, but since I feel no fear, there is no such thing. Fear is subtle that way. I only back down if I choose to, not because I'm compelled to.

A subtle shift in his stance reveals he's about to kick. I jump back, just before he does, putting all of my weight onto the back of the living room's reclining chair. The hard footrest swings out with the strength and weight of a giant's foot. With one foot sailing through the air where my head should have been, the man doesn't see the chair bottom snap out. But he sure as hell feels it when the slab of wood slams into his kneecap, repositioning it three inches above where it's supposed to be. He drops to the floor like he's been shot.

I stand on the chair, looking for the man with broken fingers. If he's any kind of real fighter, the break will just slow him down. But there's no sight of the man.

The windows all around the living room shatter. Someone shot them out.

A breeze kicks up.

The chemical fog begins to dissipate. I glance up. The ceiling fan has been turned on. Do they think fighting me in the clear will be any easier? When the haze dissipates enough for me to see the kitchen, I have my answer.

Ten men, all armed with assault rifles, fill the open-concept doorway. The red beams of their laser sights are visible in the lingering miasma. Each is locked onto my body. Behind them I see

Cobb looking concerned and Shiloh, held in place by two more armored men. They seem oblivious to the fact that she's weeping and shaking. I want nothing more than to set her free, but there isn't any amount of fearlessness that can escape this shooting squad. So I lower my guard and wait for the mist to subside.

I allow the three injured men to limp from the room. The big man on the ground behind me is still out for the count. I turn slowly sideways, like I'm preparing to take a fighter's stance, but keep my body relaxed. Moving slowly, I dig into my pocket.

The smallest of the armored men lowers his assault rifle and takes a step forward. He lowers his weapon and pulls off his mask.

Katzman.

He speaks. I can't hear him, but I can read his lips. "You can still come in alive."

I remove the headphones.

"You can still come in alive," he repeats. "But I would prefer to kill you, so please, by all means, decline the offer."

"You won't kill me," I say.

"Sure about that?" he asks.

I'm not, but there's no way to see that on my face. "Pretty sure." I lift the plastic syringe case in my left hand. "Because you need this."

Katzman eyes the syringe and seems to be weighing his options. A measure of calm seeps into his eyes. He reaches out a hand. "Please. Give it to me and you can just walk away. It was a bad idea to bring you in, and I'd be happy to see you leave."

I consider the offer. It's a fair trade. My life in exchange for the mystery syringe. But one look at Shiloh's face, now placid from the effects of a sedative, whittles my options down to one. With the last of her lucidity, she looks me in the eyes and mouths the words, "Find Simon."

Simon? The name is as foreign to me as an alien world. I file it away for later and turn my attention back to Katzman, whose patience is wearing thin.

"Take it," I say, tossing the plastic case to Katzman.

By the time he catches it, realizes it's empty, and looks back up at me, I've already depressed the syringe's stopper all the way down, emptying the liquid into my thigh. Katzman says something, but I can't make out the words.

My mind is exploding.

16.

I scream.

This alone is highly unusual. I *don't* scream. When people are injured, and all that air gets shoved against their vocal cords, it's not the pain that does it.

It's fear.

Of death.

Of injury.

Of deformity.

But not the pain itself. For the most part, shock wipes the agony away better than any painkiller. At least at first. But the knowledge that something has gone catastrophically wrong sets the imagination ablaze, and adrenaline-fueled fear blossoms like a nuclear mushroom cloud.

I've never experienced any of this, mind you, but I see it in people's eyes. And the shriek coming out of my mouth sounds afraid. But it's *not* fear. It's something else, beyond my control. As my body flails on the floor, my mind watches like a spectator. Fear, after all, is a product of the mind, not the body. My body is screaming because it's being controlled by whatever substance I just slammed into my bloodstream.

"Hold him down!" Katzman shouts. "Don't let him injure himself!"

As I suspected, I've just made myself invaluable.

But at what cost?

My mind slams back into my body.

The world feels different. Hot and then cold, soft and then prickly. For a moment, I can see the soldiers above me, and then they're gone, replaced by darkness streaked with blurry green lines. I can still feel the soldiers' weight on me. Can feel their breath on my face—my mask has been removed—and hear their shouting. But it's like they're not there.

And then they are.

"Did you see that?" one of them shouts.

"Look at his—"

"Holy shit!"

"Sedate him," Katzman shouts. "Someone sedate him!"

The hallucination returns, but only in part. The darkness flickers in and out of view. Shapes move about the room, vague but alive, dancing among the men. To my knowledge, I've never taken LSD, but I'm pretty sure this would qualify as a bad trip.

"Strange," I hear myself say. My blurry hand comes into view, reaches for the darkness, which swirls away, slipping through one of the soldiers. When the hallucination grazes him, he shivers.

"We're not alone," he says. "Katzman, we're not—"

"Stow it!" Katzman shouts. "Every single God damn one of you get a grip. Tamp down your fear and get your shit stuffed back up your asses. You know how to do this job—now do it!"

Despite the man's stature, his voice commands respect, not just from the men around him, but my hallucination as well. The flickering darkness recedes. A chill runs through my arm. Then it's free, released by the men who held it.

"Damn," a man says. He looks at Katzman, fear in his eyes.

Katzman reaches out to the man. "Give it to me." He takes a small syringe and steps above me. He glares down at me. "Sometimes your unpredictability is too predictable. You did this to yourself. I want you to remember that."

Katzman jabs the needle into my neck.

The flickering slows down.

The world feels solid again.

The hallucination fades to black.

The soldiers' voices fade.

In the silent darkness, on the edge of unconsciousness, I hear something else—whispers. And then nothing.

I wake to the grating sound of a blender chewing through ice. Despite the racket, I'm actually quite comfortable. I open my eyes to a bedroom that feels familiar but isn't. The bed is plush, the soft cotton comforter is warm with body heat. Sunlight sneaks past the shades, filling the room with a warm twilight glow. If not for the grinding ice, I might have just said, "Screw it," rolled over, and gone back to sleep.

The blender slows and stops.

Someone is whistling, but I wouldn't call it a tune. Whoever is in the kitchen is nervous.

I sit up and take in the bedroom. The décor is immediately recognizable. The funky, bright paintings. The earth tones. I'm back in "my" apartment. Back at Neuro Inc.

And I'm not sedated.

These people are crazier than me. They must know what I'll do. Unless they believe whoever is in the next room can convince me otherwise. I throw off the covers and find myself still dressed, though my shoes have been removed. I find them beside the bed and slip them on.

I'm about to stand and leave when I decide to snoop. Something about the bedroom is wrong. A detail is off. There are two dressers. I'm a T-shirt-and-jeans guy. One dresser would have been enough. Moving quietly, I tug the drawer of the nearest dresser. Boxers and socks. The next drawer reveals T-shirts. The next, jeans.

I move to the second dresser and open the top drawer.

Empty.

All of them are. So why have the dresser at all? I turn to the closet and open it. There are a few pairs of nicer pants. Button-down shirts. A pair of slippers, well worn, and a pair of dress shoes, also well worn—and my size—rest on the floor. All of it is on the right side of the closet. The left side is empty.

The bedroom holds no answers for me. Only more questions.

I step into the small master bath. The room is clean. Several items litter the side of the sink: a stick of men's deodorant, a bottle of shaving cream, a razor, and a tube of toothpaste. Hanging above it all are two toothbrushes.

Two.

One blue. The other, pink.

Someone missed a detail.

Time to meet my guest.

The bedroom door squeaks when I open it.

Whoever is waiting for me in the kitchen freezes. "Hello?"

The word, pronounced as "Alloh?" along with the gentle, feminine voice, help me identify Allenby before I reach the kitchen.

I enter the kitchen like I actually own the place. Allenby's head swivels in my direction, her wild hair swaying as it catches up with the twist of her head. There's a bruise on her cheek where Katzman kicked her. She tries to conceal her nervousness with a smile, then hides the abysmal job she's doing by lifting the glass pitcher to her mouth and taking a long drink of the pink liquid.

"Morning," I say. "Or is it afternoon?"

She pulls the pitcher away, just enough to speak. "Morning, actually. You slept through the night."

I open a cabinet. There are bowls and glasses inside. I take a glass and hold it out to Allenby. She looks a little surprised and says, "Thank you."

"It's for me," I say, nodding at the pitcher. "Whatever that is you're drinking, I know it isn't drugged."

"Right," she says, filling the glass and handing it back.

I smell the drink. "Strawberry?"

"And blueberry."

I take a long drink, quenching my thirst. "It's good."

She's probably unaware that she's squinting at me. Trying to figure me out. I decide to keep her off-balance. I motion to the small kitchen table. "Have a seat?"

She takes a chair, and I sit across from her. For a full minute, we sip our drinks. When my glass is half empty, a subtle flavor emerges. "Did you put strawberry syrup in this?"

She smiles. "A guilty pleasure."

"Yours or mine?" I've already discovered that I have something of a sweet tooth, and Allenby doesn't strike me as the kind of person who enjoys American junk food. Tea and tarts maybe, but not liquid-chemical strawberry and corn syrup.

She clears her throat and adjusts her seat. "How about this . . . I'll ask you a question. If you give an honest answer, you can ask me a question."

"If I fail whatever test you're about to give me—"

"It won't end well," she says, being honest, "for either of us, I'm afraid."

"Have they threatened you?" I ask.

She smiles. It's honest, too. "I'm afraid I'll simply be caught in the cross fire. Perhaps used as a shield—again."

I look around the apartment. I don't see any cameras or listening devices, but that doesn't mean they're not there. "Is this a private conversation?"

To my surprise, she nods. "There are ears nearby, behind thick doors. They will hear me if I scream, but if we keep our voices low, no one will hear us. We're not being actively monitored."

"Why not?" It seems like a poor security choice.

She clears her throat. "As you might have noticed, as unpredictable as your behavior might be, there are some situations in which we are able to quite accurately predict your behavior."

"How? Or is that a trade secret?"

She smiles. "It's your moral compass. Your fearlessness makes you erratic, but it's your sense of right and wrong that guides you. Having Big Brother in the room with us is not a good way to regain your trust."

"You never had it."

"Right." She motions to the apartment. "You're welcome to check, if you like."

Not sensing any trace of a lie, I decide to trust that this talk is private. "And if I decide to not have this conversation? If I decide to leave?"

"Well then, you'll have to deal with Betty and Sue."

"Betty . . . and Sue?"

She raises her fists. Shakes the right. "Betty." Shakes the left. "And Sue. Now, choose your fate. Have a pleasant chat or be emasculated by a cheeky British tart."

I smile, open my arms, and bow my head in mock subjugation. "I'm at your mercy."

"Now then," she says, "first question?"

"I'll go first," I say, then ask my question before she can argue. "How did they find me?"

She ponders this for a moment, perhaps already questioning her commitment to honesty. Then she says, "The . . . woman has a GPS tracker embedded beneath her skin."

I nod, believing her, mostly because it's not an answer she'd give if she were trying to win me over. I open my hands, motioning my readiness.

"How are you feeling?" she asks. "Any dizziness? Headaches? Nausea? Hallucinations?"

"That's five questions," I point out.

"Try to hear it with commas instead of question marks."

I take stock of my body. "I'm a little sore. The hallucinations have faded."

"So you were hallucinating?"

"That's two questions," I say. "My turn."

She groans and sighs. "Go ahead."

"Who is Simon?"

She lowers her drink toward the edge of the table. Her face is a frozen mask of shock. The glass slips from her fingers, twirls along the table's edge, and falls. I lean forward, catch the glass and put it on the tabletop. When I lean back and look Allenby in the eyes, she gives me a one-word answer. "Bollocks."

17.

Allenby, head dipped toward the kitchen table, appears to be in the midst of an argument with herself. She whispers occasionally. Shakes her head. Subtly gestures. It's like my question, which I think is a fairly simple one, has triggered some kind of mental glitch.

She suddenly takes a deep breath, shakes her hands through her gray Muppet hair, and groans. "Fine. If that's what it takes. That's the road we'll go down first."

"Are you talking to me now?" I ask.

"No. Yes. Ugh!" She pauses to collect herself. Folds her hands on the table. Puts on a smile and looks me in the eyes. "Where did you hear that name?"

"The woman," I say. "Shiloh."

"You *spoke* to her?" I didn't think Allenby was capable of looking more stunned, but her face is quite pliable. "And she spoke to *you*? What did she say?"

I decide to skip her accusations about me being a liar and keep this conversation on track. "She told me to find Simon."

Allenby's expression freezes. "Find . . . him?"

I nod. "Is he someone important?"

"He was," she says.

"Was?"

Allenby crumples in on herself. She folds her arms on the table and puts her fluffy head down. When she lifts her head again, she's got tears in her eyes. "This isn't going to be easy for either of us."

I knew Allenby before I lost my memory. There's no doubt of that now, unless she's lying, but I'm not getting that vibe. She seems truly upset. *Not upset . . . disturbed.* "We were friends?"

Allenby thumps her head against her arms three times and then sits back up. "More than friends."

This makes me flinch. "We weren't . . . ?"

Allenby laughs hard, releasing some of her pent-up tension.

"Heavens, no!" After a moment of silence, she asks. "Shall I just come out with it all? I want it to be your choice. Do keep in mind that you, the man who feels no fear, decided to forget all of this."

"Why?"

"You might not feel fear, but you sure as hell feel pain—perhaps more poignantly than most, and some pain can conquer even the strongest of us."

"That's why I have no memory?"

She nods. "At your request. The operation was performed here. Not that I was present for it, mind you. For all your fearless bravado, do you know how you told me? How you asked to keep your secrets and let you be? An e-mail. A God-damned e-mail."

Her complaints about my past actions flow through the colander of my mind. But some of the message gets stuck. *"Here?* Was I a prisoner?"

"Not remotely."

I shake my head. It doesn't feel right.

"Some part of you remembers," she says. "That you trust me." She points to the cupboard. "Where the glasses are kept." She waves her hand in the air, dismissing the topic. "We'll come back to that later."

"So," I say, "who are you?"

"I am . . . was a friend of your mother's."

"I can't remember my mother."

"You knew what you were giving up." She looks at me with hard eyes.

I have nothing to say to this. I can't remember the me she's talking about.

"We met at university," she says. "Your mother and I. We became like sisters, and then we were when I married her brother."

"You're . . . you're my aunt?"

Tears slip from her eyes, and she reaches a hand out across the table. I'm not sure why, but I take it.

She works hard to control her voice. "I'm nearly the only family you have left."

"Nearly the only family?" I ask, and then something twists in my gut. Some strange discomfort, like I've eaten something rotten. My mind may not remember, but my body does, just like it remembered where to look for a glass. The sensation moves through my torso and neck, squeezing my brain until the realization snaps into focus.

The missed detail.

"The toothbrush."

"What?"

"In the bathroom," I say. "There's a pink toothbrush."

She rolls her eyes and mutters, "Incompetents." Allenby squeezes my hand. She looks around the room like she's afraid someone could be listening. But then, believing her own claims of privacy, continues. "There's no going back from this. Not again."

"I understand."

"I'm going to tell you your name."

I nod. "Please do."

"You're not Crazy. With or without a capital *C*." She pauses, unsure. Whispers, "Bollocks," and then says, "Your name . . . is Josef . . . Shiloh."

"Shiloh." I release her hand and stand. My first name holds little interest. But the last name . . . "Shiloh." An unfamiliar rush of emotions makes me feel uncomfortable. Is this what fear feels like? I lean on the table for balance. "The pink toothbrush. It belongs to . . ."

She nods. "Your wife."

I all but fall back into my seat. "Wife . . ."

"Part of you remembered her, too. You might not remember her, but you never stopped wanting to save her, did you?"

Despite my lack of memory, I know she's right. "What's her name?"

"Maya."

"Maya," I say, trying out the name, but it doesn't sound familiar at all. Hell, my own name, Josef Shiloh, doesn't feel right. To me, I'm still Crazy.

Or maybe that's just the selfish man Allenby spoke of. My whole persona might be a fabrication. An escape. But from what? Running requires fear. What could I be afraid of?

The answer comes to me as a question.

"Who is Simon?"

Allenby looks freshly wounded by the question. This is where the story gets ugly. Where the pain begins. I can feel the invisible energy of it rolling off of her in waves. She lifts her head, twisting her mouth, and then speaks two words that radically alter the way I see the world.

18.

"Your son."

I stare at Allenby, searching for a hint of deception. I find none.

In the past year, I haven't once considered that I might be married. The idea of having a son is so totally foreign to me. And yet I smile. "I have a son?"

Allenby does *not* smile.

Her gloom robs my smile as well.

"I *had* a son."

Her nod is subtle.

"He's dead?"

Another nod.

"How?"

"I'd rather not say."

"I don't remember it," I assure her. "I don't remember you, or Maya, or Simon. If you tell me, I'll know about it, but I won't feel it. To me, we're talking about strangers."

She blinks her tears away, looking at me with glossy brown eyes. "You feel nothing? Not even a little?"

I shake my head. It's a lie.

I feel *something*. I'm not sure what. The emotions aren't connected to a thought or memory. It's deeper than that. But I can handle it, and I'm sure as hell not afraid to hear the rest, even if it was so bad that I had my memory eradicated.

"Fine," she says, sitting back. She wipes her arm across her running nose and sniffs back her emotions. "It was Maya."

"What was Maya?"

"She killed him. Your wife. Murdered your son."

"How?"

"With a shard of glass from a broken clock. It was a gift, that clock, from me." Allenby straightens her posture, steeling herself against the story. "She stabbed him fourteen times. In his arms. His chest. His stomach."

Emotions roil. I fight against them.

"She held that little boy—he was eight—in her arms and buried the glass into him over and over, into the boy who trusted her implicitly, into the son she adored with every strand of her DNA, into the young man who you would have done anything to save."

"But . . . why?"

"That's harder to answer." Allenby looks up at me and seems surprised.

"What?" I ask.

She points to the right side of my face. "Your cheek."

I touch a finger to my cheek. It's wet. A single tear has fallen. "Tell me why."

"The official ruling was temporary insanity, which is actually close to the truth. Except there was nothing temporary about it. Over the months that followed, she descended into a kind of madness. She would scream until her throat went raw and she lost her voice. She would dig at her legs, exposing muscle."

"I saw the scars."

"She returns to herself on rare occasions, as she must have with you, but we've had to keep her heavily sedated. The marks you no doubt saw on her arms were self-inflicted wounds. Someone forgot to add a sedative to her IV bag. When she woke, she used her arms as a pin cushion for the IV needle. Even when she's loopy on drugs, she finds ways to harm herself."

"Is it the grief?" I ask. "Remorse for what she did?"

"No," Allenby says. There's not a trace of doubt in her voice. "It's fear that drives her."

"Fear?" From what I've observed over the past year, fear most often has a source. It could be as obvious as a man with a gun or as subtle as an idea. But what could Maya have to fear from an eight-year-old boy whom she adored? "Fear of what?"

"This is going to be hard to understand," Allenby says.

"Because I don't feel fear?"

"Because it's bloody insane."

"I lived in an asylum," I remind her. "My life—the life that I remember—is about as insane as it gets."

Allenby stands and takes the blender pitcher to the sink. Begins rinsing it out. "You're wrong about that. That capital *C* you're so fond of is going to feel a whole lot smaller in about sixty seconds."

"What happens in sixty seconds?" I ask.

She points to the shade-covered kitchen window. "You're going to build up the nerve to pull up that shade."

"And what am I supposed to see?"

She pauses scrubbing the pitcher. "Do you remember injecting yourself?"

I hadn't thought of it since waking, but I remember it. "Yes."

"Do you remember the hallucinations?"

"Yeah, but—"

"What did you see?"

I think about the strange, distorted darkness, lined with green. She doesn't let me tell her. "What did you hear?"

I nearly say, "nothing," but then I remember. "Whispers."

She returns to her chore. "Then it worked."

"What worked?"

"The drug you destroyed and then used on yourself. Bravo, by the way, hats off." Her sarcasm is biting. "From the moment you woke up this morning, you were tested. No one knew things would go quite as far as they did—Maya and your dashing escape were not part of the plan—but the results, in the end, were predicted. All the while, your psychological and emotional states were being assessed, not to mention your physical abilities, which don't seem to have deteriorated."

"Whose horrible idea was that?" I ask. "I could have killed some-one."

"You nearly did, and I'm afraid Lyons organized the tests. I argued against it. Katzman, too. Though I think he was more con-cerned about himself." She looks back at me. "They knew you'd do it, by the way. Inject yourself. All they had to do was convince you the contents were important. They just didn't think you'd leave in a blaze of glory first."

"Lyons didn't have a heart attack, did he?"

She shakes her head. "He's a decent actor. Knew you wouldn't kill a man who was already dying."

"They were shooting to kill."

She nods. "There's no other way to test a man who is as hard to kill as you. Lyons's words. But his confidence in your abilities seems to have been well founded. Frankly, I'm surprised that you didn't burn this place to the ground."

"It was on my to-do list."

"And now?"

"I'm not sure."

"Then let's make you sure." She motions to the window. "Sur-reality awaits."

I stand and step around the breakfast table. With a tug, the shade launches up, slapping against the window frame as the powerful spring turns it too many times.

The window is vertical, part of the story-tall steps running down two sides of the building. The view outside is what I remember. New Hampshire in summer. Green and blue. And . . .

Something else.

"What's that?" I ask, pointing at the parking lot below. The lot is fairly empty now, and all signs of the previous day's battle have been cleaned up.

Allenby steps up beside me. "What do you see?"

"Someone in the parking lot." There's a shadow moving among the cars, but I can't make out who it is. "Is that a bear?"

Allenby shrugs. "I don't see a thing."

I point. "It's right there."

"The lot is empty. I don't—" There's a slap and her voice cuts off.

I glance toward the sound and find my hand clutching her wrist. That's unusual. But it's not fear. It's surprise. "What's happening?"

"Look again," she says. "Try to see more. When you feel it, push."

When I look back to the window, my eyes feel strained. Like I need glasses. Something tickles my eye, and I fight the urge to blink. Following Allenby's advice, I push forward. I can feel the stretch, like some newly formed muscle in my eye, and I will it to flex. And then, with a twitch, it does.

Blinding pain comes in waves, flowing from my eyes and down into my torso. My stomach clutches, pitching me forward with a grunt. My muscles spasm, the pain becoming systemic. "What's happening?"

"It will get easier," she says. "Look again, when you can."

Fighting the pain, I turn my eyes up.

The parking lot is gone.

New Hampshire is gone.

The land is dark, mixed with veins of shimmering green light. The sky appears as a dark purple hue. There's movement in the dark. Indistinct. Revealed by shifts in the green light. My vision flickers, pulsing pain throughout my body.

I see the parking lot.

And then it's gone. Or not. It's just dim. Less focused. And the veins of green remain.

I rub my eyes and the two views—the real and surreal—strobe back and forth. I close my eyes again. "I'm still hallucinating."

"No," Allenby says. "You're not."

"Then what am I seeing?"

"The world. But in a way no one else can."

"There's a shadow in the parking lot. Moving. But there's no source. It isn't connected to anyone."

"Just the one?" Allenby asks, suddenly tense.

I scan the lot and see nothing else moving. "Yes."

"That shadow," she says, "is your enemy, *our* enemy, hidden from the world but present. Always present. They are the shifting air that makes hair stand on end. The monsters under the bed. The sense of impending doom, great depression, and panic that has no source. Most of us feel their presence—fear without tangible cause—on a regular basis. You, on the other hand, Mr. Fearless, have never felt them."

The pain lessens and I open my eyes. The view is back to normal. Shifting movement turns my eyes back to the parking lot. The moment I see the strange shape skulking around the cars, the world goes black and green again, bringing a fresh wave of nausea-inducing agony along with it. "Dammit." I turn away from the window. The apartment and Allenby look normal.

"How do I stop it?" I ask, clutching my gut with one hand, supporting my weight on the kitchen table with the other.

"Are you afraid?" Allenby asks. She sounds concerned, but I think she's more worried that I'm feeling fear than she is about my physical state.

I rub my throbbing temples. "Is it supposed to hurt like this?"

"Try to focus," she says. "See what you want to see. See *where* you want to see."

"Have you done this before?" I ask.

"God, no."

"Great," I say, turning toward the dark window. "So your advice is—"

"Bullshit?" Allenby says. "Maybe. But it's also you're only hope, because once we step out of this building, you're going to have to control it—and the pain—on your own."

I turn back to the window and lift my head, tracking a fast-moving shadow as it sweeps by. A faint whispering tickles my ears but then fades. Allenby must see my surprise this time because she asks, "What?"

"The shadow."

"Where?" Her voice is instantly tense. Almost a whisper.

Whatever this thing is, she's definitely afraid of it. "It just passed by the window."

Allenby takes a deep breath, lets it out slow. "How did it make you feel? When you saw it."

I glance at her. "Are you asking me if I felt afraid?"

She nods.

"No."

She pulls down the shade and collapses into one of the kitchen chairs. "Did it notice you?"

Focused on the kitchen and Allenby, the pain quickly subsides. "Notice me? I said it was a shadow."

"Mmm." She's lost in thought. On another world.

I sit down across from her. "Allenby."

She doesn't acknowledge me.

"*Aunt* Allenby."

That gets her attention. She looks up with a hint of a smile. "Yes, Josef?"

"Crazy."

"Still?"

I tilt my head. Half a nod. "It was more than a shadow, wasn't it?"

"What you saw . . . however briefly, it's the reason your son is dead, your wife is lost, and you elected to forget it all. They're your enemy, Crazy. And they're right outside the windows. You're not here to be experimented on. You're not here to find Simon. Or to save Maya. All of that is in the past."

"Then why am I here?"

"Honestly? I'm not entirely sure, but I suspect it has a lot, if not everything, to do with vengeance."

19.

"Vengeance," I say, without enthusiasm. The word feels hollow. Untrue. Vengeance is an act of passion, driven by emotion. It's not even a desire. It's a need.

"And there's the real problem," Allenby says. "When Lyons offered to remove your memory, it was an act of mercy, but also refinement. You were always his preferred coconspirator. I was never sure if that was because of your potential to be a living WMD used in humanity's defense or genuine affection, but when Simon and your parents died and Maya . . . You lost focus. You nearly lost your mind. You—"

"My parents are dead, too?"

Allenby sucks in a breath. She's horrible at keeping secrets.

"Tell me about them."

"They were beautiful people." Her eyes are downcast, unable to meet mine. "Joyful. Silly, really. Laughed a lot. You did, too, for a time."

"What I meant," I say, "is how did they die?"

"Oh," she says, then a whisper. "Oh . . ."

"They were on vacation. A tropical resort. Had a suite on the top floor. Jumped off the balcony."

"They *killed* themselves?"

"That's the official report. Mutual suicide. But when you know how to look between the lines, you can make sense of the senseless. Your father, Daniel, hit the concrete walkway not far from the pool. Your mother, Lila, made it to the water but struck the bottom. When she was lifted out, she regained consciousness long enough to speak." Tears well up in her eyes. She's describing the brutal death of her best friend and sister-in-law. My mother. Lila. Though I have no memory of the woman, I find myself moved by the story. I take Allenby's hands. The gesture elicits a sob, but it's quickly crushed with an efficiency that only comes from practice. "Your mother's final words revealed the truth about their deaths. 'The darkness came for us,' she said. A monster, like the one you glimpsed outside, drove them to jump."

"Drove them?" I ask.

She nods, her fluffy hair sliding slowly forward and back, seaweed in a current. "They've turned fear into a weapon. Can push it into people. Steal their sanity. Force them to do things to themselves, to others, that . . . they can make us do horrible things."

"So my mother knew about these fear-inducing shadows? About what's outside?"

"We all did. And it made our family targets. That same night . . . that same damn night, they took Hugh, my husband—your uncle—and Simon."

*They . . . Who or *what* are *they*?*

"But you survived," I point out.

"I nearly didn't. I was tackled before I could follow Hugh into traffic. I tried to warn you, but was too late. The phone was ringing when you found them, Maya and Simon. You never answered, but it was me on the other end."

"This is what I ran from," I say. "Why I erased my memory." Losing an entire family in one night . . . It sounds like enough to break even the strongest of men. But not Allenby. I hid from it, but she's been dealing with this pain for more than a year.

"While you retreated, Lyons became even more obsessed with his research," Allenby says, lost in the past. "His theories about their intentions had been—" She stops. Looks me in the eyes. She's revealed something she wasn't supposed to. Knows what my next question will be.

Why did Lyons become obsessed over my family's deaths?

"You're not supposed to know," she whispers.

"No more secrets," I remind her.

"Except this one," she says, keeping her voice low. Despite her assurances that our conversation is private, the secret she nearly revealed has her on edge. Nervous.

I continue my argument in a lower voice. "You made opposing promises."

She shakes her head, disappointed. "Bollocks." Eyes on mine again. "Not a word."

I nod.

"Maya's maiden name is Lyons. Stephen is her father and Simon's grandfather. He never had a son. Just the one daughter and he loved that boy more than his own child. Their loss set him on a . . . refined path. He was driven before, by what he described as a cursed childhood, taunted by the darkness, monsters in the closet, unceasing, crippling fear for which there appeared no source. He spent years with psychologists and psychiatrists who rotated him through various drug cocktails. But nothing helped. And then, when he was grown and accustomed to the fear, it left him wounded, but driven to understand it and uncover its source, which he did, and they took his—our—family for it. Rabid curiosity and study shifted to preparedness and, I fear, vengeance. But . . . who can blame him? I'd be lying if I said I never thought about finding a way to hurt them. Hugh . . . the man was an angel."

"Who's left? In our family."

"Just the four of us, counting Maya. Stephen's wife passed away when Maya was still a child."

"Why would I run from all this?" I ask. It's a rhetorical question, wondering aloud because what Allenby has said doesn't feel like me.

Allenby shrugs. "God only knows, but you took Lyons up on his offer to erase your memory, which, if you ask me, was your first and only real act of cowardice. When you woke with no memory, you attacked. This part is secondhand, mind you. As I mentioned, I found out about your decision via e-mail, and the job was done when I arrived. You were subdued and drugged. Katzman drove you away, put you on a park bench, and set you loose upon the world. I don't know what the man was thinking, but within a few hours you'd been arrested. I located you when you were committed to SafeHaven a few days later."

"And left me there."

"It seemed the best place for you. Even you believed you were crazy. So, yes, we left you there."

It's a lot to assimilate, but one detail stands out. "You said I had the potential to be a living WMD."

She nods.

"I'm just a man."

This gets a laugh, like I've just told the funniest joke. "Okay," she says. "I'm going to be honest with you because it seems to be the only thing that keeps you from throwing yourself out of windows or punching people in the face."

"Makes sense."

"You were *born* without fear. Didn't shed a tear when you entered the world. While your mother and I wept, you stayed as calm as a—"

"You were there when I was born?"

"Cut the cord."

"How old am I?"

"Thirty-four. Your mum was twenty-three at the time. I was twenty-two. Turns out you were born with malformed amygdalas. Your memory was unaffected, but you couldn't feel fear. You never have."

"A lack of fear doesn't explain what I can do."

"It explains why you excelled in the military."

"What branch?" I ask. I'm not sure why I care, but I want to know who I was, and different branches of the military can shape a man.

"Army," she says. "First as a Ranger, and then Delta. But that didn't last long."

"I washed out?"

"You were noticed."

"By who?"

"Who do you think?"

"Lyons," I say. "What is this place, CIA?"

"Once upon a time," she says, "as were you. Your skill set made you the ideal operative."

"My skill set . . ." I say. "What did I do?"

"In the Rangers, and Delta, you fought alongside some brave and highly skilled men, and one woman if I'm not mistaken, but your willingness to take on *any* assignment and do whatever insanity was required to get the job done set you apart. You went into the darkest places and saw the vilest aspects of humanity, and somehow, on your own, came to understand something that Lyons had already hypothesized; that there were monsters in the world, just beyond our experience but influencing it."

If what Allenby is telling me is accurate, I was a fearless, highly skilled soldier who could experience horrible things and not be forever changed. That information, combined with my mental filing cabinet overflowing with ways to inflict pain, extract information . . . and kill, forms a picture in my mind. I know what I was. Who I was.

"Assassin," I say.

"The best," Allenby says. "The CIA would never confirm this, of course. Assassination isn't a sanctioned activity, you know. And it's not the best career choice for a husband and new father. Lyons, like you, worked for the CIA once upon a time, but the company specializes in international affairs, not . . . what we do. So Neuro was formed as an off-the-books black operation with limited oversight, and you signed up, in part because Lyons was already your father-in-law, but also because that skill set of yours made you even more qualified for what Neuro was tasked to research, and not just as a warrior. Threat assessment was part of our job, but we were also tasked with uncovering any natural resources that might exist just out of reach. Our research had the potential to change the world." She watches my face, judging my shifting expression. "What's confusing you?"

"It's just hard to believe I'm who Maya married. Who Lyons let her marry." Who would let their daughter marry someone who killed for a living?

She smiles. "First, it's the twenty-first century. She did what she wanted. Second, that's the part that confuses you? Really?" She shakes her head, still finding the humor in it. When I don't reply, she continues. "Well, I can't speak for Lyons. He knew who you were. What you did. Honestly, my best guess is that he saw you as the best man to protect his daughter. He knew you loved her. Everyone did. A lack of fear can be disastrous, but it can also be romantic. You were never afraid of telling the world, or Maya, how you felt about her." She smiles, remembering something. "You were good friends for a time, through Lyons. And then one day, at a party, you approached her, said with your usual boldness, 'You'd make a good wife. Want to get married?'"

"That *worked*? Sounds a little old-fashioned."

She laughs and wipes a tear from her eye. "She thought you were joking. Said yes, not knowing you were serious. But that boldness of yours is something she came to love. Working backwards, you then asked her out on the most nonromantic date imaginable. Really, who takes a girl bowling on the first date? But . . . it worked. And you got her a ring. And gave her a son.

"As for why Maya married an assassin, your lack of fear also meant you had no qualms about hiding the details about what you did. She knew you worked for the CIA, like her father, and understood that secrecy was part of the job. She didn't ask. You didn't tell, and you never had a problem with it, or the work, until you had a son."

"And then?"

"Neuro. Lyons had been at Neuro's helm from the beginning, some twenty years before you were brought on board, but the discoveries made with your help turned the once-small operation into what you've seen. Your job shifted from ending lives to being the point man for Neuro's . . . explorations. What you saw out there, it was our world. The Earth. But it wasn't the Earth as we know it. Another world, but not. What's important to know is that it's real. *They're* real. They might sometimes appear as a shadow, a hint of something in the dark, or a feeling of something near and impending, but they are physical beings. They're simply beyond our perception. And they're the source of all this fear that's eating up the world."

"But not me."

"Not you," she says. "And that's why Lyons wants you here. Why he always wanted you here. He eventually brought both sides of the family into the fold. Said it would be safer that way."

"And all this is funded by the U.S. government?"

"Once you and Lyons had physical evidence for the existence of other realities sharing this world, he received all the funding he asked for. Off the record. If something went wrong, the government wanted deniability. It was real, but it was still fringe science. But the possibilities for energy, environmental, industrial, and military applications are vast. That said, most employees here have no idea who they're really working for, or what the true scope of Neuro's research is. Our only true oversight is Winters, who reports to the director of the CIA. Whether or not information gets passed on to the president, I have no idea, but I'd guess that he's happily in the dark."

I tap my fingers on the tabletop, weighing what to ask next, and realize that Allenby hasn't asked me a question in a while. Her job probably ended when she confirmed I could see whatever that was outside the window. Her last statement about the dark reminds me of my mother's supposed last words. "What is it? The darkness. The shadows."

"We call them the Dread," she says with no hesitation, looking up at me. Apparently, this is information she's been cleared to give. "Capital *D*. You're immune to the fear they can instill in people, and the resulting influence on our actions, but the rest of us . . ."

"I'm officially confused."

"You should be," she says. "Showing you might be easier than telling you. Do I have your word that you won't punch, kick, or otherwise maim anyone you might encounter outside of this room?"

"As long as no one tries to kill me again and you keep telling the truth, we won't have a problem."

"Good enough for me," Allenby says, and then shouts, "Katzman, it's okay. We're green. Pack it up."

The doors to the second bedroom, bathroom, and several closets open at once. Men dressed in riot gear and armed with an array of nonlethal weapons file into the apartment and out the front door.

The last man to emerge is Katzman. His eyes linger on me for a moment and then swivel to Allenby. "You sure about this? We've got a handful of men in the infirmary already."

"You need better men," I say.

Katzman stops behind me. I can hear the barely controlled anger in his every breath. But he doesn't act, or even address my comment. I have to give him credit for self-control. I would have punched me.

"It will be different this time," Allenby says.

"How can you be sure?" Katzman asks.

"Because this time, we're telling him everyth—"

An alarm interrupts. It's the same alarm that sounded when I escaped. I lift my hands off the table. "I didn't do anything."

Katzman puts a finger to his ear, pressing the barely visible earbud down tight so he can better hear the voice on the other end. The anger melts from his face as his listens. It's replaced by fear, an emotion I'm getting really good at recognizing.

Allenby stands. "What is it? What's happening?"

Katzman pulls his finger away. Turns toward Allenby. "Incursion. Third floor."

"Here?" Allenby nearly shouts the word. "How could that happen?"

Katzman looks down at me. I'm positive he's going to blame me, and to be honest I wouldn't even argue the point. There's no doubt my actions have compromised the security of this building. But that's not what happens. Instead, he swallows his anger, and maybe some pride, and says, "We're going to need your help."

20.

Boots thud down the carpeted hallway as the men dressed in riot gear storm toward a neighboring apartment, two doors down. I follow Katzman with Allenby on my heels.

"Copy that," Katzman says, hand against his ear. He turns back. "It's in the west stairwell. Headed up."

I catch his arm and stop him. "*What* is?"

He looks from me to Allenby. She gives him a nod.

"The enemy," he says.

"One of the Dread?"

Katzman glances at Allenby, eyebrows raised in question.

"It worked," she says. "He saw one on the building. It must have found the broken window. Got inside."

He yanks his arm from my grasp. "You will either do what I tell you or stay out of the way."

While Katzman storms away, I turn back to Allenby.

"There isn't time to fully explain the situation," she says. "It's complicated. And strange. I promise you will get answers, some probably sooner than others. What you need to know now is that you're going to see something that doesn't make sense. And when you do see it, I want you to kill it."

I stare at her.

"You've done more for less in the past."

I frown. "Fine."

When I step inside the apartment two doors down, I feel like a kid who has just stumbled across Santa's workshop. It's not an apartment at all. It's an armory. The room is a mix of modern weapons, bladed weapons, nonlethal armaments, armor, and high-tech gadgets. The men in riot gear stop as I enter, watching me with suspicious eyes.

Katzman points to me. "Dread Squad, this is Crazy." He sweeps his hand toward the seven men. "Crazy, Dread Squad."

While the tough-looking men of "Dread Squad" go back to their business, arming themselves with a variety of weapons, I scout the room. A machete mounted on the wall catches my attention. The twenty-inch cleaver blade is straight with a chisel tip and the back side, which slopes in a smooth line back to the handle, is wickedly serrated. The entire weapon is black and slightly textured. Like Teflon. But it's not just the machete. A case of knives, bayonets, and less-brutal-looking swords are all black, too. A nearby Dread Squad member loads fresh rounds into a magazine. The bullets are black. So are the guns.

"It's made from an alloy called oscillium," Allenby says. She lifts the machete and its sheath off the wall.

"Never heard of it," I say.

"No one has. It's a mix of nickel, aluminum, and titanium, along with a few things I've never heard of and don't care to remember, formed into whatever we want and bombarded with intense bursts of laser light, which is what turns it black. You were part of the trial-and-error program that created it."

I'm starting to feel like I'm living in my own shadow and I'm getting pretty annoyed with my past self. I have more questions, but the alarm keeps me focused. I look the machete over, admiring the fine blade forged from some top-secret exotic alloy. The ridiculousness of the situation is not lost on me. "So what are we fighting then, werewolves? Is this alloy like our silver bullet?"

"That would be easier," she says. "Oscillium is important because of the way it vibrates, or oscillates, hence the not-so-creative name."

"So, the machete vibrates?"

"Not in any way you'll ever feel," she says. "I'm not a physicist, but the way I understand it is, all matter vibrates, but at different speeds. Different frequencies, from very low to extra high. Normally, people might talk about atoms and electrons, but around here it's all about string theory, which basically says all matter is composed of teeny, tiny strings that vibrate at different frequencies. And like the frequencies of sound waves, there are vibrations we can detect as physical matter, or light, or heat, and some we can't. What you thought were hallucinations are simply frequencies of reality that are normally undetectable and intangible to humanity and most common elements on Earth.

"Think of reality as musical notes. Each note on the scale is as audible, as *real*, as the next, but vibrating at different frequencies. The world as we experience it is an A. But the Dread experience the world in a different frequency. To them, reality is a B. On the same scale, the same planet, but distinct. The difference is that they are longtime musicians, able to move between notes, whereas we are still children, striking only a single note. Unlike us, or even the Dread, oscillium can vibrate in a single frequency, or multiple frequencies, and it can shift back and forth with ease."

"And how does that work?" I ask, unwilling to hide my sarcastic tone.

"Bioelectromagnetism." The confidence of Allenby's voice says she's up to the task of facing my scrutiny, but this is starting to feel new-agey. "The magnetic field generated by a human being pulsates up and down between .3 and 30Hz. The field measured at the hands matches the field measured in the brain, all of which can be affected by the mind. It's been shown that people can change their field simply by focusing on it. At the low end of the spectrum, the magnetic field will pull the oscillium fully into sync with our frequency. On the far end of the spectrum, the oscillium will shift out of our frequency. Everything in between will have no effect."

"Is that dangerous? Can't the Dread affect the frequency?"

"Even if they knew it was possible, their bioelectromagnetic field is different from our own. The frequency shift only works for people, and even then only with practice. Once you know what the bioelectromagnetic field shift feels like, you can change the frequency of oscillium just by thinking it.

"The weapons you see here, like the walls and windows of this building, were designed to oscillate between A and B so quickly that they exist in both frequencies at once. But they can also be in one or the other, depending on the electromagnetic field of the person in contact with them, though there has never been a reason to not have the weapons exist in both worlds. It allows us to attack them without moving between frequencies like they do and keep them out of the building. Theoretically, all matter can make the jump between worlds with a shift in frequency, but oscillium does it naturally."

"Here, there, and everywhere," I say.

Allenby pauses. Sighs. "Your uncle used to sing that song to me."

"Sorry."

She forces a smile and waves off her sudden melancholy. "It's a horrible song, but an accurate description of the alloy." She holds the machete out to me, the blade resting in her open palms. Back to business.

I accept the offered weapon. When my fingers wrap around the handle and the machete comes up in my hand, a smile creeps onto my face. "Was . . . this mine?"

She grins and nods. "Tokugawa Ieyasu, the first shogun samurai of Japan, once said that the sword was the soul of a samurai. The relationship between weapon and warrior, forged in battle, could never be broken." Her smile fades. She puts the scabbard in my free hand. "Too bad that didn't also work for family, eh?"

I slide the blade into the scabbard and slip the weapon over my back. Katzman approaches holding a belt with a holstered sidearm already in place. I identify the weapon with a quick glance: a black SIG Sauer P229. "What's inside?"

"Point forty cals," he says as I take the belt and strap it in place. "Try not to shoot any people. Your . . . senses are still adapting, so your target will most likely look like a shadow, but just because you can see through it doesn't mean you can't shoot it."

"Oscillium," I say. "Right."

He nods. "There is a chance it could also appear as something more substantial. If that happens, try not to let this throw you."

"Nothing throws me. Figuratively, though literally is also doubtful."

Not amused, he heads for the door. "Two teams! Alpha, hit the west stairwell, work your way down. Take your time. Beta, elevator down and come up from below." I'm sure he's going to leave me out, let me tag along, see how the big boys do it. It's the kind of silverback macho stuff you expect from a short man dressed for war. But that's not what happens. "Crazy, you're with Alpha. On point."

"*Katzman,*" Allenby complains.

Katzman opens the door. The four-man Beta Team rushes out. "It's why he's here, isn't it?"

Allenby racks the slide of her own handgun. Holsters it on her hip. She's got two black knives on the other hip. She quickly grabs the wild poof atop her head that is her hair and pulls it back into an elastic that rolls off her wrist, there all along, waiting for duty. "Fine."

Katzman motions to me. "Follow the hall to the right. All the way to the end and left. The stairwell door is straight ahead." With that, he lowers a pair of strange round goggles over his eyes. The rest of Dread Squad does the same. I turn to Allenby to ask, but she's pulling a pair over her own eyes as well.

"They let us peek between frequencies, but just a peek is sometimes too much. You won't need them. Hopefully." She flashes a grin. "Move it, soldier."

With a confidence born of obvious naïveté and lack of fear, I head out of the room and turn right. I feel a flash of déjà vu. It's not the hallway that feels familiar. It's the anticipation. Of battle. Of facing chaos and reining it into control. I've done this before. What does it say about me that I can remember this feeling, but not what it's like to have a son and lose him?

"Cut the alarm," Katzman says behind me, talking into his hidden mic. A moment later, the blaring whoops fall silent and I can hear the heavy breathing of Dread Squad's Alpha team behind me. They're not winded already, just amped. Or are they afraid? If they are, they're pretty good at hiding it.

Eight apartment doors later, we reach the end of the hall and turn left. The stairwell entrance is forty feet ahead. I don't know if anyone lives in these units. Maybe just the Dread Squad guys. Either way, the doors don't open. No curious eyes peek out. Could be that the residents have been trained to hunker down when they hear that alarm. Could be that they're just afraid.

I stop by the stairwell door, draw my weapon, and flick off the safety. Katzman stops next to me. "I hope Lyons is right about you."

"Let's find out," I say, and look back at Alpha Team. "Teams of two. No bunching up. Katz, you're with me." I point at the next two men in line. "You two enter when we hit the first landing." I point at the last two. "You two stay put with Allenby. If it's not us that comes out the door . . ."

The four men under Katzman's command all turn to him.

He's clearly annoyed but gives a curt nod.

I open the door and step into the stairwell. The walls are gray. So are the railings. And the concrete steps. It's woefully bland in an industrial-Russia kind of way. No windows. Wire-encased bulbs line the walls. Whoever designed the rest of Neuro's HQ really skimped on the stairwells. Of course, this is the modern world. How many people still use stairs?

The landing ahead is empty, so I track the steps down and

around with the barrel of my gun. Seeing nothing, I lean over the railing and look down.

Nothing.

The stairwell is empty.

"There's nothing here," I say.

Katzman grabs my arm. Hard. His sleeve pulls up a bit. The hairs on his exposed arm stand on end. The hairs on the back of his neck spring up, too. He puts a finger to his lips and then mouths, "It's here."

I look over the railing again. There's not a damn thing in the stairwell besides us.

Katzman slides the strange round goggles over his eyes. He inches toward the railing. Painfully slow. Then, with a quick motion, he glances over the edge, just for a moment, and springs back. His chest heaves. His weapon lowers. His eyes, behind the tinted goggles, go wide.

What. The. Hell?

Katzman is a brave man. He's stood up to me twice. But that man is gone. He's withered into a child just woken from a nightmare. He manages to find his voice, though. "Three stories down." A gasp for air. "Use your eyes. Like you did earlier."

I remember my strange look out the window. What it felt like. What it looked like. Dark. Tinged with green. Otherworldly. The living shadow. But I'm not sure how to trigger . . . whatever that was, again.

I lean over the edge, looking for a target. Eager to pull my trigger. To draw my machete. To tame the chaos.

But there is nothing in my repertoire I can do about a drab stairwell.

That's all I see.

I blink hard, trying to alter my vision. Trying to see what's not there.

Allenby told me to "see what you want to see." She might not understand how to control the changes my body is going through, but she probably knows how it's supposed to work.

I lean over the edge again, aiming down at nothing.

See, I think.

See!

I relax my thoughts. Focus my attention on what I can't see. Then I feel it. That strange new muscle. I flex. My eyes tingle, then sting, and suddenly, like a light switch has been thrown, I can see what's not there. And it hurts. The pain nearly cripples me, exploding from my eyes and roiling through my blood, but what I now see keeps me upright and focused past the physical discomfort.

I'm looking at my target, which is very much *not* a shadow, straight in the eyes.

And it's looking right back.

21.

I empty the P229 at the thing. Twelve .40 caliber rounds. It should be dead. Most everything else on the planet short of a blue whale or armor-plated rhino would be. Then again, it's about the size of a rhino, and the way it's flickering in and out of view makes the details hard to discern. It could be armored. Or thick-skinned. Or who knows what.

I have no idea what it is.

But it's there.

It's real.

And then it's not.

I blink and it disappears. I'm about to ask where it went but then realize I'm focusing on what it is rather than seeing it. I narrow my eyes, willing them to see what is unseen, and feel a shift in my vision. This muscle just needs exercise.

With a fresh wave of pain, the monster reappears, one floor higher and on the move. It's fast for its size, taking each flight of stairs with a single leap.

My hands reload the P229 without taxing my mind and despite the pain. It's a reflex, muscle memory, and I'm able to keep my eyes on the rising creature.

It's mostly black, which doesn't help with the details, but twisting green lines trace the body, helping to define its muscular forearms, powerful limbs, and arched back. It has no hair to speak of, just rough black flesh like the skin of a stealth bomber . . . or the black machete on my back. There are four glowing green eyes atop its head, two on the sides, two looking forward.

But that's all I get. The flickering effect intensifies as the creature nears.

Its massive mouth opens like a hippo's, long strands of saliva stretching out, revealing large, sharp teeth and a tongue composed of what looks like undulating worms. It appears to be roaring, its entire body shimmering, vibrating, but all I hear is a whispered hiss. Katzman reacts to the sound by yelping and scrabbling back toward the door. "Shoot it," he says through grinding teeth. "Shoot it!"

It's just one story down when I empty the second magazine into it. If I missed at all the first time, which is doubtful, I score a hit with each and every round this time. The thing bucks and reels, throwing itself back against the wall, but it doesn't go down. All I'm really doing is irritating it.

"Not working," I say to Katzman.

The creature drops back down to all fours and turns its flickering head up.

"It's a bull," he says, looking a little more put together, but still wild-eyed.

"Is that supposed to mean something?"

"They're tougher."

The bull's green eyes come into focus. The pupils are split, two vertical rectangles connected in the middle, forming an H.

"What's it doing?" Katzman asks.

"Looking at me."

"Does it know you're looking back?"

"We're having a staring contest, so that's a safe bet, yeah."

He pushes himself up, fighting against quivering legs. "You can't let it escape. If they find out . . ."

My hands eject the spent magazine and slap in a fresh one. My last twelve rounds.

I keep my eyes locked onto the beast's. The rest of its ugly face slowly comes into focus. Its domed head has no nose. No ears. Its eyes are circular, blank, but somehow also filled with loathing. The teeth in its prodigious hippo mouth are like a great white shark's, but the color of night. The only color aside from black and pale, fleshy worm-tongue is green. Thick, glowing, fluorescent-green veins twist away from its eyes, forming pathways around its body.

"Find out about what?" I ask.

"*You,*" he says. "That you can see them."

"Right. Any advice on where to shoot it?"

"I've never killed one in combat."

Great. I adjust my aim, pointing the barrel of my gun at its right eye. If a .40 caliber in the eye won't put it down, I'm not sure what will. It just stares back, as fearless as me, either not fearing the weapon or naive about its ability. I squeeze the trigger.

Far below, a door bursts open. Beta Team surges into the first-floor stairwell. My first shot misses. The bull is no longer there. Has it disappeared or did it move? A blur of movement, bounding down the stairs, is my answer. It's going for Beta Team.

"Incoming!" I shout down the stairwell, and charge down after the unreal creature. It's taking the flights down, one leap at a time, but slows to round the bend. As I keep my downward sprint at an even pace, we move in tandem, separated by a story and a half of stairs.

With one hand on the railing, I try to run faster, swinging around the corners. It helps, and I avoid smashing into the concrete walls, but I'm going to dislocate my left shoulder if I'm not careful. That said, my pace never slows because I'm not afraid of dislocating the arm. Sure, it will hurt, but I don't need it to fire a weapon and a quick slam into the wall can pop things back into place.

Screams rise up from below as I reach the building's third floor. I look over the edge. The bull is still two flights above the Beta Team, but they've spotted it, and, like Katzman, they've become useless sacks of molten fear. The four men climb over each other to escape.

There's no way I'll be able to stop it in time.

I'm just two sets of stairs above the group when it reaches them.

But it doesn't attack. It simply lands among them and vibrates. Otherworldly whispering fills the stairwell. When it does, I see it better than ever. *Its frequency is changing*, I think, *closer to A than B, having a more profound effect.*

A kind of madness grips the men. They react out of terror.

One man turns to run and careens straight into the concrete wall. The impact knocks him out cold. He tumbles limply down the stairs, bruised and broken, but still alive.

He's the lucky one.

The other three pull triggers. Unaimed bullets rip through the stairwell. The sound is thunderous. The effect, savage.

As I round the final flight of stairs, I'm greeted by bloody carnage. Despite the armor, the three men have managed to cut each other down, coating the stairs and walls with blood, guts, and brains.

And yet the monster lives.

But it's been injured. There's a splash of bright-green wetness on its back.

It turns around to face me as I round the last flight. I can't tell if it's surprised by my arrival. Those wide eyes never change, like a fish, expressionless.

It vibrates again, coming clearly into view. The whispers, like indistinct hissing, grow louder.

I feel nothing.

The thing's head reels back a bit, showing a hint of surprise, which brings a smile to my face. And it's the smile that has the most impact. The creature rears up on its back legs, vibrating furiously. Its underside looks soft.

"Big mistake, buddy." I leap at the thing, pulling my trigger twelve times in the seconds it takes to reach the monster. It falls back from the force of the bullets, injured but not dead.

Yet.

As I fall within striking distance, I swing my weapon like a club, hoping to crack its domed skull, or at least daze the creature.

But I miss.

Well, *miss* isn't entirely accurate. The weapon hits the hard skull and is torn from my hand. While the handgun makes contact, my hand goes *through* the thing. Right through its head, like it's some kind of immaterial specter.

The creature reaches out its thickly muscled arms and catches hold of the railing and wall, stopping its backward descent. Instead of slamming into the thing, I simply pass straight through it. The concrete floor greets me harshly. I roll with the impact, but there isn't much room, and my roll ends against the equally solid wall.

The bull spins around, looking down at me, vibrating. This time I hear a rattle and a whispered shriek. The sound brings fresh pain, radiating from my ears, but I'm not sure if it is the sound causing the pain or whatever is allowing me to hear it. I fight to stand. I don't think anything is broken, but I'm going to hurt in the morning.

Enraged by my nonresponse to its strange behavior, the monster leans in closer. The massive hippo mouth drops open large enough to swallow me whole, but it's not trying to eat me. It's roaring. The wormy tongue shakes. Saliva sprays but doesn't strike me.

Then the sound reaches my ears. It starts as a whistle and builds into a deep, throaty roar, like a lion's, but sustained. I catch a whiff of the thing's warm, rotten breath. The brief sense feels like a punch to my nose.

Unfazed by the freakish sight, I push past the pain, recover my dropped weapon from the floor, take aim, and pull the trigger.

The weapon clicks. I've already drained the magazine.

Stupid mistake.

The sound snaps the bull out of its intimidation display. It stops shaking and fades partially from view. The head turns toward the door. The exit.

It bolts.

As the large body passes by, I reach over my back, clasp the machete's handle, draw the blade, and swing, all in one fluid motion. While I'm sure my hand would pass straight through the thing, the weapon's black blade bites into flesh. Bites—and sticks.

The massive bounding weight of the bull yanks the blade from my hand. The creature—the Dread, capital *D*—lands on the first floor and then leaps through the door like it wasn't there. The machete, however, makes contact with the door and stays behind, tearing a green splash of gore from the monster's backside.

I recover the machete and shove through the door. The bull is already fifty feet away, running on all fours and trailing a stream of what looks like thick Mello Yello. I give chase, but there's no way to catch it. It's clearly trying to find a way out. I'm either going to be there to see how it escapes or greet it when it can't.

As the Dread approaches the end of the hall, it never slows.

Ahh, I think, understanding the creature's escape plan. But will it work?

The monster leaps a potted plant, throws its head up, and lunges at the tinted window. The window resists the monster's head but bends. Then the creature's massive body adds its weight to the impact, and the window explodes outward. The bull rolls out into the night.

I pick up my pace, machete in hand.

I can reach it. I can—

An alarm sounds. Small LED lights blink above the broken window. Just seconds before I'm through, a sheet of black metal slides down, blocking my path. Through the next window over, I see the spectral brute limp off into the darkness.

A loud ding whirls me around, machete raised. Elevator doors open. Allenby, Katzman, and four members of Alpha Team step out.

"What happened?" Allenby asks, looking around. "Is it still here?"

I point my blade at the sheet of black covering the broken window.

"Dammit!" Katzman shouts.

"I can track it," I say, but the man is shaking his head before I finish the sentence.

"Too dangerous," he says. "They'll know about you now."

"*How* could you track it?" Allenby asks.

"You're standing in its blood," I say, and, with a flick of my wrist, clear the green goo from the blade. Allenby looks down, and for a moment I see the floor the way she does—white, polished, and sparkling clean. She can't see it. None of them can.

I slip the machete into the scabbard on my back. "I want answers. All of them. Now."

22.

"Not possible," Lyons says. He sits behind his office desk, elbows resting on the mahogany surface. The room, like the living quarters, looks more like a cozy home office than something in a vast corporate, black budget headquarters. The only real aberration is that there are no windows. The office is located on the fourth floor, perfectly positioned at the building's core. I glance around the space, looking for something expensive to destroy. And there is a lot to choose from. Ancient weapons from cultures around the world cover the walls, desktop, and shelves. It's like a "history of warfare" museum. And it's all tied together by a framed quote behind Lyons's desk chair:

> *The opportunity to secure ourselves against defeat lies in our own hands, but the opportunity of defeating the enemy is provided by the enemy himself.*
>
> —Sun Tzu

"Please don't break anything," he says. To show that he doesn't know me as well as he thinks he does—even though he does—I listen and take a seat across from him. Allenby, behind me, breathes a sigh of relief. Katzman stands beside the desk, not taking sides in what started as a request for answers. And yeah, you could probably call the kicked-in door, my loud voice, and thrust index finger a demand, but I *was* holding back.

"Why *isn't* it possible?" I say.

"Because . . ." Lyons thrums his fingers over the desktop, three strokes of four. He stops and looks me in the eyes. "Telling you the truth now will set you on a path I'm not entirely convinced you can handle."

"From what I've seen today, it's not something you're capable of handling, either."

He nods slowly. "Setbacks are to be expected. Every war has its risks."

"War?"

"War," he repeats, nodding just once. "Did you know that this world has never really known peace? Not once? At every point in history, somewhere around the world, war has raged. Even today. Especially today. Here in the States, the population is insulated from this reality. We read about it. Watch it on the news. But only a select few really get their hands dirty. Men like you. And me. It becomes a part of you, mingling with your DNA, changing you from the inside out. When war rears up again, men like us see it coming before anyone else. And we can react first. Fight and win. It's what we do."

"I thought you were a scientist," I say.

"In the modern age, science is capable of killing far more people than brawn." He leans back, supporting a grim, heavyset brow. "War isn't coming. It's here."

"You make it sound like Neuro is fighting this war alone. What about your bosses at the CIA? The government will—"

Lyons picks up a TV remote. Aims it at the flat screen mounted to the side wall. "I don't suppose you've watched the news this morning?" He hits the power button and the TV comes to life, already tuned to a news channel. There are no pundits talking, just a news ticker at the bottom, scrolling tidbits of violent clashes around the world and clips of recent events. Soldiers in an eastern European city I can't identify open fire on a crowd, gunning them down. Instead of fleeing, the mob rushes through the bullets, swarming over the men while armored units roll in. These are soldiers fighting the people they're supposed to protect. The video changes to a studio. A tired-looking reporter with disheveled hair sits solitarily behind a desk like the last bastion of cable news. "That was the scene in Kazakhstan earlier today. We now take you to the White House, where the president is making a statement already in progress."

Somewhere in the White House Frank Paisley, the president of the United States, standing behind a podium, appears on the screen. ". . . have taken all possible steps to prevent domestic casualties, but no promises can be made if civil unrest continues. Make no mistake, in the defense of innocents, who are peacefully residing in their homes or places of business, the National Guard has been authorized to use lethal force. If you are in one of the twenty-three counties currently under martial law, please obey the curfew, and the property and personal rights of your neighbors. On the matter of international tensions, we are doing our best to quell fears of an imminent attack. While Russia has invaded many of its former Soviet states, we maintain a strong alliance with our border countries and are working to maintain the longtime bond with our fellow NATO members, despite unproductive rhetoric. On the subject of China, we stand behind our Japanese allies and have urged China to stand down its aggressive naval—"

Lyons turns the TV off. "The United States government currently has more tangible threats to manage. Civil unrest. External threats. Global strife. We're at the tipping point of World War Three." I open my mouth to speak, but he holds up his hand. "And the powers that be can't be fully trusted to act accordingly. They, like the rest of the world, have already been affected and influenced by the Dread's prodding fear, directing humanity towards a precipice like a herd of panicked cattle. Further exposing men like the president to the Dread could spiral things out of control even faster. Ultimately, involving outside government agencies is Winters's call, but I have made my case to her as well, and she agrees. Neuro was tasked with handling what we call the mirror world and its residents and that's what we're going to do. We're the front line in this war, and you will either be part of finding a solution or wait the crisis out from the confines of your apartment upstairs. Or SafeHaven if you'd prefer. But I can't have you punching any more holes in my building. You could undo everything."

"That possibility exists whether you answer my questions or I start looking for them," I say. "I can see them now."

"And they you from what I've heard."

I nod.

"You won't last long on your own," he says.

"Can we please stop with the bravado?" Allenby asks. "I expect it from him, but not from you."

With my back to Allenby, I'm not sure who "him" and "you" are, though I suspect I am the "him" in question.

Lyons takes a laborious breath. "I will answer your questions. All of them. But first, a request."

"What?" I say.

"Clean up your mess."

"*My* mess?"

"Security was compromised because of your paranoia-fueled egress yesterday." He motions around the room with both hands. "This building's natural defenses—"

"The tinted windows." I guess. It's the same odd tint I noticed in the ice creambulance.

He nods. "The glass is laced with oscillium particles. Not impenetrable, but solid in either world. Several of them were shattered and have yet to be replaced. The Dread typically try not to be noticed. They prefer subtlety. They won't force their way through the windows, but the breaks already made in floors not protected by the shielding you saw on the ground level must have been too tempting. And we didn't anticipate a situation where a window higher than the second floor could be shattered."

"Cracks or no cracks," Katzman says, "it was brazen for the Dread. We're running out of—"

Lyons holds up a hand, silencing the Dread Squad leader. "I want you, Crazy"—he has to force himself to use the nickname—"to track down the injured bull and kill it before it can relate what it found to the colony."

"On his own?" Katzman looks equal parts surprised and offended.

Lyons swivels around toward Katzman and, with something close to a growl, says, "You have other matters to focus on."

Katzman just purses his lips and nods.

Lyons's chair squeals as he swivels back toward me. "The bull has a fifteen-minute head start, but I'm told you wounded it. The nearest colony is an hour south, on foot. If it's moving slowly, you'll be able to catch it in time."

"And if I don't?"

Lyons's face grows dark. "You have cost this organization a great deal. Never mind the dead men lying in the stairwell. You've exposed us to the enemy. Provided a chink in our armor. Even worse, you have given our enemy advance warning."

"Of what?"

He raises a single eyebrow and points a finger at me. "Of *you*. Imagine if Japan had advance knowledge of the atom bomb. Do you think the B-29 bomber would have reached Hiroshima unscathed?"

"You're . . . comparing me to an atom bomb?" I'm seriously starting to wonder what kind of a man I was before losing my memory.

He shrugs. "Perhaps closer to the *Enola Gay*, the B-29 that carried the bomb. Either way, the choices you make will have an impact on a war that most people aren't aware of but are feeling all around them. There is no insulation from what's coming. We will prevail and live or lose and die. That is the nature of war, and your actions will have very real and long-reaching consequences. I need you— we *all* need you—to take this seriously."

I look to Allenby, knowing she'll give it to me straight. "Is he serious?"

She looks from me to Lyons and then back to me. "There is no doubt that the Dread are attacking the human race. What I would like to know is why. I would prefer a peaceful resolution, but that doesn't seem likely, and if they continue on track, with no resistance from us, it's going to be an easy victory."

"That's enough for now. Time is short." Lyons says. "If you want answers, they will be given when the bull is dead, and only if you decide to grace us with your presence."

"And if I decide to leave?"

"You can watch the world burn on your own."

I have no idea what that's supposed to mean, but if these Dread are behind the turmoil around the world, they need to be stopped. Though I don't fear them myself, I've seen the effect they have on people. If they can turn three trained soldiers against each other, they can turn a crowd into a mob or a protest into a riot. Maybe even a misunderstanding into a war.

I stand from the chair. "I'll kill it."

"You'll try," Lyons says.

"And when I do," I say. "No more secrets?"

Arms open wide, he says, "I will be an open book." He turns to Katzman. "See about the windows. I want every crack, ding, and scratch repaired within the hour. We cannot afford another incursion." Then to Allenby, "Get your nephew whatever he wants. I expect him out of our doors in five minutes."

"He's sustained some injuries," Allenby says.

Before I can wave off her concern, Lyons says, "Pain focuses the mind. He can heal if he comes back."

"When," I say. "Not if." But as I turn to leave, a strange sensation washes over me. It's not fear. It's a lack of confidence. For the first time in my short memory, I've just talked straight out of my ass, and everyone in the room knows it.

23.

Four minutes later, after a stop at a first-floor armory, I'm fitted with black body armor; have a new, sound-suppressed P229 handgun holstered on my hip—for all the good the last one did; and what I've begun to think of as my machete over my back. The new addition to my jet-black arsenal is a compound bow and twelve arrows with wide hunting tips. A bullet will punch a hole in a target, but these arrows will carve two one-inch-long slices deeper into the target's flesh than a bullet can puncture. Unlike a bullet, which fragments on impact, the arrow will slide straight through. And it will barely make a sound. Even without a kill shot, a target will quickly bleed out. Last is the up-close and personal weapon of last resort, or perhaps first resort. Nothing kills as efficiently or quietly as a garrote wire. The thin oscillium cable has a handle at each end and, once wrapped around a target's neck, can kill quickly and quietly. No one has ever tried using the device on a Dread, but it's an assassin's best friend when subtlety is called for. Or, at least, I *think* it is. I have no memory of ever using one, only that I know how. I loop the wire around my hand and pocket the weapon.

The bow and arrow clip onto the back of my ride, a jet-black ATV, the perfect vehicle for navigating the woods of New Hampshire.

"I'd offer you the helmet," Allenby says, holding a matching black helmet in her hands. "But we both know you won't take it."

When my hand grips the key already in the ignition, Allenby puts her hand on my arm.

"Last advice from my aunt?" I ask.

A glimmer of sadness makes a brief appearance but is chased away by hardened eyes. "From your doctor. The . . . changes your body is undergoing. It will let you do more than see them. Much more. If that happens, the pain you felt before, when you were just seeing them—"

"Got it," I say. "It's going to hurt like a bitch."

She smiles. "Like the mother of all bitches."

"It's rewriting my DNA or something like that, right?"

"Something like that, yeah, targeting your senses."

I nod slowly. "I've heard them."

"Good," she says. "Just remember that you're in control. You can turn it on. You can turn it off. Just like they can."

There's a hint at something in what she's told me. Something I don't like. But I can't figure it out, don't really have time, and there is a more pressing question on my mind. "You said the Dread world was like another frequency. Separate from ours."

She nods.

"So how was that creature, that bull, able to be intangible to me yet in contact with the stairs and walls?"

"There is a third frequency that is neither A nor B, but also both, where parts of each physical reality overlap. Inanimate, nonliving matter vibrates at a slightly different frequency than actively animate, living, moving matter. This zone of overlapping frequencies includes some natural elements such as older trees and man-made elements like roads and structures, with the older, sturdier variety being more common. In contrast, a human body, even when standing still, is always in motion. Muscles, lungs, heart. We are in perpetual motion. Our frequency, like those of most living things, remains rooted fully in A with no overlap. This allows the Dread to interact with the inanimate, physical elements of A—like the staircase—while avoiding contact with the animate life that resides here—such as you. It's a physical place with elements of both notes, but lacking the distinct life of each."

"B-flat," I offer.

"Exactly. What we do know is that to make real physical contact, you and the Dread have to be in the same frequency. You might be able to see and hear between A and B, but to interact physically, you can't just be sensing other frequencies, you need to move fully between the frequencies."

"Out of A and into B. And maybe B flat."

"In theory. Good enough?"

"For now," I say, "And Allenby . . . If I don't make it back, I'm glad we're family."

Her smile is the most genuine I can remember seeing. "Arsehole," she says, wiping tears from her eyes. She shoos me with her hands. "Go."

I start the ATV, give Allenby a last, quick nod, and tear off across the nearly empty parking lot toward the woods where I last saw the bull. Upon reaching the grass, I slow to a stop. The green lawn is neatly trimmed and greener than any grass has a right to be. But there is no sign of the bull, either in the grass or the dark woods beyond.

See what's not there, I think to myself, willing my vision to shift.

And it does. Painfully. I grind my teeth as an imaginary Jack the Ripper stabs my eyeballs.

My vision flickers between worlds: one bright and colorful, the other shades of black striped in green and cloaked by a purple sky. *It's like night vision,* I think, still recognizable as the world but in strange shades of color. Is this the Dread's B world? Or is it B flat?

Muscles behind my eyes twitch, each snap sending a fresh pulse of pain into my nervous system. But I can see both worlds now—the tree line has changed, a mix of recognizable trees, now leafless and large; sagging black trunks, held back by a fence; and the paved, inanimate parking lot—and the trail of glowing green blood left by the wounded bull. The bright plasma against the bleak background shines like reflective road markers, spaced every five feet, when the bull put weight on the wounded limb.

I'm about to gun the engine when a sound like whispering rises up around me. It's from nowhere, and everywhere, ambient like the wind. As I try to ignore the rising din, a smell tickles my nose.

It stings like ammonia and is foul like death, but is new. And heinous. I breathe through my mouth but can taste it, too. Fresh agony swills through my core as my other senses are . . . What? Changed? Expanded? Twisted? Whatever is happening, Allenby was right. It hurts like the mother of all bitches.

Despite the foulness of the scent and the pain of detecting it, I know it's not harmful. It's always been there, in the air, in my lungs. I just couldn't detect it before. This whole new world was just beyond reach. And if Allenby is to be believed, I came to understand that on my own once, without Lyons's help. These things are real and apparently observable to those not afraid to look. The problem is, that's pretty much just me.

I glance back at the building. Allenby is there. The staggered pyramid behind her is like an obsidian megalith, a sheet of impenetrable black, except for two squares of light marking my escape route and the failed attempt to stop me. There are men inside, trying to position new squares of tinted glass.

Attuned to the world just beyond our own but still physically present in the real world, I gun the throttle and follow the long drive out to the security gate, past the fence. The guards must be expecting me, because they just wave me past the newly repaired gate. Beyond the fence, I speed into the woods. Happily, the scent of crisp pine needles, which carpet the forest floor, still exists and helps drown out the foul tang. The pain eases, too, diminishing to a dull headache. It's the shifting of senses that hurts. Maintaining the shift is easier.

The forest, cast in shades of gray shadow and purple light, is strangely beautiful. There are pine trees, but they're intermingled with other, strange black trunks rising up to empty branches. Some of the trees occupy the same space, twisting in and out of each other. Some stand solitary. Green veins, like those on the Dread bull's hide, but not nearly as bright, cover the ground, connecting everything. Am I just seeing both frequencies at once, or is this a separate place? I can't tell, but I'm pretty sure I'm still physically located squarely in my home frequency, not in Lyons's mirror world.

I follow the trail of blood for twenty minutes, crushing a path through dense forest. While the many streams, saplings, and fields of ferns don't stand a chance against the ATV, I have to navigate around fallen trees, two ravines, random granite boulders, and a hundred-foot cliff, which, if the blood trail can be believed, the bull scaled.

The beast fled in a straight line, due south. According to Lyons, it was headed toward a colony. While he didn't explain what that is, I get the implication. If I don't catch the bull before it reaches the colony, I'm going to be facing more than just one of these things.

But what can they do?

Their weapon of choice seems to be fear, to which I am immune. It appeared to be capable of significant physical harm, but what good is all that nasty potential if it can't touch me? Maybe it's not a matter of can't, but won't. If that's the case, the oscillium weapons provided by Neuro give me an advantage, provided the bull doesn't come across some hunters and frighten them into shooting me.

Or a mob, I think, remembering the people in Manchester. *Could all of that fear, and the resulting anger, really have been fueled by these things?*

My rumination is cut short by a cloak of black rising into my field of view.

The bull! It swipes out with one of its thick arms.

I swerve left, but the shape moves with me, blocking my view.

Then it leaps aside, revealing a thick pine tree, five feet ahead. I hit the brakes, but I'm moving at forty miles per hour. There's no avoiding the impact. The front of the ATV slams into the pine's armorlike bark. For a fleeting moment, I think that I should have worn the helmet, but then I'm lifted up and propelled forward, straight into the tree.

24.

There shouldn't have been time to think about the pain I would feel upon kissing the tree, but I do. It's not long, just a second, but when the words, *this is going to hurt,* flit through my thoughts, I realize I've somehow passed the point of impact unscathed.

And then the pain comes late. My body arches, going rigid as though in the grip of fifty thousand volts. The pain is so overwhelming that I think I should be dead, or at least unconscious, but there is no escaping it. So I do my best to reach beyond it.

I'm airborne, spinning like a flung action figure.

I feel the subtle pull of gravity, identify which direction is down, and reach out. The simple movement comes with a wicked sting, like my muscles have atrophied in the past second, never used and withering. My hand grazes the forest floor, which feels wrong. The rest of my body responds, muscle memory acting despite the severe discomfort, turning me over. The fall becomes a roll. It's not something you'd see in a movie. I don't spring back to my feet. But after three bouncing somersaults, I'm not dead, though I seem to be experiencing the torment of the damned. The bodywide ache makes self-diagnosis difficult. While it's possible I could have survived an impact with the tree, I would have most certainly broken bones and been on the receiving end of a concussion. The pain is equally distributed throughout my body, but I'm mobile. This isn't broken bones; this is something else. The headache of shifting vision has enveloped my entire body. But why?

My tumble ends as I slide to a stop in what feels like cold mud. The goo hugs me in place. When I try to stand, the gunk—and the muscle-numbing pain—holds me down. I strain to move, lifting an arm. It spasms from the effort, drawing an angry shout from between my clenched teeth. When the arm comes free, I fight through the pain, knowing that my body isn't broken. Snapped bones would undo me, but I can fight past pain. With a growl, I pull free, climb to my feet, and draw my handgun. A quick spin reveals nothing.

And everything. What I was seeing before, without a doubt, was the mystery world in between. B flat, or whatever. Overlapping frequencies, like the chunky chocolate layer between two sides of an ice cream cake, connected to both but also separate. It was only a hint of something still beyond my experience. Now . . . now I'm seeing—and feeling, and hearing, and smelling—more. A *lot* more.

The pine tree that should have ended my life is missing.

The ATV is gone.

The whole damn forest is gone.

All that remains of the world I knew is the gentle rise and fall of the earth itself. There is a new, dark forest replacing the pines. The trees are just as tall but bowed and laden with thick, gelatinous, black tendrils of what looks like pulled pork. If it's vegetation, it's unlike anything I've seen before.

I'm fully immersed in Lyons's mirror world, existing in an unknown frequency of reality.

A chill runs over my arms and legs.

Could full immersion in this world right next door to mine actually be generating some kind of fear in me?

I look down at my bare arms. Goose bumps cover my skin. But it has nothing to do with fear.

My clothes are gone.

The machete, with its black strap, remains over my back. The belt and holster hang loose around my waist. But that's it. If not for the layer of black muck covering my body, I'd be fully exposed.

"What the f—"

My hand goes to my chest, grasping at nothing. I claw at my neck. The chain and pendant are gone. "No!" I shout and fall to my knees, scouring the muck, the pain giving way to my mania. "No, no, no!" My mind slips toward oblivion. I dig and crawl through the mud, desperate and pitiful. It's not that I'm afraid without the pendant, I'm lost. Body, mind, and soul.

For an unknown amount of time, it's just me, the mud, and my frantic search. It could be five seconds or five minutes. But then I see it, a glimmer of brass color mixed within the dark, wet soil. I dive for it, grasping the chain and lifting it free. The chain and pendant are coated in sludge, but a quick swipe of my thumb reveals the word, "evidence."

My mind snaps back into place. I put the chain over my head.

Movement behind me.

I recover my dropped gun, spin, and pull the trigger.

The charging bull, green blood spraying with every pump of its hind legs, flinches with each impact, but the bullets fail to puncture the thing's thick forehead. I adjust my aim, my stance unwavering despite the oncoming mass, and snap off a single round toward the monster's eye. The creature flails, diving to the side like it can dodge the round now buried in its head.

A moment later, I discover that Allenby was right. While fully immersed in the Dread's frequency of reality, the bull is fully tangible. I can now see, hear, smell, taste, and *touch* this other world.

And it can touch me.

Hard.

A flailing limb catches me in the gut, lifts me out of the muck, and flings me against a tree. I fall to the wet ground, thinking the pine tree might have been a mercy. At least this is pain I can understand. Injuries can be assessed. The agony of shifting between worlds, now fading some, is disorienting. Gasping for breath, but knowing there isn't time to rest, I try to use the tree for leverage, and push myself up. But the bark, if there is any, is smooth and slick. I wrap my arms around the trunk, lock my fingers together, and hug the tree. My body slides up even as my feet sink into the muck.

But I get to my feet again.

So does the bull, though this time it's not exactly right. I don't know if it's dying or if the bullet lodged in its head is screwing with its thought process, but when the thing charges, it's not in a straight line.

With my handgun missing, knocked away when I was struck, the machete is my only weapon, unless . . . I look back to where the pine tree was, to where the ATV should be crumpled up. The bow and arrows are there, floating in space, held by an ATV that can no longer be perceived by any of my senses but that exists nonetheless. These oscillium weapons can exist in both worlds or just one at a time. Sounds like a bunch of science fiction hoo-ha, but there they are, floating by the tree.

There's not enough time to get the bow, and the machete—I draw it up and out of the scabbard hanging on my bare back—feels like an extension of my arm. Not that it will help if the bull manages to throw its full weight into me. The Dread bellows oddly, its voice slick and warbling. Confused. *It's going to miss*, I think, and prepare to strike as it passes. But then it stumbles and is suddenly back on track, green blood–coated head lowered to ram the life out of me.

See what's not there, I think. *Be somewhere else! Go home!*

A pain like melting flesh surges up from my feet, rises through my chest, and explodes from my mouth as a scream.

The bull's head slams into the machete first. The blade bites deep, severing the thickly armored skull in two. The creature's battle cry is silenced, but forward momentum carries it *straight through me.* I've passed, painfully, back into the world between, still able to see the bull but no longer physically interacting with it. The pine trees are back. The wrecked ATV, too. The only hint that the Dread world is just beyond my perception is the green veins scattered about the ground like a loose net.

I duck as the machete, which still exists in both worlds, is caught in the beast's skull and wrenched from my hand. The side of the blade slips past my head while the bull crushes his face against a mirror-world tree I can no longer see.

Black fog covers my vision as the bull slumps down dead. While my body is free from the bull, my vision is stuck in the lightless insides of the bull's body. I try to step out of it, to the side, but am held in place. It's my belt and the scabbard strap. The Dread is still interacting with them, pinning them against a tree that's no longer there.

Wrenching the machete back and forth, I tug it free. Then I slip the blade beneath the strap over my chest but stop before cutting it free. Oscillium can be here, there, *or* everywhere. And I can bring it with me. Change its frequency. Bioelectromagnetism. Rage moves it into the mirror world, calm pulls it back. I turn my attention to the strap, will it to leave the Dread world while thinking pleasant thoughts, which is hard to do while trapped, naked, and covered in mud inside the body of a monster. Rage would be easy, but calm? My free hand comes up and clutches the plastic pendant. This is my calm. My center. I focus on it. My chest burns with such intensity that I expect to see smoke and smell roasted me. I breathe through it, like a woman in labor, maintaining mental calm despite the body's signals that something is wrong. And then the pain fades and the pressure on my chest disappears. The oscillium strap has shifted back into my reality, or rather left the mirror world behind.

I shake my head. *Bioelectromagnetism. Who would have guessed?*

Granted, it's mild pseudoscience compared to the discovery of varying frequencies of reality, but learning about weird shit and actually *doing* weird shit are very different experiences.

I try to move again, but there's a tug around my neck. The pendant. It's not made of oscillium and shouldn't be able to move freely between worlds. I consider leaving it behind, but a deep sense of loss, like a nail pounded into my chest, forbids it. It's a part of me. I have no idea why, but I think I'd stay here and rot before leaving it behind.

So I decide to take it with me. I did it once before, when I fell through the tree. Allenby mentioned that such a thing, in theory, could happen, probably with some kind of concerted effort, but I somehow achieved it instinctually. But can I duplicate the effect on purpose?

This is different from the oscillium. The pendant's metal and plastic weren't designed to switch frequencies in response to a change in bioelectromagnetism. But that doesn't mean it's stuck in one frequency. Allenby said it was theoretically possible, and I proved it by somehow bringing the pendant with me. But how?

Force of will, I think. The object around my neck feels like part of me, so when I fell through the tree, whatever part of me has changed took the pendant along for the ride, letting it piggyback through the frequency shift. *Just like the food in my stomach,* I think. It's not technically part of me, but it comes along for the ride. I'm no scientist, but it's the layman's explanation that makes the most sense. Maybe Lyons will be able to explain it? What's important is that it *is* possible.

I close my eyes, will with all my heart and soul that the plastic charm will stay with me, and lean forward. For a moment, I feel nothing but the pull of the chain on my neck. The tug becomes a strangle, the chain taut, stuck inside the bull. *C'mon!* I think, hoping the chain won't snap. *C'mon!*

A sharp sting, like a razor's cut, or how I imagine a tight garrote must feel, slides across my throat. Am I killing myself? Am I sliding my body through the chain? These possibilities cause me no fear, but I'd prefer not to have a metal chain embedded in my neck. A sharp tingling sensation seeps out of my neck, and for a moment I can feel it reaching out, stretching along the notches of the pendant.

I pitch forward, freed from resistance. My first thought is that the chain broke, but when I open my eyes again, I'm free of the bull and the pendant hangs around my still-tingling neck. I clasp my hands around the rainbow-colored mystery, more thankful for its presence than surprised I've just moved a nonoscillium object between worlds. My hands travel to my neck next. There is no wound. The pain was caused by the shift. Back in the world between, closer to my original sensory self, the discomfort is once again a dull ache.

With all of my accoutrements freed from the Dread world and the bull's body, I'm able to step away and look at my fallen foe. It's dead, that's for damn sure.

And I'm as naked as a hairless cat, but not quite hairless. The mud from the other world is gone, left behind when I shifted back home. Machete in hand, I scramble back to the pine tree, body protesting with every movement because of the lingering effects of shifting between worlds, not to mention getting clubbed by the bull. My clothing is plastered around the trunk where my body should have struck. I peel the articles away and quickly dress.

After slipping on my second shoe and tugging the laces tight, I sense a presence and, without thought, focus on the world around me, in multiple frequencies. The sudden surge of extrasensory input hits the inside of my forehead like a sledgehammer, but I manage the pain with the knowledge that it is temporary. Clicking screeches, which I can clearly hear, mix with the strange whispering that feels more . . . in my head. I plug my ears. The clicking stops. The whispering continues *in my head.* I turn slowly, keeping my body concealed by the pine tree and ATV.

Several small Dreads, the size and energy level of pugs, swarm around the fallen bull. They're focused on the wounds, twitching back and forth, sniffing the body and the air. *Are they scavengers?* I wonder, but the things never take a bite.

I count seven of them.

A shriek interlaced with frantic clicking turns me around.

Make that eight.

The small creature inspects me, oblivious to the fact that I can see it, too. Its four eyes match the bull's, two vertical rectangular pupils joined in the middle to form a ragged H surrounded by luminous green. Its body is small but armored, like the bull, and a lattice of glowing veins coat its hide. *Is it a baby bull? Did I kill these things' mother?*

The rest of the pack tears around the tree, checking me out.

Then, one by one, they vibrate. *They're trying to frighten me*, I think. But why? Do they want me to run? Am I supposed to panic and fall to the ground? Or are they hoping I'll lose my mind and fall on my sword?

Whatever it is they're expecting, I don't do it, and suddenly they're on to me. They've switched from casual inspectors to on-guard watchdogs, each facing me, coiled to spring. But in which direction?

While I have no fear response, I'm careful to not look the things in the eyes. That, I've learned, is a dead giveaway. Right now, they're just confused, but—*damn*. I turn away from the bunch on the ground and face the pine, where a ninth mini-Dread clings to the bark, upside down, staring straight at me.

I try to look away, but it's too late. Our eyes connect.

Moving slowly, I take hold of the bow, and nock one of the black arrows. Though none of my movements are aggressive, the small creatures are backing away. If they're any kind of smart, and I think they are, they've put two and two together.

"That's right," I whisper. "I killed your big—"

The things grow rigid.

Surprised.

Annnd fuck—they understand me. Good to know.

I draw back the bow and send an arrow into the Dread clinging to the pine tree, pinning it to the bark. The body goes limp. The top half flops to the side, swivels down, and hangs in place.

There's a beat of silence and then the Dread pugs bolt. But they don't scatter, which would be smart; they all head south. I nock and fire two more arrows, slaying two more Dreads, but there are too many, and they're too fast. I sling the arrows over my back and pursue the things up and over a rise.

For a moment, I see just the real world. The tall pines of the forest are replaced by gravestones on the other side of the hill. It's a cemetery, empty and peaceful, but old and unused for a long time. I shift my vision back to the world between, the pain less severe now. A network of glowing veins cuts across the ground, along with the scattering pugs, but nothing else. Nothing, at least, in this reality.

It takes just a moment this time, focusing on what I can see and feel, expanding it all, like taking a deep breath. The world bends and flexes, like I'm looking through warping plastic, and then it snaps back into focus. The pain sucker punches me and drops me to my knees. The raw pain of changing my perceptions is equally intense, but the duration is shorter . . . or maybe I'm just getting better at coping.

I look up, seeing the Dread world. My eyes widen. The shrieking Dread pugs race toward a black mound, like a giant wart on the surface of the purple-skied earth. The whispering I've been hearing now fills my head, loud but unintelligible. Bulls pour out of the mound's arched entrance, meeting the smaller creatures, touching noses with them. There is a familial feel to the way they're interacting, but the differences in their appearance are obvious now that I'm seeing them together. The bulls have longer limbs, barrel chests, and longer necks, not to mention those massive jaws. The pugs have short, thin limbs that don't seem well proportioned to their wide, squat bodies.

I don't know if the bulls can see me. If they can see in all frequencies, or only one at a time, or if, like me, they're able to peek from one world into another. But if they're not looking now, they will be soon. So I duck down and crawl away, shifting my vision back into the real world. I complete the shift so quickly that the sudden pain knocks me to the ground. It takes all of my willpower to not shout out. Instead, I bury it all, rolling on the pine-needle carpet, clutching my head while the pain subsides. It takes just seconds, but given my predicament, feels like a lot longer.

I might not be afraid, but I'm not stupid, either. Being found by multiple bulls without any understanding of what they really are, and can do, is likely a death sentence. With the quiver of arrows over my back, the bow in one hand, and the machete in the other, I break out in a run. I slow my pace ten minutes later, confident I'm not being followed. Not only have they not attacked, but I've looked back, in both worlds, and seen no sign of company. That said, I'm following the trail of blood north, back to Neuro, the same trail of blood those bulls will have no trouble following. The supernatural shit is going to hit the fan, and I'm going to be the only one who gets to see it coming.

25.

"Is it dead?"

I stop in front of Lyons, who is waiting just beyond Neuro's main entrance foyer. He's dressed for work, in slacks, a white button up, and a lab coat, split at the middle by his belly. He cleans his glasses with a fold of his coat while waiting for my answer. Two men from Dread Squad Beta flank him, warily eyeing my disheveled state.

"It's dead," I say.

Lyons raises his eyebrows. "That's all? You have nothing else to say?"

"It's *very* dead."

I'm not going to tell him about the pug Dreads, about the world on the other side, or my ability to fully immerse myself in that place. The flow of information needs to come in my direction first.

He watches me for a moment, then puts his glasses back on. "Follow me." He strikes out, and the guards stay in place, watching the entrance.

We head for the elevator, walking in silence. Inside, he pushes the button for the seventh floor. The doors slide shut.

"Before we start," I say, "I want you to know that all of the previous unpleasantness could have been avoided if you'd just told me the truth from the beginning."

"You sound like Allenby," he says.

"Wisdom must be a family trait."

I want to see if he'll be honest about us being family. About his daughter being my wife. I've given him the perfect segue, but he just grunts. Or was it a laugh? He could have been clearing his throat for all I know.

The elevator stops with a ding and the doors slide open.

The level outside the elevator is easy to identify. There are bullet holes in the wall, a sheet of black covering the window I leapt from, and a familiar set of doors. While Lyons turns left, I head the other direction, for Maya's room.

For *my wife's* room.

I look down at my ring finger. There isn't even a hint that I wore a ring on that finger. Assuming we married before having a child, the ring would have been there for at least eight years. But it's been a year since the ring was removed. There must have been a mark before, but I just never thought to look, and whatever indentation the band created has since faded.

"What are you doing?" Lyons asks.

I ignore him, open the door to her room, and step inside. She's lying in bed, just like she was the first time I saw her.

This is my wife . . . The concept is surreal. As distant from me as the solar system from the galaxy's core. And though the urge to free her remains, I have no memory of her, no feelings for her. How would that make her feel?

A shuffle of feet announces Lyons's arrival.

"Does she know?" I ask.

"Know what?" Lyons asks.

"That I don't remember her."

The man shrugs. "I'm not sure what she does and does not know."

"Because she's out of her mind, or because she's sedated around the clock?"

His face seems to melt, some invisible force tugging his lips into a frown. This *is* his daughter. "Both, I suppose."

We stand there for a moment, watching the motionless Maya. Once upon a time, the two of us were a part of her life, but now . . . now she's an anxiety-ridden, self-mutilating vegetable and I'm what? I'm a mystery. Time for some answers.

"I'm done," I say, and leave the room.

He lingers for a moment but then follows, overtakes me with the awkward shuffling walk of a man whose knees don't work well anymore, and heads for a pair of doors I recognize. We stop in front of the *Documentum* door. He swipes his key card and we enter.

The vast, dark room glows dully from the light provided by the glass tubes. The space looks the same as it did before, a collection of dead people floating on the left, empty vessels awaiting occupants on the right.

I'm confused when he stops. "I've already seen this."

"You have seen the victims," he says, motioning to the bodies. "Like Maya, they got too close to the other side, saw too much, or were driven to madness for any number of reasons I can only guess at. You've witnessed the effect the Dread can have on people who lack your fearless nature, which is nearly everyone on this planet."

Lyons waves his hands at the empty tubes. "But did you see the collection?" He looks at me. "Granted, all I can see is empty containers, but you . . ."

He wants me to look with my new senses. I blink, shifting my view. Invisible icicles impale my eyes, the pain like brain freeze, but far worse. The jolt makes me flinch, but I'm ready for the pain this time and look beyond it, peeking, once again behind the veil. When I do, Lyons steps away from me a touch but says nothing. And I pay him no heed. I can't. The sight before me is unholy and captivating.

Lyons walks up to one of the tubes, which to him appears empty, and raps it with his knuckles. "The glass, like the windows on the outside of this building, is laced with oscillium."

All but seven of the tanks contain a Dread. I see three bulls, crammed inside their tanks, several of the smaller pugs, and another four or five different types, all dead but without any obvious wounds. Like the living Dread, they're all shades of dark gray and black, but the mesh of glowing veins is now the color of rotting spinach.

"If you can't see them, how do you know they're here?" I ask.

"The goggles you saw earlier filter and shift frequencies, allowing us to see them. Only partially. Like shadows," he says. "Unless they're already close to our frequency of reality, then they become clear. But even in death, viewing them for extended periods is not advisable."

I remember the effect a quick look in the stairwell had on Katzman. "Because you might go nuts."

He nods. "In death, the Dread no longer actively project fear, but there is residual . . . discomfort created by viewing their frequency of reality. Researchers who have spent even a short amount of time studying the corpses are far more susceptible to their influence. As a result, we have very limited data on their physiology and haven't been able to perform any experiments of note . . . aside from you. I have only looked once. Those who have risked more . . .

Well, an excess of fear can break the human mind. It's what happened to the people you see in this room. It's what happened to Maya."

"You knew her well," I say, luring him toward honesty.

"Who?"

"Maya. Not even Allenby used her first name."

"We were close," he says and turns to me. "As were you and I."

He's nearly being honest now. Perhaps the subject of Maya is simply too painful for him? Despite knowing he's my father-in-law, I have a hard time picturing the two of us kicking back with a couple of beers or playing a game of Cranium—Shotgun Jones's favorite. "If you can't see them, how do you know they're still there? Or that they aren't simply unconscious? Or biding their time?"

"Sensors," he says. "We've learned how to detect their presence."

"Bioelectromagnetic fields?" I guess.

He squints at me. "Allenby has told you a lot."

You have no idea, I think, and say, "But how did you kill them?"

He twists his lips for a moment. "The foyer you passed through at the main entrance. Did you notice the delay?"

I nod. The second set of doors took a few seconds to open.

"You were being scanned. Had your bioelectromagnetic field registered as Dread, you'd have been bombarded with microwaves. The roof elevator is the same."

"Microwaves?"

"Various types of radiation and electricity have the same effect on them as they do on us. Unlike most elements, some forces exist in all frequencies, to some extent or another."

"And if there had been a Dread inside with me?"

"Alone, the beast would be killed. If a human presence is detected, the first set of doors would have opened again, allowing you and the Dread to leave."

"And each of these walked into your trap?"

"Slow learners," he says, but he's still not being fully honest. Many of the dead Dread have wounds that being cooked from the inside out doesn't explain. I let it slide, though.

"They follow people, you know. Torment them." His voice takes on a dark tone. "I know that fear is lost on you, but for the rest of us it can be a nearly insurmountable force. The Dread seep into people's lives, pushing fear, breaking minds. And they don't discriminate. Men, women, children. Everywhere in the world.

People try to ignore them mostly, and often succeed, blaming their presence on the wind, a settling house, coincidence, imagination, nerves. Or we create stories, myths, about fairies, aliens, ghosts, and other things that, while frightening, are easy to write off. We have hundreds of defense mechanisms that keep us from acknowledging the Dread are real and present. And who can blame us. Life is easier for those most able to ignore the truth. But for those who acknowledge the darkness and who refuse to cower to it, they become targets, trying to stand but being stepped on, pushed down again and again."

He's seething, talking about himself now. The trials of his youth. The passion that drives him. More private information set free by Allenby's loose lips.

He takes a moment to catch his breath, then motions to the collection of Dread. "Most of this bunch came in following employees. After a few months, they stopped trying. Neuro Inc. is currently the only place on Earth you can be truly free of their presence." He frowns at me. "Until you exposed a chink in our armor. We're lucky it was just the bull. He was hard to miss."

"What was it doing?"

"Based on the data from sensors around the building, we think it was just excited to be inside, like an overactive dog. It was running about because it could."

I'm not so sure that's true, but the time to open that can of worms hasn't come. "Then you don't think they're smart?"

"Oh, they're intelligent. There's no doubt about that, but they're also instinctual, reacting on primal urges, to intimidate, bully, and dominate their rivals."

"Humanity," I say.

He nods and starts toward the laboratory doors at the back of the *Documentum* room. "It's more complicated than that, but there is more evidence than you'd expect. We've gathered a database of statistical and anecdotal evidence. But it's the testimonial evidence that's most intriguing."

"You've talked to survivors?" I ask.

"Some," he says. "But most are like Maya, locked in a permanent state of catatonic terror. Much of our testimonial evidence came from *you,* before the . . ." He points at his head. "I should have never let you do it."

I'm not at all interested in hearing more about that past decision. "What kind of evidence? Had I seen them?"

"Most of the physical descriptions we have came from you. The Dread kept trying to frighten you, but couldn't. The more they failed, the more persistent they became, revealing themselves to you nearly completely while attempting to send their fear into your fearless mind. In all the years I've studied the mirror world, you were the first person to corroborate what I believed was there and was observing mathematically and electronically." He stops by the lab doors. Swipes his key card. The light flashes green. "Not that you're the only person to have seen the Dread. Ever heard of the Mothman?" He pulls open the door.

26.

Before I can answer, we're inside the lab where several familiar faces wait. Allenby is there, a look of relief in her eyes. She takes my hand and gives it a pat but says nothing. Next is Cobb. After abducting him, forcing him to care for my kidnapped patient, and putting him in danger, I didn't think I'd ever see him again. Most men would have run the other way. But here he is, sitting in a chair, eyes on the floor. Not that he looks happy about it. He's so pale it looks like Dracula had a go at him, but I suspect he's just been told the truth. Then there is Katzman, the Dread Squad leader who managed to corner and capture me. I can't remember if that's ever been done before, but it still impresses me. He's all business, leaning against a counter. He offers a professional nod. I think my victorious return has earned a little respect. That will probably change when I tell them about the pugs, but I don't care. Behind Katzman, but towering over him—in scale more than presence—is a new face. Standing at least fifteen inches taller than Katzman, the man's shaggy face is easy to see, despite his best attempt to not make eye contact. He's young, lanky, and dressed like it's still the '90s—jeans, T-shirt, open plaid flannel. The way his brown eyes dart everywhere but toward me says that he's like Cobb and doesn't really belong in this group. Looks more like he should be playing video games than discussing monsters that live just beyond our perception. I decide to spare him some social discomfort and not introduce myself just yet.

Last in the line is Winters, the CIA overseer and my former . . . what? The tightness of her scowl matches her crossed arms.

"Not happy to see me?" I ask her.

She huffs. "You knocked me out, gagged me, and cuffed me to a bed."

"The gentlest way I know how," I say. "And you did try to kick me in the face. And tase me. Do they know why you're really upset at me?" I motion to the others.

A circle of confused eyes stare at me. Except for Winters. She looks something close to mortified. I think. I can recognize fear, but the subtleties of it are hard for me to pick out. But she definitely looks uncomfortable.

"Was it after Maya lost her mind, or before?" I ask Winters.

Her eyes slowly widen. She's trying to tell me to shut my mouth without making it too obvious. But the implications aren't hard to miss. Even the new guy gets it. He's folding in on himself, trying to disappear.

"*Josef,*" Allenby says, shaking her head.

"Do you remember?" Lyons asks. He either knew already or doesn't care.

I shake my head. "She didn't flinch when I groped her breast."

"You *didn't?*" Allenby says to me, covering her mouth with her hand.

"I lack impulse control," I say.

Winters pounds her fist into a desktop. "We're not here to discuss the past."

"It was just a few days ago that—"

"Josef!" Winters's use of my real first name somehow confirms that we once had a relationship of some kind.

"The transgressions of your past are not why we're here," Lyons says, though I can see he's not thrilled about the development, either. He might even be hiding his reaction so I don't learn that we're family.

I hold up my hands to Winters and offer a peace-treaty smile. "It's ancient history, right?"

She forces a grin that says it isn't, but we both move on.

I approach Cobb. "So, did they blow your mind?"

He looks up at me. "You could say that."

"Still up to being a paramedic?"

His slow nod doesn't exude confidence, but he's here, and I trust him. "Great. Paramed me." I pull off my T-shirt to gasps of surprise. My stomach and back are bruising from impacts with the bull and the tree.

Cobb stands, the cobwebs of confusion cleared. "Medical supplies?"

Allenby points to a tall cabinet. "There."

Lyons leans in close, inspecting the purple skin. "What did this?"

"The Dread bull."

He reels back. "It *touched* you?"

"Hard," I say. "Is that unusual?"

"It's rare," he says, deep in thought. "But it's not unheard of. Despite their ability to move between frequencies, they seem to avoid moving fully into our perceptual realm. We think it makes them uncomfortable. It might even be painful. It must have fully understood the threat you present. That is, unless . . ."

I know what he's thinking and nod. "We weren't here."

Lyons seems both surprised and pleased. But he stays quiet, letting Cobb do his job.

Cobb throws a sheet over an operating table. One by one, he squishes four instant ice packs, mixing the chemicals inside. Then he lays them out on the sheet. "Lay down on these. Fifteen minutes."

I climb on the table and lay down. The ice packs are frigid against my back but hurt far less than the bruising will if it goes unchecked. Once I'm down, Cobb hovers over me, crushing two more of the flat ice packs. He lays them on my stomach and ribs, which makes me flinch a bit, but the discomfort is all but forgotten when Lyons stands over me.

"Know your enemy," he says. "I assume that's not a concept that's lost on you."

I nod. "But isn't the second part of that quote to know thyself?"

"The only self you need to be concerned about is the one capable of defeating our enemy. The rest is background noise that you can worry about if we survive."

It seems like a harsh point for Lyons to make, but I can't say I disagree. Distraction is dangerous, and in this case not knowing myself might be the best thing.

Lyons steps back and motions to the newcomer, who's leaning so hard against the wall that I think he's trying to shove himself through, one molecule at a time. "This is Jonathan Dearborn. He's an expert in mythology, both ancient and modern, as well as history and anthropology."

Dearborn closes the distance between us with one long stride and extends his hand, rigid and fluid at the same time. "I specialize in differentiating history from mythology. In this case, identifying which myths bear enough resemblance to known Dread variants to be considered witness testimony rather than conjured tale or misguided belief."

"To what end?" I ask.

"Knowing the enemy," Lyons says. "Looking for patterns. Identifying goals. Hot zones. Potential targets. He's helped us identify colony locations and has provided a comprehensive study of the Dread's influence on human affairs." He swivels his head toward Dearborn. "Start with Mothman."

"Mothman, right," he says. "Reports of the . . . creature were common in parts of West Virginia during 1966 and 1967. All black. Red eyes. Large wings. Those who saw it, only briefly, were terrified. There are many theories about what it was, including a giant crane. A folklorist named Brunvand came closest to getting it right. He believed the details present in the Mothman sightings were so similar to older folk tales that he'd cataloged and studied that the creature wasn't something new, but something *old* being seen by a fresh audience."

"I suppose you've identified a few of those myths?" I ask.

"A few *thousand* dating back to the beginning of human history." Dearborn is emerging from his shell like a turtle that's just had an energy drink. There's an excitement in his blue eyes that wasn't there a minute ago. "Many, like Mothman, have names. Ōmukade, the giant man-eating centipede in Japan. A real nasty one. Barguest, the black dog of northern England. The name comes from the German, Bärgeist, which means 'bear ghost.'"

"Sounds like a bull," I say.

Dearborn snaps his fingers and points at me. "Sasabonsam in West Africa. A man-sized black spirit with a twenty-foot wingspan that terrifies people with its cry and has bloodred eyes. Sound familiar?"

I nod. It's a similar enough description to Mothman.

"Ahamagachktiat," he says next. "Native American tribes had thirty-seven different names for what we now call the Bear of North America, not to be confused with an actual bear. This black apparition, which terrified tribes across the country, appeared as a horrifying, shadowy bear. Again, sound familiar?"

He knew it did and continued. "The Duende, with alternate names like Muah, Dominguito, and Duenos del Monte—the mountain lords—haunt South America. They're small black creatures with flat, wrinkled faces."

Pugs, I think, and understand what he's getting at. "So, they've been around for a very long time, and they're everywhere."

"On every continent, living among us," he says. "And they're as old, if not older, than the human race."

"But what do they want?" Cobb says. "And if they hate us so much, why don't they just kill us?"

"Because they can't," Lyons says. "Not overtly. Fully entering our world and engaging us is against their nature. They prefer to hide between frequencies. At heart, they're cowards."

"We don't know that for sure," Allenby says. "It's possible they simply don't want to kill us."

Lyons waves the comment away like a foul smell. "They're bullies whose longtime victim is on the cusp of growing stronger. They might have enjoyed tormenting the human race for centuries. But the writing is on the wall. We're going to expose them. We're going to fight back. And they mean to stop us." He turns back to Cobb, shifting gears. "Just a hint of a Dread is enough to make people afraid. We feel them around us all the time. As a cold draft, or an unexplainable feeling of being watched, or a creeping paranoia that someone means you harm. We've all felt those things. Some of us more than others."

"Can you see them out of the corner of your eye?" Cobb asks.

Lyons eyes the man. "Only if they are close to our frequency. Why do you ask?"

"Nothing," Cobb says, looking a little sheepish. "Just something from *Doctor Who.*"

"Doctor *Who*?" Lyons asks.

"The TV show," Dearborn says.

Lyons sighs and rolls his eyes.

"We most often attribute their actions to ghosts," Dearborn continues, oblivious to Lyons's annoyance. "Or if they do affect the physical realm, poltergeists. They're also often reported as UFOs and/or aliens, but if there is a Dread species resembling the typical gray alien, we have yet to encounter it. But the abject, paralyzing fear most abductees report is consistent with a Dread encounter."

"So the Dread are abducting people?" Cobb asked.

Lyons shakes his head. "Abduction reports are likely a result of fear-induced hallucination. Shifting between frequencies of reality is taxing, and taking a body along for the ride, while theoretically possible, is probably not what the Dread can do."

It's not theoretical. I've already proved that but decide to keep my cards close to the vest. I don't know if it's something the Dread can do, but if I can figure it out in a day, it seems likely the Dread would have figured it out by now.

"Probably," Cobb says. "But you're not certain."

"We're not certain about much," Lyons says. "Other than we can no longer afford to ignore our neighbors, and they are not happy about it."

"Humanity's brief encounters with the Dread are simply a by-product of sharing the planet with them," Dearborn says. Because they live in another plane of existence, or frequency—another dimension, for lack of a better word—we can literally occupy the same time and space. And we often do, accidentally. Most day-to-day interactions with the Dread are coincidental, but some, the ones that result in the creation of mythology, especially sustained mythology ranging hundreds of years, is intentional on the part of the Dread."

"Why?" I ask.

"To frighten us," Lyons says. "To harm us. Asserting dominance. It's a natural instinct for most lower life-forms on Earth, like hyenas harassing lions."

"So they're asserting dominance by frightening people?" I ask.

Lyons raises his voice a little. Clenches his fists. "Fear is more powerful than you could possibly know, especially given your condition. It is the perfect tool to keep the human race from reaching our full potential. It keeps us primal. Afraid of the unknown. Flight wins out more often over fight. And it sets us against each other. The Dread don't need to touch us to kill us. We happily do that for them with the right motivation. Lives are lost. Wars are waged." There's a little bit of fire in Lyons's eyes. "Every person on this planet is a puppet to be played with. Or discarded. When they want to hurt us, all they really have to do is get close enough to our frequency of reality and push their fear into our minds. Sometimes, when it's dark, we don't see them. But when we do, when that shadowy thing rears up, combined with the fear they implant . . ." A shiver shakes the old man's body. He's speaking from experience.

The whispering that isn't actually sound, I think. *They get in your head.*

"That's how you found them," I say. "They found you first."

Lyons's head lowers to the floor, lips twitching. Finally, he says, "Yes. I suppose, like many children, I experienced their presence through the frequencies as typical unexplained events. What child doesn't have stories of hidden monsters, of being watched, or stalked, of fearing what lurks in the dark. But on one particular night, after seeing a shadow slip from one side of my room to the other, I made a terrible mistake—I confronted it. The fear I felt when that shadow stopped moving . . ." He shakes again. "I tried to stand up to it. It was *my* room. *My* world. I believed the monsters were real and wanted them out. So I told them that. Demanded it.

"It was ten years before they got bored with me. They left me alone long enough to join the CIA, rise through the ranks, and gain access to some of the most amazing minds on the planet. Many of the first people working on string theory were actually working for me. By nineteen seventy, we had a basic and rough string theory model that suggested the existence of other dimensions. Over the next twenty-five years, our research led to the first and second superstring revolutions that revealed eleven dimensions of reality, otherwise known as M theory. At this point, the math revealed the potential for pocket universes, but it was just numbers and symbols without concrete evidence. That would come later . . .

"By seeing them for what they were, I invited their torment. Other people might have been driven insane, but they only strengthened my resolve. I knew they were real. I just needed to prove it. They set my path all those years ago. This is still my world. And I still want them out."

The room is silent for a moment, but Lyons recovers, lifting his head and turning toward me. "A quick burst can freeze the bravest man in his tracks. Sustained exposure can drive the most strong-willed person mad, or even stop a heart. Whether or not they can, or would, invade our reality isn't the point. The point is, they don't *need* to. We are already at their mercy, defeated without ever really knowing the enemy. But we know them now. The only reason humanity didn't find them earlier is because we never thought to look."

"So, these things," Cobb says. "The Dread. They're in another dimension. I get that, but how are they able to move between them?" He points at me. "How is he? Is it like an Einstein-Rosen bridge to parallel worlds kind of a thing?"

Several surprised gazes turn to Cobb.

"*Doctor Who*?" Lyons asks, a trace of impatience lining his voice.

Cobb just grins.

"It's nothing so grand," Lyons answers. "And it's not really a parallel world. They live on the same planet Earth as we do. They're just . . . immaterial to us, to our perceptions, like high and low frequencies our ears can't detect, or wavelengths of light our eyes can't see. Humanity, and most of our animal counterparts, are capable of detecting and interacting with a limited number of string frequencies. The frequency, or dimension, the Dread inhabit is just beyond our sensory reach. Do you know anything about string theory?" Lyons points at me and speaks to Cobb. "Him, not you. Maybe a documentary while sitting on the SafeHaven couch?"

"Not that I can remember," I say.

He continues. "String theory proposes that the universe is composed of miniscule vibrating strings of energy."

I glance at Allenby. "So I've been told. Like musical notes."

He seems to not hear me. "It's a mathematical theory of everything that attempts to explain how the universe is bound together, including the vast amount of energy that must exist but is unobservable. According to string theory, the world as we know it is just a small part of something larger and unseen. Unexperienced. Traditional string theory reveals there are at least six more spatial dimensions that are hidden from us, on Earth and throughout the universe, though I believe there are more, where the frequencies overlap."

"B flat," I say, getting Lyons's attention. "I call it the world in-between."

"Exactly," he says, his eyes moving from me to Allenby. "You told him more than we agreed."

Allenby raises her eyebrows in defiance, up to the challenge. "That was before we were facing a bull and you sent him off after it."

Before the conversation gets off track, and I stop getting my answers, I pull it back on course. "So no one has actually seen these dimensions? Not even with computers?"

"There are computer models, and at Neuro we've developed methods of detecting the Dread, but when it comes to the larger world they inhabit, we're still trying to interpret the data in a way that our senses can understand. Based on our limited data, we believe they inhabit a mirror dimension of reality. String theory predicts the existence of pocket dimensions, which would be imperceptibly small, but contain bits of reality beyond our perception. As it turns out, the theory is only partly right. Pocket dimensions exist, but they're a match for our own, a reflection of our reality. Not a perfect reflection, mind you, but a physical one, meaning the physical laws governing the mirror dimension, time, gravity, mass, etcetera, match the laws of our reality. The rest of it, like life, evolved in its own unique way."

"But you really don't know any of this for sure, do you?" I lean up a little to better look Lyons in the eyes. "Everything you think you know is based on what, mathematical models and computer simulations? Even Michael Crichton didn't believe things like that qualified as scientific evidence."

"You remember Crichton?" Allenby asked. She's a little surprised.

"I did a lot of reading over the past year," I say, and then decipher the true meaning of her question. "Wait, I *met* Crichton?"

"At Caltech. January 2003." She smiles. "You were always a fan, but on that day he gave a lecture called 'Aliens Cause Global Warming' and warned about using computer models to make scientific predictions."

"You were there, too?" I ask.

"And Maya." She smiles. "It was a good day, despite the long cross-campus line."

Lyons clears his throat. "Josef's past is hardly relevant to our current situation, and in response to your query about mathematical predictions of the mirror dimension, you are correct. They're educated guesses, at best. To really observe and interact with the other world in a way that allows us to make real measurements and observations, we have to alter *our* physical state. We have to become capable of interacting with all frequencies of reality."

"We would have to become like the Dread," I say.

Lyons stares at me, curious. "Precisely."

His confirmation hangs in the air for a moment, until the implications of what he's said sinks in.

"Is that what you did to me?"

27.

"It's what *you* did to you," Lyons says, "when you decided to inject the—"

"But that was the plan all along, right? Turn me into one of them?"

"Not one of them," Allenby says. "We need people like you to fight them. And we needed you to still be human."

"So who else but me could?" I ask. "That's your justification."

"Once again," Lyons says. "It was you who decided to—"

"You brought me here under false pretenses," I say. "Created a scenario that you knew would end the way it did. You didn't put the needle in my leg, but you convinced me it was the only course of action I had left. There isn't much difference. All because I'm the only guy who can fight these things."

Katzman takes a step forward like a recruit volunteering for duty. "Dread Squad can fight them. It's not impossible. Fear can be overcome, through training—"

"I've seen how well that works."

Winters speaks up for the first time since I embarrassed her. "*And* drugs that temporarily block the amygdala's function."

"Drugs?" The question comes from Cobb.

Winters rolls her neck, cracking the tension from it. She's got an edge, and is undeniably beautiful, almost sculpted. I can see what I liked about her, physically at least. We haven't exactly hit if off yet, but that's my fault. "BDO. It's a mix of benzodiazepine, dextroamphetamine, and OxyContin."

"Geez." Cobb laughs a little "Sounds addictive as hell."

"It is," Winters concedes. "But the Oxy inhibits the amygdala."

"And the rest?" I ask.

"Makes you feel like Superman," Katzman says. "The cravings for more after a single hit can take months to go away, so it's a last resort."

Katzman has clearly tried the stuff. The thirsty look in his eyes as he speaks reveals the truth: the craving for more *never* goes away. Good thing I don't need it. Of course, I'm now part monster from a hidden dimension. A drug addiction might be preferable. I doubt the genetic changes made to my body can be undone.

Speaking of which. "If you can't really see or interact with the Dread, how did you change me?"

"The process of genetically altering a human being is actually quite simple. Dread cells are broken down though a process called sonication. We add a detergent to remove the membrane lipids, remove the proteins by adding a protase, then the RNA. We purify the remaining DNA, isolate the genes with traits we want to pass on and—"

I wave my hand around in circles. "Fast-forwarding . . ."

"Transgenesis, the process of taking genes from one organism and injecting them into another, was accomplished using a gene gun."

"That sounds horrible," Cobb says.

Lyons waves him off. "The DNA is combined with a genetically altered retrovirus that causes no outward symptoms but modifies the host's DNA with the new code."

"But that's not what Crazy used on himself," Cobb says. "That was an ordinary syringe. And how could DNA injected days ago already be changing his body? That would require—"

"Time." Lyons turns his attention from Cobb back to me. "The changes made to your DNA were made *four* years ago. You stuck yourself with *that* needle, too, though it was a far more informed decision. You volunteered."

Of course I did. A lack of fear is sometimes the worst enemy of sound decision making. Even now, the revelation that I've been part Dread for four years hardly fazes me. I don't appreciate the not knowing. The lies. My feelings of right and wrong begin to fuel a smattering of righteous indignation, but the ramifications of being not fully human for years don't rattle me. The biggest reaction I can manage is a simple question. "How did I not know?"

"When we took care of your memory," Lyons says, "we also inhibited your new genes. The drug you injected, the one we let you *believe* was important and irreplaceable, simply unlocked those latent abilities. It's why you felt them right away."

All of this makes a strange kind of sense. I get what he's telling me. But it doesn't answer the original question. "What I meant was, if you can't really see or interact with the Dread out there"—I motion toward the *Documentum* room—"all you had was mathematical theories, and I hadn't yet been . . . altered, where did you get your original DNA sample?"

"That . . . came from you, too." Lyons stands above me. Points at my chest. "Do you remember how you got that scar?"

I glance down. There's a large round scar from a puncture wound in the meat between my shoulder and heart.

"One of them slipped partially into our world and put a talon in your chest. It was aiming for your heart. But unlike you, it had no experience physically killing a human being, let alone a fearless special-ops-trained CIA assassin. You rolled, took the blow to your chest, and then removed the digit with a knife. The whole encounter lasted just seconds and left us with a Dread finger. Once in our dimension, separated from the body, the finger remained. You packed it in ice, brought it to me, and voilà, Dread DNA. That moment was like a quantum shift for Neuro. Physical proof at last. It changed everything."

"You said the Dread avoided entering our frequency physically," Cobb points out.

"I said it was rare," Lyons says. "Not impossible. In this case it was likely the lack of a fear response that instigated a reaction."

Something in me wants to argue this history lesson. It feels too simple. Too clean. But I have no memory, so how can I argue? "The severed finger didn't have a negative effect on the people who saw it?"

Lyons shakes his head. "Once fully in our world, the Dread's effect on the human psyche is mostly negated, at least to a point where it can be overcome and recovered from. Some of the fear projected from a Dread comes from the way they vibrate. Their frequency. When so close to our reality, we can feel their presence in the very strings of reality, like the universe is suddenly out of tune. It makes us uncomfortable, disoriented, and, most often, afraid. But there is something else. Something more. We don't understand it yet, but they are able to magnify, and even direct, that fear response. To fully enter our frequency of reality, the Dread must be in sync with it. So the natural fear created by their presence is negated, and when they're dead, well, they can no longer push fear at anyone."

"Are you sure about that?" I ask.

Dearborn raises his hands, eager to share. "Not all myths are about specters and demons. Some include physical confrontation."

"Couldn't they just be ancient 'big fish' stories made up to get into a girl's pants . . . or tunic?" Cobb asks.

"Since many of the stories end with the heroes' death, I'd venture at least some of them were genuine confrontations. There is Humbaba the Terrible, an ancient Mesopotamian beast whose job was to inflict human beings with terror. It had a face that looked like coiled entrails, or a lion's, depending on which hieroglyphs you believe. The monster was confronted by Gilgamesh and slain. Then there is Scylla, the Greek cave-dwelling sea monster described as a 'thing of terror.' The monster was slain by Hercules, who is undoubtedly a creation of legend, and recent information obtained by Neuro suggests the true slayer of the monster was a man named Alexander.

"These are all mythological battles with creatures that I believe were likely"—he raises a finger—"real, physical events." He raises a second finger. "Lacking any real knowledge of the Dread, ancient peoples attributed those events to already-existing myths, or brand-new ones conforming to whatever belief system or religion was prevalent at the specific time and place. And, of course, there is always a good amount of embellishment, or legend, that is added to these things over time. A Dread bull with no horns might have the huge horns of a Minotaur after two thousand years of oral tradition. So all we can really glean is that physical confrontations with Dread, while rare, have occurred in the past—in your case, the recent past—and the human involved had the wherewithal to fight back. Ipso facto, the fear effect generated by the Dread is negated or substantially reduced when they're fully immersed in our frequency of reality."

Dearborn's depth of knowledge is impressive, but is he overreaching? Who's to say that all those stories about monsters weren't just created by the ancient horror authors of the time, spreading their tales through oral tradition rather than the printing press? "Maybe it's just that a dead finger isn't that scary? Or the mythological heroes who fought back were born like me. I can't be the only one in the history of mankind to be born with deformed amygdalas."

The old man twists his lips back and forth, which I now know means he's thinking. "I believe we've answered enough questions for now." He stands over me, breathing.

"You sound like Darth Vader," I point out.

He grins. "Most overweight men do." The operating table groans when Lyons leans over and uses it to support his weary-limbed girth. "Now then, tell me what *you* saw."

While I haven't been told everything, Lyons has been forthcoming. I decide to keep the exchange of information going. "I can see them in several different ways. First, in our world, or dimension, or frequency. Whatever you want to call it. Then there is the world between. It looks similar to the real world, but is intercut by glowing green veins, which also cover the Dread. I think it's blood, like an external vascular system. The sky is purple. There are also black trees, some intermingling with the trees from our world. Basically, all the really solid, immovable stuff from both sides is there."

"It all matches his previous description," Katzman says.

"Yes, yes," Lyons says, nodding quickly, moving his hand around in circles, urging me to continue on. "Stationary objects of concrete reality tend to stretch between frequencies further than living, moving matter, overlapping with the next fully realized frequency. We know all this already."

I pick up the ice packs on my stomach, flipping them over one by one. They're getting warm.

Lyons loses his patience. Snaps his fingers at me. "The mirror dimension. *That's* where you went, isn't it?"

"I killed it there, yes."

Lyons steps back a bit, finds a chair, and sits. He doesn't seem surprised, and I think I know why. Despite his claim that all the specimens were trapped while entering Neuro, some of them came from me. I've killed them before. "Good," he says. "This is good. Give me details."

"I'll give you the whole story," I say, and I break the details down for my entranced audience, telling them about the trail of green blood, the veined trees and earth, and my crash with and travel through the pine tree, and the muddy landing in the Dread's world, which I describe in detail. I tell them how I killed the bull but leave out the pugs and colony. We'll get to that soon enough. I finish with an explanation of how my pendant made the leap between worlds with me, confirming that all matter can change frequencies; oscillium just does it more easily.

"Show me," Lyons says.

"Show you what?"

"Look into the world between."

"Isn't this old news?" I ask.

"You were very private about this before," Lyons says. "Didn't want Maya to know. Or Simon."

With a flex of my new eye muscles, I feel the shift in my vision into the world between. The pain caused by this subtle shift—though slightly less intense than my previous experiences—forces my eyes shut, but I grit my teeth and push past it, opening my eyes again. The room's structure is the same, but the people are gone, as are the less solid elements of the room—chairs, supplies, papers. I focus on my vision, shifting back to my home frequency without instigating a physical change, seeing the real world with Dread eyes. The room appears again. Everyone in the room, minus Katzman and Lyons, has taken a step back.

"What?" I ask.

"Your eyes," Winters says.

Katzman is the least shocked, and Lyons just looks interested. He produces a small flashlight and shines it back and forth between my eyes. "Have you noticed any other changes? Perhaps less overt. Increased strength, or stamina, or—"

I shake my head. "I didn't even know my eyes could look different." There's a mirror above a sink at the back of the room. I slide off the table, letting the now warm ice packs fall away, and head for the mirror. I can see something is wrong with my eyes, even from a distance. Up close, the truth is revealed. My once-circular pupils have split into two vertical rectangles, connected by a small dash. Like the bull. But they're not glowing from within. My blood, it seems, is still human.

Not all of me, though. I really am part Dread.

But how much?

I still feel human. Like myself. My experience of the string-theory frequencies I call home hasn't changed at all.

Except that I can choose to change that experience. I can see, hear, smell, taste, and feel what a Dread can, but can I really do those things *like* a Dread? And if so, are there other things I can do?

Only one way to find out. I decide to make the others my guinea pigs. I turn, face the group, and try to intimidate them. At first, nothing happens. Everyone just stares.

"You're kind of freaking me out, man," Cobb says.

"What are you doing?" Winters asks.

Katzman, hand on his sidearm, is nervous but tries to relieve it with humor. "Looks like he's trying to shit his pants."

Cobb steps closer to me, hand reaching out. "Are you feeling all r—"

A vibration slips from my limbs and into my core. My gut twists with agony, and I suspect the pain might be caused by the physical changes taking place, tapping underused muscles, or organs. But I turn the negative feelings outward, willing them toward the others . . . until five voices shout with surprise—and fear.

That's when I hear it, in my head. The whispering. But it sounds more like static, lacking the cadence of the Dread whispers.

The vibration stops quickly as the pain becomes so intense that I nearly buckle and fall to the floor. When I look up, sweat dripping in my eyes, everyone in the room has backed away. I only managed to conjure up and project a brief moment of fear, but it's had a clear effect on the others. Cobb is on the floor, scrambling to his feet. Katzman has his weapon drawn, aimed at me. Allenby is pale. Winters looks ready to fight, which I admire. And Lyons has a hand over his heart, not acting this time. Sweat on his brow.

"How?" Lyons says, before taking a deep breath. "How did you do that?"

Feeling winded, like I've just run several miles, I sit down. The pain begins to fade as I let my body become its old self. "Maybe I'm more Dread than you thought."

Lyons pushes past his fear, and the others. With excited eyes, he says, "You've certainly never done *that* before."

"Could his DNA have continued to change over the past year?" Allenby asks, sounding more concerned than scientifically interested.

"It's possible, but it's also likely the old Josef never thought to try." Lyons looks at me. "Or perhaps he just kept it from us. Show me more."

"I'm not sure what else a Dread can do."

"Enter their world," he says. "I want to see it happen."

"It hurts," I tell him. "A lot."

"Does the pain linger?"

"Fades over time, but the initial shift is like getting kicked in the nuts. If you want to see it, you're going to have to answer one more question for me."

Lyons nods. "Anything."

"What do they want? Aside from dominance. Because from what I can see, they're moving away from primal dominance and closer to a kind of psy-ops war."

Lyons leans back against a counter, twisting his lips, eyes on the ceiling.

"It's a simple question," I say.

"With a complicated answer, in part because we're not entirely sure."

"So let's skip to the end game for now. Ignore the why. They're spurring on violent mobs around the world, building a fear-fueled frenzy between governments, turning the whole world on itself. But to what end?"

"Isn't it obvious?" Lyons says. "Fear is one of the strongest emotions. Enough of it can destroy logic and fuel paranoia. When this happens en masse, we see genocides, mass murder, and war."

"They've done this before?" I ask.

Lyons nods. "Undoubtedly. But not at this scale. The human race will soon be at each other's throats. Brother against brother, neighbor against neighbor, nation against nation. There will come a point when world powers fear each other more than they do the mutually assured annihilation their nuclear arsenals provide." He pauses for a breath. "Do you understand what I'm telling you?"

"They want us to do their dirty work for them," I say.

Cobb, still steadying himself, asks, "But why? Two weeks ago, the world was fine and dandy. Then everything went nuts. What changed?"

Lyons turns to Cobb. "I have no idea." Back to me. "But it started when you took that finger all those years ago."

"This is *my* fault?"

"How would you feel if the animals in the slaughterhouse suddenly understood why they were there and who was responsible for it? They know *we* know. That we can detect them." He raises a hand toward the *Documentum* room. "That we can collect and study them. Kill them. Consider what we do in less severe situations. When an animal population gets out of control, maybe it's predators attacking livestock, or deer wrecking cars, what do we do? It's a tradition going back through all of recorded human history, and is likely responsible for the extinction of several ancient species as well as several more recent extinctions—wolves in the U.S., sharks off of Australia, deer in the Northeast."

I see where he's going, and in a horrible way it makes perfect sense. "It's a cull."

Lyons nods. "I think they mean to set the human race back. Reduce our numbers. Remove our technology, without which we have no hope of detecting them or resisting their influence. They're going to return us to the Stone Age, and themselves to the shadows, where they're safe from us."

"From me," I say.

"It's a preemptive strike against humanity before we can really fight back." He looks at me with deadly serious eyes. "Now, show me."

I take a step away from him and focus my whole body and all of my senses on what is just beyond reach. I can feel it now, the change within my body and mind, as I let the Dread part of me, and its senses, become dominant. At first, it's subtle, like the stretch of an elastic band that then snaps, painfully. I feel the shift to the world between, and then, with a shout of muscle-shaking pain, darkness. I'm fully in the other realm but still inside the oscillium confines of Neuro. The building is jet-black in all directions, lacking any kind of light. There are no interior walls—and no floors.

But in this mirror dimension, where physics are the same, there *is* gravity. And it tugs me downward. My stomach lurches as I fall from a height of seven stories.

28.

I reenter the dimension of reality I call home, seven feet lower than I'd been standing, just in time to collide with a desktop. The internal discomfort of shifting between frequencies is temporarily overpowered by the external impact. I hit the surface hard, crushing stacks of paper, a lamp, a stapler, and other odds and ends. Momentum carries me and most of the desktop debris over the side and three more feet down to the floor.

Pens spill from a jar and roll across the cold linoleum. I watch them race away and stop against a pair of white shoes. An African American woman dressed in white pants and doctor's jacket stands a few feet away, leaning back against a counter, where she must have leapt upon my arrival. Her hands are covered by blue rubber gloves and her hair is tied up in a tight bun. A glass slide is clutched between her fingers. She might be cute, or not, but I can't really tell because the eyeglasses she's wearing, with round, light-blue magnifying lenses framed by LED lights, make her look like some kind of sci-fi cyborg.

I push myself up, grunting from various ailments, and stand. "You're not a cyborg, are you?"

"W-what?" the woman says.

I'm standing, but her eyes are still looking down. I follow the angle of her magnifying eyeglasses. "Ah," I say. "It's far less impressive without the magnification."

That snaps her out of it. She looks up and lifts the lenses away from her eyes. "You're naked."

"You *are* cute," I say, now able to see her wide, dark-brown eyes. And she's right: I've once again left my clothing behind, taking only the plastic pendant and chain, the nonliving extension of myself.

She looks around the lab. It's empty except for the two of us. "Where did you come from?"

I point to the ceiling. "Seventh floor."

She looks at the laboratory door, then me. "You don't have a key card. You're naked."

I smile. "Don't get a lot of naked men in the lab?"

"Not live ones," she says. "How did you get in here?"

"I'll show you." I point to the door. "That the way to the elevator?"

She nods. "Hey, wait, you're Crazy, right?"

"With a capital C?"

"Yeah."

I look down at my naked self, not a trace of embarrassment. "Kind of obvious."

"Yeah," she says again. "I've looked at your brain cells under a microscope."

I step back toward the door. "How do my cells look in the macroworld?"

She smiles. "Far more interesting."

"But not quite human?"

The smile fades. "There are . . . aberrations, but I don't know why . . . Do you?"

"I'm starting to," I say. "Ready for a demonstration?"

Buck naked, I sprint toward the door without getting an answer.

"Wait," she calls after me. "You need a key c—"

I leap at the wall.

Focus.

Shift.

Pain.

The woman's voice drops away as I slip into the mirror dimension. Just as gravity starts pulling my jump back down, I return to the real world and land on the other side of the wall.

Inside a lab table.

The sudden, jarring stop is like a punch to the gut, accentuating the systemic revolt created by slipping in and out of dimensions. I nearly vomit on the tabletop, but my surprise at being stuck inside a table helps distract me from the pain, which, if I'm honest, isn't as powerful as before. In fact, most of the pain is now in my body. My head and eyes are mostly pain-free.

"This isn't good," I say, looking down. I'm waist-deep inside a black granite-topped table with two sinks.

A gasp turns me toward the door behind me. The woman scientist is there, hands over her mouth. "Oh my God, are you okay?"

"Not sure," I say. I wiggle my toes. Can feel them. I haven't been cut in half.

She rounds the table, squats down, and opens the cabinets.

"Am I there?"

There's a pause, and then, "Uh, yeah."

"Any blood?"

"Not that I can see."

"Good news," I say. "Matter moving from one dimension destroys matter in the other."

Eyebrows furrowed, she looks up from the cabinet peepshow. "What?"

"Means I'm not going to die in this table." I try to lift myself out of the granite slab, but the hole is perfectly conformed to my waist. I can't squeeze my butt up or my ribs down. "What's beneath us?"

She looks down. "The floor?"

"On the fifth floor."

After a moment of thought. "Living quarters for the security teams, I think."

"Thanks," I say, and then slip into the world between, stretching that elastic band until I'm snapped into the mirror dimension. The whole process is fast now. Gravity yanks me down. I let a second pass, reenter the world, and brace for impact. My legs hit the squishy surface of a top bunk. The rest of me hits nothing. I'm flipped over backward, spinning to the floor and landing hard on my ass. Hurts like hell but is nothing compared to the ache of snapping between frequencies so quickly. I'm not sure if it's doing any permanent damage, but I don't think so. The pain fades fast enough once I'm settled in one reality or another.

The bunk room is empty, which is probably a good thing. I'm not sure the guards would be as receptive to a naked man as the bespectacled scientist had been. I sit up on the side of the bed feeling like I've just gone for a run. I wipe my arm across my forehead and it comes away wet. I'm sweating. Using my Dread . . . self is a physical thing. And it's currently out of shape. But it gives me hope that, with a little exercise, I can reduce or remove the pain associated with shifting. I head for the door, think about leaping through, and then remember how that had worked out last time. I turn the handle and step into a hallway.

Several people turn my way. Some of them gasp. One hurries away.

"Which way to the elevator?" I ask.

The distant chime of an arriving elevator beckons me past the onlookers, who turn and point to the opening doors. My scientist friend from the sixth floor leans out, spots me, and waves me toward her. She holds the door for me as I enter.

"You know," I say, "most people would have brought something for me to put on. A blanket or towel or something."

She clears her throat with a smile. "Seventh floor, right?"

"Don't get out of the office much?"

She pushes the button. The doors shut. "I'm Stephanie, by the way." She holds her hand out. "I'm a neurologist."

I shake her hand. "They call this place Neuro for a reason, right?"

The elevator ascends as Stephanie nods.

"Are you aware of what Neuro really does?" I ask.

"You mean, like why you're able to fall through floors?"

I wait for an answer.

"No idea. We're all kept pretty separate. My expertise is memory, but I don't think that's high on our management's priority list. I'm pretty far out of the inner circle."

"You knew who I was," I point out.

"My predecessor is the one who . . ." She taps my head. "I've studied your file. What they did to you. Your photo was in it."

"When did you look at the file?" I ask.

"They gave it to me a week ago."

"Why?"

She pauses, unsure about whether she either can or should reply. "They wanted to know if it could be undone."

The idea of having my memory returned has never occurred to me. Sure, I've daydreamed about it. Wondered who I was. But, realistically, I thought memories, once lost, couldn't be regained. The trouble is, I'm not sure I want to remember. Seems like all I knew was pain, anger, and death. "Can it?"

"I don't know. My access was pulled two days ago. I was given a new assignment . . ." She lowers her voice like someone is listening, which could be the case. "But I think the answer they were hoping for is no."

Huh, I think, and then the elevator stops.

"So there is no way to access that file now?" I ask.

She shakes her head. "Not for me, but all my results were

inconclusive. You wouldn't learn much about yourself that you don't already know."

"You might be surprised," I say.

"Right." A sheepish smile emerges. "No memory."

The doors slide open. I take a step toward the waiting hallway and stop. "You seem like a good person. Not afraid to look where you want. Didn't lose your mind when I fell through the ceiling."

"And the floor."

"I respect that. We friends?"

"You available?" she asks.

"Married," I say. "Not that I can remember it."

"Then yes," she says. "We're friends."

I lean closer to her. "Then as your friend: get the hell out of here. I don't think it's going to be a safe place to be for much longer."

"O—okay . . ."

"Now."

She takes off her white lab coat and hands it to me.

"I don't think it will fit," I say.

"Tie it around your waist."

I do as instructed, making myself a little more appropriate, and step backward out of the elevator. She gives a wave, and the doors close.

Alone in the hallway, I turn toward the sound of voices. A door before the *Documentum* room is open. I pad my way over, bare feet silent on the floor. It's a security center. Everyone from the lab, minus Cobb, is there, huddled together, backs to me. Monitors display images of the inside and outside of the building. But a large screen at the center of the display shows an angry mob. They're watching the news?

"Hey," I say.

The group turns around as though one entity with a unified mind.

"Where were you?" Winters asks. She sounds genuinely concerned.

"Sixth floor. Then fifth." I turn to Lyons. "You were right about the laws of physics. They definitely work the same on the other side."

"You *fell* two floors down?" Allenby asks.

"One at a time," I say. "But yes."

"Awesome." Dearborn grins. "Our very own demigod."

"Hardly," I say, and point at the monitors cycling through images of the building's interior. Stephanie appears on screen, talking to some people, a smile on her face. Probably joking about me. "You should have seen me on the screens."

"We were distracted." Katzman sounds tense. A little angry, which is nothing new, but you'd think he'd also be impressed. I did just fall through a solid floor. He motions to the angry mob on the big screen. Like the march in Manchester, I see protest signs, masks, and weapons. The people in whatever city this is plan to get violent.

"Where is this?" I ask, thinking it must be somewhere in New Hampshire. Concord or Nashua, maybe.

Lyons, red-faced, eyes like an angry bull's, rounds on me. "This is right outside our doors! In the parking lot!" He leans toward me. "What didn't you tell me?"

29.

I'm about to explain that I came across pugs in the colony to the south and that the Dread understand English. Probably all human languages if they've been around for as long as Lyons thinks. But when a security guard enters, pale with fear, freckled face dripping sweat, I don't need to.

"They're here!" the man shouts. He's hysterical. A real mess. Right up until the moment I punch him in the face. He drops to the floor, out cold.

"Whoa!" Dearborn says, raising his hands and stepping away, like he might be next.

"Hey!" Katzman yells, shoving me out of the way as he assesses the damage.

"Josef," Allenby says. "You promised!"

She's right. I did promise her I wouldn't knock anyone out. But the guard isn't just a guard.

"You have a security problem," I say to Lyons.

"No kidding," Katzman says, glaring up at me. He turns to Lyons. "He's out of control."

"Stop," Winters says, stepping between Katzman and me, but the emphasis is directed toward me. She knows that if an altercation is unavoidable, I'll act first, and that I'll win. She also knows that's not going to help anyone. "Please, everyone stop and think. We all know he's impulsive, to say the least, but he never does something without good reason . . . or at least what he thinks is a good reason." Looking back and forth between Lyons and Katzman. "You've read my profile of him. You both know this. So why not have a little talk before resorting to violence, which we all know is going to end poorly for anyone who isn't a fearless world-class assassin, who, may I remind you, can move through solid objects."

In the silence that follows, I whisper to Winters. "Thanks for calling me Crazy."

"It's what you prefer right now."

"So you wrote a profile on me?"

"Part of my job is to psych eval the people that—"

"Do you normally sleep with—"

She puts her hand on my chest. Speaks quietly. "I know you have no fear, and that leads you to say whatever is on your mind, but that's not an excuse to be inconsiderate of others. What we had . . . We both needed it."

"Sorry," I say. She's right. And though I have no memory of what there was between us, the tension that exists when we're together says that some part of me remembers. The feel of her hand on my chest is . . .

Distracting.

I lift her hand away. "Later."

Lyons and Katzman still haven't made up their minds, so I decide to give them a visual aid. I kneel down next to the fallen guard.

Katzman is giving me a "don't you dare touch him" stare, but he should know that such tactics have no effect. I turn the guard's head away from me.

"Did you notice how the guard—what's his name?"

"Magnan," Katzman says. "Mike Magnan."

"Did you notice how Mike was acting when he came in the room?"

"Squirrelly," Dearborn says, and I think he already understands what the others have failed to grasp. When he takes two steps back, I'm sure of it.

Katzman motions to the video screen showing the angry mob, who is now encircling the building. "Everyone in this building should be afraid."

"Mike was a security guard here. Trained to deal with tough situations, yes? With the Dread?"

I take Katzman's lack of reply as confirmation.

"But he was acting like a panicked mouse. I don't know the man, so I'm just guessing, but that's a bit out of character for Mr. Magnan."

"It is," Katzman says. "You think the Dread got to him."

"I *know* they did." I stand up and turn to Winters. "Help Katz stand Mike up."

She listens, and the pair hoists the unconscious man up.

I walk behind them. "Try to keep him still or I might not be the only person with a part of his brain missing."

"Wait, wh—"

Ignoring Katzman, I slip into the world between, focusing past the pain. The small Dread, like some kind of headless bat with hooked talons on the ends of its leathery, red-veined wings, hovers in the air, little tentacles lowered into Mike's head. Whether the tendrils are making physical contact inside his head, I can't tell, but it looks that way. I snap out with my hand, grab hold of the Dread, and yank. It comes free in my hand, flailing without a sound. The thing has no mouth.

Clutching the Dread in both hands, I slip back out of the world in between, focusing on the little creature, feeling its frequency resisting my influence, and then bending to it. I'm winded, tense with pain, and once again naked except for the plastic pendant. I really need to start trying to bring my clothes along for the ride.

But this time, no one is interested in my statue-of-David impersonation. They can see I'm holding something, and I can feel it, still struggling to escape.

"Fair warning," I say. "There is a small Dread in my hands. I think only one of you should take a look, just in case. Would be a shame if all of you went mental at the same time."

"Don't look at me," Dearborn says, already peeking through his fingers.

"I'll do it," Winters says, while she and Katzman lay Mike on the floor.

"Not a chance," Katzman says. "It's my job to—"

"You've been exposed too many times already," Winters argues. "I'm your shrink, remember? I know how hard the strain is, and I know more coping mechanisms than—"

Fuck it.

I open my hands.

They all see it.

There is a fraction of a second when everyone leans back, collectively draining half the room's oxygen, when I think I've made a mistake. But they recover quickly, one by one, leaning in to look at the small Dread, whose natural ability to instill fear has been negated by being fully present in this frequency. But it's also not pushing fear at the moment. There's no whispering. Maybe that won't work here, either?

"Why isn't it going back?" Allenby asks.

"Perhaps the Dread need to be tethered to the mirror dimension." Lyons looks excited, on the verge of discovery. "Even when they physically attack, they never *fully* emerge from their world."

"That would explain why physical confrontations in myth never end with the monster simply disappearing," Dearborn says. "If they fully enter our world, maybe they're stuck here? That would also explain why they don't launch a full-scale physical assault."

"But I can move between worlds," I point out. "Why not them?"

"You are no longer just human," Lyons says. "Though you are no less human than you were before. You are more than human, in tune with multiple frequencies."

"So it can't leave?" Katzman asks.

I pinch both of its wings, about to snap the life out of it.

"No!" Lyons says. "Don't! I need to study it." He reaches out his shaking hands, and I drop the little creature onto the soft flesh of his palms. It tries to flap free, but he folds his meaty digits over the thing, holding it in place.

"Josef," Allenby whispers to me. She points at me and then the floor, waggling her finger up and down, without actually looking directly at me. *Clothes, right.* I quickly cover myself with Stephanie's lab coat while Lyons heads to the door. Slightly more decent, I take hold of his arm and ask, "What should we do about them?"

"Huh?" He's lost in thought, more confused by his return to the here and now than I am when I move between worlds. Granted, my quick adjustment to the strangeness that is my life is thanks to a malformed amygdala, but you'd think he wouldn't have forgotten the angry mob ready to reenact the storming of Dr. Frankenstein's castle. "Oh," he says, looking at the large monitor. "Right."

"Reasoning with them will be impossible," Winters says. "If they were driven here by the Dread, they're already beyond logical thought. Whatever fears they might have had about this place already—the strange building with armed guards and an electrified fence—have been magnified to an irrational level."

"Have we heard from the guards at the front gate?" I ask.

"They fell back to the building," Katzman says. "Even if they were authorized to open fire on the public, which they're not, there's nothing they could have done against that many people. We're cut off."

"*You're* cut off," I point out, and then ask, "How do the Dread

operate? To drive a mob of people like a herd of cattle, they
have to be coordinated, right? Something is in charge. Giving the
orders."

They just look at me. It was a stupid question. How could they
know? They can't even look at the things, let alone understand
their command structure, if there is one. So I offer up my own theory. "On the other side, anytime I'm near a Dread, I hear whispering. But it's not in my ears. It's in my head. I also hear it when they're
pushing their fear. I think it's a kind of psychic communication
that's broadcast out to all Dread, or people, in the area. It might
be how they boost fear and direct it. It was the most powerful near
the colony."

"You *saw* the colony?" Lyons spits the words like he's just gagged
on hot coffee.

"To the south. Like you thought."

The old man squints at me, looking suspicious. "How many other
details did you leave out?"

At least nine small ones, I think, but shrug. "Slipped my mind."

Katzman sits down at the security console. Mashes some keys.
The video feed minimizes, replaced by a map of New Hampshire.
He zooms in, zeroing in on the square shape of the Neuro build-
ing. "How far did you go?"

"I'm not sure," I say, "but it was the first real clearing I came to.
Never crossed a road. It was a cemetery in the real world."

"Yeah," Katzman says. "The colonies you found . . . before, were
built atop our dead." The map scrolls south. Endless woods, patches
of pines, birch, maples and oaks.

"It's why people feel an impending sense of doom while inside
a graveyard," Dearborn says. "Well, that and all the dead people.
We're not sure why they built colonies on top of cemeteries,
though."

"Stay objective," Allenby says. "We don't know if the cemetery
comes first, or the colony. It's just as likely, given the feeling of supernatural dread we feel in the presence of a colony, that we are
drawn to bury our dead in the earth where their colonies already
existed."

The satellite view suddenly shifts between fall and summer, the
barren trees suddenly full of thick green leaves. I wonder if the
foliage will make the clearing harder to see, but then it appears

on the screen, impossible to miss, several miles across. The green grass is pocked by hundreds of gray rectangles.

Katzman zooms the image in closer. Gravestones. "Got it."

I turn to Lyons, who still looks ready to run out the door with his prize. "I think we should hit the colony. If it doesn't stop the flow of information, at the very least it might distract the mob. At best . . ."

Whispering tickles my ears.

My eyes snap toward the Dread bat.

Shit.

Before Lyons understands what I'm doing, I've crossed the room and crushed the small creature between my hands and his. It's as frail as it looks, cracking beneath the pressure. The whispers stop.

Lyons reels back. "W—why?"

"Word to the wise, I'm pretty sure they understand English."

"You think that little thing can speak English?" Katzman says.

"They don't speak at all," I say. "Not like us. I said it could understand English."

"They're smart," Dearborn says. "Probably smarter than we think. They just think differently than us. We view them as savages, the same way the first New World colonists viewed Native Americans. But it wasn't their intelligence that was different. It was culture, and values, and ours most certainly differ from the Dread."

"Exactly," I say, offering the lanky man a nod of thanks. "I heard the whispers . . . in my head. I think it was trying to warn the colony. Or whatever is outside. The bull might have even made contact before the . . ." I stop myself. There's no time for an argument. "The point is, if we can disrupt whatever is coordinating the Dread from the colony, they might stop instigating this little rebellion."

"But there's no way to test your theory," Allenby says.

I grin. "There's one way."

30.

"Are you sure about this?" Allenby hands me a freshly loaded magazine, which I tuck into a pouch on my belt. I've got two more just like it already in place next to the black sound-suppressed P229 handgun on my hip. But the rounds aren't for that gun, they're for the .50 caliber Desert Eagle handgun on the countertop. Like everything else in this armory, it's made of oscillium. Even the clothing and body armor I'm now wearing were created using thin fibers of the stuff. It's flexible and light, but strong, and because of the ease with which it changes string frequencies, it will shift between dimensions without any extra effort, which is good because we won't have a bodiless suit running around revealing my location.

After stowing three magazines, I slap a fourth magazine into the Desert Eagle and slide it into a chest holster. "Would it matter if I wasn't sure?"

"I might worry less."

I pick up my machete and inspect the weapon. There isn't a knick on it, in any frequency. I run my thumb across the blade. Razor-sharp. The encounter with the bull's armor and thick bones didn't leave a mark. Oscillium is tough stuff.

"Were we close?" I ask. "Before all this?"

"Yeah," she says. "We were. When you were young."

"And after that?"

"You . . . grew up. Joined the military and got serious. Saw things no one should see. Did God knows what, too. We—your family—didn't know what you did. Not really. Not even Maya. It wasn't until after Simon was born that the old you began to resurface. Then, the Dread happened, and Neuro, and suddenly we were all brought within the fold. Lyons's idea, but you supported it. Some of us had skills or experience that helped. I was a medical doctor. Your father was an engineer. Helped design this building. But the others, your mother, Hugh, Maya, and . . . Simon, who was just a baby at the time; they were supposed to be safer . . ."

"For what it's worth," I say. "I'm sorry."

She offers a weak smile. "We all are." Her eyes find mine. "Do you think it will help?"

I sheath the machete on my back and start perusing the automatic weapons for something powerful but mobile. "What?"

"Fighting them. Killing them. Does vengeance ever help?"

I pause to look at her. "I thought we were defending ourselves? Defending everyone."

The armory door opens before Allenby can respond. Katzman enters, dwarfed by the rifle he's carrying. "I have what you asked for, but I think it's a stupid idea."

I can't contain my smile when I see the sound-suppressed 20 mm Anzio Ironworks mag-fed rifle. It's a beast with a five-thousand-yard range, low recoil, and enough power to reduce a man to red Silly String. And its three-round magazine means you can fire three shots fairly quickly, putting the fear of God into an enemy, whether they're in the open or in a tank. The downside is that it's nearly seven feet long from butt to barrel, but I don't need to be mobile, I just need to turn a few Dread into chunky stains and be on my way.

"You want to get your people out of here, we need to disrupt the mob. That means injecting some doubt. If I can pick off a few Dread, the rest might head for the hills. If not, it might still be enough to create an opening."

"I don't like it," he says.

"Is any part of war likeable?" I pick up two World War I trench knives—foot-long blades with knuckled handles—and attach them to my belt. A sound-suppressed KRISS Vector CRB .45 ACP assault rifle goes over my shoulder. It's a high-tech, mobile, and hard-hitting automatic rifle with essentially no recoil. Three spare magazines go in my vest. I finish arming myself by reclaiming the compound bow and a fresh quiver of arrows. I smile at Katzman. "Except for weapons. I think I like weapons." I look at Allenby for confirmation. She's nodding. "These weren't mine, too?"

"We knew your preferences," Katzman says. "Anything else?"

"A question," I say. "Microwaves."

"What about them?" he asks.

"All the weapons here are made of oscillium," I point out, "which can hit a target in another frequency—if you can see it—but everything here is conventional. Bullets and blades."

Katzman gives an impatient sigh. "Did you have a question?"

"Why don't we have microwave guns?"

"They don't work," he says. "In any capacity. The military has developed several directed-energy weapons using microwaves. MEDUSA, the mob excess deterrent using silent audio, interacts with a person's head. Creates a scream no one else can hear, unless they're in the target zone, too. Then there is the active denial system, which is basically a pain gun that made people *think* they were being cooked. Both were deployed and then recalled for safety and humanitarian reasons. But the flaw with all microwave weapons is that the target either needs to be standing still and cooperating, or the beam so broad that a blast of microwaves large enough to kill or injure a Dread would have the same effect on both worlds."

"Anyone in the target zone would go poof," I say.

He nods. "And the target zone would have to be large to kill something like a bull. They're tough. And fast."

"Unless they're trapped in a foyer that's actually a microwave oven," I say.

"Exactly." He heads for the door. "I'll be on the roof when you're done getting dressed for your funeral."

31.

From the roof of the staggered pyramid that is the Neuro building, there are clear views of all four sides. But we're only concerned
about the parking lot, which is full. There are at least five hundred
people, more trickling in, but the drive to the main road is mostly
empty.

Shouting voices of the protestors, who seem to believe Neuro
is polluting the groundwater and performing animal experiments,
rise up from below. The human din is mixed with an otherworldly
whispering that only I can perceive. If I could understand Dread,
then we'd have a nice tactical advantage, but cognition wasn't part
of the DNA-altering package.

There are still thirty nonessential employees inside the building. Lyons wants them out. The official reason is for their own protection, despite assurances that the building is impenetrable—by
means available to civilians. Oscillium plates have slid down beneath the windows on the first two stories. The entrances are
locked, and anyone or anything that breaches the foyer will then
have to get past the electrified floor, which I've been told has been
reduced to a nonlethal voltage. Of course, anything Dread—if
alone—will be cooked by microwaves. The oscillium-tinted windows on the higher floors are still vulnerable, but Lyons believes
the Dread will stay true to form, remaining in the shadows, acting through influence rather than an overt physical assault.

The warm summer air is heavy with moisture. Dark clouds loom
in the distance. Leaves all around the building flicker between
shades of green as the wind kicks up. If there is any doubt that a
storm is coming, the low rumble of thunder rolling through the
sky erases it. According to Katzman, the storm won't be enough to
deter the Dread, despite lightning being a threat to denizens of all
dimensions. They'll pour on the fear until people ignore the instinct to flee from open spaces during a storm.

"This is a bad idea," Katzman says, a slight quiver in his voice.

Thus far, he's been the pinnacle of bravery, except for the one moment he saw the Dread bull in the stairwell. I'm hearing that same kind of fear in his voice right now.

I turn around casually, glancing at the people with me—Allenby, Katzman, and two men from Dread Squad Alpha. As I turn, I let my vision slip into the world between frequencies, my shifting pupils hidden behind a pair of reflective sunglasses. The pain from the subtle shift in my physiology is intense, but lessoned, and I manage it with no outward sign of discomfort. My Dread muscles are getting stronger. The whispering grows louder, but I block it out. Four Dread hover above the others, vibrating waves of fear into them. It's subtle enough that their emotions are being manipulated without setting off alarm bells.

Hello, mothmen, I think, as I look at the red-eyed, four-winged creatures. Like other Dread, veins cover the outsides of their bodies, but they're not green, they're luminescent red, a similar shade to the small Dread bat. Like the bull, their heads are domed and lacking noses and ears. Their four red eyes are positioned two on the outside, two in the middle, providing a wide range of vision. While vaguely humanoid with short powerful legs and long skinny arms, the thing also has an array of small hooked limbs lining the center of its torso, twitching madly. I can't imagine what they're for until a mothman descends on one of the Alpha Team. The tiny legs wrap around the man's body, shaking in a way that reminds me of the way bees communicate. The man shivers and breaks out in a sweat.

"Katzman," I say, casually. "Have you ever been to a magic show?"

"What?" He's instantly annoyed. Fidgeting.

"My favorite act is the knife throwing." This is all made up. I have no memory of going to a magic show. But I know the tricks and need to communicate cryptically. The Dread understand English, but might not be able to decipher a message cloaked by human context. "I know some are fake. The knife pops out of the backboard. But some are real."

"You better be going somewhere with this. We're on a schedule."

I turn back quickly, like I'm looking over the roof, but I'm actually confirming that there is a mothman hovering behind me as well, vibrating fear toward me but not into me. That I haven't been attacked outright means they don't know who I am. They might know about me, but they don't recognize me as the guy that can see them—yet. To keep that from happening, I shiver, doing my best to act mildly afraid, which is a stretch, like pretending to be a shark. But the Dread haven't pounced, so that's encouraging. Good thing they can't see my eyes, though. The razor-sharp focus would broadcast my intentions.

"Know what the secret to that act is? *Not moving.*" I see Katzman's eyes widen, just a twitch. He gets it. I turn to Allenby. "Not a muscle." To the Alpha men. "You hear what I'm saying? Understand it?" They nod.

"Good." With my left hand I draw my sound-suppressed P229, casual and slow. With my right, I lift the machete from the sheath on my back. While I would love to use the Desert Eagle strapped to my chest, the hand cannon would be heard for miles. To do this right, we need to stay quiet. If the people down below catch wind, it could be like dropping a match in a gas can.

"Care for a demonstration?" I ask Katzman.

A hint of a smile erases some of the fear gripping him. "Please."

I swing hard with the machete.

From Katzman's perspective, it probably looks like I'm going to lop off his head. But that's kind of the point. I need it to look like he's the target, not the Dread. To his credit, despite being fearfueled by the mothman, Katzman holds his ground. The heavy, straight blade slips just over his neatly trimmed hair and bites into flesh that only I can see. When the swing completes its arc, a headless mothman falls to the rooftop, landing on the oscillium surface. I spin around, swinging at the monster behind me. The blade draws a line across its chest and I turn away before it hits the rooftop.

I open fire with the sound-suppressed handgun, coughing bullets into the back of a third mothman, until it falls dead, which also happens to be the same time the magazine runs out of rounds.

The last two Dread take to the sky, their whispers coming closer to being shouts. Beating their wings hard, the pair splits, heading in opposite directions.

I drop the machete and handgun, pick up the bow and quickly nock an arrow. I draw the compound line back, take aim, and—

One of the Dread Squad crew shouts in surprise.

Allenby chimes in with, "Look out!" She's talking to me, but looking over my shoulder.

Shit.

I leap to the side, keeping the arrow nocked, visualizing my roll and counterattack, but nothing goes as planned. I'm struck in the side and land awkwardly. The arrow springs from my fingers and launches into the distant woods. Before I can even think about getting up, something wraps around my ankle, cinches tight, and pulls. I'm dragged across the rooftop and then lifted up. I see the ugly mothman upside down, the digits on its torso wriggling madly. The thing has fully entered our world, perhaps knowing it's going to die from the gushing wound on its chest, perhaps just willing to sacrifice itself for its brethren now flying away. Either way, it's making a mess of my plans and continues on this track by tossing me over its shoulder and the side of the roof.

As I sail over the small wall at the side of the roof, I reach out for it. My fingers slide over the surface and find a small amount of friction. The tug swings my body around and then down. I land hard on the angled glass, which holds my weight. Not falling through the window is a good thing, but it also means that all of the impact's force is absorbed by my body. Coughing for air and trying to ignore the pain, I splay my arms and legs wide, clinging to the window. Despite my efforts, I start to slide. *No*, I think, *not yet!*

I hear the cough of silenced weapons above, and then a shadow falls over me. The mothman leans into view, its long arm slapping my body. For a moment, I think it's attacking, but a slick of bright-red blood starts flowing over the glass, just inches from my face. I grasp the Dread's arm and roll across the glass, avoiding the blood that will turn the side of Neuro into a gore-covered playground slide.

I try to pull myself up, but the body, which is lighter than me, slips. I'm sure we're about to fall together when I'm grasped from above. Katzman. Working together, I reach the short wall and climb over. I take in the scene while catching my breath. The Dread has been peppered by countless rounds. "Holy overkill. Which one of you shot it?"

Allenby, Katzman, and both Dread Squad men raise their hands.

"Thanks," I say, and pick up the bow. The two remaining Dread are fleeing, one far closer than the other. I nock an arrow, draw it back, and aim. I release the string and the black projectile cuts soundlessly through the air, striking a mothman's back before it clears the far side of the roof.

"Holy . . ." one of the soldiers whispers. Though the others can't see the mothman, they can see the arrow stop in midair and fall to the roof. A second arrow is nocked and the string drawn back, but the second Dread is moving fast and climbing, too far for me to hit with the bow. I let the bowstring go slack and remove the arrow.

"Get that thing out of sight," I say to the Dread Squad men while pointing at the dead Dread, stuck in our world. While they move for the monster, I pick up the 20 mm sniper rifle and run toward an air-conditioning unit.

"How many were there?" Katzman asks.

"Five," I say. "Now just one, but it's getting away." I pull down the bipod and lean it on the metal cube. Angling the several-foot-long barrel into the distant sky, I get behind the weapon and peer through the scope. It takes a few seconds of shifting back and forth, but the adjustable zoom allows me to spot the fleeing Dread and lock on.

I chamber a round. At its base, the munition is an inch across so just one will get the job done and then some. I focus on the target. Mothman number 5 is fleeing south, but at an angle. I gauge the distance. Half mile. Moving fast. I pan slowly, following my target, then lead it, aiming at the open air, where it will be in the next second.

I exhale.

Finger on the trigger.

The weapon bucks hard and coughs loudly when the round tears off through the sky. Compared to other sound-suppressed weapons, it's loud, but the noise isn't sharp. Pinpointing its origin would be difficult, especially to the people far below us.

The Dread continues on its way, unmarred.

I chamber a second round.

"You *missed*?" Allenby says. It's the most surprised I've heard her.

"I've been in a psych ward for a year, and though I seem to know how to operate this beast, I have no actual memory of doing so." I look through the scope. "But I'm not worried."

"That's because you don't *get* worried," Allenby says.

I pull the trigger. The big gun kicks, sending a second round tearing toward the Dread. I'm hoping to see the thing twitch and fall to the ground, but that's not what happens. The damn thing *explodes,* bursting into a mash of black and red goo that rains down into the forest. I chuckle in surprise and lean back. "Got him."

"What did they look like?" Katzman says. He's got goggles pulled over his eyes. Can see that we're in the clear now. But if reinforcements show up and he's wearing them, he'll be useless.

I point at the goggles. "Better to take those off. Let me handle this."

He lifts the goggles.

I point at the Mothman being dragged up onto the roof by the two Dread Squad members, who are doing their best to not look at it. "All five were like that one. Mothmen."

"Hey!"

We all turn toward the voice. It's Dearborn. He's running toward us from the elevator, waving excitedly. He's got a damn smile on his face. "I saw it from the security room."

"Are you nuts?" Katzman asks. "You're supposed to be leaving with the others."

"No way, man," Dearborn says. "This is modern myth in the making, demigod and all. I need to see this. I need to bear witness."

"I'm no demigod," I say.

"The Dread have been worshiped as gods," he says. "You're part Dread. Ipso fa—"

"Ispo fuck off," I say. "You're going to get yourself killed."

He ignores me and leans over the mothman's body, which has been laid out on the roof by the Dread Squad guys. It's very dead and covered in its own gore, but that doesn't seem to bother Dearborn. "It's a mothman." He looks up at me. "You're lucky you saw it."

He's clearly not going anywhere, and I don't have time to force him. I lift the sniper rifle and lug it back toward the roof's edge. "Why's that?"

Dearborn walks beside me. "The amount of fear generated by different subspecies of Dread varies—we think. Looking at the history of Dread encounters and comparing sightings of various species with the resulting effect on humanity, we can paint a rough picture of which Dread can do what. While bulls can instigate people to violence, it takes time. Mobs and confusion are their territory. Historically, mothmen most often lead to dramatically violent events. The 1967 encounters in West Virginia culminated with the collapse of a bridge that killed forty-six people. They're also more likely to enter the physical realm, as you just saw."

"The claw I took?"

He nods. "A mothman."

I turn to Allenby, who is on my other side. "Maya? And Simon?"

"Most likely," she says. "Hugh and your parents, too."

Assassins, then. Like me. I'll keep that in mind next time I come face-to-ugly-face with one.

I crouch by the side of the roof. Moving slowly, I put the rifle down, leaning the bipod on the top of the foot-tall wall surrounding the rooftop. "Anything worse than a mothman?"

"Not that we, or previous you, has seen or captured thus far," Dearborn says, "but it seems likely. While humanity divides race by skin color and facial features, the Dread vary far more widely. It's more like different species of Dread, rather than races, though each species might also have its own geographically separated races. We don't know, and thinking we've experienced all of them would be like going to a mall and assuming all races of humanity are represented." Dearborn peeks over the wall. "From what we know, the Dread we've encountered are just the grunts. Following orders. They're closer to trained animals than intelligent beings. I suppose you might find out when you visit the colony, eh? If you're still keen on playing G.I. Joe."

I lift the sniper rifle, placing the stock against my shoulder. "Just need a little target practice first." I look through the scope and take aim at the crowded parking lot.

32.

"Triangular-shaped head, wider at the top. Tall but hunched body. Kind of like Lyons. Its legs are covered by some kind of cloth. Black. Wispy. Almost like a skirt. Has four eyes like the others. Two on the outside, two nearer the middle. Bright yellow veins all over. Two arms, but they split into tentacles. Too many to count. Each ends with a glowing yellow tip, and it's poking them into the backs of people's heads as it passes through the crowd." I lean away from the sniper scope and look at Dearborn. He's shaking his head, a hint of a smile. Allenby just looks mortified. "Something new?"

Both nod. My past and forgotten experience with the Dread is starting to appear fairly limited. Bulls, pugs, and mothmen seem to be the limit of Neuro's Dread-related knowledge base. Of course, back then, the Dread weren't trying to instigate rebellions and world wars, so I suppose it makes sense that we're encountering previously unseen species.

I return my eye to the scope. "There's only one of them down there. Eight bulls. Maybe twenty pugs."

"Pugs?" Allenby asks.

"The little ones. They look like alien pugs. The dog breed."

"You said the new one was wearing clothing?" Katzman asks, standing behind us, far enough away from the roof's edge to not be visible.

I focus on the monster in question as it flits about the agitated crowd, moving from one person to the next, pausing just long enough to . . . what? "That unusual?"

Katzman kneels behind the wall, peeking over the top. He slowly lowers his goggles into place. His body goes rigid just from seeing the thing. He curses, yanks the goggles up, catches his breath, and says, "According to your past accounts, it's a first."

"Whatever it is," I say, "it's not really scaring anyone." I watch the way the bulls and pugs shimmer closer to our frequency and the effect their brush with our reality has on the people nearby.

They're pumping fear and paranoia into the crowd, keeping them on the edge. But Medusa-hands seems to be directing the flow of ideas. Those it touches move forward, toward the front doors. If this goes on much longer, they might have this mob storm the building. Lyons has faith in the building's defenses, but I have my doubts. If there is anything a mob is good at, it's finding a way through a building's windows, even if those windows are three stories up. And these people are supercharged by fear. Some of the most heinous and desperate acts in human history have been fueled by fear. If these people get inside, anyone left will be in serious trouble. Of course, so will those who get inside. Once we evacuate the remaining staff, the people left inside will either be inner-circle scientists or heavily armed guards and Dread Squad members. The pristine hallways beneath us could very quickly get a fresh coat of red.

"Can you take it out?" Katzman asks.

I center my scope on the thing's wide head. It's always moving and, despite the creature's size, remains ducked down behind the people it's affecting. I could shoot it, but not without risk of hitting someone. While I'm fairly certain I could squeak a round between some protesters without hitting them, I don't know if the massive round will be stopped by the Dread's body. It could very easily pass straight through the Dread—and whoever is behind it. I might drop the monster and a line of ten people with it. War between overlapping dimensions is a complicated thing, especially when the bullets exist in both worlds.

But do they have to?

I grip the large rifle with both hands. "I'll be right back."

"What are you doing?" Allenby asks.

"Just make sure the drivers are ready to go." To Katzman. "We're leaving in one minute."

I slip into the mirror dimension, skipping right past the world in between. I force my shout of pain to come out as a gasp. My body lurches, spasms, and then feels whole and normal again. *Much better,* I think. But still far from a painless experience. Still, the transition from one world to the other is getting easier. *How much more like the Dread will I become?* Right now, I still look, feel, and think like me, but will those things change as well? If I keep flexing these Dread muscles and perceptions, will they overpower my humanity?

Questions without answers. No one knows.

From my low position on the oscillium rooftop, all I can see is purple sky. I search it for mothmen and see nothing but the storm approaching in both dimensions. I lean up over the edge. The Dread below flicker in and out of view, slipping into the world between before returning to their own frequency. They do it without effort or obvious pain. For them, it's like walking.

On this side of reality there will be no people to keep the Dread's attention. I will be easy to spot, especially when I open fire. For a moment, I debate this strategy. Open myself up for attack or let the chaos of the crowd hide me? Since I have no desire to accidentally kill innocents, and no concern for my own well-being, it's a short debate. I lean up, raising the rifle in position. Before taking aim, I focus on the weapon, willing it to exist only in the mirror universe. While I know it's possible, there's no way to know if it worked.

Or is there?

I put the weapon down, flash back to the real world with a grunt, and confirm that the sniper rifle is gone. "Nice," I say, only partially aware that I've just surprised the others, and then slip back into the mirror world, grunting once again, but never slowing.

I retrieve the weapon and peer through the scope. The bulls and pugs are all there, running and slipping back and forth between frequencies, pushing their fear between worlds. So is Medusa-hands. I can see it fully now. The way it moves is unnatural, which I suppose isn't surprising given the fact that it's from a dimension beyond human perception. I can't see its legs because of the sheet of black hanging from its waist, but given the way it moves smoothly across the ground, which is now thick muck, I'd guess the same tentacles writhing at the end of its arms also serve as legs.

Ignoring the pugs, I search for my targets. Medusa-hands will be the first. It's most likely the brains. I figure I can take two or three of the bulls before they figure out where I am, and another two if they come for me. But then I'll need to move. There's no way I can take out all of them, but I think it will be enough to disrupt the mob. At least, I hope it will be.

I slip my finger over the trigger, zero in on Medusa-hands, and expel my breath. Before pulling the trigger, I hear an uptick in the whispering that permeates the mirror dimension. This time, I sense a direction.

Behind me.

I turn back slowly.

Mothmen.

Ten of them. And something else. Something larger. They're at least a mile off, but closing fast.

Nothing like a little external motivation, I think, and look back through the scope. Medusa-hands is no longer moving. Its broad head is turned up toward me. I pull the trigger. The gun coughs. A massive oscillium round pokes a clean hole in the front of Medusa-hands's triangular head, right between the eyes. The round mushrooms inside the beast, expanding and creating a wave of pressure of flesh, bone, and yellow blood, all of which exits the back of the thing's head through a basketball-sized hole. But the pressure wave also moves outward in all directions, and the explosive force shatters the thing's head like a stick of dynamite inside a pumpkin.

I slap in a fresh magazine and shift my aim to the next target, a bull, now looking back and forth. I pull the trigger. The thing detonates as the round moves through its thick body, front to back. The pressure is so great that gushing wounds erupt from its torso, outlining the round's path through the monster's body.

A second bull fills the lens as I turn to the right. This one has spotted me. It takes a step forward and then ceases to exist, its head folding in and then erupting out—explosive red gore and green blood.

I find my next target already charging, which means the others are, too. But it's not stupid. The bull ducks and weaves as it runs, slowing its charge but making itself a harder target. Too bad for the bull; it's big as hell. I pull the trigger. It loses a leg and falls into the mud, trailing a luminescent green streak of blood. It moans in pain, drowning out the frenetic whispering now filling my mind.

I look back. The mothmen are closing in. The thing with them now looks like some kind of bus-sized flying centipede, undulating up and down while gliding on pterodactyl-sized, fleshy wings. Maybe this is the Japanese, man-eating centipede Dearborn mentioned? Ōmukade. But with wings. Could this, as he guessed, simply be a different race of that species? Maybe in Japan this thing doesn't have wings? Or maybe the poor souls who saw it just couldn't remember the wings? It pulses with veins of color— green, yellow, red, and purple. Four wide eyes stare at me. I have no idea what this thing is, but, fear or no fear, I don't want to find out.

Back in the parking lot, two bulls rush toward the building. The rest stay put, pushing their fear into the mob outside Neuro. With little time to spare, I abandon the rifle and step out of the mirror and back into reality.

I'm back for just a fraction of a second, recovering from the painful shift, when Allenby shouts, "What did you do?"

33.

I look out over the parking lot, expecting to see the remains of people whom I'd mistakenly shot with bullets from the mirror dimension. But there are no bodies and no blood. Even the Dread remains are gone, back in their home dimension. It's the living who have Allenby spooked. The mob is marching forward, just one hundred feet out and closing.

"You need to get back inside," I say to Allenby and Dearborn before turning to Katzman and the two Dread Squad soldiers. "Hell is about to rain down on this place from the north. If you're out here when they arrive, you'll all be shooting each other or jumping off the building."

"Back inside," Katzman says to his men, who eagerly obey.

Allenby lingers. "What's coming?"

"Bunch of mothmen and some kind of giant flying-centipede thing."

Dearborn gasps. "Ōmukade."

"I think so, yeah." I grasp Allenby's arm. She doesn't want to leave. Probably thinks she'll never see me again. And she might be right, but if she stays here, distracting me, we're both going to die. "Go. Now."

When Katzman takes her arm and pulls, she relents. With one last look of concern cast in my direction, she flees past the immobile helicopter and toward the rooftop elevator doors.

Without watching to make sure they make it, I pick up the bow, cinch the assault rifle's strap tighter, and leap over the side of the roof. I land on the slanted windows and quickly pick up speed, doing a repeat performance of my previous escape, this time with more guns and a clearer purpose. Nine stories slide past in seconds. When I near the bottom, the crowd is within thirty feet. I splay my arms and legs, pushing my palms and boot soles hard against the glass.

My drop off the edge is controlled, and I land on my feet. The mob is upon me, just fifteen feet. Running now. Arms outstretched, eyes angry.

Or is it fear?

If it is, it's a kind of fear I've never seen before. Afraid or angry, the violent intent of this group is impossible to miss. Their fingers are either hooked or clenched. Some hold weapons—bottles, tools, whatever happened to be nearby when the Dread tore them out of their lives and sent them on a rampage—but all of them look ready to kill.

No time like the present to test the crux of my plan. Rather than draw a weapon, I must become one. Same as the Dread. I siphon all of my anger, all of the frustration I feel about not remembering my past, and I channel it. My body tingles, and then explodes from the inside out. Or, at least, it feels like it does. The first and last time I tried this, the pain nearly dropped me. For this plan to work, I'm going to need to redefine the boundary of my pain threshold. The discomfort moves from my extremities to my core and then—outward. I don't think the mob can "hear" what I can—the static whisper of broadcast fear—but they sure as hell feel it. The burst of fear is quick, snuffed out by pulsing agony that stumbles my feet and slows my pace, but the effect is powerful.

With a unified shriek of surprise, the leading wave of the stampede skids to a halt, fighting to go back the way they came. But they're met by their still-charging counterparts and collide like two waves of human flesh. People scream. Limbs snap. Bodies are trampled.

Will any of them remember why they were here? Why they were crushed? Why they were propelled to violence, or why they collectively feared a single man? I decide it doesn't matter and leave them to their self-inflicted turmoil.

Running along the side of the building, I continue pushing my own brand of fear on the encroaching masses, creating a ten-foot buffer between them and the building. I'm slowed by the electric, muscle-tensing pain brought with each output of fear, but my hobbling progress is, at least, steady. The trouble is that each push is harder than the last, the cumulative effect heading toward a crescendo that might rob me of consciousness. Thinking of the lives at stake and the greater threat to humanity, I grind my teeth and growl through it. Behind me, the mob has now reached the building and is pounding on its side, demanding entry. Those I

pushed back have either rejoined the crowd or have been trampled by it.

Movement ahead focuses me. A garage door opens. A black ATV
sits idling, waiting for me.

Soaked in sweat and near collapsing, I stop broadcasting fear
as I approach the ATV. I'm going to need to recover from the effort if I'm going to have any chance of getting through the crowd.

The bow and quiver of arrows attach to the back of the ATV. I
keep the rest of my personal arsenal wrapped, clipped, and
strapped to my body. The four-wheeler is idling, so I just slip it into
gear and pull out.

The vehicle's engine draws attention from both sides of the mirror. Shifting my view between worlds, I see the crowd of people
and the Dread nipping at their heels turn their focus to me. Here
comes part 2 of the plan, or is it part 3? We never really broke it
down like that. It was all just one long, crazy idea.

I speed toward the crowd, racing to meet the wall of humanity. Seconds from impact, I pour on the fear and push the mental
whisper out in front of me like a tidal wave. That's how I envisioned
it happening. In reality, the automatic reflex of my body to undo
intense pain turns the tidal wave into a sputtering garden hose.
Screaming through the ache, I push harder. Something inside my
body shifts, physically, like an organ has just slid out of place. The
muscles in my gut spasm. My mind says that I'm killing myself, that
something catastrophic is happening to my body, but my will ignores the screaming warnings. They don't frighten me. Then, all
at once, the coughing emotional engine roars to life, and I feel the
wave of energy flow outward.

People scream as they're sandwiched between the fear pushing them forward and the fear now rolling out in front of me like
a pressure wave. They leap in the only direction that no longer
terrifies them, to either side and out of the way.

A path clears. Mostly. The Dread don't move.

But they should.

With one hand on the steering bar, holding the throttle, I draw
the Desert Eagle from my chest holster. No longer concerned about
noise, I aim the .50 caliber gun at the nearest Dread, a feisty pug.
It all but vaporizes when I pull the trigger, the significant recoil
absorbed by a special wrist guard developed by the military for a
Delta unit that had a penchant for the big gun. A second pug snaps

to attention, turning its body and four round eyes in my direction. It's the closest thing to startled I've seen a Dread. Then I pull the trigger and wipe the look off of its face, along with the rest of its head.

The Desert Eagle's kick sends a jolt through my body that intensifies the torment of pushing fear. It takes all my concentration to keep the ATV moving in a straight line. The fear flowing from my body flickers and ceases, the whisper fading, but the path ahead is clear of humanity. Unfortunately, the pain remains as whatever shifted inside my body slides back into place, moved by an invisible sadist stirring my insides with his hand.

A bull closes in from the side, a pug scurrying close behind it. I fire three .50 caliber rounds at the bull. It takes the first two and keeps coming, despite the fact that half of its right side is trailing bright-green loops of entrails. The third shot caves in the thing's domed skull and drops it.

The pug lunges for me, its jaws open wide enough to envelop my face. Its teeth are small but sharp, and the inside of its tongueless mouth is lined with small, undulating tentacles. Like the four eyes and external vascular system, some form of tendril seems to be a common trait among the Dread. It's about to cling to my face like an *Alien* face hugger, so I lean to the side and let the thing sail past.

The path ahead is clear of anything large, so I aim for the far end of the parking lot. Pugs scramble out of the way. The remaining bulls keep their distance, focusing on fueling the mob, which is now behind us.

I'm in the clear, I think, looking back at the now-fading mass of people and Dread. Then I turn forward and realize I've underestimated the scope of the assault.

34.

Eight mothmen swarm toward me. I brace myself for their attack, but then they're beyond me. My eyes track them over the parking lot, where they merge with a cloud of mothmen circling the Neuro building like the Wicked Witch of the West's flying monkeys around a volcano. At the center of the Dread cyclone is the centipede thing—Ōmukade—which angles itself downward and falls. The impact shakes the earth in all dimensions as the massive body strikes the oscillium frame. While the building is well defended against the Dread, I don't think anyone planned on facing such a colossal specimen. How could they? It's never been seen before.

But Ōmukade isn't just a heavy hitter. It's a transport. Bulls, pugs, and Medusa-hands jump from the thing's sides, where they'd been clinging. Lyons said that the Dread are driven by a territorial nature, that they're ruled by emotions, feelings, instincts. But what I'm seeing looks like a very well thought out and coordinated attack plan. Military precision and forethought. This isn't purely instinctual behavior. We already know the Dread are highly intelligent, but Lyons has underestimated their capabilities and intellect.

They're ignoring me. I'm the guy who can move between dimensions. Who can kill them. Reveal them. But they're not interested in me. Not right now.

They're after something else.

Some*one* else.

This leaves just one possibility in my mind. They're here for Lyons. Like me, they're ignoring the foot soldiers and aiming for the guiding mind. It's a strategy as old as warfare. Cut off the head, kill the leader, and the enemy no longer functions. Definitely intelligent.

I rev the engine and speed off. The long driveway is empty now, not a person or Dread in sight. The mob has either served its purpose or the Dread met their human quota for how many people are required for a successful assault. The security gate is in ruins, ransacked by the mob. I work my way through the debris, hit the road, and speed south, pushing the ATV toward its fifty-mph top speed.

The thickly treaded wheels buzz over the pavement. I keep an eye on the woods to either side of the road but see nothing of concern in either dimension. And for a moment, I breathe. The air smells of pine. And water. And deep-woods rot. My body relaxes. I haven't forgotten the stifling chemical scents of SafeHaven. Despite all that's happened and is about to happen, I'm still pleased to be free of that place and smelling real air again.

With a clear mind, I turn my thoughts to my route. Follow route 202 south for three miles. Turn right onto Old Pine Road. A mile farther, the road ends at the Old Pine Memorial Cemetery. I'll be there in four minutes, tops. It's not a lot of time, but it might be too much. I'm in a race with the Dread, but the odds are stacked against me. They have two armies, human and Dread, one on each side of the mirror. I have me. Both sides are vying for the other's leadership, and whoever reaches that target first and kills it wins. Though the stakes are higher for humanity. Should Lyons and Neuro be taken out today, the war will essentially be over. After my four-minute journey, the plan gets shaky, but it's basically "find and kill anything that looks in charge," with the hopes of disrupting the Dread's psychic network of communication, which out here, in the woods, is silent.

The windy road bends to the right. I take the turn fast, tires screeching and then biting, keeping me in my own lane, which is good. If I'd slid across the double yellow lines, I would have plowed right into a brown state-trooper cruiser heading in the opposite direction.

When he speeds past me, driving equally fast in the opposite direction, I'm positive he's heading for Neuro. He'll probably just become part of the problem when he gets there, but at least he won't be my problem.

A surge of whispering fills my head.

It's followed by the sound of screeching tires.

As I round the bend, a look back reveals the cruiser, in a cloud of tire smoke, spinning back around. There's a Medusa-hands half in, half out of the car, very close to our frequency of reality, its yellow-tipped tendrils buried in the officer's head. Two bulls bounce around the vehicle, filling the roadway with intense fear. They're coming for me, and they're using the policeman as a weapon.

Then I'm alone on the road again, speeding down an empty strip of New Hampshire. Movement to the left catches my attention. Deer fleeing the ATV's loud buzz. Movement to the right now, a bull, running just inside the tree line, keeping pace, but not attacking. Lines of green veins covering the world and tall black trees appear as my vision shifts into the world between. The solid road continues here, as well, its solid, unmoving nature stretching between frequencies. The ache in my eyes is dull, like a fading headache. It hurts, but the severity has dulled, reaffirming my belief that the parts of me that are Dread just need exercise. The bull is alone, but not for long. The roar of the approaching police cruiser grows louder, and the car will soon overtake me or smear me across the pavement.

I jerk to the left.

The cruiser flashes past, doing at least eighty.

Momentum carries me off the road to the left. I swerve around three tall pines and then crank the ATV back toward the road. A bull is there, charging alongside me, staring at me with its four round eyes. For a moment, I feel a connection to the thing. Then its face implodes as a .50 caliber round punches through. I holster the Desert Eagle on my chest.

Brakes squeal.

The rear end of the police cruiser races toward me, or me toward it—either way, the effect is the same. I veer right, racing up a bumpy, root-covered incline as I round the cruiser. While I would love to enter the woods and speed away, the tree line is too thick. Following gravity's pull, I angle the four-wheeler back down to the pavement and skid to a stop. I draw the Desert Eagle, twist back, and fire into the police cruiser. Three rounds. The heavy bullets pass through the glass like it's not even there, each one hitting its Dread target.

Tires squeal as the cruiser brakes hard and spins around to face me.

The officer leaps out, gun drawn, aiming over the door. "Don't move!" He's no longer being directed by the Medusa-hands I shot. He's just doing his job and is hopped up on fear.

I look around the cruiser. The Dread fell back through the car and now lay twitching on the ground. As it dies, it fades out of the world in between and returns to its mirror world. I look for the remaining bull, but it's nowhere in sight.

"Hey!" the officer yells.

He's lucky my lack of fear is *sometimes* kept in check by my strident moral code. Instead of simply shooting the officer, I blow his mind and shift fully into the mirror dimension. To him, I've just winked out of existence.

I crouch down, holding my side as the invisible sadist goes to work again. The ache fades faster, though, and I'm able to stand a moment later, feeling more normal, or at least the new normal, with each breath of the tangy, ammonia-scented air. The earth around me is soft and moist. Puddles of liquid with swirling, oily rainbows seep into my footprints as I walk toward the cruiser. Once I'm sure I'm past the car, I slip back into reality. I'm just five feet behind the officer, and he doesn't hear me coming. Three pressure points later, he's unconscious. I lay him in the backseat, steer the car to the shoulder, put on his hazards, and leave.

As I return to the ATV, the whispering in my head grows louder. Almost frantic. But I don't think it has anything to do with me. *It's Neuro,* I think, and understand what the suddenly excited and frantic tone of the hissing voices means: *the Dread have made it inside*.

35.

The rest of my drive is uneventful. Three minutes after leaving the officer behind, I pull to a stop, one hundred yards from the cemetery, and park behind a stand of trees. On my feet, I stalk a little bit closer, allowing the shadowy forest to cloak my approach. I keep track of both worlds by taking quick looks between frequencies, noting the ease with which I can now shift my vision. It's not really a tactical advantage since the Dread can also view both worlds, but at least I'm not at a complete disadvantage, like most people. And if the Dread aren't also monitoring both worlds, I might be able to walk right up to the front door.

Fifty yards from the cemetery, I lay at the fringe of a fern patch, totally concealed by the lush, three-foot-tall foliage. Of course, all this effort might be for nothing. I have no idea how the Dread see our world. While my eyes can see like them, I'm still human, and still have two eyes instead of four. For all I know, my presence might shine like a beacon, though I don't think so since I'm still alone.

I put a pair of binoculars to my eyes and check out the real world first. If there are any human beings guarding the place, I want to know about it. The graveyard is ancient, the headstones smooth, slate-gray, worn by time and rain. The names are weathered, some of them erased completely. The remains of a church lay to the side of the cemetery, having been consumed by fire long ago but never rebuilt. Given the amount of graffiti and shards of broken glass, it's probably been a teenage hangout for years. The graveyard is surrounded by a wrought-iron fence. Black paint curls back from the posts, revealing patches of maroon rust. There isn't a single flower by any of the graves. The dead here have been long since forgotten by whatever distant relatives survived them.

Keeping my body in the dimension it belongs to, I let my eyes gaze into the mirror. I feel my eyes shift, the pupils splitting and stretching. It's like moving a colored lens in front of my eyes and then removing it. The pain is negligible. The clearing is still there, but the cemetery is gone and everything else has changed. The forest is now a moist, black jungle streaked with luminescent veins of color, not just green. And the sky is purple, casting its weak glow through gathering storm clouds. I haven't seen the sun here. Maybe there isn't one. Or maybe the strange sky just filters out different wavelengths? Could be why nothing grows green here, other than the veins. But really, who knows how this place works? No one, that's who.

What I do know is that there isn't a Dread in sight.

The giant wart that is the Dread colony sits atop the cemetery's location. Closer this time, I can see that it's a dry husk of a thing, like a beehive. It looks almost brittle, but it's big, a diameter of two hundred feet, at least.

I sit still for a full minute, each second putting Neuro in greater danger. I consider some of them new friends, and, while I can't remember her, one of them was—*is*—my wife. I'd like to think I'm honorable enough to fight for her, memory or not.

I stand from cover. Leaving the bow and arrows clipped to the ATV, I unsling my assault rifle and jog toward the nearest arched colony entrance. Armed with two trench knives, a machete, a P229, a Desert Eagle, and the Vector, I'm close to a walking arsenal, but there's no way to know what I'm going to find in the darkness beyond or what it will take to kill it.

I step inside the colony without a second thought and let the rest of my body slip into the mirror world. The sudden pain staggers me, but my body soon adjusts to this distant world just beyond our reach and I'm moving. My eyes adapt to the shade with typical human efficiency—slowly. But it's not entirely dark inside. Veins of color line the walls. It's like everything in this world is alive, pumping luminous blood through exposed veins.

The floor is hard-packed, dry soil, not like the mush outside. Countless oddly shaped footprints litter the dusty top layer. It's normally a busy place, but right now no one seems to be home.

Whispering rises in pulses powerful enough to daze me. Whatever is generating the mental "sound" is nearby. I can feel it, and I'm pretty damn sure it can feel me. Probably did the moment I slipped fully into this world.

The shuffling of scurrying feet confirms it. While most of the colony is away, probably part of the assault on Neuro, some pugs have remained behind. It's a horrible defense, and the sound gives me a direction to head. Assault rifle up and against my shoulder, I head left, toward the scratching.

The sound of small feet ebbs and flows through the tunnel, but the small creatures making the noise fail to manifest out of the gloom. They're just out of sight, darting away before I can see them. But I can hear them. The passage leads downward, following a subtly tightening spiral. Alcoves line the outer wall, each one filled with a variety of mirror-world brush twisted into nests. I take aim into each as I pass, but the chambers are devoid of life.

Ten minutes later, toward the end of what I believe is my fourth full revolution around the colony, at least fifty feet underground, the incline levels out. The air is like a giant's armpit: warm, moist, and rank. The smell is hard to describe. Part ammonia, part rotten egg, part decaying flesh. There's nothing redeeming about the odor.

The whispering surges and then stops.

The scampering quiets.

They're waiting for me.

A large arching entryway looms on the right. I stalk toward it, glancing into the last empty alcove as I pass. There are a number of tactics for entering a defended space. I ignore them all, waltzing out into the open, weapon ready. And while I don't fear what I find, I can't say I'm not surprised by it.

There are twenty of the little black pugs. They're holding their ground, bodies stiff, jaws sprung open to reveal writhing maws. The little veins webbed around their bodies pulse with green light as the luminous blood circulates quicker. Behind them are two bulls, their posture similar to that of the pugs, their hippolike mouths agape and ready to swallow me up. None of this is what's strange, though. It's the mound of undulating flesh rising from the earth at the center of the circular chamber that catches me off guard. Tendrils, similar to those of Medusa-hands, but thicker, rise out of the ground. Hundreds of them, writhing and dancing like charmed snakes.

But the rubbery tentacles aren't the only thing coming out of the ground. Veins, pulsing with color—red, green, yellow, and purple—rise out of the earth around the fringe of tendrils, stretching across the floor and rising up the walls, disappearing into the earth. Whatever this is hidden beneath the colony seems to be supplying the blood, for lack of a better word, to the veins covering the floor, and possibly the land surrounding the colony, maybe for miles in every direction. I glance at the nearest pug. Small veins of green rise up from the floor, commingling with those on the pug for a moment. The pug brightens and the veins fall away. This thing controls the Dread *and* sustains them, at least in part. While individual species of Dread might have varying degrees of intelligence and sentience, allowing them to do things like fight, direct people's fear, and understand English, this thing is the mastermind. It's the source of the big whispers, linking its mind with theirs. I can feel this truth as much as I can logically deduce it. I've found my target.

"Well," I say. "What are you waiting for?"

The tendrils twitch. A pulse of whispering makes my mind whirl. While I don't understand the various sounds and syllables moving through my thoughts, I somehow feel the message in my core.

Don't . . . Or is it, *wait . . .*

Either way, it's feeling a bit of trepidation.

And it should be.

I'm firing before I know it, sending quick bursts of sound-suppressed automatic gunfire into the pack of pugs. Five are down by the time they react. Half dive for cover. The rest lunge for me. Those that hide are the smart ones; the others are quickly cut down, the last of them twitching to death at my feet.

I eject the spent magazine and slap in a fresh one.

The tendrils writhe frantically. Frenetic whispering fills the chamber.

It's panicked.

It's *afraid.*

The irony of this isn't lost on me, but there's no time to dwell on it. The two bulls charge while the remaining pugs flank me.

Focusing on the clearest threat, I turn the Vector toward the nearest bull and introduce it to a barrage of oscillium projectiles. The monster bucks and shrieks but never stops. It lowers its head, preparing to ram me. But it can no longer see me. While firing the vector left-handed, I draw the machete from my back with my right hand and sidestep the beast. As it passes, I swing hard, chopping the machete into the bull's squat neck. I'm not sure what Dread anatomy is like, but it appears that severing the spine behind the head has the same effect it does on creatures in my home dimension. The bull slumps to the floor, silent and still as green fluid pours from the external veins severed by my cut.

High-pitched shrieking fills the air as the pugs launch their assault. Some jump; some come in low. There's no way I can defend against them all, so I don't. While four fall to gunfire and two meet the end of my blade, the rest make contact. I feel the pressure of their powerful jaws latch onto my body, three on the legs, one on my waist. The squeezing on my legs is painful, but the thick plates of oscillium armor on my limbs do their job. My waist is a different scenario. While the pugs' teeth fail to puncture the oscillium fabric, the sharp points and high pressure are still puncturing my skin. I can feel the hundreds of short tendrils in its mouth, writhing against my side.

I cleave the pug at my waist in half, but it remains clung to me in death. Green blood and bright-red innards spill on two of the pugs attached to my left leg. They spasm away from the gore, revolted by it, shaking their little bodies as they stumble oddly away.

I'm about to shoot the fourth pug when I realize the pint-sized attack was never meant to inflict harm. It was a distraction. I turn around in time to see the remaining bull leap clear over its fallen comrade, land in front of me, and throw its armor-plated head into my already-bruised gut.

36.

I saw a rodeo once. On TV. It's a bona fide memory and not just random knowledge left over from my previous self. I sat on the couch in the SafeHaven lounge with Shotgun Jones. We'd been the only two who stayed out of a ruckus at lunch—Seymour never could resist a good scrap when everyone was involved—and we had the place to ourselves. Normally, sports with any kind of violence are forbidden, but we'd had our fill of figure skating and tennis and convinced the security guard to put on something else. He was originally from Texas and quickly found a rodeo show on one of the nine-hundred-something channels we normally couldn't access. At first, we were less than enthused. Watching men cling to the back of a raging bull for all of five seconds wasn't exactly a sport. But then one of those bulls got loose. Caught a clown running. With a quick snap of its head, the bull struck the clown's backside and propelled the man into the stands. Shotgun laughed and laughed.

As I sail through the air, I understand how that sorry clown felt. Of course, he was gored in the process, but being in a mirror dimension that is fifty feet underground and full of angry tentacles, I think I've got him beat. And he had a crowd of worried onlookers to catch him. All I've got is the papier-mâché-like wall, which is about as strong as you'd expect. I crash through the layers of crisp wall and spill back into the hallway.

I'm twenty feet up the round hallway, out of view for the moment. The machete is gone. So is the assault rifle.

Grunting as I stand, I draw the Desert Eagle. One good shot and the fight will be over. I take aim down the tunnel, back toward the chamber entrance, waiting for the bull to come tearing around. But he doesn't show. Can't even hear him running.

But I can *feel* its approach rumbling the ground beneath my feet.

From the side.

I spin and squeeze the trigger three times, but the wild shots miss the bull exploding through the wall. I'm hit hard and shoved back into one of the alcoves, tripping and falling into a Dread nest. The prickly den is warm and full of gelatinous goop. My feet slip as I get back up just in time to face the bull again, this time without a hard-hitting weapon. All I've got left is the P229, which I've had limited success with, and the two, foot-long, World War I trench knives.

I unclip the blades and slip my fingers into the oscillium knuckles. Then I charge. I've faced off against a good number of these things now and they're never accustomed to my fearless approach. This one hesitates, just for a moment, before meeting my charge head-on. But it's too late to stop me. I plant a foot atop the nest's edge and vault up and over the bull's four-eyed head.

There's no way I can clear its entire body, but I don't intend to. As I drop toward the thing's hindquarters, I thrust one of the blades down, punching the blade through the armored plating. The blade catches. My motion is arrested and I snap to a stop, falling atop the bull.

As the bull rears up with a howl, I start to slide away. But I have no intention of squaring off with this giant in close quarters again. I stab the second knife down hard, puncturing the bull's flank. With two handholds, my fall stops, and I cling to the bull's back like an honest-to-goodness mirror-dimension bull rider.

Yee-haw.

The bull fulfills its role in this mock rodeo, bucking and thrashing, trying to kick me off. But as mean as this son of a bitch is, I'm meaner. And the armor, which has helped me sustain much of the beating thus far, continues to protect my body. All of this allows me to keep my grip, though the metal knuckles wrapped around my fingers help, too.

A surge of whispers makes my head spin but has an immediate reaction on the bull.

It runs. Downward. Back toward the central chamber, right where I want to be. But when the bull charges around the bend and enters the round chamber once more, I only have enough time to register the changes in the room, think *what the fuck,* and open my eyes a bit wider. Then the bull snaps to a stop. Its forelimbs bend, its hind legs thrust. I flip up and over the bull. My fingers feel like they're about to break, stuck inside the knife knuckles, but the blades slip free with twin slurps and finish the rotation with me.

I land on my back.

Correction, I'm *caught* on my back.

The landing is soft. Undulating. The bull has deposited me right into the mass of tendrils. They *planned* this.

I swing with both arms, aiming to cut myself free, but my limbs only make it a few inches before being yanked to a stop. Pressure envelopes my body, holding me in place, my arms extended and legs straight down like a mirror-world crucifix.

I stop struggling. It's a wasted effort.

One of the ten Medusa-hands, whose appearance in the chamber surprised me, slides closer. It looms above me, taller than the others. Its four wide yellow eyes stare down into my eyes. Its head cocks to the side, no doubt wondering how I have the same split pupils or how I'm here at all. If they're as intelligent as I think, it will see that I'm part Dread.

It leans closer, just inches from my face.

Whispering fills my thoughts. It feels like questions, but I don't understand.

"I don't understand you," I say, knowing it can understand me.

It pulls back a bit, surprised by my words, or perhaps by the revelation that I can hear the whispers. The Dread turns to the others. A sound like wind fills my head as all the Dread start think-talking at once.

A voice, louder than the others, drowns them out, and the mental storm falls silent.

The tall Medusa-hands leans over me once more.

I decide to reason with it. "Why are you attacking people?"

It leans closer.

"If you just left us alone, I wouldn't be here," I say.

My words have no impact.

A hint of a whisper flits through my mind. I'm not sure why, but I fall silent and watch the Medusa-hands above me.

It whispers at me, the cadence familiar, pushing fear.

I feel nothing.

It tries to instill its fear in me again, the whisper louder.

Still nothing.

Moving slowly, it comes in closer. Tendrils from its hands snake toward my head. The tiny tips tickle my skull, looking for entry but finding none. I'm as material here as they are. Getting those tendrils into my brain is going to take physical force.

The Dread pulls back, the tendrils snaking away. With a bow, it slides back.

Now wha—

There's a sharp crack and pain at the back of my head. I feel movement for a moment, and then confusion. *What's happening?*

It's in my head, I think. The tentacles are beneath me; one of them actually punched through my skull and is probing around in my brain. This should terrify me, I know that, but I feel nothing beyond curiosity and anger for being violated. Killing an enemy is one thing, sticking a tentacle in his brain . . . It's just not acceptable. It's *wrong.*

The skin on my legs suddenly goes prickly. Then stops.

I taste popcorn.

I feel love.

This thing is screwing with my brain, I think, growing angrier.

I'm cold and then hot and then, for a flash, I remember a face.

And its name.

Simon.

And then it's gone, the memory lost once more. But the anguish that accompanied that brief flash lingers for a moment. Then it, too, is gone, replaced by a painful spasm of each and every muscle in my body.

My skin chills. Goose bumps pock my body.

"Get out of my head," I grumble. "Get the fu—argh!"

The scream that replaces my words is primal and physically painful as it tears the very fabric of my throat.

I feel the tentacle retreat.

And scream again.

I suck in a deep breath. It's not controlling me now, but a third scream tears through the chamber.

And a fourth.

I've never felt anything like this before. My body and mind are like strangers, each vying for control, each propelled into senseless action, but by what? I don't know what this is!

And then I do.

"Oh God," I shout. "Oh God, no!"

It's not just fear I'm feeling.

It's terror.

37.

I wake slowly. Dazed. Half aware of the world around me. Events replay in my mind. I screamed for I don't know how long. Then passed out. I've seen fear do strange things to people, including fainting, but to me? Not a chance.

The memory drags me from sleep a bit. I'm comfortable. In a soft bed. But moving. Undulating.

Carried.

I'm not in a bed at all.

Adrenaline surges. My pulse quickens. My heart feels like it will explode.

I've always kind of looked down on people who panic. I've never understood it, in the same way the average person can't understand what floating in zero gravity feels like. Fear was foreign to me.

Was.

Control it, I tell myself. Though I've never been good at controlling my impulses, I'm not without discipline. I should be able to wrestle my emotions down enough to act. With building confidence, my pulse slows. A measure of control returns. Now I just need to see where I am.

I open my eyes.

Four bright-yellow split-pupil eyes of a Medusa-hands peer down at me, hovering just a foot above my head. I suck in a tight breath as my whole body seizes. I struggle to move but am still bound. I fight for freedom, fueled by a fresh adrenaline dump in my veins.

I'm scared out of my mind, but I haven't *lost* my mind. Yet. I've seen the effect the Dread have on others, and this isn't it. I'm afraid—there's no doubt. Nearly paralyzed, but I haven't lost myself to it. This knowledge fuels my defiance, and I return the Dread's cold stare.

Then it whispers in my head.

Waves of fear wash through my body. My insides twist. I scream, but my voice is raspy and raw. The sound that escapes my mouth is a crackling, ragged thing. My mind slides toward oblivion, shouting, *Run! Hide! Escape!*

And then some instinctual part of my mind that has been unneeded since the day of my birth asserts itself.

In a flash, I'm free of the tentacles' grasp.

Pain worms its way through my body, but the fear destroying my mind is gone. That's the good news.

The bad news is that I can't breathe.

Where am I?

I'm held still. Perfectly still. Unable to move. Unable to expand my chest to even attempt to breathe. Absolute darkness surrounds me. Grit stings my eyes, so I close them. I manage to exhale and pull a short breath. If there is oxygen in the breath, I don't feel it. Instead, I get light-headed and detect a trace scent of something familiar.

Dirt.

The reality of my situation snaps to the forefront of my mind, and fear grips me once more. I've slipped back into my home dimension—fifty feet below the surface. I'm buried beneath the Old Pine Cemetery, deeper than anyone would ever think to dig.

And if I stay here much longer, I'm going to suffocate.

Think! I will myself. People overcome fear all the time.

But not against the Dread.

They're ugly as sin, but I can look at them if they're not trying to inject fear into me. If I take them by surprise, I might be able to escape. They feel fear, too. I've seen it. And they seem just as uncomfortable with the emotion as I am.

My lungs burn for a breath, hungry for air.

Not yet, I tell myself. *Focus.*

Am I armed? I have no memory of the Dread taking my sidearm, but that doesn't mean they didn't. Nor do I have a memory of them removing the knives from my hands. I was bound in place, the blades useless.

I try to wiggle my hands, but can't. The earth hugs me tight. When I slipped out of the mirror dimension, my body replaced the matter that was here and carved out a perfect me-sized space in the soil. But I still should be able to shift my body subtly—unless . . .

It's not dirt I'm encased in, it's solid stone. Most of New Hampshire sits atop a bed of granite, and now I'm inside it, trapped like a fossil.

Focus!

I turn my attention to my hands. While cold is seeping into my body from all directions, my fingers feel colder. But is that a circulation issue or are the oscillium knuckles wrapped around them conducting the cold into my fingers? *It's the blades,* I decide.

My body quivers and then contracts, unable to even wiggle.

Ignore it.

I visualize my return to the Dread world. There will be a moment of surprise. Just a moment. And if I let fear paralyze me then, I'm done. They'll probably kill me before I can slip back into my perfectly formed tomb.

Attack, I tell myself. *And then run. Run and don't stop.*

My pulse quickens in anticipation.

My lungs scream for air.

Now, I think, *now!*

Part of me resists the idea of facing those monsters again, but this fate is far worse. I'd rather die fighting and horrified than suffocating as a coward. And only one course of action offers a chance for survival.

I slip back into the mirror dimension and fall atop a bed of flesh.

The tendrils surrounding me snap back in surprise, as do the collection of Medusa-hands who have come close to inspect the location of my disappearance.

Act! I think. *Before they do!*

I get my feet under me and spin. I haven't seen the trench knives yet, but I feel the resistance of flesh on their blades as I turn and swing.

Tentacles fall to the floor, spraying purple.

Several Medusa-hands flail back, shrieking, missing tendrils of their own.

I'm close to puking in fright as the tendrils come for me again. I swing twice more, carving a path. I dive free, roll to my feet, and run. Halfway to the exit, I spot my machete on the floor. I scoop it up and return it to the scabbard on my back. As I reach the arched exit to the long circular path, I make a mistake and glance back.

Two of the Medusa-hands, eight eyes locked on me, send a wave of fear in my direction. I scream when it hits me and stumble to the floor. But they're not the only thing frightening me. At the center of the chamber, the tendrils, some of them hacked in half, bleeding bright purple, rise out of the ground, pushed up from beneath by something larger.

I crush my eyes shut, pushing tears free, and fight the Dread's fear-inducing effect. My feet slip over the dry floor as I peel out like some kind of Warner Bros. cartoon. Then I'm off, running up the slope. I open my eyes and find the path ahead clear.

The ground shakes. It's subtle at first, but then powerful enough to stumble me. Fear and adrenaline drive me onward. With every staggering vibration, I gasp in fright and run faster. I'm not sure I've ever run so quickly, but the fear also makes me clumsy and more apt to flounder.

Whispers fill my head.

A chill runs up my spine, warning of unseen danger, urging me to turn around.

I look back not really expecting to find anything, but a Medusa-hands is right behind me, tentacles outstretched.

With a shout of surprise, I lash out, burying the trench knife in my right hand into its skull. The body falls slack, pulling me down to the ground. I try to pull the blade free, but it's stuck. I slip my fingers out of the knuckles and stand, leaving the weapon behind.

Movement catches my attention. The tunnel behind me is alive with motion. An army of Medusa-hands writhes toward me, their external veins and eyes glowing in the semidarkness. All around me, the veins that fill this world pulse with frantic energy. I turn away from the Dread stampede before they can paralyze me with fear and run.

The slow incline frustrates me as the rumbling grows more violent. Whatever was buried in the chamber below is rising.

Coming for me.

A warm, wet breeze makes my cheeks sticky. The smell of rot tickles my nose. *Almost there.*

Feeling a presence behind me and a chill on the nape of my neck, I draw the P229 and fire blindly. Shrieks fill the tunnel. I don't know if I'm killing them or just injuring them, but they don't catch me.

The entrance is just ahead.

A bull appears, its head twitching back and forth, no doubt summoned by whatever is still rising from the earth. Its eyes lock onto me, but before it can react, I act, driven by desperation and guided by instinct and skill. The remaining trench knife stabs up through the Dread's chin and into its brain. I slip my fingers out of the os-cillium knuckles and continue running, leaving the blade behind. The bull mewls and staggers away, not quite dead, but on its way.

I run out into the swampy clearing, slipping in the muck.

As the mob of Medusa-hands charges out behind me, I slip back into my reality and partially out of their grasp. But not completely. If they get their tendrils in my head, who knows what kind of thoughts they'll put in there. If there is pain from the frequency shift, I don't notice it. Fear, and its by-product, shock, can numb the mind from physical pain—I've heard.

Back on firm ground, adrenaline pumping, vision narrowed, I cover the hundred yards to the ATV in twelve seconds. I jump on the seat, turn the key, and rev the engine. One last peek into the mirror world reveals eight Medusa-hands, twenty yards back and closing fast. Behind them, the lobotomized bull staggers but can't chase.

None of that fills me with as much trepidation as what happens next. The colony bursts open like an overfull aluminum-foil Jiffy Pop pouch. Massive flakes of the hivelike walls burst into the air. A giant limb, the size of a thick tree trunk, rises from the ground. Its foot, a triangular-shaped pad with long, thick, hooked claws de-scends to the ground. I can't feel the impact in this dimension, but I can see the Medusa-hands stagger.

Having seen enough, I blink and see only the cemetery. I know the Dread are still there, coming for me, but not seeing them al-lows me to calm down. Focus.

I turn the ATV around and tear down the old road, back toward route 202. Despite my escape, return to reality, and speedy retreat, I can't fight the building fear gripping my chest. Whatever that thing was rising out of the ground, it's coming for me. *Dammit*, I think, *it's coming for me.*

38.

Trees blur past as I speed north on 202. I've got the needle pegged, but the speed now makes me nervous. I brake around the same corners I tore around on my previous journey. I stay locked in my lane. I think I should have brought a helmet. A *helmet*! In New Hampshire! Where almost nobody wears a damn helmet!

I am not a fan of fear.

It might be the most powerful force I've ever felt. It controls the body despite what the mind thinks. But the mind isn't unaffected, either. I'm thinking things I never would have before. I'm considering driving north until the tank empties, stealing a car and driving until the world freezes. Part of me is a coward, and it shames me.

I don't run away. It's not who I am, fear or no fear.

I repeat the thought like a mantra, trying to keep myself on course for Neuro. They might be screwed, too, in which case I probably *will* head north and not look back. But they've also got weapons. And if I die, it won't be alone.

Why do I care about dying alone?

In the past two years, the subject of my death, immediate or future, never crossed my mind. The topic just never held my interest. I knew it would happen. That life is finite. Quick, even. But now, thoughts of death, dying, and ceasing to exist—or not—threaten to undo me.

I swerve hard to the right as the road bends left, shouting in surprise and fright as I nearly cross over the lines and plow into a car. I cut hard back to the left, narrowly avoiding a tree. The driver lays on the horn, flipping me off as he speeds past. My heart beats hard. I slow the ATV. I was so wrapped up worrying about death that I nearly brought it about.

Moving at just twenty miles per hour, I catch my breath. I'm not sure why I'm winded. I'm sitting. The ATV is doing all the work, but I feel like I'm running a marathon.

Tires screech behind me. The high-pitched sound is followed by a sharp crash, the sound of metal striking wood.

It's coming.

It's still coming!

I gun the engine, speeding up the road, fear of what's behind me overpowering my fear of crashing.

I see the police car up ahead. The officer is just now climbing out of the vehicle. He sees me. Goes for his gun. But he's still dazed. Has trouble unclipping the weapon. As I zoom past, I shout, "Run!" But the officer just stands there, fighting for his weapon.

I'm just two hundred feet beyond the man when a shrill scream tears from his mouth. I glance back. The man convulses in the street, struck down by some unseen force.

It's right there.

I can't see it. I *refuse* to see it. But I know it's there. The giant Dread. Closing in on me, ready to unleash a fear powerful enough to destroy a man's mind.

I increase the ATV's speed. I have no choice now. Driving like a maniac—like I used to be—is my only option.

Be Crazy, I tell myself.

I'm still that guy. I can still do the things he did. My skills, my knowledge—none of that has changed. I'm just afraid.

Despite the summertime warmth, a chill spreads over my body. *It's close.* With a mile of road left to go and the long Neuro driveway, I'm not going to make it. Make it to what? If the Dread are inside the building, where can I hide?

Hide?

Dammit, I hate being afraid. The emotion is intolerable.

The short hairs on my head stand a little taller. All over my body, hair attempts to stand on end. A chill shakes through my core and nearly sends me off the road. I have just seconds.

With a scream wrought by the nearness of the Dread and the action I'm about to take, I cut hard to the left, cross the yellow lines, and launch into the woods. If it wants to reach me, it's going to be in the world between, where the trees will obscure me. And if it wants to enter this world and kill me physically, the forest will slow it down.

In theory. I'm basing all this on a day's worth of experience and secondhand, untested knowledge provided by my previous self.

I swerve in and out of trees, making myself a hard target. There's no sign that anything is behind me, and while the chill gripping my body has faded some, it's still there. It's just harder to notice since I require nearly all my attention to keep from slamming into a tree.

The trees thin ahead. I can see the sky. I'm approaching a clearing. Almost there . . .

A tree cracks behind me.

I glance back. Bark has been shredded from a pine.

The air shakes.

The giant Dread is pushing itself into our world. It doesn't want to scare me to death, it wants to smear me on the forest floor.

A blur of motion pulls my attention to the right. A tree explodes, bark peppering my face. The tall evergreen topples over, falling diagonally toward me. I hunker down and speed onward, determined to beat the tree's descent. The splintering wood and loud whoosh are hard to hear over the ATV's whining engine, but I can feel the thing coming, just as surely as I can feel the Dread.

Pine needles slap my head. A small branch whips my scalp, opening a wound, but I manage to escape being struck by the tree's girth.

I look back again, expecting to see the Dread or another falling tree, but the woods appear empty, save for the dust kicked up by the felled pine.

When I look forward, I scream.

Adrenaline surges again. I move faster than I have before, turning the ATV hard to the right. The crackle of the electrified fence tickles my ears as I narrowly avoid slamming straight into it. I hadn't seen it up close before, but I now recognize the black, weaved metal for what it is. Oscillium. No matter which world the Dread is in, it's going to hit that fence.

And then it does.

The fence rattles as it's lifted out of the earth by an unseen force. Electricity cracks over its surface, surging into the Dread.

I slow and look back, peering into the mirror world.

My eyes widen. The Dread is there, still alive but tangled in the fence, shrieking in pain. It's a blur of movement, giving me no clear view of itself beyond giant limbs. I shift my vision back to a more comfortable frequency without getting a good look at the thing. All I really know is that it's the size of a monster-truck 18-wheeler, with wide, squat legs; really long, hooked claws; and streaks of glowing purple veins.

While the monster tries to free itself from the fence shooting electricity into its body, I speed north, using the chain link as a guide. A minute later, I speed out of the woods in front of the ruined security shack. I head past the broken gate, back onto smooth pavement. I twist the throttle as far as I can.

As I near the Neuro building, I let my vision slip into the world between. The black pyramid-shaped building is still under attack. Mothmen fill the sky. The centipede thing is smashing its head into the elevator doors. Bulls and pugs scurry around the parking lot, driving the mass of humanity, who are now pounding on the outside of the building, trying to get through the metal plates. To the right of the entrance, a group of people have laid out a collection of ladders. At the top, several men with hammers, bricks, and shovels attack one of the third-floor windows, punching a hole through its surface.

A respectable amount of fear punches me in the gut, tempting me to turn and run before I'm noticed. I let my vision see just the real world again. Ignorance really is bliss. Then I have an idea. It's insane. It's . . . crazy.

I'm still that man, I tell myself.

No. I can't do this.

Fuck off! I think at this new inner voice. *Just shut up.*

Fear, I realize, is like a little cartoon devil on your shoulder. You can listen to it, argue with it, or fight it like a son of a bitch.

Be Crazy. Just one more time.

I let go of the throttle, slowing the ATV. As the engine idles and the four-wheeler slows, I hear the chain-link fence rattling. I glance back in time to see the fence lift high up into the air and fall back down.

It's through, I realize, but don't look at the mirror frequencies. I can't. My will to fight is a skipped heartbeat away from becoming flight.

Turning back toward the building and the mob surrounding it, I draw my handgun, exchange the cartridge for a fresh one, and spin the sound suppressor off. Gun in hand, I steer toward the ladders and twist the throttle. As I near the back of the crowd, I fire the pistol. By the third shot, people are looking my way. When I point the weapon at them, they move. When I push the fear I'm feeling toward them, using my own Dread abilities, they shriek. The pain is nearly as intense as I remember it, but its effect on my mind is dulled because I'm so distracted by the danger approaching from behind. Fear, at least, is a powerful motivator for overcoming lesser discomfort. The effect moves up the ladder as I near. People dive away, some straight to the ground, others onto the angled building, where they slide away.

When the ATV strikes the ladders and climbs, the men up top see me coming and abandon ship. I'm sure the Dread bulls and pugs have seen me now, too, but since I haven't been struck by a limb sliding between dimensions, I've made it past them before they could act.

The ATV rattles up the ladders, which form a perfect ramp. When it reaches the window, the tires squeal over the smooth surface for a moment but then catch. I lean forward as far as I can to keep from falling backward and rocket up the side of the forty-five-degree slanted wall.

I take a peek into the mirror world to make sure I'm not driving into the jaws of a giant centipede. Mothmen high in the sky are coming my way, but the roof ahead looks empty.

Then I'm airborne, clearing the top. The ATV drops to the roof with a jolt. I hit the brakes and skid to a stop.

Everything on the roof stops and turns my way.

Shit.

Shit, shit, shit!

I hop off the ATV, thinking, *Please be right! Please be right!*

Lyons believed that something at the colony was leading the Dread, maybe controlling them. I think that thing is the giant that's been chasing me, directing the others with its omnipresent whisper.

I slip fully into the Dread dimension, wince against the sudden pain, and dive to the discarded 20 mm sniper rifle still leaning against the short wall. I bring it back to reality with me, but not fully out of the mirror world, and remove the spent three-round magazine, pull a spare from a pouch on my hip, and slap it in.

I blink sweat out of my eyes, knowing that Dread are approaching from all directions, lift the heavy weapon up, and plant the bipod on the short wall. I lean into it, resting the stock against my shoulder, and peer through the scope.

The behemoth is there, staring right back.

39.

Seven round eyes look up at me as the massive Dread lopes toward the building. Five of the eyes arc across the top of the monster's head, just above the other two, all of it surrounded by pulsing purple veins. Unlike other Dread, these eyes are solid black, like a shark's. Beneath the eyes is what looks like an exploding mass of flesh—the tendrils that invaded and rewired my brain. Seeing the tentacles on the front of this thing's face reminds me of a star-nosed mole I saw in a *National Geographic.* Ugly as hell, but the Dread mole's horrible face and long hooked claws are definitely designed for subterranean living. Which might be why it moves so awkwardly over land. Its wide legs have a short reach. Its spine arcs with each lunge forward, almost like an otter on land. But the strangeness of its movement does nothing to negate the effect its hideous appearance has on my psyche.

My eyes twitch, spasming muscles mixed with stinging sweat. My vision is questionable, but I keep my eye to the scope, aiming between the triangle of eyes at the center of the giant's head.

I slip my finger over the trigger.

And squeeze.

The Dread mole shimmers for a moment. I see it through the scope and shriek as something cold reaches through my chest and clutches my heart. The shot goes wild, tearing up into the atmosphere.

Gasping as unbidden thoughts of suicide bounce through my skull, I lift the rifle again.

The building shakes.

The Dread mole has thrown itself against the side. It swings one of its massive clawed hands out and shatters the oscillium window. Pulls itself higher. Slams its other clawed hand through the building. Higher. Climbing.

I'm shaking, muscles out of control, obeying the fear impulse driven into me by the Dread, ignoring the commands of my fracturing psyche.

The monster pushes its powerful fear up at me again. I close my eyes against it, but a wave of torment spills over me. I scream in emotional agony, eyes to the sky.

The building shudders.

Then again.

I can't look.

It's *right* there. I know it is. It has to be.

I consider running. But where? And how? I'm locked in place by fear-induced rigor mortis. My muscles tense and release, twitching. My head throbs, skips, and races. Pressure builds in my sinuses. The physical manifestations of fear are debilitating.

You can't miss.

The voice is familiar. Confident. Crazy whispers from some hidden nook in my mind.

It's *right* there. You *can't* miss.

I open my eyes.

Look down.

Scream.

My arms work on autopilot while my voice fills the air with a raspy squeak that is my ruined voice. A round is chambered. My shaking hand pulls the trigger. I can't hear the gun fire over my scream, but it kicks hard. I nearly drop it, but my arms, directed by muscle memory I can't remember learning, chamber the third and final round. The weapon kicks hard. I drop it to the roof and pitch forward as the last of my strength is torn from me.

Through blurry eyes, I look over the short wall.

The Dread mole is gone from the world in between. It's difficult, but I force my eyes to see the mirror dimension. Whatever pain the shift causes is insignificant compared to the effects of being afraid. The giant is there, slowly sliding back to the swampy ground.

The Dread mole is motionless. One of its eyes has burst. Purple and white fluid oozes from the ruined socket. A 20 mm round can punch through a tank, so I have no doubt the bullet continued through the head, creating a pressure wave that destroyed whatever it came into contact with. To the right of the ruined eye is a clean hole, dead center, between the triangle of eyes. I hit it twice.

I'm a good shot, even when I'm out of my mind. I choke out a laugh that becomes a cackle and fall into a shaking fetal position. My body convulses uncontrollably, outwardly reflecting the turmoil that has become my mind.

This is what the Dread do to people. This is why even strong men like Katzman can't even look at them. I've lost control. I've lost myself.

But I'm not dead. And I'm not being attacked.

My eyes clench shut, but I need to see. I need to know if there is anything left to fear. As my body quivers, I let my eyelids slip open. Purple light filters through my lashes. I'm still viewing the mirror world. I open my eyes and come face-to-face with a Medusa-hands. My voice sounds like tearing paper as I shout. I try to push away from the creature, but I'm already up against the wall. Nowhere to run.

But I don't need to.

Like me, the Dread is on its side, twitching. Alive, but no longer in control. Or maybe no longer *being* controlled. I don't know which is the case, but the thing appears to have been lobotomized by the Dread mole's death. Then it goes rigid, its limbs snapping still for a moment before falling to the roof, still and dead.

It must have been right behind me when the strings were cut, when the Dread mole died. Had it reached me . . . I'm clutched by horrible images. My head pounds.

I look beyond the wide head of the Medusa-hands and take in the rest of the rooftop. Mothmen litter the oscillium surface, shaking like dying bees, some spinning in circles. A few more are still falling from high up in the sky, fluttering madly like actual moths that flew too close to a lightbulb. The large centipede undulates and thrashes, snapping its large wings in the process. The uncontrolled movement brings it to the side of the roof, where it rolls over and falls from view.

It's over, I think.

My body quakes, still gripped with fear despite the danger's passing.

Get a grip.

The small voice of my former self has no power.

Stand up.

Like a swimmer pulled from arctic waters, my muscles contract and release of their own accord. Images of death and pain and blood race through my thoughts, unhindered.

Stand the fuck up!

I squeeze my eyes shut, shaking my head back and forth. "No!" When I open them again, the sky is blue, and the Dread are gone. I'm safe.

But *still* afraid.

I roll onto my stomach, forehead resting on my folded arms. I've won, and yet I feel like a frail creature that has lost everything. Where do feelings like this come from? How can my mind conjure such torturous emotions having never experienced them before?

Because it has.

I just can't remember them.

I *have* lost everything. A wife. A son. Thirtysomething years of memory.

None of those things were created by the Dread. They simply drew to the surface what existed, no matter how well hidden by my lack of memory, and magnified it. The realization does me no good.

I can't remember what I've lost. Not really. But there is nothing in my life, absolutely nothing, that can combat this sorrow. No love. No real friends. And just this one, hollow victory, if you can even call it that.

I'm done, I think, and close my eyes. With a final spasm, my tired mind and even more exhausted body quits, and I slip into merciful sleep.

40.

I wake up screaming. The sound cracks my raw throat, combining with the exquisite pain that comes from sitting up too quickly. My body is beaten and bruised.

Something brushes against my forearm. Squeezes. I don't so much flinch from the touch as catapult. Arms flailing, I reel away, spiraling out of bed and onto the hard floor. An IV needle tears from my arm. The floor punishes me for the clumsy descent. But I barely notice as I scramble backward across the floor, still running from that touch.

My head hits the door. Then my back. My legs continue to pump, but there's nowhere left to go.

Through my still-screaming voice I hear a name. It's being shouted at me. Slowly, it sinks in.

"Josef!"

My eyes snap up to the sound of the voice.

Blue eyes stare back at me. They have an immediate calming effect. My voice falls silent, but my legs are rigid, pressing me against the door.

"Josef," the voice says, gently. "It's me. It's Jess."

Jess?

"Winters," she says.

My eyes wander. Her blond hair is a mess. Her face is partially covered by a bandage. "I know you," I say.

She crouches in front of me, smiles, and puts her soft hand on my cheek. "Better than you remember."

As she strokes the side of my face, I close my eyes. Memories and tears surface, none of them pleasant. I can feel the Dread mole, projecting fear upon me, crawling through my mind. I put a hand behind my head. There's a bandage taped in place.

"You're okay now. You're safe." Her voice is calm and soothing. "We haven't detected any Dread activity in the region since—"

"They're all dead. I think. The whole colony."

She says nothing. Just keeps rubbing my cheek. The repetitive caress calms me, my head sagging a little farther with each downward stroke. I take a long breath and let it out slowly.

"Can I take your pulse?" she asks.

I nod.

She takes my left hand in hers and places two fingers on my wrist. The touch is gentle.

Twenty seconds later, she says, "Good," and lifts her fingers away, but my hand stays in hers. "Can I ask you some questions?"

"You're here as my psychologist, then?"

"You're still direct," she says.

"Habit."

"Then . . ."

"You're wondering if I'm afraid."

"Yes."

I look her in the eyes but have trouble not looking away. Her gaze is intense. "Do I look afraid?"

Sadness sweeps over her face. "Very."

"There's your answer."

"How?" she asks.

I put my hand on the bandage at the back of my head. "They got inside my head. Fixed what was broken."

"Allowing *you* to be broken, but why not just kill you?"

"They weren't done with me, but I escaped. I think they were trying to understand what made me fearless. Apparently, they figured it out."

She slips her hand out from under mine and stands up. "I'm sorry, Josef."

She heads for a counter, opens a folder, and jots a few notes. "There are clothes in the bathroom if you would like to get dressed."

I look down. I'm wearing a paper-thin gown. Again. The hospital garb once again matches the room. If I didn't know better, I'd think I was staying at Average Hospital USA.

I stand slowly, my body protesting each movement. Winters offers no help. I don't know her well, but this seems a little out of character, especially in light of the affection she just offered . . . which ended the moment she knew the truth: the fearless Crazy is now just a regular guy—who can pass through dimensions, but that is something I have absolutely no interest in doing again. Ever. Was she really only attracted to my fearless nature, or is her sudden change somehow meant to protect me? If so, I wish she wouldn't. For the first time that I can remember, I feel in serious need of moral support.

A draft reveals the gown's open backside. Fueled by embarrassment, a new emotional delicacy, I hurry into the bathroom, close the door, and lock it. All of this is new to me. I can remember who I was and how I would have done things—who cares if she sees me naked—but now . . . now half the thoughts in my head make me squirm. My memories of SafeHaven, seen through this new fear lens, are traumatic. What I've experienced since leaving that place is even worse. I shake my head at it all, trying to keep my thoughts empty, but I can't. There isn't much that I've experienced in the year of remembered life that doesn't now haunt me, including things I did, thought, and said.

The small bathroom doesn't provide a whole lot of room, and it's impossible to miss myself in the mirror. My brown eyes are framed by upturned eyebrows above and dark circles below. My face is covered in stubble and scabbed-over scratches. If I turn my head, just a little, I can see the bandage taped to the back, over my close-cut hair. I slip out of the gown. More bandages cover wounds I have no memory of receiving, and my ribs are wrapped. The broad ache suggests bruising rather than breaks, which is good, I suppose.

Despite all the fresh wounds, I notice that the past injuries—the self-inflicted puncture wound and the vast bruising across my midsection—are nearly completely healed. *That was fast,* I think, probing the stab wound. The flesh is mostly nit together, the swelling and bruising all but gone. Two weeks of healing in a day. I'm also far less sore than I think I should be. In fact, I feel strong. Almost energized—physically, not emotionally. Lyons had asked me if I felt any different. *Am I becoming more Dread?* As my throat constricts at the thought, I lean forward, looking into my own eyes like it was the first time. *What was I thinking?* I've done so many stupid things. Every punch, bone break, harsh word spoken, and rude action from the past year flits through my mind. But the worst decision might be the one I don't remember. I altered my DNA. Made myself something not human. I close my eyes, willing the endless barrage of cringe-worthy thoughts from my mind.

Focus on the here and now, I tell myself. *Just get dressed, say good-bye, and leave.*

But to where? I still have no memory. No home. No job. There's no way in hell I'm going back to SafeHaven.

I start to feel light-headed and realize I'm not breathing.

Fear, in all its nuanced forms, is hard to manage.

With a steadying breath, I turn away from the mirror and look at my clothes. At least they're familiar and comfortable. I slip into the perfectly fitted ensemble of jeans, T-shirt, and brown sneakers. Fully dressed, I splash cold water on my face and look in the mirror one last time. A little more human. A little less mousey.

"Everyone on the planet lives like this," I say to my reflection, the words coming out as an unintended whisper. "You can handle it."

I leave out the fact that everyone else on the planet has had a lifetime of learning to manage fear, and even then people fail at it all the time. But I'm a trained assassin, right? A killer. I've conquered the unthinkable. I can conquer fear.

Standing a bit taller, I grip the door handle, give it a twist, and push.

A ball of gray snaps around, revealing two wide eyes. I jump back, bark out a raspy shout, and raise my arms defensively.

"She wasn't kidding."

I recognize the voice. Allenby. I lower my arms. She stands on the other side of the door. Her hair, freed from the elastic that had been taming it, billows around her head. A bandage covers half her forehead, but she seems otherwise unscathed.

"W-where's Winters?"

"Probably headed back to Lyons," she says. "She was just here to make sure you were actually . . . you know." She frowns in a sad sort of way. "Come out of there, poor boy." She reaches her arms out, and I all but fall into her embrace, her hair tickling my ear. "It will get easier. With time. Practice. And some hardening."

Her hand rubs slow spirals over my back, and I feel myself calming again. A lack of fear means I've also never been comforted before. This is all new. And not bad.

She pushes me back, looks me over. "There's something I think you should see."

I barely register her comment. "Where's Lyons?" I thought the man would want to know every detail of what I saw and did, about the new Dread, about the colony's insides. I don't take his absence personally, but it *is* confusing.

"He's not here."

"Not here?"

"They've relocated." She raises her hand, stopping the question forming on my lips. "I didn't know about the second location. I found out an hour ago. From what I understand, it has more of an . . . offensive focus. Whereas Neuro is primarily research focused."

"And he didn't want me to—"

"I'm afraid he's cast you aside. There was security footage of what happened on the roof . . ." She pauses to give me a sympathetic look. "For the record, few people have stood against a full Dread onslaught and recovered, let alone had the wherewithal to take action. I think it's too soon to count you out, but now that you can feel fear again, Lyons sees you as a liability, and not able to take part in whatever he's been cooking up at this second location."

"Even with my ability to move between worlds?" Despite the question, I'm feeling a bit of relief.

"Strangely, yes."

I sit on the bed. "Well, I agree with him. I can't do this."

She leans down, hands on knees, and levels a hard gaze at my eyes. "You can. And will."

I find a drop of bravery left in the once-full bucket and return her stare. "Not. A. Chance."

"Aren't you curious about what happened while you were gone?"

Now that she mentions it, I am.

"First, the larger ramifications." She sits on the bed beside me and lifts a tablet from her pocket. She turns it on and accesses a saved video. The image is split down the middle showing two locations. I recognize both, but Allenby explains anyway. "The footage on the left is from New York City. On the right is the security footage from the roof. Pay attention to the time stamps."

She hits PLAY. The videos have no sound, but it's not required. On the left, an angry mob marches down 42nd Street. It's a familiar scene, and the people are framed by riot police and sky scrapers on either side, though the mob contains a good number of police officers, too.

The video on the left shows an empty rooftop, and then me. I zoom into the picture atop an ATV, taking to the air and landing in dramatic fashion. And then, in a blink, I'm gone, disappeared into the mirror world. I watch the time stamps, keenly aware of what is happening in the now-empty security feed.

And then, I reappear, curled up on the rooftop, looking pitiful and afraid.

Motion in the left video feed draws my attention. It started just before I reappeared. The scene in New York has taken a turn for the worse. Chaos erupts, but it's not what I expected. The mob has turned violent, but the brawling isn't between mob and riot police, it's every man and woman for themselves. Even the riot police are taking part, attacking the mob and each other.

Allenby switches the video to a playlist of saved videos. She scrolls through various video clips, some from phones, some from the news, and some from security cameras. Those with time stamps show different hours, but the minutes match up. They're videos from around the world. In different time zones. But I understand what I'm seeing. They were all recorded at the same time. Angry crowds, in all of them, seem to snap and go wild all at exactly the same time. The psychic bond shared by the Dread allows them to stay in contact instantly and globally. Killing that monster set off a global response from the Dread.

"Where there was violence before," Allenby says, "there is now chaos. Cities are burning. War is imminent. The world is on the brink."

I look away from the videos. "What happened here?"

"They got inside," she says. "Those who were caught either went mad or killed themselves or the person closest to them. Some of us made it to the oscillium-walled panic room. Sealed ourselves inside. They were nearly inside that when you . . ." She sighs. "Not everyone made it to the panic room."

She holds my gaze, waiting to see if I'll understand.

"Not everyone could walk. Not everyone was *awake*."

"Maya," I whisper. "Is she . . . dead?"

"Worse," she says.

"Worse?"

"I went for her. Carried her by myself. But they reached right out . . . There were tentacles. I dropped her. Couldn't look. Couldn't control myself. But I could see her. She was here, and then she wasn't. Just like you." She takes my chin in her hand, squeezing hard, forcing me to look at her. "They *took* your wife, Josef, and, God damn you, you're going to get her back." She lets go of me. "You're the only one who can."

41.

Allenby sets a stalwart pace down the hall. I struggle to keep up at first but push through the aches, and my body limbers up, feeling strangely renewed. I'm not sure where she's leading me, but the innards of Neuro are a mess. Burn marks, bullet holes, and smears of dry blood mar the floors, walls, and in some places the ceiling. Allenby told me that fifteen people died when the Dread infiltrated the building through the elevator shaft. Would have been worse if the mob had gotten inside. Speaking of which . . .

"What happened to the people outside?"

"The Dread influence faded. Slowly. But within an hour, most of the people outside lost steam and left. When only a few remained, I went out and spoke to a woman. She was just sitting on the pavement, rocking back and forth. Her knuckles were bloody from pounding on the walls." She glances back at me. "She was twenty years old. A college student. Poor thing had no memory of why she was there or what had happened."

"Why the big show?" I ask.

"What do you mean?"

"The Dread can make neighbor turn on neighbor."

"Family against family," she adds.

I motion to a spatter of blood. "To the death."

She stops walking. "What's your point? Or is it a question?"

"Both." I use the pause to stretch. "They could turn everyone against each other, like they are in the cities, but not everywhere. The human race could literally murder itself into oblivion. So what's with the mobs? The government standoffs? The slow build toward global chaos? What's the point?"

"I'm not sure there is a—"

"They're smart," I say. A chill runs through my body as the memory of the Dread mole's mental intrusion surfaces. I push the images from my mind. "If they've chosen to attack us with such a slow build to annihilation, there's a reason."

"You might be right, but it's too late for speculation now." She starts moving again, double-timing it.

"What do you mean?"

"There's a reason you're still here, and I'm here with you. Lyons hasn't said so outright, but I think he's done studying them. He's out for blood."

"He can do that?" I ask. "I thought I was—"

"I'm not sure you're as unique as we believed, at least in terms of being able to move between worlds. If the fear can be overcome with drugs, he might not need you . . . at least not for a single assault. He has spoken, in the past, about creating a kind of mirror dimension WMD. Something that would affect their world but not ours. I didn't think he'd done it, but now I'm not so sure. It makes sense that he'd keep it from me. I always opposed the idea, which is probably why I'm here now. Left behind, as it were. Mass destruction in either dimension will be catastrophic. The effects are totally unknown. Not even theoretical. But extermination is never the solution."

"Then what is?"

She stops at the stairwell door, hand on the knob. "I don't know." She opens the door and steps into the stairwell, maintaining her pace while heading up.

I stand still, eyeing the stairs.

Allenby stops at the first landing. "What are you waiting for?"

"I'm in a bit of pain."

"They made you feel fear," she says. "I didn't realize they also made you a whiney bitch." She glances back, grinning wide.

Despite the circumstances and pain, Allenby manages to get a smile out of me and to sufficiently motivate me to tackle the staircase. Like the walk down the hall, each step simultaneously hurts and helps. By the top of the second flight, I'm in pain, top to bottom, but also feel stronger, more focused, and a little less fearful.

A little.

By the top of the sixth flight, I've worked up a question that's been nagging at me. "How did it happen? With Maya."

Allenby stops next to a door labeled 6. "What?"

"How was Maya taken?

She frowns. "All I saw were tentacles—"

"Medusa-hands."

"Right. It reached out of thin air, wrapped her body in those . . ." She shivers. "It just yanked her away from me, and they both disappeared. I couldn't do anything. They got to me with the fear." She stares at the floor, shaking her head in shame. "I ran. Didn't even look back."

I haul myself up the final step. "It's all in our heads. The fear."

"What do you mean?"

"The Dread communicate without speaking. It's like a network. Sounds like whispering, but it's in your head. Not your ears. Thoughts are broadcast. The closer you are, the stronger the signal, and the louder the whisper. Their presence makes people uncomfortable. It's like pressure waves moving through frequencies, rippling through to our world, where we feel them as brushes with the supernatural. The closer they are to our frequency, the stronger the overlapping ripple and sense of being watched, or followed, or hunted."

Allenby grins. "Did they also make you smarter?"

"Just guessing. But that wasn't the important part. It's the whispers, the . . . psychic communication that does the real damage. It's how they trigger the deep, irrational fear that drives people to do horrible things. But the Medussa-hands . . . they can get inside your head and push specific thoughts. Working together, they can make a person do anything."

"Like kill their son or run into traffic," she says.

"Right."

Allenby pauses. Looks back like she's waiting for more. "And?"

"What?"

"Was there a point to this revelation? A way to stop it? Happy thought or something?"

I shake my head. "I . . . just don't want you to feel bad about Maya. There was nothing you could do."

She looks a little stunned.

"What did I do?" I ask, feeling nervous.

"The intricacies of fear have always been lost on you," she says. "You wouldn't have noticed how I was feeling, and certainly wouldn't have spent the time explaining things to make me feel better."

"Do you?" I ask. "Feel better?"

She opens the stairwell door. "Not at all. But thanks for trying."

We step into the sixth-floor hallway and turn right.

I walk beside Allenby, the exercise having limbered me up. In fact, the pain has almost completely subsided. I consider telling her about it, but Maya's disappearance weighs more heavily on my mind. "The real question is, why did they take her at all?"

"To get at Lyons, I'd guess," she answers. "They've infiltrated Neuro in the past. You revealed as much with the Dread bat. How many of them have made it inside over the years? They must know he's in charge, that without him, Neuro will be less of a threat. That they took Maya reveals they know a lot about us. About all of us. Lyons never said he suspected this outright, but he spent most of his time locked in here. Over the past few months, he'd been leaving, traveling in the oscillium-protected vehicles—I suspect visiting this second sight. But I don't think he's stepped outside since . . ."

"A year ago," I say.

"A year and a half," she corrects.

"Is that when . . . ?"

"The attack on our family, yeah. It affected you both. You became distant. Angry. Six months later, you retreated from reality and had your memory wiped."

It still doesn't feel right. "We're missing something."

She raises her eyebrows at me, waiting for an explanation.

"Lyons became Dread target number one. I erased my memory. You've been kept out of the loop on this second location. Something happened a year and a half ago. Something bigger than the attack on our family. Something that changed everything. What was it?"

"I wish I knew," she says.

"When did the world start going haywire?"

"Two weeks ago."

"Before that, was Lyons here?"

She shakes her head slowly. "No. He returned a week after the first riots. Insisted on retrieving you."

"To what end?"

"To . . . bollocks. I see where you're going. He compared you to the *Enola Gay*. You were meant to be the delivery system. But now—"

"I'm obsolete. And they know who I am. They'd see me coming."

"I'm sorry, Josef. I didn't know."

"I'm getting used to it," I say.

"To me not knowing things?"

I shake my head. "My name."

She smiles. "I've noticed."

"I just wish I could remember something—anything from the past that might help."

Her smile widens. "So now you want to help, do you?"

"Help, yes, but I won't be jumping between worlds and fighting Dread." I feel the sharp shame of cowardice, but know in my core I won't be able to face another Dread and survive. "I'm not capable of that anymore."

"Not in your current state," she says, stopping by a door labeled NEUROLOGY. "But perhaps if you were properly motivated." She pushes through the door, revealing a prepped operating table and three faces—Cobb, Blair the ice creambulance driver, and Stephanie, the woman who had been trying to determine whether my memory could be returned. Given the operating table and her presence, I think she found the answer, and it terrifies me.

42.

"Crazy," Stephanie says with a knowing smile. "Good to see you again."

I have a hard time looking her in the eyes as I now remember our first meeting with severe discomfort. That I could just strut around naked, in front of a woman I'd just met, now seems like a distant impossibility.

"You two know each other?" Allenby asks.

"We've hung out," the neurologist says as she approaches. She elbows my arm like we're pals, but the best I give her admittedly funny joke is a sheepish smile.

"When I fell through the floor, I landed in her lab." I spit out the words, finding myself taking deep breaths despite a lack of physical effort.

"Ooh," Allenby says. "Hung out. I get it now. You were in the buff."

I grip Allenby's arm. My throat feels like its swelling, my breathing growing labored. "What's happening to me? Feels a little like I'm being strangled."

She looks me over, still grinning, but also concerned. "Looks like a touch of embarrassment-induced anxiety. You're not used to being teased."

Cobb puts a gentle hand on my back. "Take a deep breath. Count out seven seconds."

I do. My chest feels about to explode it's so full.

"Hold it for seven seconds." He counts this out with her fingers. "And now let it out for seven seconds."

I exhale slowly, feeling a measure of calm return as the breath seeps from my lips. I repeat the process twice more until I feel better. When I look up again and see the operating table, my throat starts to close up again. Visions of Stephanie opening the back of my head mix with memories of the Dread mole probing my brain.

Allenby puts her hand on my arm. "You won't be having surgery if that's what you're worried about."

"I won't?"

"Just one injection," Stephanie says.

"But in my brain."

"From what I understand, there's already a small hole in your skull." She pauses for a moment, when I quickly find a seat and all but fall into it. "There are no pain receptors in the brain. You're not going to feel a thing."

"But something could go wrong." I point to Cobb. "That's why he's here."

"And because you trust him," Allenby says, and gives the man a look.

"I wouldn't support this if I thought your life was in danger," Cobb says, and I believe him. Out of everyone at Neuro, he's the only one whose integrity I don't doubt to some degree. I don't even fully trust dear ol' Aunt Allenby.

I turn to Stephanie. "You're not touching my head until I understand what you're going to do."

"I'm going to restore your memory," she says.

"How?"

"It's complicated."

"Humor me."

"The way your memories were erased . . . the procedure was . . . archaic. I can't actually believe you requested it." Stephanie glances at Allenby, who nods for her to continue. "Memories are stored in the cerebral cortex, which is the outer layers of the brain. Sometimes, when the cortex is damaged, like in a car accident, neurons will die or degenerate. Glial cells, which are most easily explained as the nervous system's overprotective glue, swarm to the injury sites, protecting the brain against bacteria or toxins. The side effect of these reactive glial cells rushing to protect the mind is that the scar tissue they form effectively blocks the growth of new, healthy neurons, trapping memories in the cerebral cortex. So memories aren't lost so much as blocked. By studying and comparing numerous traumatic-injury amnesia cases, my predecessor was able to identify the specific neural pathways used to recall memories as well as the regions of the cortex itself that store long-term memories."

She looks uncomfortable with what comes next.

"I can handle it," I tell her, only half believing it. But I have seen and survived worse, including what she's now explaining. If I keep reminding myself, maybe I won't curl up on the floor.

"They basically raked the surface of your brain in the regions controlling memory. And they caused trauma to the areas responsible for transmitting those memories. They couldn't really destroy the memories without killing you, so they forced your cerebrum to do the job itself, creating vast amounts of memory-blocking glial scar tissue."

The news makes me uncomfortable, but since it happened to a version of me I can't remember, it doesn't feel any different than if I'd read about it in a magazine. "And you're going to what, remove the scar tissue?"

"In a way," she says. "We're going to turn those glial cells into functioning neurons, which will reopen neural pathways to the portions of your cerebral cortex that have been segregated."

"How?"

Stephanie sighs. "Seriously?"

"It's my brain."

"It's not going to sound fun."

I stare at her until she complies.

"Fine. We're going to inject the glial cells with a retrovirus."

She's right. That doesn't sound fun at all. "You're going to give my brain a virus?"

"Retroviruses can—"

"I know what they can do," I tell her. "I'm part Dread, thanks to a different DNA-altering retrovirus."

Stephanie just shakes her head. "Well, this retrovirus contains the genetic code for the NeuroD1 protein, which, in the hippocampus, turns reactive glial cells into nerve cells. The virus can't replicate for long. It doesn't destroy healthy cells. And it can only infect glial cells. The rest of your functioning neurons will remain intact."

"That . . . doesn't sound too bad, but I'm not sure I want my memories back. I forgot them for a reason, right?" I turn to Allenby. "You said that life had become so painful I opted to erase my memory rather than live with it. What good will come from me regaining memories so painful that even my fearless self couldn't handle them?"

Allenby is suddenly in my face. "Because pain hones us." She shoves my chest. "It gives us purpose." A solid slap across my face staggers me back. "It makes us stronger." She slaps me again. I try to dodge, but she's fast and I'm on the defense. "Pain teaches us lessons." She swings hard once more, but this time I catch her wrist in my hand. She glares at me. "And sometimes, if we're lucky, or brave, pain can push us past our fear."

She yanks her hand out of my grasp. "You can't run away from your past, and I don't think you ever intended to."

"What do you mean?" I ask.

"Why would a man without fear run away? Sure, it hurt. We lost your parents, your son, who happens to be my nephew, and we lost *my* husband. I've been living with that pain all these years. It's what drives me to keep fighting. But you . . . you retreated from it? Bullshit. That's not you. It never was. You wouldn't have gone through with it without a good reason. Or a bad one. It wasn't the loss of your family you were meant to forget, it was something else."

"What?" I ask.

"I have no idea," she says, "but I hope you remember."

Looking at Allenby, this fifty-five-year-old woman whose small stature belies a powerful resolve, I'm inspired. She has suffered deep loss, is fully aware of the kind of enemy we're facing, and is willing to stare defiantly in the face of fear. But can I find that strength in myself, even with my memory returned? I'm not sure. Fear is new to me, and it will be new to my old self, too. I have no natural defenses against it or coping mechanisms to help me recover from its effects.

And what if I'm an asshole? What if my memories return and the thing I wanted to forget was something horrible I did? I already know I was a CIA assassin, but what if I was a murderer? What if I *enjoyed* killing? Who knows what my past self did. I have trouble believing it was anything but horrible.

I clench my eyes shut against the tide of what-ifs.

Allenby is right. It doesn't matter who I used to be. Or what I'm afraid is going to happen. With countless lives and an outright war with the Dread looming, any help I can offer should be given without hesitation, even if it hurts. Even if it frightens me.

I turn to Stephanie. "How fast will it work?"

"It will be a slow spread as the retrovirus works its way through the damaged areas. The change will be one cell at a time." She holds her hands up. "And before anyone complains, this is a good thing. Picture a lifetime of memories like a lake. Right now, all that mental water is dammed and frozen. We're going to be thawing the ice, but we're also removing the dams bit by bit. If it happened all at once, the flood of information would overwhelm your mind. The effects could be catastrophic."

"Total time," I say. "How long? Months?"

"Oh, no." She waves her hand dismissively. "Days."

"What's it going to feel like?"

"If I could ask the lab rats, I'd be able to . . . tell . . ." She looks at my wide-eyed expression. "Probably should have left that detail out, huh?"

"Probably," I say, but try to ignore that we're talking about a procedure that's only been done on lesser mammals. "When it's done, if it works, will I still be me?"

"You mean, will you still be Crazy with a capital *C*?" Allenby asks, but doesn't wait for an answer. "You'll still remember the past year, so those experiences will shape who you are, but you'll also be Josef, too." She takes my hand. "Look, I know I've painted an unappealing image of your old self, but you really weren't . . . I've been angry at that man for a long time. For running away. You were a good man, and a great father, despite your previous occupation. If I didn't think bringing the old you back would help, I wouldn't do it."

"Why not?"

She pats my hand and steps back. "If you really did volunteer to forget, with the intention of never restoring your memory, I'm not sure you'll be happy to remember."

"So you're counting on Crazy to balance out Josef?"

"Something like that."

"Okay," I say, and climb on the table. "Let's just do this so you don't have to draw that gun behind your back and force me to."

All eyes turn to Allenby. She offers a fake apologetic smile, draws the weapon from behind her back, and moves to place it on a countertop. She stops halfway when the door behind her opens.

Winters steps in. "Just what the hell do you all think you're doing?"

Allenby swivels around, leveling the gun at Winters.

The one-woman CIA oversight committee / psychotherapist doesn't even blink at the weapon. She glances around the room, at who's there, at the equipment, then at Allenby. "Let me help. He's going to need someone . . . close . . . to help him transition when he wakes up."

"Wait, what?" I ask. "What do you mean, wake up?"

Allenby nods to Cobb. "Do it."

I feel a pinch on my neck, hear a whispered apology from Cobb, and then drift into a dream.

43.

Heads shift about randomly, a mix of dark hair and darker-colored abayas. There's no pattern to the clogged marketplace, just movement as thousands of people buy, sell, and steal for their families. They don't call the Chor Bazaar the "thieves market" for nothing. There are as many stolen goods being sold as there are pickpockets working the crowd.

My view is from far above the action, a half mile away and sixteen stories up, on the roof of a hotel that provides a line of sight straight down Mutton Street, right in the middle of Muslim-populated Mumbai, India.

I scan the street, looking for my target, who should be easy to spot, despite the fact that all I can see are heads. And motorcycles. Cars won't fit up the narrow street with all the people, so the vehicle of choice in this part of the city is of the two-wheeled variety. Except for the black BMW parked across the street from the used-instruments shop. It sticks out as obviously as my target will.

"There you are," I whisper, as a blond woman steps out of the music shop. She has an edge to her. A seriousness that, despite her age and aquiline beauty, says she's not someone with whom to trifle. Too bad for her; trifling is kind of my job.

I put her head in my crosshairs as she speaks to someone still in the shop.

The dossier I received said she runs a human-trafficking ring, smuggling women out of India and into the Middle East. But she recently expanded her business and now smuggles arms to a variety of terror organizations. Bad career move.

It's a hard shot. Her head, while squarely focused at the center of my crosshairs, is occasionally blocked by a passerby. I could pull the trigger only to have someone step in front of the bullet.

But this doesn't frighten me. If the bullet does strike someone else first, the high-caliber round will pass straight through the unfortunate's head and still find its target. Ignoring everything but my target, I slip my finger behind the trigger, exhale, and squeeze.

"Do you, Josef Shiloh, take Maya Lyons to be your lawfully wedded wife, promising to love and cherish, through joy and sorrow, sickness and health, and whatever challenges you may face, for as long as you both shall live?"

"I do," I say.

The words come fast. Fearless. I love the woman standing across from me. She's perfect, and I make the promise with no concern about later breaking it.

The minister turns to Maya and smiles. Who couldn't smile at a woman like this? She's strong and sharp, like a sword, but also soft and gentle in a way I've never experienced. Her black hair, spilling from a bun in curly loops, looks even darker against the stark white of her wedding gown. She smiles at me, and I want this day to be over so the night can begin.

"Do you, Maya Lyons, take Josef Shiloh to be your lawfully wedded husband, promising to love and cherish, through joy and sorrow, sickness and health, and whatever challenges you may face, for as long as you both shall—"

"I do," she says.

"She can't even wait for me to finish the question," the minister jokes, getting a laugh out of the full church. I glance to my parents. My mother's tears are matched only by those of Aunt Allenby. They hold hands, sisters-in-law who seem more like two halves of the same soul.

Uncle Hugh gives me a thumbs-up, a far less traditional man than my father. Speaking of my father, he actually looks proud, wearing his black kippah hat emblazoned with the Star of David so everyone knows the gentile woman is marrying a Jew. He will welcome religious arguments after the ceremony, but for now he's happy to be happy.

I clap my hands together and rub them in anticipation. "Okay, who's got the rings?"

Hanging upside down for any length of time is a fairly uncomfortable affair. Hanging upside down for four hours, inside the ventilation system of a penthouse, sixty-eight stories above Ramat Gan, Israel, is nearly unbearable. But I do it in silence, waiting patiently for the whores in the bedroom below to finish their job. My target lies between them, moaning like a wounded mule.

And then, he's done. Wants nothing more to do with the women. Shoos them out of the room like he never asked them there in the first place.

I don't know much about the man, other than that he has close associations within Al-Qaeda, and someone in the company wants him dead, immediately, and disappeared for three days. I don't know why. I don't care.

The man stumbles around, mumbling about the whores' lack of abilities and attractiveness. I nearly laugh when I realize he's speaking to his own nether regions, which apparently hadn't performed as hoped. All that mewling was a show, but for whom? The women are no doubt having a good laugh at his expense right about now.

He wanders around the room, clearly drunk and pouring himself another glass. For a man with ties to Al-Qaeda, he's the worst example of a good Muslim I've ever seen. He curses toward the door, his accusatory hand sloshing the drink.

He gasps. Stands suddenly still.

Has he detected me? The air-conditioning flowing past me shouldn't carry a scent. I'm too careful for that.

No, I decide, *it's them.* They're here. Making my final job a little more difficult. I never had a problem with what I do, or keeping the details a secret from Maya. But in the year since the birth of my son, I've had an increasingly difficult time believing that being an assassin, government sanctioned or not, is an acceptable job choice for a father.

So I'm taking care of this last job, retiring from my life as a killer, and joining Neuro Inc., Lyons's CIA-funded black organization, to help study the creatures I suspect are currently in the room below.

I'm not going in with blinders on. I've been part of enough black ops before. Lyons—whose military background and employment at DARPA have been covered up well enough that even my friends in the CIA couldn't find anything substantial—has given me a way out of this line of work, and I appreciate it. More than that, I'm convinced, like Lyons, that the Dread are a greater and growing threat that needs to be addressed. For the first time since Maya and I married, her father and I have a common interest beyond fishing.

The trick is that the Dread also seem to be interested in me. Lyons thinks it's because they have no effect on me. Whether or not he's right, I do see their influence while working. Sometimes they go after my target. Sometimes they disrupt the scene. Sometimes they reveal themselves to me, trying their damnedest to get my knees quivering. This should probably unnerve me, but Lyons believes it gives us a better shot of studying them. My new job description might as well be "bait."

A shadow flits through the room. My target spins with a yelp as the Dread work him up. *Assholes*, I think. They're going to draw attention and delay the op or, worse, send him out the window.

The man drops his glass and bends to pick it up.

A monster flickers in and out of reality, hovering on wings, its four red eyes locked onto the man. When he turns around, my op will be ruined.

What are you? I think, and then drop.

The square ceiling vent clangs open. The man snaps to attention, not thinking to look up. As I descend behind him, I position a noose above his head with one hand and flip off the monster with my other, which is also holding the pulley system's remote. The Dread flickers and disappears. I slip the noose around the man's neck and push a button on the remote.

The noose snaps tight as the line is yanked up by the pulley bolted to the inside of the air duct. While the man gurgles and kicks, just two feet from the floor, I unclip from the carabiners holding me upside down and take out a hundred-foot-long roll of plastic wrap. Like a spider, I spin the dying man around, wrapping him in layer upon layer of clear plastic.

In the time it takes him to die, I've got him fully wrapped in plastic, head to toe. When he's done wriggling, I push a button on the remote. The man is lifted into the vent. Once he and the line that had been holding me are inside the ceiling, a thin line attached to the vent cover retracts, pulling it back into place.

Dead and disappeared. That's how it's done.

Between the cold air from the air-conditioning and the plastic wrap, the room shouldn't smell like death for a few days, and, even then, most people won't think to check the ceiling vent. I pick up an old room-service tray, pile on some plates, and head for the door.

Before leaving, I turn the thermostat down and take a look back. There isn't a hint of the Dread, but I don't think it's actually gone. Just hidden. I flip it the bird one more time and leave next week's crime scene, and my career as an assassin, behind.

"Daddy!" The kid runs like a wide receiver and hits like a linebacker, despite being eight years old and sixty-five pounds. The tackle turns into a hug as Simon, whose undying affection for me is dwarfed only by his never-ending reserve of energy, wraps his arms around my waist and squeezes. I return the embrace and lift him off the ground, spinning him in a circle before depositing him back to the oriental rug in our home's foyer.

"How was school?" I ask.

"Boring," he says. "Duh."

"Duh?" I reach to tickle him but stop when the door upstairs slams shut. I look at Simon. "Where's your mother?"

"In the basement," he says.

We both look up. "That been happening more often?"

He nods. "Kitchen cabinets, too. And cold spots in the house. I don't go in the basement anymore." He pretends to shiver. "Are you sure it's not ghosts?"

While I am most definitely sure it's not ghosts closing doors, making rooms chilly, and turning nights into nightmares for Simon, I'm not about to tell him what it *really* is. Ghosts would be preferable to the Dread, who have been harassing my family for months. In a few days, it won't matter. We'll be living in the Neuro apartment full-time. We would be already if the moving company hadn't screwed up the scheduling. Not that it's all bad. We weren't ready anyway. Boxes waiting to be filled litter the house. Maya's not happy about the move. Doesn't know about the Dread, and so my fabricated reasoning—closer to work, to family, and free—doesn't make a lot of sense. She wants a normal childhood for Simon, but what kid wouldn't want to live in a top-secret laboratory? She'll understand when Lyons gives me the green light to tell her everything. "I told you before: the house is drafty. If you're feeling cold air, that's why."

He rolls his eyes. "It's okay if you're afraid of ghosts. I won't tell anyone."

"You won't?" I say, reaching out to tickle him again. He shrieks as my fingers find his belly.

Maya appears in the doorway, frying pan in one hand, knife in the other. She's panicked. On edge. She sees me and lowers her weapons. "Dammit!"

"You swore!" Simon shouts, still laughing.

"Sorry, baby," I say, and kiss her cheek. She's been on edge these past few weeks. The Dread taunting is getting to her. Moving will be a good thing.

"I wasn't expecting you for another hour," she says.

"I know . . ."

"But?"

"I have to go back in. Going to be a late night. We're close to a breakthrough."

"And then maybe you'll tell me what you two have been working on?"

"That's up to him," I say.

"You're my husband!"

"And he's your father, and my boss." I want to tell her she's safer not knowing, but that will just make her feel less safe. I suspect that's the reason why Dread activity in our home has remained docile for the most part. They know I can't be affected, and they tend to leave the ignorant alone. Until they don't.

Simon leaves the room, sprinting through the living room.

"I don't feel safe here," Maya whispers. "It's getting weird. Seriously. You know I'm not one to cry ghost, but—"

I point in Simon's direction. "Did you tell *him* that?"

"No!" She's still whispering, but on the verge of not. "You know I wouldn't. He's having enough trouble sleeping."

"Look," I say, putting on my perfectly calm smile. "There's nothing to worry about."

Her laugh is brief and sarcastic. "Easy for you to say."

I take her face in my hands. "You're safe."

"Promise?"

I kiss her lips. "I promise."

Grass tickles the back of my neck. I smell lilacs. The sky above is nearly intolerably blue, the late-afternoon sun low on the horizon, deepening the tone. Spring has arrived, at last, and I'm at the park with Maya and Simon. I can't see him, but I can hear him chirping away and laughing when Maya tickles his belly with her nose.

The past six months have been transformative for me. I've been so accustomed to taking life and watching death that being part of the formation of something new, alive, and delicate never occurred to me as something worth pursuing.

But here I am, lying in the grass, hands behind my head, enjoying . . . everything.

Simon's face hovers over mine, the wetness around his smiling, toothless mouth threatening to drip down on me.

"Dadu," Maya says, doing her imitation of what Simon would sound like if he could talk, wiggling him back and forth. "Dadu, you must hold me now. Hold me, Dadu. Mamma wants to lie down."

I reach up and take the boy, holding him above me while Maya lies down beside me and snuggles in.

I'm still getting used to all this. I'm not a natural with babies. With gentleness. At first, I pretended he was nitroglycerin. Shaken too hard, he would explode. But I got better at holding him. I treated his dirty diapers like live mines and learned how to disarm the worst of his bombs. But the silly-voice strangeness that possesses most people when holding a child is still foreign to me. I haven't mastered it yet, but I try, and his smile helps.

"Who's a funny boy?" I say, lowering him to my face so our noses touch for a moment. Then I lift him back up and repeat. Repetition seems to be the key to eliciting a laugh. They don't usually find humor in something the first two or three times, but after that each repetition gets a bigger reaction. I repeat the up-and-down motion, saying, "Who's a funny boy?" three times before he squeals with delight, kicking his legs and flapping his arms, saying, "Ooh, ooh, ooh!" Then he stops, wide-eyed, and turns to watch a dog walk past with its owner, that openmouthed smile locked in place.

While he watches the dog, I turn to his mother and find her eyes just inches from mine. I kiss slow and gentle, interlocking our lips. I hang there for a moment, feeling a crazy kind of closeness that I now share with two people. When we part, I say, "Thank you."

"The kiss was that good?" she asks.

"For him," I say, glancing up to Simon, who's once again trying to fly away as he says "Ooh, ooh, ooh!"

"You helped. A little." She squeezes my arm, and in that moment I decide I've had enough killing. Enough fighting. I might not be afraid to die, but there is no way I want to risk not being around for Simon or Maya. Her father hinted that Neuro might have a place for me. As a fellow company man, he knows what I do, more than Maya does, and if he says I can leave behind my days of violence, I might just take him up on it.

I turn back up to Simon. He's somehow managed to grab a fluffy white dandelion. He blows on it twice, mimicking what he's seen Maya do several times already, and then stuffs the thing into his mouth. He looks down at us, a little shocked when his open mouth is suddenly full of clinging debris. The smile fades and tears quickly come. Laughing, Maya and I sit up, working together to clear the dandelion bits from his mouth, while distracting him from the confusing feeling ratcheting him up to a high-pitched scream.

Most of my career, I've worked solo, depending on myself more than anyone else. Now, I'm part of a team, and it feels right. More right than anything before it.

With the dandelion cleared away, I lift the crying boy and stand. I put him on my chest, lean his small head on my shoulder, and do what Maya calls the "daddy bounce," shifting my weight side to side while gently bobbing up and down. Simon quiets quickly. I kiss the back of his head and look down at Maya. She's got tears in her eyes. Whispers, "I love you."

I wake suddenly, sitting up in bed. "Maya?"

I'm in a hospital. "Maya?"

She's not here.

This isn't a memory. I'm awake. Back at Neuro in the present. I only remember bits and pieces of my previous life, of Maya, but it's enough.

They have her. My wife. My son's mother. And I'm going to get her back.

44.

The door behind me opens. I spin to greet whoever it is, saying, "We have to—"

It's Winters. Her face and hopeful blue eyes act as a catalyst. I grip my head, suddenly at the mercy of a raging migraine. Images flow past my eyes. Smells. Sounds. An entire sensory barrage of what once was. I feel Winters's embrace. Her comforting words. Feel the closeness of her friendship. Her support. And then something deeper. Something forbidden and guilt frosted.

I loved her. Briefly.

But I was going to put a stop to it. In the wake of Maya's collapse—and Simon's death—I was weak. And lonely.

"What's on your mind this morning?"

I look up at Winters, confused for a moment before getting lost in the memory. She's dressed in a loose-fitting silk negligee. Her hair is messy. No makeup in sight. She's gorgeous, standing in front of the bathroom sink in my Neuro apartment.

I can't do this anymore.

As I lay in bed that morning, watching her sleep, I came to a conclusion. Our relationship, no matter how good it feels or how much comfort it provides, is wrong. I'm still married, and, despite what Maya did and the anguish I feel about Simon's death, it wasn't Maya's fault.

She didn't murder our son.

The Dread did.

When she recovers, I need to be there, till death do us part.

Death do us part.

But I'm not ready to break things off with Winters now. Not standing half-naked in my bathroom. Not immediately following last night. She deserves better than that. "Just distracted."

She brushes her teeth, speaking between strokes. "About what?"

I wave off the question. I need to speak to Lyons. It's about something important. Something critical.

But . . . I can't remember what.

She spits in the sink, rinses, and places the pink toothbrush in the wall-mounted holder.

I gasp out of the memory, returning to the medical room. Winters has a steadying hand on my arm.

"It was *your* toothbrush," I say.

"What?" She guides me to a chair. Sits me down. "Are you okay?"

The headache is gone, but memories are surfacing one by one. Most are insignificant, days and events lost in time, things I wouldn't have remembered even before losing my memory. The cascade of history is like background noise. Voices, whispers really, of days gone by. Riding my childhood bike. Military training. Endless school days, each nearly identical to the previous. I can ignore these memories, but the more recent and powerful ones return with painful urgency.

"I don't remember everything," I tell her. "Bits and pieces. But . . . I do remember us. Parts, anyway."

She crouches in front of me. Takes my hands. "What do you remember?"

"I'm not sure you'll want to know."

She offers a sad smile. "I'm good at reading people. It's part of my job. I could see it in your eyes that morning. Also, it's been a year. So, let's hear it."

"I'm still married," I tell her, voicing Josef's old conclusion and Crazy's newly formed opinion. "And I was then. It shouldn't have happened."

She nods, either in understanding or acceptance.

I place a hand on her cheek, and she leans into it. "I'm sorry," I tell her. Then my body goes rigid as a fresh cascade of memories is unleashed.

She pulls my hand from her face. "Did you remember something?"

"A lot. But nothing important." I rub my head, feeling a fresh headache brewing. "I didn't . . . break things off before. Why not?"

She stands, returning to her usual professional demeanor. "That was the day you decided to forget. About me. About Maya. Your son. And everything else that mattered to you."

She's growing angry. Borderline pissed. These are the emotions that fueled her earlier attempt to physically subdue me. Given what I now remember about her, I'm glad she wasn't seriously injured during that failed effort.

"That doesn't make sense. Doesn't sound like me," I say, but I'm still not positive. Out of a lifetime of memories, I think I've recovered maybe thirty percent, most of that being from childhood.

"How is he?" It's Allenby, in the doorway. Her hair is loose and billowing. The sight punts pain into the side of my head and sends me back.

"What the hell did you two do?" Allenby's voice is loud in the phone. I pull the device away from my ear.

"What are you talking about?" I ask. "What happened?"

"They got Hugh!" she shouts.

"*Who* got him?" I ask, but I already know the answer. There's only one *they* she'd associate with me. The Dread. "Are you safe?"

"Don't worry about me, you—"

The office door—*my* office door—bursts open. It's Lyons. His cheeks are flush.

I point to the phone, "It's Kelly, she's—"

"I know," he says, moving past me to my computer. I can hear my aunt shouting but can't make out the words. Lyons steps away from the computer, revealing the screen and a single photo. The phone lowers away from my ear. I have a thousand questions but am too stunned to ask all but one. "When?"

"Ten minutes ago," he says.

I stare at the photo depicting my parents, both dead. My father lies on a concrete walkway, a pool of blood around his supine body. I recognize the hotel in the background. They were on vacation. I helped pick the spot. In the background is a second body, soaked and surrounded by a puddle of water.

"They're targeting our family." He says it calmly, like the danger has passed for the rest of us.

He doesn't know. He thinks they're still here.

Lyons must see the shift in my face. He asks, "What is it?"

I stand. "Maya and Simon went back to the house. Simon wanted one last night in his room."

"But . . ." He looks bewildered. Panicked. "They were supposed to be here. I told them to stay here!"

I can hear the distant voice of Allenby on the phone. She's heard and is shouting at me to go. "Get Simon, Josef! Get them both!"

I'm on my knees, gripping my head.

"What happened?" Allenby's voice is clear now. Present.

"A memory," I say. "A hard one." I'm glad I don't yet remember what happened next. My stomach clenches with the knowledge that it, too, will soon be unleashed. The memories I've regained are already enough to spur me into action. I remember my son. The depth of my love for him and the pain of his loss. I know what the Dread took from me. From my family. And, like Allenby hoped, it is enough to make me face my newfound fears.

No, I think, *I don't want to face them. I want to obliterate them.*

The unanswered question is, *Why did I run from them in the past?*

Knowing that the answer will eventually be freed by changing scar tissue, I decide to waste no time or energy trying to uncover it. Given the look in Allenby's eyes, I think time is something I don't have.

Allenby gets her hands under my arms and lifts. I stand with her. "We need to go."

I understand her urgency. Maya's kidnapping now weighs heavily on me. The idea of losing her, for good, and in such a horrible way, after betraying her trust all those years ago, is unacceptable. But where there was urgency before, there now seems to be a ticking clock. "What's changed?"

Allenby heads for the door. I follow, shakily at first, but then steadied by Winters's hand on my back.

"They're on their way here," Allenby says, looking over her shoulder.

"Who is?"

"Dread Squad."

I'm about to say that's a good thing when I realize the implications of her fear. They're not on their way to help; they're coming to stop us.

"I spoke to Lyons," Allenby says. "He sounded . . . different. Angry."

"He thinks they killed Maya?" I ask.

She nods. "But I think it's more than that. He seemed more upset about the attack. Compared it to Pearl Harbor. Said the Dread had awakened a sleeping giant."

"He's been comparing the Dread to World War Two Japan," I say. "Sees this as the first wave of an invasion."

"His war has finally begun," Winters says. "I knew he was preparing for the worst, but I didn't know he was actually ready to strike. While I'm sure he has support from people above my pay grade, this is war, and I doubt he has the president's stamp of approval. This was all supposed to be a process. Build evidence. A game plan. Present it all to the president and let him decide."

"I think that this was the plan all along," I say. "Something started two weeks ago. It's why he brought me back. I was going to be his *Enola Gay*." My eyes widen. "I was going to deliver a bomb."

"What bomb?" Winters asks.

I shrug. "I have no idea, but I was his delivery system." I turn to Allenby. "He's found someone else to do it."

This is something he's been working on for a long time at that second location, and if the World War Two analogy is accurate, I don't think Maya will survive it . . . *if* she's alive. Whether or not Lyons's actions are impulsive, misguided, or on target and justified, Maya's life is at risk. "What's the plan?" I ask, strengthened by my increasing resolve.

"Maya's embedded tracker is transmitting. You're going after her," she says. "You're the only one who can. I'm going to let the Dread Squad take me in so I can have a chat with your father-in-law. See if I can't talk him back from the brink. There has to be another way to do this, or at least do it with the full support of the U.S. military."

I nearly point out that the U.S. military might be compromised already, that under Dread influence they might be more likely to shoot each other or us. This is probably the same conclusion Lyons has come to. If so, he can tell Allenby himself. Let them debate strategy and protocol. I'm going after Maya.

I notice a slight tremor in Allenby's hands. It started when she mentioned Dread Squad. "You seem a little nervous. You don't think Katzman will—"

"I don't think it will be Katzman," she says, "or anyone else we might know. Dread Squad isn't just the handful of men you saw here." She stops in front of an armory door. "There are hundreds of them."

"Three hundred thirty-three," Winters says. "I helped vet them. They were supposed to be a defensive force, like the Secret Service, protecting VIPs from Dread influence, but I think they've been trained for something else."

"They're not your problem." Allenby enters the armory.

The armory has been picked over, but an array of familiar clothing and weapons has been laid out for me. I pick up the machete and whisper, "Faithful."

Winters looks at me like I just passed gas. "Excuse me?"

"The best weapons have names," I say, speaking as old Josef, who I now recall had a habit of naming prized weaponry, and apparently still does. I hold the machete up. "This is Faithful." *Which makes it better than me,* I think, but keep to myself. I turn to Allenby. "You said Maya's tracker signal popped back up. Is she nearby?"

Allenby frowns. "Louisiana. New Orleans. Hope you're not afraid of flying now. Lyons sent a team in that direction an hour ago, so they've got a head start."

"You said Lyons didn't think Maya was alive," I point out.

"It's not a rescue mission. It's an assault."

"If they're already in the air, how are we going to catch up?"

"I've made arrangements," Winters says. "Lyons might have vast resources, including planes, but Neuro is just a small cog in the larger machine that I have access to. We'll get there first, *if* we leave now."

"This might be a stupid question," I say, "but why don't we have a couple of F-22s force them to land?"

"Lyons has a lot of friends," Winters says. "In Washington and the military. He's probably got F-22s *escorting* him. Our best play is to beat him there, get Maya to safety, and see if her survival takes the wind out of his sails."

I appreciate that Winters and Allenby think there is an alternative to the coming violence, but I'm not convinced. Not by a long shot. Conflicts like this are ended by violence, an opinion that is, thus far, supported by my returning memory. If I'm able to get Maya clear, I might even give Lyons my blessing. I have no love for the Dread, and he's the only one capable of responding to the threat.

Allenby seems to think I've been cut out of the loop because a fearful Crazy wouldn't approve of war—of fighting the Dread. But the opposite is true. By taking Maya, they've rekindled my hatred for them. I appreciate Allenby's position, but Maya is my only concern. Not only did she love me, unconditionally, but she also made me feel more . . . human. I lived in darkness so vast that I was able to see the Dread, not with my eyes, but with my heart. I recognized the effect they had on people because it was the same effect my presence so often elicited. Maya freed me from that, and now I'm going to free her from it.

Voices, firm and professional, slide into the room from the hallway beyond. Commands and confirmations. Dread Squad. They're already here.

Allenby picks up and shoves the oscillium armor at me. "We can't let them take you. It's time to be Crazy."

45.

The plan is simple. Allenby, a trusted higher-up at Neuro, will claim I've left, and she'll request an audience, via phone or video, with Lyons. Winters, whose oversight of Neuro gives her authority separate from Lyons, will vouch for her. If granted, she can try to talk him out of whatever endgame he's working toward, or at least glean some intel, which could help my rescue effort. If we can't do that, Allenby thinks Lyons might have the sleeping-giant comparison backward, that he might instigate the end of humanity at the hands of the Dread. I'm not convinced, and until Maya is safe, I'm not taking sides.

Some of what I remember about Lyons isn't encouraging. On the surface, he's a good grandfather and devoted father. He's also a tortured soul, deeply feeling the frightening events of his youth, when the Dread visited him at night, nightmares made real. He didn't talk about those dark times often, not that I can remember yet, anyway, but when he did . . . The emotional scars are deep. But there is another side to the man, kept from plain sight, that is emerging in my memory. After his time with the Dread, before the CIA, he saw war as a young man. In Korea. I now remember a conversation with him, during which he reminisced about the firefights, the confusion and sound and adrenaline of battle. He waxed about battle the way an ex–football star fondly remembers game-winning plays. While he's been content to research his life-long enemy, collect war trophies from around the world, and oversee his own private army, perhaps the events of the past two weeks have freed him to relive his glory days, if only vicariously through Dread Squad? Has Maya's abduction pushed him over the edge and thrust him to wage war he can't win?

He might even view himself as some kind of noble hero, a modern-day George Washington, crossing the rift between worlds to free humanity from the Dread tyranny. It's not even that much of a stretch if he could pull it off. But Allenby thinks he's more likely to doom us all. She might be right, but if the Dread could wipe us out, why haven't they done it already? That alone says a conventional victory might be possible.

My part of the current plan is simple. Hide and wait. Cobb and Blair have transportation ready and waiting. Once Allenby is away, I'll be off to New Orleans with Winters and whatever help she's summoned. Like I said, simple.

"Don't move," a man shouts. I can't see him from my hiding place behind a weapons counter, but I can see Winters and Allenby. And I don't like what I'm seeing. The looks on their faces, along with their suddenly raised hands, tells me two things. They don't know these men, and they've got guns pointed at them.

My heart starts pumping hard. I can hear the rushing blood behind my ears. My vision narrows. Muscles tense. Even if nothing happens, I'm going to need a little time to recover from the adrenaline dump.

"I'm Dr. Allenby, and I would like to—"

"Don't care who you say you are, so shut it." The gruff man's voice carries an unsaid threat. His next words are spoken into the hallway beyond him. "Are they on the list?"

"Both of you know me," Winters says, glaring at them. "Lower your weapons, now, or—"

"Yeah, they're on the list," someone else replies. A hand slips into view, holding a small tablet. I can barely make out a photo of Allenby on the screen. The man holding the tablet swipes his thumb a few times. I see Cobb's photo, and mine, and then Winters's.

Winters clenches her fists. "Listen, you two—"

"ID confirmed," the man says, pulling back the tablet. Winters takes a step forward, violent intent barely contained. She's stopped by the muzzle of a gun, leveled at my aunt's chest. "Stay where you are."

"Why are you here?" Allenby asks, still defiant.

In reply, the man taps his finger on the touch screen and turns the device around. It's a video of Lyons. He's in a hangar. Men rush back and forth behind him. He leans in close, face slick with sweat, eyes unfocused, but angry. He doesn't look well. "Josef, Kelly, and anyone who happens to be aiding your unsanctioned endeavor, I am aware of your efforts to restore Josef's memory, and I'm afraid I cannot allow you to continue. Your actions and plans are tantamount to treason. And in times of war, such as this, the only acceptable response to this crime is of the harsh sort."

What? My mind reels. This man is my father-in-law. We worked together. What he's saying doesn't fit with what I know of the man. But that's still an incomplete picture. What are we missing?

"Dr. Winters," Lyons continues, "if you are present, you have been a trusted colleague until now. Please decide which side of this you want to fall on. Josef. Kelly. I tried to avoid this, I really did." He sighs. "Family has always been my core . . . but now, what we're doing is for all the other families on this planet. I'm afraid our broken house has become a liability. Kelly, you oppose my plans. Always have. Josef . . . I'm sorry, son, but even the best soldiers become expendable eventually, and I can't let either of you stand in my way. Good-bye."

Before I can fully register the threat, a sharp report of a gunshot contained in a small space stabs my ears, but the physical pain is nothing compared to the sight of my aunt, whom I've only just begun to remember, but who I know I adore, falling back through the puff of pink that has exploded from her back.

I'm rooted in shock, processing surprise slower than I used to, but Winters acts before Allenby hits the floor. She brings her foot up hard, kicking the unseen soldier's wrist. The gun falls free, clattering to the floor, just a few feet away from me.

"Crazy!" Winters shouts without looking at me. Her voice snaps me into action. I pick up the dropped gun and aim it at the backside of the door, looking to fire thirteen rounds into whoever is on the other side. The problem is that Winters is also on the other side. I know my old self would just aim to the right and fire, but I can't risk hitting her. She follows the kick with a punch. I hear it connect. The struck soldier falls, but he's not alone. Whoever is behind him is now free to act.

And he does.

A perfect three-round burst punches a triangle of holes into Winters's chest. She stands frozen, looking down at the red plumes of color growing on her blouse. She starts turning her startled eyes in my direction but never gets the chance to make eye contact. She deserved so much better than this.

"Bitch," the soldier says.

A single shot snaps Winters's head back. She crumples in on herself.

My old self—Crazy—would have handled this differently. Sure, he might have shot Winters, too, but maybe not fatally. At least with that version of myself, she'd have a chance of survival. As rage overcomes any traces of fear, I dive forward and slide into view in the last place they'd expect it, underfoot. I fire a single round. The bullet slips neatly through the man's soft throat and explodes out through the back of his head.

The mix of blood and brains spray on the second man's face, causing him to flinch. I put a hole in his forehead before he can recover.

A third soldier slides into view, firing an assault rifle from the hip. He sprays bullets into the armory, hitting everything at waist height, which is nothing. Wisely, he hasn't fully entered the doorway. But that can be corrected. I shoot his leg, punching a hole through his shin. He topples to the side, shouting in pain. But his voice, and life, are silenced by a bullet before he lands atop his deceased comrades.

I lay there, breathing for a moment, waiting for more soldiers to enter the room. But no one comes.

I don't even need to look at Winters to know she's dead. And I'm not sure I could handle seeing her like that, not after remembering what she meant to me. But Allenby . . . I drop to my knees, put a hand behind her head, and check her pulse. It's faint, but there. I glance down at the wound. The Dread Squad soldier aimed for her heart, but missed, punching a hole through her shoulder instead.

Her eyes flutter open.

Our eyes meet for a moment and she smiles. "Are you all right?"

That she's worried about me when she has a bullet hole staggers me. "*I* am."

She sees me glance at Winters and follows my eyes.

"I'm sorry," she says. "I know you cared for her."

Part of me wants to linger, to mourn for Winters's death. She did mean a lot to me. But there is still a chance that I can save Maya, and when all of this is done, kick Lyons's teeth in. His war might be justified, but this kind of violent paranoia is uncalled for. There will be a reckoning for Winters's death. "Do you know her CIA contact?"

My aunt nods. "He's a good man. She's already been in touch with him. Understands the situation and our part in stopping it.

Help me up." I lift her by her good arm. Ignoring the still-bleeding wound in her shoulder, she digs into her pocket and takes out her phone. She snaps a photo of Winters and the men who killed her. I nearly ask why, but then realize Winters's contact is going to want confirmation that she's dead.

When she looks up at me, I must look a little shell-shocked. She pockets the phone and puts her hand on my face. "There is more strength in you than you know, Josef. You just need to remember."

Her eyes drift downward. She reaches out and takes hold of the chain beneath my shirt. She tugs it, and the strange melted pendant that is my security blanket falls out. She lifts the rough, circular, color-swirled mystery up so I can see it. "Remember."

I'm about to tell her that's not how it works, that the memories come back randomly, but then, with quick breath, I realize that I *already* remember this. It came in a cluster of information, hidden until now, freed and brought to the forefront of my thoughts.

Something's burning, I think, and stand from my home-office chair. The chemical scent in the air is subtle, but so out of place in my home that I react immediately. There are several things in this world that produce similar odors, none of them good, and I wonder for a moment if one of the CIA's enemies has figured out who I am. Recovering and unlocking the handgun hidden in my desk drawer, I hurry through the house, following the scent toward the kitchen.

I pause at the open doorway, no danger in sight, but with Simon home I'm not going to take any chances. Right now it's just the two of us. Maya is out shopping. Moving slowly, I lean into the room and quickly spot my target—a panicking six-year-old boy who has melted two action figures on the stove top. A cookie sheet covered with chicken nuggets and french fries lays next to the mess.

I tuck the gun behind my back and hurry into the room. Simon turns toward me, eyes wide and overflowing with tears. He's waving his hands at the rising toxic smoke. "I was trying to make lunch for us! I turned on the wrong one!"

The action figures are now a puddle of colorful swirling plastic sitting atop the smooth-topped stove.

"I'm sorry," he says, now blubbering and snotty. His abject despair breaks my heart.

I quickly turn off the burner. "Hey, hey, it's okay." It's really not okay, but I'm pretty sure he's learned that on his own.

"I melted my guys," he says, revealing the true source of his sadness.

I kiss his forehead and stand up. It's an ungodly mess. And nothing I do now is going to change that. I get two knives from a drawer and return to the cooling stove top. Using, and ruining, the two blades, I carve the liquid, still-fuming plastic into two gooey mounds. Then I form them into thick, colorful masses. I open two windows, letting the cross-breeze clean the air, and we spend the next ten minutes it takes for the burner and plastic to cool in silence. When everything is cool to the touch, I wedge a metal spatula beneath the two circles of plastic and chip them off.

Simon is no longer sad. He's curious. I lead him down to the basement, set up two spots at the workbench, and take out some tools. After drilling holes in both plastic circles, I set to work with a wood burner, melting words into the back of both chunks. The air fills, once again, with the stench of melting plastic, but the work doesn't take long. When I'm done, I turn them around so Simon can see my handiwork.

"What do they say?" he asks.

"It says, 'evidence,'" I tell him, and then slide old neck chains through each. I put the first over his head and the second over mine. "This way we'll never forget what happened . . . and your mom will never know."

That gets a smile out of him.

And me.

Until I return from the memory, lift the plastic pendant, and turn it around. The word is still there. "Evidence." So neither of us will ever forget. I nearly start crying, in part because of the sweet memory, but also because I chose to forget it. It's unforgivable. Then I hear footsteps. Rushing. Whispered commands. More soldiers moving down the hallway, no doubt rushing to inspect their dead.

I recover the Vector assault rifle I'd failed to remember before.

Allenby takes my arm. "Are you okay to do this?"

I chamber a round, slip my arm out of her hand, and step into the hallway. It takes just a moment for me to confirm the targets are not friendly, and then I sweep the muzzle back and forth, finger held down hard over the trigger. It's some of the poorest, old-world-style gangster shooting I've ever done, but the sheer number of rounds makes it effective. All three soldiers drop.

I take one last look into the armory, at the woman who might have loved me, and then turn to Allenby. No words need to be said. We're going to get Maya back and rain down hell on anyone stupid enough to get in our way. She nods and we head out together.

46.

After meeting Cobb, Blair, and Stephanie, we race to the airport. While Allenby coordinates with Winters's CIA contact, Cobb tends to her shoulder. Stephanie, who's already done everything she can to help, parts ways with us at the airport, taking the car and heading west to stay with family in Vermont, one of the few places on earth to still be largely free of violence.

After passing through a security check, we're escorted onto the tarmac by two silent men in suits and head for an open hangar. Blair stops, mouth open, when we reach the doors. "Is that a—"

"Concorde," Allenby says.

The plane's sharp, downward sloping nose makes it easy to identify. The Concorde is the fastest passenger plane to have every crisscrossed the Atlantic. It was decommissioned after a few well-publicized crashes and more than a few complaints about the sonic boom generated when the plane breaks the sound barrier, tearing through the sky at Mach 2, more than twice the speed of the fastest troop transport.

Ten minutes later, we're in the air, cruising at 1500 miles per hour and escorted through the FAA-emptied skies by three F-18s. Our man at the CIA is getting things done, and quietly. Lyons will have no idea we're coming.

I spend part of the three-hour flight catching up on global news, which is dramatically grim. The way global events are being presented leaves little doubt that a nuclear holocaust is imminent; the government is days, if not hours, from being overthrown; and better make friends with your gun-carrying neighbors because militia frontier life is the only hope for survival in the soon-to-be nuclear wasteland. For once, all the drama is justified. Cities are imploding, the violence chaotic and without reason. Militaries are still largely under control, but there are troop movements on the borders of too many countries to count. The Dread need to be stopped through whatever means necessary, meaning there is a chance that Lyons's aggressive option is justified. It is, after all, a proven tactic. If Maya is safe and her father really has a way to remove the Dread threat from our world, then I hope he succeeds. And when he's done, he'll answer for Winters.

Violence has escalated out of control in major cities around the world, and tensions between nations are reaching the point where a few navies and air forces have skirmished, leaving nearly two hundred dead and a Japanese maritime self-defense force destroyer limping back to port, courtesy of the Chinese. If it weren't for the trouble brewing in the major cities of most nations, I think the world would have already rushed headlong into war. The threat of civil war seems to be the only thing tempering militaries, just in case they're needed at home. Alliances are breaking down as paranoia runs rampant. An every-man-for-himself mentality has taken hold of governments.

It's a brilliant strategy. No one outside Neuro would even think to consider the real cause of all this chaos. People are afraid and, like good mammals, are focused solely on the clear and present dangers, rather than the ones lurking just beyond perception. All the Dread need to do is pull their influence from one area and apply it to another. Send the rioters home, and the world goes to war. Turn government attention inward, and the riots become civil war. Maybe they'll do all of the above?

Allenby thinks that the only way out of this for the human race is for the Dread to back off. I'm not totally convinced, and the memories of what they took from me and how they did it fuel a deeply personal desire for vengeance.

When I'm not watching the news, I'm remembering.

This isn't my first trip to New Orleans. In a cruel irony, the city is where Maya and I spent our honeymoon. Not the usual place for a pair of newlyweds, but we both like the food, music, and atmosphere. We spent two weeks exploring the bayou, the city, and the culture. When the memory returned, it felt like recapturing some of the happiest days of my life . . . a life I want returned.

My childhood is almost a complete picture, much of it fading back to the recesses of my mind. My years as a young man are spotty, but I remember my training and a good number of special ops missions, and CIA . . . assignments. More recent memories are fewer, but several early years of my life with Maya and Simon are nearly complete. Each new memory—a birthday, anniversary, quiet night at home—stabs a fresh pang of sadness into my gut. But the knowledge that my sweet boy was brutally slain by his own mother's forced hand transmogrifies grief into rage.

And I welcome it.

I'm going to need it. The memory of what the Dread can do, the kind of fear they can push into a human mind, is still fresh. But anger, I've learned, is one of the best ways to overcome fear. And right now, I've got anger to spare.

The most recent years of my life, a year ago, are still full of holes, some small, others gaping. I decide not to worry about them. My path is already set and they'll come in time, if I survive.

Allenby pulls my eyes away from the TV, showing what appears to be a vicious gang fight, but is actually the British Parliament. I point to the small screen mounted to the seat in front of me. "Have you seen this?"

She glances at the screen but seems almost uninterested. Her downturned lips hint at grim news. "What is it?"

"I've just got word," she says, motioning for me to move over. I do, and she slumps into the seat beside me, wincing from the effort of sitting down. "The president has given Russia an ultimatum."

"Let me guess," I say. "Putin needs to pull his troops back from the borders of former USSR states."

She shakes her head. "I'm afraid it's too late for that. Russia invaded Ukraine, Georgia, and a handful of 'stans' this morning. They've been waiting for the chance, so it didn't take much prodding. The only silver lining is that those nations were smart enough, or maybe too afraid, to fight back. The real problem is that, as of twenty minutes ago, Russia's nuclear arsenal went hot."

She doesn't need to finish the thought. If Russia was prepping for launch, so was every other nuclear nation in the West. Things are escalating. "The Dread know Lyons is coming," I guess.

Allenby says nothing, which I take as agreement.

"How long did the president give them?" I ask.

She looks at me, fear in her eyes despite the absence of Dread on this plane. "Three hours."

"How long until we land?"

"One hour."

"Shit."

"Indeed."

"And if they don't back down?" I ask. "What was the threat?"

"Open-ended," she says, meaning that all cards were on the table. In two hours, things are going to get out of hand.

I set a timer on my watch. Two hours and fifty minutes, adjusting for the time it took for the news to reach me. Then I say, "I'm going to sleep," knowing I'll need all the energy I can get when we land.

She chuckles, pats my knees, and grunts as she stands. Despite the news she's just delivered, I'm out in five minutes.

Cobb wakes me as we begin our approach. I look out the windows, shifting my vision into the mirror world. The world above is purple, the land below hues of darkness, pocked by several small colonies, almost the size of houses, but nothing significant. In the real world, it's all swamp. Our approach to the airport brings us in east of the city, and flying around it for a look will take time we don't have. *We'll recon from the ground,* I decide.

According to Allenby and corroborated by my returning memory, Lyons had identified New Orleans as the location for what could be the largest Dread colony in North America. Allenby believes he's out to destroy it with the hopes that the loss of a large colony will essentially switch off the smaller colonies and hordes of Dread in the same way that the destruction of our local colony did to the Dread in the area. But it's not really the colony that needs to be destroyed, it's the Dread mole hiding inside. They're the taskmasters. If he's right, and this can be done, it could work, instantly freeing the United States from their influence. But then what? Could we act fast enough to free other nations, focusing on the ones with nuclear arsenals? Or would the attack have the same effect on the Dread as the nuclear assaults on Nagasaki and Hiroshima had on World War II imperial Japan? *That's what he's hoping for,* I think, and wonder if I shouldn't resume my roll in his plan—after Maya is secured.

Knowing New Orleans might someday become a target, Lyons kept a fleet of oscillium-encased vehicles in the company's private hangar. One of them, a red SUV, is waiting for us. As the door opens and the staircase descends toward the tarmac, I take my first breath of city air tinged with the rot and salt of the nearby bayou and ocean. The familiar smell brings back memories of my honeymoon and nearly relaxes me.

Ed Blair gives me a slap on the shoulder. "Let's move." He flew in the cockpit, making sure the pilots went where they were supposed to. Had they received conflicting orders from Lyons or his friends in the military, they would have completed the flight at gunpoint. The short man hurries down the stairs, gets behind the wheel, and starts the engine.

"Here," Cobb says, handing me the black duffel bag that holds my assortment of weapons.

"You can wait here," I tell him. "Stay with Allenby."

He lifts a large first-aid kit complete with a portable defibrillator and gives it a pat. "You might need me. And your aunt is fine here without me."

"But not well enough to join you?" she asks from the top of the stairs.

"Not a chance," I say. "That's a bad wound and if you move around too much, you're going to reopen—"

"I'm a doctor," Allenby grumbles. "And I can—"

"You're also on morphine."

"Oh," she says, and grins. "That's why I feel so good."

"Riiight," Cobb says.

I head back up the stairs and help Allenby to a seat. "I'll be fine. I'm going to find her and bring her back."

She smiles and pats my face twice. "Always such a good boy. Don't dally."

I kiss her forehead and head back to the door, stopping to glare at the two pilots looking back out of the cockpit. "If she leaves this plane, it'll become your coffin."

Their rapid nodding reminds me of bobbleheads.

The SUV horn honks twice, beckoning me down the stairs. Blair is all business.

We drive in silence, following interstate 10 west, heading toward the tracker's mirror-world position and avoiding the clogged streets of the city's core, where large angry crowds fight each other, loot storefronts, and burn the city. Police vehicles, SWAT trucks, and other emergency responders are everywhere, sirens blaring, lights flashing, racing in multiple directions. I can't tell if they're helping or simply joining the fray. There's more tension in the air than humidity. But there's no sign of the Dread. I have no doubt that they're out there, moving among the crowds, but they leave the SUV alone.

We exit the highway, turning left past a car that's been left to smolder. Whatever happened here has moved on to another part of the city.

"Whoa," Blair says as we pass under the highway. "That's not good, right?"

I look ahead. There's a cemetery on the right, known as a "city of the dead" in this part of the world because of the rows of sun-bleached, aboveground tombs. New Orleans is below sea level, built atop land that should be a swamp. Dig a few feet down and you hit the water table. So you have three options for burying the dead: weigh the bodies down and let them sink through the four feet of water filling their six-foot grave, bury the dead in shallow graves to be uncovered by harsh weather and floods, or build them a concrete, granite, and marble city aboveground. Since no one wants moist cadavers floating around the city every time it floods, the dead reside in endless rows of bleak structures ranging from economy stacks to opulent mansions, the inequality in life retained in death.

But this city of the dead is not our destination. That doesn't mean it's not populated or a risk, however.

I steel myself for a fright and gaze into the mirror dimension, noting that the shift in my vision now causes no pain at all.

There's a colony at the center of the graveyard. A small one. And while the swamp has been held at bay in our dimension, the mirror world is under a layer of water. Trees, laden with heavy coils of black gunk, rise from the liquid, which is reflecting the dark purple sky. Despite all the water, there isn't a ripple of movement. There are no Dread here and haven't been anytime recently.

"They're everywhere," Cobb says as we pass another small colony. I look ahead, to the right, and see more, all just as empty as the first. Turning my eyes back to the real world, I see what Cobb does. Cemetery after cemetery. Drawn to bury our dead on the colonies, this stretch of swamp held back by concrete has become littered with tombs and mausoleums. Tall willow trees, heavy with hanging Spanish moss, sway in the wind, creating a landscape that is eerily similar to the mirror world. I find myself trying to slip farther out of that place, but the trees are here, rooted in my home frequencies. There's no escaping them.

"It's just up ahead," Blair says, turning right. The tracking device last showed Maya in this part of the city. It uses GPS positioning, so once she was pulled back into the mirror world, it stopped working and, since there are no satellites in the mirror world, won't work there, either. If we get within a half mile, a local transmitter in the embedded device will do the job, but until then we're relying on her last-known location.

"Stop," I say. "Pull over."

He stops short of a bridge that crosses one of many ocean inlets cutting into the city. On the other side of the bridge is St. Louis Cemetery No. 3. Of the three big cemeteries in New Orleans, this is the largest and most opulent in terms of crypt construction. Just two miles from the French Quarter, it was flooded during Hurricane Katrina, but, thanks to the heavy stone tombs, the dead stayed where they were supposed to.

I climb out of the car, eyes on the still-distant cemetery. It's a typical summertime New Orleans day. Mid-nineties. Humid. The sky is blue and clear. But there's no denying something feels off. While this part of the city is relatively quiet, I can hear sirens in the distance. The drone of an angry crowd rises and falls with the wind.

But not here.

I take a deep breath, count to seven, let it out for seven, and then let myself see the mirror world again.

Something's wrong.

I climb atop the SUV, its roof bending beneath my feet. I have a clear view of the mirror world beyond the inlet, which is now pea-soup green and clogged with glowing seaweedlike veins extending out of the muddy banks.

"What is it?" Cobb asks. I hear his voice and the car door opening, the shift of the vehicle beneath my feet as he exits, but I can't see him. "What do you see?"

"This can't be the right place," I say. There's a colony, but it's just like the others, small, devoid of life, and partially lost to the swamp. Abandoned. I turn to look at Cobb but forget to shift my vision.

That's when I see it.

The colony.

It's so vast that I take a step back and slip on the SUV's windshield. I tumble back with a shout, landing on the hood and rolling to the concrete. When I open my eyes, I'm under the bleak water of the mirror world. For a moment, I panic, but then remember that I'm only seeing this world. I haven't fully entered it yet. I shift my vision back to the real world and stare at the blue sky above.

Blair and Cobb appear above me, their concerned looks blocking out the sky.

"What happened?" Blair asks.

"It's not at the cemetery," I say, and point back the way we came. "It's behind us."

They both turn around.

"The park?" Cobb asks.

Maya and I spent two full days exploring the park and its variety of tourist-friendly locals. Twice the size of New York's Central Park, the thirteen-hundred-acre City Park is a massive collection of park greens, willow and oak trees, two stadiums, botanical gardens, an art museum, *Storyland* for the kids, a lake, several golf courses, and more, all featuring New Orleans's telltale old-world style mixed with hints of bayou. In the mirror dimension, it's populated by one single structure.

The colony.

47.

The structure is massive, resembling a half-sized black and gray version of Australia's Ayers Rock—Uluru to the natives—an 1,100-foot-tall, six-mile-circumference sandstone formation. While Uluru rises from the flat plains of the bush, the colony is partially concealed by the tree-laden swamp, but it still manages to tower above it all. While looking at the closer, smaller colonies, I'd missed the one looming over them all, so big that it could be mistaken for landscape. I hadn't seen it before because the cemeteries and smaller colonies kept my eyes on the right side of the road.

Several of the large six-winged centipede Dread lazily circle the perimeter above the colony. A few mothmen, just distant specks, flit about, entering and leaving the colony via one of many tunnels hewn in the outer wall. The base of the structure is hidden from me by the vast swampy jungle that is the mirror world.

I slip my vision back into the real world. Instead of the colony, I see a straight road leading to the New Orleans Museum of Art, which, with its Roman-style columns, looks like it would be more at home in Washington, D.C. Three colorful banners hang behind the columns like an afterthought, added when someone realized the parliamentesque style of the exterior didn't scream, "art." Beyond the museum is the park: endless trees with hints of buildings hidden within. I shiver at the idea that all the people using this park, to play with their children, watch a game, or experience a little culture, are surrounded by Dread, unknowingly moving through the heart of a colony. Of course, this also explains the many reports of hauntings within the park, and probably accounts for the prevalence of black magic, voodoo, and New Orleans's dark history.

"Are you okay?" Cobb asks, helping me to my feet.

I take stock of my body, paying attention to aches and pains, and find . . . nothing. "I'm . . . fine."

He shakes his head, unbelieving. "Don't be macho." He reaches for my head, pulls me down to inspect the fresh stitches. "What the . . . this was a good gash, right?"

I never saw it, but remember the tree branch cracking against the top of my head. "Allenby stitched it?"

"But there's no wound," he says. "There's just a line of stitches. Lift your shirt."

I comply and am surprised when Cobb flinches away from me. "Holy shit."

I don't look. I can't. "I'm still changing, right? Becoming like them?"

He shakes his head. "You look . . . normal. Better than normal." He motions for me to look, and I do. My body is healed. No cuts. No scrapes. No scabs. And the vast amount of bruising covering my torso is gone. I might not look like a Dread, but this kind of healing must come from them. And now that I'm thinking about it, I feel stronger and more energized than I can remember feeling ever before.

"So, I guess that's good news," he says, then changes topics, perhaps sensing my discomfort. "What did you see?"

"You don't want to know." I head for the back of the SUV, pop the back door, and open my gear bag.

Before I can dig inside, Blair steps up next to me, holding out a smartphone. "Still nothing on the local tracking app, but—"

The phone chimes. We all flinch.

"It's got a signal," Blair says, as I take the device.

A map of New Orleans centered on my location is displayed on the phone. A blue dot reveals my position just before the bridge. Using my thumb to move the map, I scroll upward. A red dot appears, dead center in the park, on the north end of Scout Island, surrounded by Couturie Forest, the only swath of forested bayou to be found in the city. On the plus side, she's not far. Not so much on the plus side, it's going to be a slog reaching her, in either dimension. Despite the good news of locating Maya, something confuses me. "This is more than a half mile away."

Blair looks at the screen without taking it from me. "It's a GPS signal. She's in our frequency again."

Why? I think. *What's the point in bringing her back and forth between frequencies?* The answer is obvious. "They're luring us in."

"Us?" Cobb says, sounding as worried as I feel. None of us wants to walk into a trap.

"Lyons," I say, hoping I'm right. "They don't just know he's coming; they want him, too."

A sudden chill runs over my arms. The hair stands on end.

"Do you feel that?" Cobb asks.

I don't answer.

I can't.

The Dread are near, and some unlocked primal part of my mind says that if I acknowledge their presence, they'll acknowledge mine in a horrible way. It turns out, that is their intention, regardless of my actions.

"Ah!" Blair shouts. He's by the driver's-side door, looking about for something that isn't there, or at least can't be seen. I haven't shifted my vision yet, but I know we're not alone.

Suddenly, Blair starts scratching at his face, like someone's just dumped a bucket of spiders over him. He shouts and hops, his cries warbling. For a moment, I'm paralyzed as fear spilling over from Blair takes hold. He screams, and it feels like a lightning bolt has struck my chest.

I hate fear. Even more than the Dread, it is my enemy.

"What do we do to our enemies?" The voice belongs to a drill sergeant, his words returning as a fresh memory.

"Kill them," I respond, both in memory and in the present. "Fucking kill them."

I step around the side of the SUV, weapons forgotten, fists clenched, but am stopped by Blair. He levels a shaking handgun toward my chest. I nearly retreat but manage to stand my ground. A subtle shift in the frequency of my vision reveals Blair's company. A Medusa-hands has its tendrils buried deep in his head while a mothman hovers above, whispering waves of fear into the man, the little limbs lining its abdomen shaking frantically. It's a lethal combination, and for a moment, I think it's directed toward me. But it's not.

"Don't let . . . them . . . win." They're Blair's last words before he turns the gun on himself and pulls the trigger.

The sharp report of the handgun and sight of this brave man's brains bursting out of his skull both increase my fear and galvanize my course of action. With a scream, I charge, lunging at the Medusa-hands as it retracts its tendrils from Blair's head.

Halfway to the creature, I realize I probably should have taken a weapon. But it's too late now. I'm committed. And I'm not exactly defenseless.

I leap into the air, painlessly shift my body between frequencies to the world between—which I note is a mix of Dread world trees and New Orleans city—cock my fist back, and drive it into the bottom of the thing's triangular head, impacting the yellow vein-covered flesh beneath two of its four eyes. The impact is solid. The monster flails away, sliding smoothly at first but then stumbling and falling. As it falls, the black shroud covering its lower limbs falls aside, revealing at least twenty thin, triple-jointed legs, all ending in sharp barbs.

If the Medusa-hands were alone, there might be time to rush back and grab a gun or knife, but it's not alone, and there isn't time. Before I can even think about what to do next, a wave of fear tears through me, scouring away my fragile emotional defenses the way a nuclear blast would remove my skin.

But I stand against it. Maybe it's the rage, or the part of me that's becoming more Dread, but the fear, while powerful, doesn't completely undo me. It does, however, freeze me in place, all my energy going toward overcoming the effect.

A memory surfaces. My first kiss with Maya. In the rain. Like some Hollywood cliché except soaking wet, cold, and out of our heads in love. I scream, but not in fear. A vibration moves through my body, curbing the effect of the Dread's influence. When my mind clears enough, I turn my eyes up toward the mothman. It's ten feet away, four wings beating, hovering beyond the reach of my physical body. Its four red eyes narrow almost imperceptibly. I'm not sure the things can even blink, but this slight expression of emotion, of doubt, in the monster's split-pupil eyes is the last bit of encouragement I need.

I stand on shaking legs. Feels like I'm lifting a bulldozer. But the harder I fight, the less the weight, until suddenly I'm free. Like a snapped elastic band, the wave of fear generated by the mothman pulls back, the whisper cut short, pursued by an attack of my own. My body buzzes with energy, static whispering-roaring. And the Dread . . . it arches back and clutches its head. The furiously beating wings go rigid and the monster plunges from the sky, landing in a heap. The pain of pushing fear is gone, replaced by a sense of power.

I slip back into the real world for a moment to check on Cobb.

He gasps at my return, clutching the side of the SUV, Faithful in hand. But rather than take the weapon from him, I decide to enable his recovery from the fear effect. "Cobb, I'm going to bring one of them to you! Get ready for a fight!"

"What?" he shouts in what I now easily recognize as terror.

I slip back into the world between and bend over the recovering mothman, grasping its arm, which is covered in short, thick hairs. I pull it up, lean back hard, and propel the thing toward the side of the SUV. Before letting go, I force it into our reality and slam it into the vehicle. It crashes against the door and falls to its hands and knees.

Cobb shouts in surprise, jumping back, but quickly realizes the monster isn't affecting him. With a battle cry, Cobb raises the machete into the air.

I don't watch it come down. Back in the world between, the Medusa-hands is back on its many feet, scrabbling toward me over pavement, tendrils stretching for my head. There's no avoiding it—by conventional means. I slip fully out of the world between and dive forward, passing through the Dread's location. I feel a chill through my body, but nothing more. I roll to my feet just as I re-enter the world between, coming up behind the not-so-spry Dread.

I sweep its legs out, snapping some of them. The Dread retreats fully to the mirror world before hitting the ground, and I follow it. The thing lands with a splash, much of it now underwater. I jump on its chest, which feels like thin skin wrapped over bony nodules, and stare into its yellow eyes, seething with anger.

Tendrils snake out of the water, glowing yellow, eager to influence my thoughts. I don't give it the chance. A burst of fear, sent into the thing's core, makes it shake. The four eyes widen, just a touch, the rectangular pupils narrowing.

Armed only with my bare hands, I flicker out of the mirror dimension, punch downward into empty space, and then reappear atop the Dread. My fist has occupied the space at the center of the Medusa-hands's head, shifting matter, destroying stationary matter. I splay my fingers out, further shredding the Dread's brain. The monster spasms and falls still.

Then I'm back in the real world, no trace of gore coming with me. That is, until I turn around. Bloodred gore, glowing and inhuman, covers the street. The mothman lies beside the SUV, hacked to pieces. Cobb stands there, breathing hard, Faithful in hand.

"Feel better?" I ask him.

"Much," he says.

I push the mothman parts back into the mirror dimension. I don't think seeing a dead bogeyman lying in the streets of New Orleans would do anyone any good. When I'm done, I turn my attention to Blair. He's definitely dead. I place my hand on his chest, offer up a prayer for his soul, and hide his body beneath the waters of the Dread world swamp.

"We can come back for him if we survive this," I tell Cobb, upon seeing his surprised look.

I take one last peek into the mirror world, watching the colony and the air around us. There are no reinforcements en route. The two Dread must have stumbled across us, perhaps having recognized the significance of a vehicle made of oscillium. I heard no whispering communications, so they must have acted without instruction and without calling for help.

With the bodies taken care of, I have Cobb drive back toward the art museum and pull over. Checking to make sure we're alone in both dimensions, I head for the back of the SUV, gear up, and then approach Cobb, who is sitting behind the wheel. He rolls down the oscillium-tinted window. "Don't get out of the car. Don't do anything to draw attention to yourself. Better yet, pretend you're asleep. You're not going to feel the Dread unless they make physical contact with the car, so don't assume they're not around just because you can't feel them."

He nods. "I'll be ready when you need me."

"Cobb . . . thanks. For everything. You've done more than anyone could have asked."

"Protecting life is my business," he says, and I realize that in many ways, Cobb is my antithesis, not just physically but professionally. Where I once took life for a living, he saves lives. And I've learned a lot from him, about facing fears, about honor and trust. He's a better man than me. Unfortunately, I'm not yet done taking lives, and that probably means that Cobb isn't going to get a break from saving them.

"Besides," he says, "helping you has been the most important thing I've ever done. No matter who you used to be, I know who you are now, and am glad you took me captive."

I smile. "I did give you beer."

He nods. "You were a conscientious captor."

I pat the door twice and step away. "Stay safe."

The window begins rising up. "I'll be here when you need me."

I give a wave and step off the road. The slap of my boots on the sidewalk picks up speed as I jog, then fall silent as I move to the grass, hoping no one spots the armored man with two handguns, an assault rifle, two trench knives, and a machete, about to wage a one-man war.

48.

The distance from our parking spot in front of the art museum and the edge of Couturie Forest is nearly two miles if you follow the roads. I reduce the distance a little bit by cutting through patches of woodlands, but there is no avoiding the several bridges along the way, not without going for a swim. The trip takes me fifteen minutes, all of it spent in the real world, visually monitoring nonhuman frequencies. Each passing minute weighs on me, drawing my eyes to my watch again and again, watching the timer tick down to ninety minutes. So far, I seem to be moving unnoticed. The colony is either not afraid of being attacked, has defenses I can't see, or is too busy elsewhere. Possibly all of the above.

I stop at the edge of the forest, hiding in the foliage at the center of a roundabout, the last real road I'll see once I enter the trees on the other side of the street. But before I do . . .

I take out the phone and, with a swipe of my finger, open the tracking app. Maya's position hasn't moved. She's definitely inside the colony, smack-dab at the middle but still registering on the GPS, still in this world. Or maybe it's just the tracking device. They could have taken it out of her. I slip into the mirror world and watch the signal disapear. I nearly drop the phone in the foot-deep water when someone speaks behind me.

"You shouldn't be here."

The voice is distorted, gravelly, and deep.

Hair on the back of my neck stands tall. *The Dread can speak?*

"Turn around," says the voice. "Slow."

I comply, hands out to my sides.

I'm expecting a bull to lunge or tendrils to stab into my head, but the figure behind me, while all black, is human. The oscillium armor matches mine, but the man's head is covered by a mask and he's wearing the round goggles that allow humans to see the Dread, which is generally a very bad idea. He's pointing a sound-suppressed handgun at my chest, shaking slightly.

"The hell are you doing here, Crazy?"

While I'm glad he's not Dread, the gun at my chest makes me nervous. I have a hundred memories of situations far worse than this. In them, I'm cool, collected, and thinking about solutions, most of which are absolutely nuts. Now, I'm having trouble looking away from the weapon's barrel.

"Who am I talking to?" I ask.

The man tugs his mask up with one hand.

Katzman. And he looks even more nervous and squirrelly than me. So much so that I ask, "Are you okay?"

"Fine," he says, his head twitching. "It's the drugs."

I nearly ask, but then remember BDO, the mix of benzodiazepine, dextroamphetamine, and OxyContin. Makes the user feel invincible, even in the face of the Dread. That's when I realize something startling: *Katzman is in the mirror dimension.* He's got split pupils just like me.

He sees the surprise in my own Dread eyes and explains. "All of Dread Squad can move between worlds."

"How long have—"

"A year. We've been training for D-day ever since."

A year... I think, but ask, "D-day?"

"Dread-day. You were supposed to lead this little party, but last I heard, you had lost your marbles, which makes me wonder, why are *you* here?"

"You mean, why am I not dead along with Winters?"

He's genuinely startled by this news. They had, after all, been his colleagues. Maybe even friends. *"What?"*

"Lyons had her killed. They tried to get Allenby, too."

"Bullshit."

"Right after they restored my memory." Speaking of which, I have a few memories of Katzman. There was a time when he served as my second in command. Dread Squad had been my idea. "You were already on your way here."

He doesn't argue the point. The timing fits.

"I don't blame you," I say, letting him know I'm not here for personal vengeance. I hold up the phone, allowing him to see the tracking app. Since we're in the mirror world, there is currently no signal, but it's still a useful visual aid. "Maya is here."

He shakes his head. "She's dead. Lyons wouldn't lie about that."

"There's a chance he believes it," I admit, "but there is no proof.

He could be wrong. Why would they bring her here if she was dead? Also, he killed Winters and tried to kill the only family he has left. I'm not sure he's seeing things clearly."

"Doesn't matter," he says. A thick vein on his forehead twitches. "We're doing the right thing, and I have my orders. We've been planning this for—"

He closes his mouth.

"Planning *what*?"

I follow a subtle shift of his eyes and see the strap of his backpack. When he looks back at me, his face is twitching, his mouth pulling in and out of a smile. He shakes his head like he's having a seizure, but I think he's refusing to answer.

"Destroying the colony might not stop a war with the Dread," I tell him. "It could start one." I don't know if Allenby's position on this matter is right or not, but if it hasn't been considered, it needs to be.

You'd think I just told him I was pregnant. He gapes at me, the drugs exaggerating his reaction. Then his mouth slaps shut, and he pulls himself together. "We're *already* at war. Once upon a time, you knew that, too."

I can't argue about what I don't yet remember, so I ask, "What if everything happening around the world is a warning? A shot across the bow."

"A warning?" He scoffs. "For who?"

"Who do you think?"

It takes him only a moment to understand. "You think all of this . . . everything that's happening around the world is a warning—for Neuro?"

"Not Neuro. Lyons. You don't find it odd that they took his daughter? That they brought her here, to his first target?"

"If she really is here, they're using her as a human shield. They're desperate. Afraid. We can end this today, and they know it."

I don't argue. He could be right. The tracker signal might just be exposed to let us know she's here, because they think that will stop Lyons. "I'm not going to get in your way, and I hope you're right about all this, but if there's a chance she's alive, I need to at least try to get her back. How long do I have? Give me that much."

"Ten minutes," he says.

"Until what?"

"Let's just say we're going to do this the old-fashioned way first."

"World War Two–style," I guess, and he doesn't argue. "Just tell me it's not a nuke. There's already enough talk of that."

"Not a nuke," he says, lowering the weapon. "What do you mean? Enough talk about what?"

"Russia's nukes are on standby. Ready for launch. Which means everyone else's are, too. The president issued an ultimatum: stand down in . . ." I look at my watch. "Eighty-six minutes, or else . . ."

"Or else what?"

"Nothing good," I say, "but it won't take much more than a nudge from the Dread to make sure it's the worst possible 'or else.'"

Katzman slowly shakes his head. "Then we need to stop them. Here and now."

He's right about the here and now, but the method is still up for debate.

"Look," he says, "if you're not out of here in ten, you probably never will be."

"Anyone else I should worry about?" I ask.

He shakes his head. "We're holding a perimeter until the—" He closes his mouth, realizing he almost gave me too much information. "No. Beyond me, it's just th—"

His eyes go wide. The weapon comes up. I dive to the side as he fires, feeling the zing of bullets passing inches from my cheek. My roll is slowed by the foot-deep water, but I manage to get my feet under me and draw my sound-suppressed P229 handgun. Too bad it's the wrong weapon for this fight.

Four bulls charge through the swamp, their massive mouths hanging open with worm-covered tongues, and green veins pulsing with energy, charge through the swamp.

"Oh my God," Katzman whispers. "Oh my God." The drugs do the trick. Katzman stands his ground and fires. The problem is, he's about to become a mirror-world pancake.

49.

Katzman pulls what I like to call "a Hudson." Like the space marine in *Aliens,* he stands his ground, firing and swearing, out of his mind while still inflicting damage. The drugs he's on keep him from running but, mixed with adrenaline, are sending him into a manic state of mind.

"Fuck you!" he shouts, emptying his handgun and *dropping* it into the foot-deep water. To his credit, the bull he emptied the clip into is now limping and slow, but it's still coming. "Fuck you!" he shouts again, unslinging his assault rifle and spraying an arc into the rushing monsters.

While he's doing a horrible job killing the Dread, he *is* drawing their attention, freeing me up to act, which I appreciate because, unlike him, I'm not on any fear-fighting drugs. I suppose that's lucky for both of us. It wouldn't do anyone any good if we both fearlessly drained our magazines into a mirror-world swamp and died.

I consider leaving Katzman to face the bulls alone. Both fearless versions of myself probably would. I wouldn't have been afraid to let Katzman face the result of his actions, even if he died. The ramifications of making a morally wrong choice wouldn't scare me. For the first time in my life, I'm afraid of what the choice will mean for my soul. So I take a moment to think about it and come to a different conclusion.

I draw my Vector assault rifle, take aim, and pull the trigger. A full magazine peppers a Dread bull's gaping mouth, shredding its innards and dropping it to the ground. A cascade of water explodes around the monster, sending sparkles of luminescent blood in all directions.

One of the three remaining bulls turns on me. The other two, including the limper, continue toward Katzman, who is struggling to reload his weapon. I have no trouble switching out the magazine but am very aware that if it takes a full magazine to take down a bull, I'm going to run out of ammo very quickly.

Think, I tell myself with just seconds left to act. The Dread bull is thirty feet out, pulsing fear at me. A wave of nausea sweeps through my body. I fight it, strategizing. Aiming. I pull the trigger, popping out a three-round burst. Bright green geysers of blood erupt from the bull's right knee, just as it puts its weight down on the limb. With a warbling shriek, the creature spills forward and to the side. An arcing wave of water rises up to engulf me, but I slip out of the mirror world and move forward. The bull flinches as I reenter the mirror world, weapon already aimed down. Once again, I realize the Dread, while physically superior, are not accustomed to combat—their world is all about mental warfare, psyops. Nor are they used to using multiple dimensions in a strategic way. It catches them off guard. While they are comfortable with humanity in general, they've never seen anything like me, and it scares them, maybe as much as seeing a Dread in the flesh would frighten a person.

I pull the trigger. At close range, all three rounds punch through the eye on the side of the Dread bull's head, shoving the monster's brains out the other side. A plume of glowing green bursts into the water beneath the bull's head.

A cough of sound-suppressed gunfire, drowned out by the wild shout of a man, turns me around in time to see Katzman's final moments. The bull, even if it was shot and killed, will plow into him.

Katzman's eyes go wide as even he realizes this. And then, he's gone.

Not dead. Just gone. Returned to his home dimension. The bull passes through the empty space.

But Katzman, perhaps just reacting without too much thought, slips back into the mirror world before the bull has fully passed by. As a result, he reenters this world partially *inside* the bull. His legs are yanked up off the ground and pulled along for the ride, but the bull, whose gut has now been replaced by a panicking man, spasms and topples forward.

Get out of there, I think.

Katzman's kicking legs suddenly disappear, leaving a gaping wound behind. The bull splashes into the water, dying slowly, mewling pitifully. I feel a moment of pity for the thing and then turn to the fourth bull, already injured by Katzman. It has pulled up short, shifting its four eyes between the most recently slain bull and me.

Whispering fills the air.

I take aim and fire, emptying the clip. The bull flinches back, turning to run, but then a round hits something vital and the monster falls limp. The whispering stops.

Katzman hasn't returned, so I chase him back to the real world. He's on the ground, coughing and sputtering, panicked and furiously wiping at himself. He's covered in bright green gore, viscous slime, and chunks of Dread organs. When he left the second time, he took a lot of the Dread with him. I note that he's not writhing in pain, either. They've trained for this but, unlike me, lack the ability to push fear. I volunteered to be the first guinea pig. I remember that now. The rest of Dread Squad must have received a more-refined batch of the DNA-altering retrovirus, leaving them more human than Dread, not fully both like me and not able to do everything I can.

"Calm down," I tell him. He flinches when I stand over him but slows down a bit when he sees it's me. "They're all dead."

I don't know if he hears me. The foul-smelling guts covering his body have his undivided attention.

"Katzman!"

His eyes lock onto mine, wide with fear and drug-induced focus.

"You can leave all this behind when you slip between worlds." I've been leaving the blood of dead Dread behind. Katzman, it seems, needs a little practice. "Just focus on what you want to take with you. Everything else will stay behind."

He stares for just a moment, then gives just a hint of a nod.

"Go to the world between first," I tell him.

"I—I don't know if I can."

I crouch beside him. "I trained you better than this. I remember that now. Just focus." I shrug. "Or you can stay covered in gore."

Strands of florescent-green slime dangle from his arms as he lifts them up, inspecting his situation. His stomach lurches. He's about to wretch. I put my hand on his back and do the job for him.

Faster than you can blink, we're in the world between for just a moment, and then back home, leaving the gore behind. Katzman is dry again, patting his body down with his hands. We're surrounded by lush green willows.

"Thanks," he says. "For helping."

I move my hand from his back to his shoulder. "Tell me what's going to happen."

"I can't."

"I could have left you," I say. "I saved your life."

After a beat, he says, "It's a weapon."

"What *kind* of a weapon?"

He looks unsure for a moment, but a word bubbles out of him when I lean a bit closer. "Microwave."

"I thought microwave weapons in the field were a no-go."

"Not guns," he says.

"A bomb," I say, finishing the thought. "A microwave bomb."

I knew that microwaves and radiation affected all frequencies of reality, but I never considered what that really meant. I don't really consider them now. They kind of just barrel into me. "When we detonate a nuclear warhead, the effects are felt in both worlds."

"You have a point?" Katzman asks.

"They're bluffing," I say, more to myself than Katzman.

"What?"

"They don't want to push the president into nuclear war with Russia. It would kill them, too." I want to believe this, but I'm not sure. The Dread, and the way they think, is still a mystery. "But if they're pushed . . . If we leave them no choice . . ."

His forehead scrunches up, the depth of his wrinkles exaggerated by the drugs flowing through his veins. "You think they'd kill themselves, intentionally?"

"Maybe the World War Two Japanese analogy is more appropriate than Lyons knows? We really know nothing about the Dread. Who's to say they wouldn't rather burn with us than let us win?"

"What's the alternative?" he asks. "Let *them* win? Screw that."

"Can you stop it?" I ask. "If you had to?"

He shakes his head. "There are five of us carrying microwave bombs. Only one of us actually needs to make it inside."

"That's what's on your back?"

He nods. "But it's really just a backup plan, in case the assault goes FUBAR."

Assault? Lyons *is* out of his mind. "Why?"

"Honestly . . ." He looks me in the eyes. "I'm not entirely sure."

That Lyons hasn't shared all his plans with the man in charge of Dread Squad is a little disconcerting. What could he be planning that a loyal soldier like Katzman might not carry out?

I look at my watch. Eighty minutes until the president's deadline. This is going to be tight.

"How much longer?" I ask.

He points to the sky just as a faint whine begins to tickle my ears. I look up and to the north. A massive black Boeing C-17 Globemaster III flies toward our location. The huge transport plane is capable of transporting over a hundred paratroopers, dropping them into a battlefield with precision.

Then I see another.

And another.

Lyons's covert, black operation is about to leap into the light of day and into the arms of the Dread.

50.

"Can you delay the assault?" I ask, already suspecting the answer. He barely gets a chance to start saying no when I wave off the question and sprint across the traffic circle.

As I leave the macadam behind and enter the lush Couturie Forest, he shouts to me. "They're going to shoot anything that moves! Don't be in there when they arrive!"

I don't doubt his warning. Amped up on BDO he very nearly shot me. Probably would have if he hadn't recognized me. The potent mix of chemicals might help a human being overcome the Dread fear, but when there's nothing to be afraid of, the drug sends the user into a manic state. Facing the Dread without it allows me to think more clearly, which is essential, but it also leaves me more susceptible to their effect, not that the drug did wonders for Katzman's performance.

My pace is slowed by the thick vegetation growing everywhere, but it's faster than slogging through the mirror-world swamp. I speed up when I come across a footpath headed in the right direction, but I only get thirty feet before I'm struck by an invisible freight train. I'm lifted off the ground and thrown into a marsh.

I've pulled my body and armor fully out of the mirror world. They shouldn't be able to strike me, unless . . . They're pushing themselves into this world, just for a moment, just long enough to strike.

I stand, dripping wet, and ready my weapon. Then I slip between worlds, ready to put another Dread out of its misery.

Nearly waist-deep in water, I spin, searching for my target and finding absolutely nothing. I'm just a hundred feet from the curved wall of the colony. Like all the others, a series of arched entrances lines the outside wall, one every fifty feet, raised up just above the waterline by an earthen ramp. Like the city of New Orleans, the Dread colony is barely keeping the water out.

After ten seconds of searching for whatever struck me, I lower my weapon. I'm alone, and the entrances to the colony are un-guarded.

A sudden fear clutches my insides.

I spin again, ready to pull the trigger, but am still unable to find a target. With my back to the colony, I search the black, hanging tree line. I see no motion, just bunches of dangling, wet foliage.

A ripple of water rolls past. I spin and fire three shots—into the water.

I'm being toyed with, my fear increasing with each close en-counter.

But encounter with what?

I get my answer as the water, twenty feet away, bows up and slides away from a rising form. Four yellow eyes, all atop a flat head, break the surface. Four feet closer, a snout rises, blowing a hiss of air through two nostrils.

I take a step back. If you'd asked me, at any point in my life up until yesterday, whether I was afraid of crocodiles, the answer would have been no. Today the answer is yes; I am most definitely afraid of crocodiles. I don't think that what I'm seeing is an actual croc, but if it's anything like the man-eating reptiles, the distance between its snout and eyes mean it's absolutely massive. A good thirty feet long.

The eyes glide toward me, unblinking, moving through the water so smoothly that they don't create a ripple.

A metallic-purple light slips through the water to my right. It's in my periphery, but I don't look at it. I can't take my eyes off the monster coming my way . . . until it stops. The submerged Dread freezes, going perfectly still.

I glance at the purple thing moving beneath the water, gliding casually between the Dread and me. I can't see much of it, but it looks like a long fish of some kind, its shiny scales reflecting the sky's purple light.

The four large yellow eyes flicker and turn black as the thing slides beneath the water.

I'm paralyzed, watching the fish swim by, oblivious to the dan-ger. When it's ten feet in front of me, a shadow moves over the fish and snaps down. Water explodes into the air. The Dread rises from the water, thrashing the fish back and forth. Its eyes flicker brightly, and then the veins covering its wide body come to life like irides-cent bulbs, blinking before going solid.

I was wrong; it's not like a crocodile at all. It's much, much worse. The mouth is not only deep, it's also six feet wide, with long black teeth that extend outside the mouth, like a Venus flytrap. The long teeth have skewered the fish. It clamps its wide jaws shut, the teeth forming a perfect seam, carving the prey in two. Rough, glossy skin, crisscrossed with yellow veins, rises up from the curved mouth to the four eyes, allowing them and the tall nostrils positioned *halfway* to the end of the mouth to protrude from the water without revealing the rest of the beast. The body is, as I suspected, at least thirty feet long, but with legs long enough for it to stand clear of and move quickly through the water, though I suspect its flat tail can move it through the water pretty quickly, too.

In the ten seconds it takes the Dread croc to trap the fish, sever it in two, and swallow the halves, I've completed my assessment of the thing: I'll be just another meal in fifteen seconds if I don't kill it in the next five. Knowing my magazine is half empty, I eject it, letting it fall into the water. I slap in a fresh magazine with three seconds left.

A loud snapping sound turns the monster's, and my, attention upward.

A Dread Squad soldier descends through the sky, held aloft by a black parachute, no doubt made of oscillium. He's made a mistake by entering the mirror world before landing. He's probably too hopped up on BDO, itching for a fight. But he has captured the croc's full attention for the moment.

I look into the real world. Three Globemaster transport planes circle the forest. Small black figures spill from the back of each, which are like deer shitting pellets rapid-fire. Soldiers, hundreds of them, fall toward the ground, their black parachutes deploying at what appears to be the last second, and then, one by one, they wink out of reality.

They're parachuting *into* the mirror dimension. It's not a bad tactic, really, except for the fact that they're going to land in several feet of Dread-croc-infested water. It's going to be a bloodbath, on both sides, as the drug-amped soldiers unleash their weaponry.

Not that I'll be around to see it. When the soldier sees the Dread croc, he shouts a battle cry and opens fire. The croc responds by submerging itself and pumping its tail. It surges through the water, heading for its new target.

I can do this, I think.

And then the water to my right flickers yellow.

Then to my left.

Flickering yellow bodies, each as big as the first, come to life, one after another, stretching as far as I can see. I stand still as the light grows brighter.

No, not brighter . . . Closer to the surface.

An array of glowing yellow eyes emerge from the water.

Feeling what I believe is an appropriate level of earth-shattering fear, I burst back into the real world and sprint forward like a white Bronco from the LAPD. It's just a hundred feet to the colony entrance.

Luckily for me, all eyes in the mirror world are now looking up.

After a few-second sprint, I slip back into the mirror world, just feet from the colony entrance.

Screams erupt behind me.

A Dread croc rises out of the water, propelled by its powerful tail. Its wide jaws open and shut over a man's pelvis. He's severed in half. While his legs are carried away, the still-living man shrieks, out of his mind, his insides splashing into the water below, acting as chum. Monsters swirl through the water, vying for position as the nearly lifeless man continues his descent.

Two Dread crocs make their move at once, each catching a portion of the man, silencing his screams. It's only a second before a fresh holler of pain fills the air, this time followed by the staccato roar of automatic gunfire. It's followed by more and more, nearby and distant, thunderously announcing the arrival of the human race in the mirror world. The battle for the colony's perimeter has begun.

I want no part in it.

I step inside the colony and am greeted by darkness. It lasts just a moment as my eyes adjust, faster than before. Luminous veins line the walls and ceiling, providing a rainbow of ebbing, flowing light. I take the smartphone out, intending to check on Maya's position, but the screen is black and dripping water. I put the device away and move quietly, stepping down the smooth, curving grade. It appears this giant colony is designed similarly to the smaller one in New Hampshire, spiraling downward toward an open core. This means I've got a long journey ahead of me. I think the colony is a thousand feet across, give or take a hundred, so the perimeter is just over three thousand feet. After just my second revolution, I'll have traveled a mile. At a run, I can cover the distance in six minutes, but there's no way to know how many circuits the tunnel makes before reaching the bottom. As wide as this colony is, I might have to run several miles before reaching the bottom, and I don't have a half hour to spare.

But what other choice do I have?

Throwing caution to the wind, I run, setting a fast but not impossible pace. The air smells rank, strong with ammonia, and stings my throat, but I haven't passed out yet, so there is still enough oxygen to keep me alive.

Three minutes into my run, I haven't encountered any resistance.

At three minutes, five seconds, everything changes.

Alcoves line the walls on both sides up ahead. In the last colony, these spaces contained empty nests. With all the action outside and the commotion in New Orleans, I expect the same here. As I run by the first alcove and glance inside, I realize my mistake. With the closest thing I've seen to a stunned expression on a Dread, a bull watches me pass by.

For a moment, I think it's just going to let me pass, but then a cry rings out, echoing down the long, curved tunnel. The bellow is joined by a sharp surge of mental whispering.

Barks from far beyond me and all around me explode into the air.

I pour on the speed, instinct telling me to run from the danger while my intellect screams at me to stop because I'm simply putting myself deeper in Dread territory. My flight into danger is short-lived. Thumping feet turn my attention to the left.

A Dread bull charges from an alcove, head down, perfectly aimed. A wave of fear explodes from the monster, tearing through my body, twisting my insides like a giant corkscrew spiraling through my gut. Its four eyes lock on target, confident. With only a second before impact, I freeze in place.

51.

Muscles spasm and lock.

Lungs seize.

My body becomes a statue. Unflinching. Unmoving.

And still alive.

I can't see, smell, hear, or feel anything. That's not entirely true. I feel cold. And wet. Trapped tightly on all sides, moisture seeping past my clothing to chill skin.

And then I realize I have felt this before. Once. Locked in stone beneath the New Hampshire colony. I've left the mirror world and leapt into the very earth itself, which in New Orleans is so far below the water table there is actual water pressure. It squeezes in on me. My nose stings as water fills it, threatening to spill down my throat and fill my lungs.

In a blink, it's all gone. The pressure. The water. All of it. I'm standing in the Dread-colony hallway, no doubt looking a little stunned. The charging bull has just passed. It felt like minutes trapped in earth, but was just a second, maybe two. The bull, having already lunged, sails through the air and into an adjacent alcove, where it careens into the back wall.

The thick but papery structure is no match for the bull. The wall tears, spilling the Dread into the space beyond. Hundreds of thin layers flutter away, butterflies in flight. A gaping hole is all that remains.

As more bulls leap from their alcoves, turning their heads back and forth, huffing and sniffing, most craning their gaze toward me, I run. For the hole. Not only is it my only hope of escape, it should also help me avoid an entire revolution around the colony, saving me a long run.

I sprint toward the alcove as the floor vibrates from the impact of so many charging bulls. It's full of bunched-up debris, swirled into black nests, intertwined with glowing veins of surging liquid.

A head rears up.

I pull Faithful from my back, prepare to swing.

But there is something in the Dread's four large eyes that holds me back. Not anger, or hate, or even fear.

It's innocence. A complete lack of understanding of the danger I present. It merely regards me with interest. *A baby*, I realize, and then, *a litter*, as more heads rise. Dread or not, the rules of engagement still guide my hand, and I will not attack children. I have, in the course of my career, had my fair share of collateral damage. People get in the way sometimes. But the CIA is careful to avoid situations with children and would never actually target a child. Even secret agencies and assassins have standards. But what moves me most, when my eyes meet those of the Dread calves, is how they remind me of my son.

It's no wonder these bulls are out of their minds trying to kill me. I've just invaded their home and put their children in danger. The trouble for them is that I'm just the start. If any of Lyons's drugged-up Dread Squad get inside, they'll kill everything. But this *is* war, and the Dread are ultimately responsible for what happens here today. They should have moved their young from this place. Even if they didn't know Lyons had targeted this colony, they've been inside my head. They must have known that *I* would come when Maya's tracker signal began transmitting.

Hopping from the edge of one nest to the next, I bounce through the alcove and leap toward the ruined wall. I'd like to say this is the old fearless Crazy shining through, but it's really just desperation, hoping that whatever lies on the far side of this wall is less horrible than a horde of enraged, rhinoceros-sized parents.

The remains of the papery wall slap against me but provide little resistance as I plow through. When I see what lies on the other side, I shout in surprise, not because some horrible monster awaits me, but because I've jumped out over a twenty-five-foot drop.

It turns out that my fear of falling is misguided. As soon as my descent begins, it's arrested. The bull, now clinging to the backside of the wall, has caught me. With a grunt, it slams me into the wall, once, twice, and then a third time, rattling my thoughts and snapping me into the past.

I'm with Lyons. It's my first day with Neuro and he's just told me his long-term game plan for the Dread. He's looking for a way to repel them and end what he calls their "reign of terror." Without their influence on mankind, he thinks wars will end, fear will dwindle on a vast scale, and global peace will be attainable. He speaks with energy bordering on frantic. Hungry. Unable to understand the subtlety of fear at the time, I missed the cues that this fight was personal for him. It always was. The "better world" scenario he presented me was simply justification for a vendetta that began during his childhood.

He asks my opinion.

"In my experience," I say, "the only way to truly squelch a long-time enemy is to beat them into submission and then reverse the flow of influence. Post–World War Two Japan is a good example."

His only response is a smile.

The memory fades as my body is jolted.

In the present, my new surroundings overshadow the surprise I feel about the World War II analogy, of which Lyons is so fond, which originated from me. I'm hanging sideways in the grasp of a bull as it lumbers down the tunnel on three limbs. Its grip is solid, my arms pinned by my sides. I'm stuck, and while the creature is moving in the right direction, I have no intention of reaching Maya as a prisoner. The sound of several sets of heavy footfalls tell me the bull is not alone. I open my eyes and confirm it. Bulls, pugs, and Medusa-hands. Too many to count. A mob of Dread is escorting me downward.

Seeing no other option, I pull what is becoming the oldest trick in my "How to Outwit and Outmaneuver Dread" book. The quick plan is to hop into my home dimension and, while the bull is distracted by my disappearance, return to the mirror dimension, push the mob back with a burst of raw fear, put a few Desert Eagle rounds into the nearest alcove wall to weaken it, and dive right on through. It's insane. I recognize that, but it's all I can come up with, so I go for it.

The plan falls to pieces the moment I put part 1 into action. I'm expecting moist but solid earth to hug and hold me in place. Instead, I get a raging torrent of flowing liquid. I'm yanked forward instead of stopping, spun around, slammed against hard stone, and lost in complete darkness. Near drowning, I reenter the mirror world, hoping to be tossed to the floor farther up the tunnel. But that's not what happens.

When I enter the mirror world, I'm not deposited on or above the tunnel floor, I'm embedded *in* it. Half of my body is locked in stone. The other half, lying sideways, is left to flail. With my one free eye, I see the bulls snap to attention, snorting at my return. The closest of them raises its thick foot to stomp on me.

Choice is removed once again. I manage to suck in a breath through my one free nostril and then slip back into the raging waters far beneath New Orleans. I'm swept away again and brutalized by the tunnel walls. I cling to the air in my lungs, but the rapids seem determined to knock it free. Bubbles burst from my mouth with every jarring impact.

Then my head hits something solid.

I black out for a moment.

When I come to, thrashing awake, the air in my lungs is gone.

I reach out, hoping to feel open space, but how will I know it? Moving so quickly, spun like a pebble in a rock polisher, how will I ever recognize that fraction of a second of cool air being different from the water?

I won't.

But then, as the raging water takes a sudden turn, I do.

I don't feel the change so much as I *hear* it. The gurgling, muffled cacophony of flowing water suddenly echoes in a tight space. The sound actually hurts my ears when I take a gasping breath, and then another, calming the burn in my lungs.

The surface beneath me changes to a slanted solid stone. I can't see it, but I claw my way over the surface, fighting to pull myself free of the devil's waterslide. The gap is small, just enough room for me to pull my torso out of the water, but my legs remain wet, tugged at by the rapids, urging me to my death.

The rock bed is cold against my head, but so very welcome. With each breath, my body normalizes. *Calm down,* I tell myself. *Start thinking. What options do I have?*

Option one, check out the mirror world. I peek without moving my body between worlds. It's a surreal experience. I'm encased in the black earth, but it's intercut by thin, glowing roots. I don't clearly understand the Dread or their world, but one thing is for certain, it's all connected. Free to move, I look in all directions and see the same thing: earth, right in my face. I rub my eyes after returning to the pitch black of the underground river. I only looked into the other world, but my brain still thinks there's dirt in my eyes.

That means I've got only one possible escape route—the river. And who knows if it will even bring me in the right direction, or if I won't have my back broken against a stone five seconds after getting back in the water?

But no choice means no choice. As much as I don't like the idea of being battered by the rough waters or drowned beneath them, I refuse to give in now. Sure, I could survive in this little world for a time. I'd die from hypothermia long before I starved, and I certainly wouldn't die from lack of water. But I'd be letting the Dread have Maya without a fight, and if she's still around when Dread Squad arrives . . .

I sigh and roll onto my back.

Despite the pitch black, I close my eyes and see Maya. Her smiling face. Her hands full of pumpkin gore, dripping freshly pillaged seeds. I wait, holding a carving knife, while Simon digs his small hands into the open gourd. He's the closest thing I've seen to a true Halloween zombie. I smile at the memory. It returned recently, probably while I was being bashed about in the river.

"I'm sorry," I say into the darkness, warm tears on my cheeks. *Dammit. I miss that kid.*

Miss his mother, too . . .

I see the entire past year, spent in SafeHaven in a new light. Despite the company of Shotgun Jones and Seymour, I was very alone. My lack of fear and memory prevented me from experiencing it, but now that my memories are returning and I'm able to feel a full range of emotions, remembering that time is heartbreaking, lonely, and desperate. Looking back even further, I can see that my life before Maya was much the same. I depended on myself, leaned on my fearless nature to get past struggles. My own strength carried me. But when I found Maya, that changed. I was still fearless, but she removed the burden of self-sufficiency. She became my strength. So did Simon. Is that why I ran away? Despite my lack of fear, did I become powerless? Weak? It's not impossible, and I certainly wouldn't have feared ridicule for my mental retreat.

But Maya wasn't gone. She was alive. She needed me. Why would I have run from that? I still can't remember, but I'm not going to make the same mistake again.

I'm coming, baby. I'm coming.

I roll myself into the river, content that it will either carry me where I need to go or usher me into the afterlife, from which I will do my best to torment the Dread for what they've taken from me.

52.

Relaxing my body, I let myself drift through the darkness. I'm slammed into a side wall as the river takes a sharp left turn. That's when I start checking the mirror world for open spaces. With my vision in the Dread world, I watch scores of glowing vein-roots slip past in a blur.

The river batters me. The pain radiating through my body hides the burning in my lungs for a minute, but the ache to breathe soon dwarfs all other feelings. I crush my lips together, clinging to the air, absorbing each and every molecule of oxygen.

I hold on, watching the subterranean mirror world slide past. I'm seconds from taking a breath. Seconds from death. Lights appear in my vision, choreographed twirling spots. It's almost beautiful. But I can't see. My view of the mirror world slides to black.

No time left, I think. *No time!*

I shift.

And stop.

Locked in densely packed earth. The only question left is, Which world do I want to die in? *Home,* I think. I'll drown and be carried by the river, maybe ejected out to sea and found by a fisherman. Maybe I'll even get a burial. Or perhaps just feed a hungry shark. As my mind starts to slip away, I focus on returning home one last time.

Then I feel it.

My foot can move!

I slip back into the river, am tugged down hard. My mouth opens, sucking in water. As my body goes rigid, I shift back to the mirror world, leaving the river behind but carrying along the water in my lungs.

I fall for just a moment and land on a hard surface.

My body shakes, desperate to breathe, but unable to because of the water in my lungs. Still fading, it takes all of my remaining energy and willpower to roll myself over onto my hands and knees.

My gut and chest convulse silently, pumping water out of my lungs, and then I can breathe.

That first breath of ammonia-scented air fills my lungs so hard and fast that I sound like a broken trumpet, announcing my arrival to any Dread in the area. I cough hard, expelling more water and the precious air too soon. My vision fades. I breathe hard a second time. The veins covering the floor beneath me come into focus. After three more gasping breaths, I get my body under control, still heaving but no longer doing an impression of a wounded wildebeest.

It's a full minute before I can even think about doing something other than breathing. And then a single thought explodes into my mind. *I'm alive.* Rewinding recent history, I faced down four bulls, a swamp full of Dread crocs, and angry Dread bulls, and I was nearly drowned and/or buried alive.

And *I survived.*

While feeling fear. It's a nice confidence boost, if only for a moment. My body aches from head to toe. While my past wounds might have healed, I've taken more than a few beatings since arriving in New Orleans. I can't see all my wounds in the dark, hidden by armor, but I can smell my own blood, even after my cleansing dip in the river, which means I'm bleeding from somewhere. Identifying the source of the wound would be easier if the pain wasn't everywhere.

I push past it all, for Maya, and for myself. I'm not Crazy anymore, but that doesn't mean I'm not still the deadliest son of a bitch the Dread have ever encountered. I look around and find myself in an alcove. It's short and full of small nests. *A pug den,* I decide. I crawl slowly toward the opening and peek out. Nothing in either direction. No sound. No wave of pressure to indicate the approach of a Dread welcoming party.

I step out and take stock. I've got Faithful on my back, both trench knives on my hips, and the Desert Eagle holstered on my chest. The weapon can fire underwater, so the river trip is no concern. I swap out the magazine for a fresh one and slide the big gun back in place. I've managed to evade the Dread defenses. With stealth back on my side, using the hand cannon would be counterproductive.

I pull Faithful from its scabbard. The black blade is almost invisible, not just because of the dim light, but because it doesn't reflect the light. Still, I can feel the chisel-tipped blade's weight in my hand. I head left, following the path ever downward. At the top of the colony, the tunnel's curve was almost imperceptible, always far off, but here it twists around so tightly that I can't see more than fifty feet ahead. I hug the right wall, moving quickly and quietly but checking every alcove and nest for signs of life before tiptoeing past.

Despite my efforts at stealth, the thump of my boots on the hard-packed floor feels loud. The colony is silent.

Did they abandon the colony? It seems unlikely, but if the Dread mole can burrow as well as I think it can, there could be a network of tunnels connecting all the colonies in New Orleans.

Or maybe I'm in one of those other colonies? Could the fast-moving river have swept me out into a neighboring colony? This could also be a tunnel between colonies, though that seems un-likely. The continual curve suggests a colony . . . but is it still the right one?

I stop.

The tunnel levels out ahead. A fifty-foot-tall arching entryway stands to the right, just before the tunnel's end. Whether or not this is the right colony, I've reached the bottom. Remembering what I found inside the main chamber of the New Hampshire colony, I slide Faithful back into the scabbard and draw the Desert Eagle. It lacks the ridiculous power of the 20 mm sniper rifle I used to drop the Dread mole, but it can shoot a round through twenty-five watermelons and drop anything short of an elephant in one shot. With nine rounds in the gun and nine more ready to go, I should be able to punch a sizable hole in just about anything I encoun-ter—I slide up to the archway and peek around—except for maybe that . . .

I duck back, considering my options, which are fairly limited. I can fight and die. I can run, and probably die. Or I can give up . . . and die. Running, while perhaps my only chance of survival, isn't an option, because as dire as the situation is on the other side of this wall, I saw Maya. There's no way in hell I'm going to leave her. I came here for Maya, and if I'm going to die, I want her to know that I'm me again, that I remember her and that I came for her. That, at least, will provide a little closure before I'm slain.

I step around the archway into full view and stop. My eyebrows slowly rise, cresting halfway up my forehead. The Dread . . . nearly a hundred of them . . . are all looking right at me.

So much for not being noticed.

The chamber resembles a coliseum with staggered seating, wrapping around two sides, stopping before a second archway on the far side. Dread of all types, including some I've never encountered, line the benches. I feel like I've just walked onto the field of a football stadium, only no one is clapping and the opposing team is straight out of a nightmare.

Against every instinct, I take another step forward. Then another. By the third step, I've managed to insert a little confidence into my stride. I head for the center of the chamber, where Maya is being held. She's framed by two of the largest Dread I've seen, only smaller than the Dread mole. The behemoths look almost elephantine, but where their trunks should be are writhing masses of short, pale tendrils resembling a bull's tongue. The tendril length tapers up the thing's head, forming a line between its *six* eyes and a moving mane along its back. Its massive body pulses with green blood and ripples with muscles. The jaws, which split at the bottom, stretching a translucent sheet of flesh between the sides, are slung open like a baseball catcher's open mitt. I turn my attention away from the giants—the mammoths—and back to Maya.

She's conscious and watching me with red, swollen eyes, but her mouth is clamped shut. At first I think they've frightened her into silence. Then I see the wriggling tendrils of a Medusa-hands behind her head. It must sense my attention because it skitters out from behind one of the mammoths, slowly wrapping even more tendrils around Maya's waist.

Behind all of this, a squirming mass of tentacles, each as thick as my thigh and nearly fifteen feet tall, rises into the air. I know they're connected to a Dread mole hidden beneath the surface, but I can't help see each of them as a separate living thing. Given the thickness of the tendrils, the beast beneath this chamber must be huge. The word "kaiju" comes to mind. If such a thing got loose in the world of humanity, they'd make movies about it.

I stop halfway between the archway and Maya. I glance back, confirming what I already suspected. The exit is blocked by six bulls, four Medusa-hands, and a pack of wary pugs. I won't be leaving.

"Don't be afraid," Maya says, and her words, clearly those of the Medusa-hands controlling her, make me laugh.

Maya and the Medusa-hands behind her cock their heads to the side in unison. "You are afraid, are you not? This is new to you, Josef Shiloh. We have felt it."

"What do you want?" I ask, picking targets. My goal right now is to free Maya long enough to beg for her forgiveness.

"Understanding."

"I understand you well enough," I say and nearly open fire, but don't. If there is even a tiny fraction of a hope that Maya can survive this, I need to play along. For now.

"And then what?" I ask.

"Your help."

I laugh. I can't help myself. The idea of helping the Dread feels like Hitler asking me to help build a gas chamber. Why on earth would I help these bastards?

"We will free your wife," Maya says, referring to herself. "We saw your past. This is acceptable to you."

"Don't tell me what I think," I say, but know they're right. They peeked into my mind and scoured my memories before they'd been returned to me.

The mammoths take two long steps to either side. The thick tendrils behind the Medusa-hands and Maya turn toward me, snaking forward.

"We will help you remember," Maya says.

"Remember what?"

"*Everything.*"

"My memory is—"

"Fractured," she says.

"How do you know?" I ask.

There's no reply. They don't need to explain, because I have no choice. I have to do it. Killing a few more Dread won't bring Simon back, and it would be a fairly hollow revenge. But saving Maya . . . that is something worth dying for. I have no idea if the Dread can be trusted. Probably not. But picking a fight guarantees her death.

I slide the Desert Eagle into the chest holster, hold out my empty hands, and walk toward the outstretched Dread-mole tendrils. I stop a few feet short. "Fix her."

Maya and the Medusa-hands cock their heads in the other direction. "Explain."

"Undo what you did to her mind. Setting her free will do nothing for her if she spends the rest of her life in a hospital bed. Take away her fear."

Maya twitches suddenly, then stops and says, "It is done."

"Let me talk to her."

Maya blinks and then looks around, showing no reaction until her eyes land on me. Then she smiles the way she used to. She reaches out a hand. "Josef. You—" And then she's gone. Silenced again.

"That's not enough," I say, thinking twice about my gun. I'm being played. They'll never let her go. She could be dead already for all I know. A puppet. Before I can make a choice, it's made for me.

I turn around at the sound of a scuff. There's no avoiding the tendril that has snaked around behind me. It springs up like a striking snake, splitting open to reveal a mass of smaller tentacles that open and engulf my face. The twisting limbs cushion my fall, just a fraction of a second before they invade my mind for a second time.

53.

"You're okay," I say, bicep-deep in water, supporting my wife's weight. "Just breathe. Take it easy."

The midwife, Deb Fairhurst, standing on the other side of the birthing tub, stares at me, incredulous. I can see the question in her eyes. *How can you be so calm?* Despite having aided in hundreds of births, Fairhurst is amped. She's doing an admirable job of forcing calm into her voice, speaking slow, soothing words into Maya's ears while monitoring her vitals, which is harder now that Maya decided to get in the tub. But there are subtle cues revealing the tension she's hiding. She's sweating. Her forehead is locked in place, wrinkles unmoving. I wonder if, when she's older, her heavily wrinkled forehead will be a reminder of all the children she helped deliver, or if they'll just be unwanted lines? Her movements have become sharp and quick when she's out of eyeshot of Maya.

I flash Fairhurst a calm smile. Her forehead flattens a bit and she grins back, shaking her head. She'll ask how I stay calm later. It's the number one question I get asked. For now, there is a baby about to be born.

Maya crushes her nails into my shoulder, drawing the first non-calm expression from my face. If she's trying to share the pain of childbirth, she's doing an admirable job, though I'm sure it's nothing compared to what she's enduring, so I keep this thought to myself.

"Breathe, baby," I say. "Move beyond the pain. Control it."

"And push," Fairhurst says.

From my position behind Maya, I can't see what's happening, but Fairhurst's attention is suddenly more on the water than on Maya. In a moment, she'll have two patients to care for.

"Good," Fairhurst says. She's grinning now. "Just one more push and we'll be done."

As the contraction ends, Maya releases my arm, then taps it several times. I lean down to her.

"Go," she says.

"You want me to leave?"

"Go." She waggles a finger toward the tub beyond her basket-ball belly. "Watch."

That she's thinking of me in this moment of pain, not wanting me to miss witnessing the birth of our first child, is a testament to her strength, love, and selflessness. I kiss her wet forehead, slide my arms out from behind her back, and move to the side of the tub, opposite Fairhurst.

"Anything I can do?" I ask.

"Just watch," the midwife says.

Maya tenses, gripping the sides of the tub. Her forehead fur-rows, but it's the only outward sign of pain I can see. She's doing this drugless, focusing her will and body, letting things happen naturally. I didn't think it would be possible, but here she is, over-coming pain I can only imagine and fear I will never know.

My jaw drops when a small, naked body appears in the water, flowing up and out of the water, carried aloft by Fairhurst's skilled hands. And then she says three words that put a permanent chink in my thick armor. "It's a boy."

Before this moment, if you had asked me if I wanted kids, I would have shrugged and said, "I don't know." I was indifferent. I felt happy when Maya told me she was pregnant, but wasn't moved by the news. I saw a child as just another one of life's challenges to overcome. Fairhurst announced the sex because we chose not to find out earlier. But something about those three words: "it's a boy . . ."

I weep for the first time since joining the military. It's just a single tear, but its presence feels like Noah's rainbow, a promise of something greater than myself, of continuing generations of Shilohs and . . . a son.

My son.

I reach for him and find only darkness.

I'm out of the memory, which was returned to me by the Dread mole. I can't see or sense the world around me, but I can feel it in my head. But why would it give that memory back to me? Of all my memories, that poignant moment reminds me of exactly what I lost. What the Dread took from me. And why I hate them. If they were looking for brownie points, they don't have a very good under-standing of what makes people tick.

An image begins to resolve. Another memory.

I'm walking with my son. Just the two of us, out experiencing the world, sloshing through a swamp. He steps up beside me, rubs his head into my side.

"Are you ready?" I ask.

"Yes."

"Your strength and courage honor me," I tell the boy.

He bristles with pride. "Now . . . let's go."

We move together, pushing through the mire until we reach the other side, where a desert awaits. It's flat, brown, and barren. But there has been activity here lately, and I've been tasked with understanding it. Walking casually, son by my side, we head for a collection of buildings. They're new but lack all the other things that normally indicate habitation—power lines, paved roads, and other types of infrastructure.

We stop a mile out, watching the activity in and around the small collection of buildings. And then, at once, the people there leave. A parade of vehicles heads north. Curious, I start toward the buildings but notice my son isn't following.

"What is it?" I ask him.

"I'm afraid," he confesses.

"No one will see us," I tell him. Though he is young, he understands this. He just hasn't experienced it yet. "You will be safe. They cannot harm you."

"But I don't like this place."

"And you shouldn't. But we have been asked to understand it. To ensure it is not a threat."

"Could it be?" he asks.

"They have sought us out in the past," I tell him. "But they cannot see the world as we do. They are limited and lost to emotion, conflict, and primitive thoughts."

"Like we were." My son is intelligent for his age, which is why the matriarch requested his training begin early.

"Yes," I say. "During the dark years, we . . . tormented these people. Made them afraid of us. And as you know, some of us still choose this path. But not me. And not you. Understanding is more important than control, and making them afraid of us only draws their attention. Our worlds are connected, but our paths must remain separate."

My son begins his reply but cuts the thought short with a huff.

His head snaps up, eyes wide. He's sensed something I missed. Danger. Intense and close.

Before I can give the command to run, a distant light blazes on the horizon. It locks us in place, blossoming in all directions, full of raw and terrifying energy, the likes of which I have never seen and have no knowledge about. As the distant buildings are enveloped by the explosive light, I feel warmth on my skin.

No . . .

I take hold of my son and return us both to the swamp. "Run!"

But it's too late. The energy rips into our world, boiling the swamp. Anguish fills me, not because of my blistering skin. I have been trained to withstand pain. It's my son's agonized wail that stabs my soul. He's dying, painfully, curled up in the flash-dried muck beside me. Before my vision fades, I catch one last look at my son, his sleek and noble domed forehead, his brilliant green eyes, now flickering. I send him on his way with one last push of affection. Then he's gone. No longer part of me.

Why? I think. *Why is this happening?* And then, connected to the matriarch, I send one last request: *avenge us.*

The memory ends as my life fades. But it wasn't my life. It was a Dread bull and his son. The location was the Jornada del Muerto desert, better known as the White Sands Proving Ground. The explosion, which I recognize from recordings made of the event, is known as the Trinity explosion. It was the United States' first test of a nuclear weapon. In 1945. That memory is seventy years old but still feels fresh to the mind of the matriarch. And now it's fresh in mine.

A new surge of memories begins, but, unlike the last, they're overlapping, snapping into my mind. I'm not just witnessing the events, I'm living them through the minds of the Dread, who are connected to the matriarchs. Sometimes it's individual Dreads, sometimes entire colonies. Bombs explode. Nuclear fallout poisons both worlds. Species of Dread I haven't yet seen, living in the oceans and on island colonies, are decimated by more than 2,011 nuclear tests and scads of accidents. I see Three Mile Island, Chernobyl, Fukushima, and the SL-1 meltdown in Idaho. There are also a number of less famous radioactive accidents in Costa Rica, Zaragoza, Morocco, Mexico City, Thailand, and Mayapuri, India. The stories of these events are well known in my frequency, but the human race is naive to the vast and horrible effects these events have on the Dread world. I experience these events the way every Dread around the world does. I feel the network of minds connected through the matriarchs. They are separate and with free will but connected and unified, though some—mostly immature youths— still act outside the network, following in the old ways of haunt- ing humanity.

The explosion of memories, coupled with the overwhelming emotions of hundreds of thousands of Dread cut down by human ingenuity and warfare, tears me apart.

It's no wonder the Dread would see us as a threat. We've been waging war on them since 1945. While test sites might be empty in our world, in the mirror world we're wiping out entire colonies.

Like I did.

The deaths I've caused, even in the past hour, weigh more heav- ily now. But they still killed my son and still have Maya, which means I would make the same choices. That Dread bull would have done the same for his son. But would the matriarchs do the same?

The matriarchs . . . I only have a vague sense of what they are, and I think the word is really just a loose translation enabling me to make sense of an alien memory. I suspect the Dread mole whose tendrils now embrace my still-senseless body is one of them.

Three new memories that belong to me begin to surface. They hit me all at once, snapping back into my mind. And they change *everything.*

54.

Darkness resolves slowly, giving way to dim red light, both from my surroundings and the ruby-colored flashlights attached to the sides of my head, allowing me to see without killing my night vision. I'm crouched inside an alcove near the bottom of a small Dread colony.

But it's not me. It's someone else. This is a recording. I'm watching it on a large flat screen from within Neuro. I'm overflowing with raw emotion, not only from what I'm seeing but also because it's been two weeks since the deaths of Simon, Hugh, and my parents. After two weeks of heartbreaking agony, funerals, and the commitment of my wife to a violent-offender psyche ward, all I was left with was a single question: *Why?* A thin trail of suspicion led me here, to Neuro's field-ops monitoring center.

The name of the man, whose voice I recognize, slams back into my memory—Colby . . . Rob Colby. He is hunched over a small black device, pressing a button. Colby is like me, born fearless and recruited to Dread Squad straight out of boot camp. He's just twenty years old and has no business inside a colony. I never met him, but I knew he'd been vetted by Winters and was being trained by Katzman. When he was ready for active duty, I would have finished his training, in both worlds. The device's black domed top begins to hum. Colby toggles his throat mic and whispers. "DS Home, this is DS Active, over."

"I hear you DS Active. You are on with DS Home and Bossman. Over." It's Katzman's voice on the other end.

"Copy," he says. "The TV dinner is cooking. Over."

"Copy that, DS Active. Let us know when you're out of the kitchen and clear, but be aware: if we do not hear from you in twenty minutes, we'll assume you're not coming to dinner and cook it without you. Understood? Over."

"Solid copy. Beginning exfil now. Out." Leaving the device behind, Colby makes his way through the colony, undetected, using a mix of traditional stealth—hiding his scent by smearing his body in Dread waste and ducking behind natural or Dread-made elements. And when that fails, he slips out of the mirror world, calmly waiting in solid earth while various dangers pass. Moving efficiently and without conflict, he exits the colony and then the mirror world, strolling away through an old cemetery. He even pauses for a moment, pretending to mourn by a gravestone. The kid is good. A natural. The kind of calm ability that can only come from someone born without fear.

"DS Home, this is DS Active. Over."

"We hear you DS Active. Over."

Colby stands and walks out of the cemetery, stopping by a black car. "I am out of the kitchen. Feel free to cook when you're hungry. Over."

Colby slides behind the steering wheel of the already-running car, the hiss of air-conditioning audible.

"Stand by, DS Active. Over."

"Copy that." Colby waits, tapping his fingers on the steering wheel.

"DS Active, this is DS Home. Bossman is requesting visual confirmation that dinner is cooked. Over."

Colby turns his attention to the empty cemetery, the camera mounted on his head revealing what he sees. There are fifty-odd gravestones spread out among tall pines and oaks. He shifts into the Dread world, taking the camera with him. In the dim purple light, a papery domed colony is surrounded by strange-looking trees, all of it covered by green veins. "Copy. Watching the oven now. Over."

"Stand by . . ."

It's just fifteen seconds before wisps of smoke seep through the top of the colony. Then the roof bursts into flame. Dread spill from the exits, stumbling, falling, grasping as their bodies are cooked and cracking, seeping bright fluids.

A microwave bomb, my present mind realizes, despite the weapon being unknown to my past self.

They fall into the swampy water, but there are no flames to extinguish. No amount of water can stop the microwaves blasting the area. In fact, the water around the colony has begun to boil. Inside sixty seconds, the colony has imploded. Not one of the writhing Dread has escaped alive. And then, the colony rises up again, shattering outward. A massive creature resembling a giant mole rises from the colony. It spasms hard, its back arching, and then spills forward, into the boiling swamp, as still and motionless as the rest of the now-dead colony.

"DS Home, this is DS Active. I have visual confirmation. Dinner is cooked, goose and all. Over."

"Copy that, DS Active. Come on home. Over."

Colby shifts back to the real world to find the cemetery in flames. The blaze is violent, swirling high in the sky and already leaping to nearby trees. "DS Home, this is DS Active, cooking also burnt the crust. I repeat, the crust is burning."

"Crust is burning," Katzman says. "Understood. Bossman wants to know if you were ID'd."

I'm expecting a negative reply, but Colby says, "Affirmative. I let one of those snake-handed bastards get a look at my face and gave it time to spread the word before putting three between its four eyes."

Why would he let the Dread ID him? my present self wonders, while the me in this memory seethes with anger. He's expecting something I don't yet remember.

Just then, Colby turns and looks into the rearview mirror. Instead of a young man with close-cropped hair and a killer's eyes, I see a more familiar reflection—my own. Colby pushes his hands into the perfectly molded mask of my face and starts peeling it away. "Think this will keep him on board?"

"The Dread will seek retribution." The voice is new. Lyons. *Bossman.* He speaks more openly, unaccustomed to the cloak-and-dagger speak used by Katzman and Colby. "My daughter and grandson are safe here. But the others . . . Their loss will force a change of heart. I will mourn them, but perhaps it's for the best. After all, a wounded predator is far more dangerous."

As the memory starts to fade, I ask myself, *When did this happen? When!* I see the video's time stamp. This was *the day before Simon died.* Before Maya killed him. Before the Dread . . . avenged what Colby, *what Lyons,* did that day, in *my* name. The blood of my son, my parents, and Uncle Hugh, along with Maya's sanity, is on *his* hands.

The memory comes clear again, just for a flash, which is long enough to see Colby turn to the left and see a steaming, cracked-open, and bleeding mammoth charge between frequencies for just a moment and crush the young soldier. The mammoth is just a blur really, but I recognize it, and that Colby died for his actions that day.

A fresh memory replaces the last.

I'm in an office. Lyons's. He's ranting about the attack on our family. Fuming about how the Dread have just declared war. How he will do everything in his power to destroy them. He doesn't know that I know the truth. He doesn't know I'm seconds away from using the handgun tucked behind my back. But he quickly figures it out when I raise the weapon toward his head. "The Dread are not to blame for what happened. You brought this on our family. *You* killed my son."

Lyons stops his tirade and looks at me. I can see he's about to play dumb.

"I saw the video. Colby wearing my face. You killed him, too, you know." My finger slides around the silenced weapon's trigger.

He slumps and sits, the ruse up. His feigned anger melts away, replaced by honest despair and tears. "They weren't supposed to be there."

"What are you talking about?"

"Maya and Simon. They were supposed to be here. I *thought* they were here! They would have been safe."

"But they weren't," I say, but it comes out closer to a growl. "Because of you." I'm not sure if he thought this information would quell my anger, because while he might not have meant to get Maya and Simon killed, my parents, along with Hugh and Allenby, whom he knew would not be at Neuro, since he'd insisted they all take vacations, were clearly his intended victims.

Instead of begging for mercy, he digs his grave a little deeper. "The Dread have been waging a war against mankind from the very beginning, frightening us, keeping us afraid of the dark, of the unknown. You know what they did to me. All those years. And it's not just me. They've held us back and influenced history in tragic, murderous ways. Despite all this, you were going to walk away. The fearless killer who lost his taste for blood."

The gun in my hand raises from his chest to his head. "I was trying to protect *our* family. There are other paths to peace than war."

"My daughter made you soft."

I nearly pull the trigger, but am not yet done trying to understand. "You and I both know that their world has been—"

"I don't care about their world." He leans forward, fists pressing into his desk, face red. "I don't care how much they've suffered."

"You should," I say, and squeeze the trigger.

A pinch in the back of my neck stops me. As I slump to the ground and lose consciousness, I see Katzman standing above me, looking sullen. "Sorry, Josef."

The memory fades, picking back up a day later.

"Stephen, I swear to God, if you don't let me go—"

Lyons leans in close. "I am no longer Stephen to you, and you are no longer my son-in-law."

"What are you talking about?" I ask.

He works the wedding ring off my finger, nearly breaking the digit as I resist.

I try to slip into the mirror world, preparing myself for a drop. But it never happens.

He looks down at me, a mix of sorrow and anger in his eyes. "You don't think I would overlook your abilities, do you?"

"What did you do?" I ask. "Am I—"

"The DNA is dormant." He stands up straighter, as much as his hunch allows him to. "You no longer have the ability to move between worlds."

"I won't need Dread DNA to—"

"You won't *remember*. You're too important to actually kill, but Josef Shiloh is dead." He steps away from the table. "I sincerely hope that whoever it is you become will someday see me as a partner once more. Perhaps even a friend."

"*Stephen . . .*" I speak his name as a warning. Whatever he's about to do will have consequences.

"I'm going to forget you, Josef . . . and so are you. You've left me no choice." He walks away. "Good-bye, Josef." A drill spins loudly behind my head. A door opens and closes. I can sense the medical team around me but can't see anyone. A mask slides over my nose and mouth. Ten seconds later, the memory ends and Josef Shiloh is erased.

Realization takes the memory's place. I never *chose* to forget. The e-mail to Winters was fake. Lyons erased my memories. Erased my son. And Maya. My entire life . . . because I *opposed* conflict with the Dread.

I wake up in the mirror world. I'm on the floor. Two Medusa-hands stand above me. They no longer look threatening or concern me. I look from one to the other and ask, "What do you need me to do?"

55.

"Stand up," a voice whispers. I turn, looking for the speaker, but see no one. I'm still in the large chamber, surrounded by Dread. Maya is there, too, but now stands far to the side, still flanked by mammoths, but no longer controlled by a Medusa-hands. She meets my eyes and gives a very lucid nod. *Is she urging me to listen?*

I obey the voice and stand while two Medusas slide away from me. The thick Dread mole, or matriarch tendrils protruding from the ground, undulate slowly, very nonthreateningly. They're just ten feet away.

"Do you remember?"

I spin around, looking for the source of the whispered voice. My eyes widen with realization. The whispering is in my head. I can understand it now. I turn and face the tendrils. "Did you do this to me?"

"Your mind has been restored, but it is not you who is understanding our language; it is I using yours."

"Can all of you communicate in English?"

"Yes." The tendrils slow. *"Do you remember?"*

"Remember what?"

"Your life. All of it?"

I think for a moment. For the first time in a long time, my memory feels complete. I know that I'm Josef Shiloh, I remember my decisions, and the true sequence of events that led to the deaths in my family. I also remember my time as Crazy, and living in Safe-Haven, where I learned how to be compassionate and patient with broken people, and not just Shotgun and Seymour. Everyone, I realized during my yearlong stint in the loony bin, is broken to some degree, including me. Most people contain it, or drown it, but other people, like Lyons, are masters at hiding it. In the end, Simon's grandfather is really a man obsessed with war, whose very human fear of the unknown and childhood trauma at the hands of independently acting Dread pushed him to make a horrible mistake. It left him broken and has driven him to seek his own kind of retribution, blaming the Dread for his pain, both externally inflicted and self-inflicted. I'm not convinced the Dread *aren't* a threat, but where there are no doubt countless shades of gray, Lyons only sees black and white.

I don't know if the Dread mole buried beneath my feet can see me through those tentacles, but I nod anyway. "I remember." My thoughts drift to the Dread bull memory at the Trinity nuclear test. "I remember everything."

One of the tendrils stretches out toward me in a nonthreatening way. An outer layer of skin peels back, unleashing a mass of smaller tentacles, similar to a Medusa-hands but tipped in glowing purple rather than yellow. The snaking things come right up to my face and stop. I don't flinch away, despite knowing what they're capable of. "What do you want me to do?"

"Remember . . . more."

"What else is there to remember?"

"History."

I'm not positive, but I think it means their history. Dread history.

"Why didn't you do this before?" I ask.

"You were still our enemy."

"And now?"

"You remember."

"I remember that you killed my son." A twinge of anger surfaces, but not enough to propel me toward violence.

"We have known you for a long time, Josef Shiloh. We have watched the man who did not fear. Such a curious person. You understand war. How they're started. And how they're prevented. You have been a party to both in the past."

The matriarch is right. My actions have both started wars and ended them. The . . . jobs I carried out affected thousands upon thousands of lives, both as a CIA killer and while working with Neuro.

"You are responsible for the deaths of many," the Dread whispers. "But you now have the opportunity to save even more."

Distant gunshots echo into the chamber from somewhere far away in the colony. My head snaps toward the chamber entrance, looking for danger and seeing none. The tendrils remain focused on me.

"*If* I remember . . ."

"Understanding is fear's—and hatred's—most powerful adversary . . . and it must be accepted willingly, not forced." The tendrils spread open, awaiting me.

I'm having trouble accepting that this ancient enemy of humanity is being genuine. The Dread *are* monsters, in every sense of the word, horrible, ugly creatures that have plagued mankind from the shadows. But we are not much different in their eyes.

"And if I don't?" I ask.

"You will lack the determination to do what you must, and both of our worlds will burn."

"You'll do it, won't you?" I ask. "Nuke the world?"

I feel the yes more than hear it. "You have felt the network that connects us all," the matriarch says. "You have seen what happens when a colony loses its matriarch."

I remember it clearly. All of the Dread connected to it die.

"I am the oldest of the matriarchs. Every colony, as you call them, is connected to me. If my life ends before another ascends . . ."

"Your world ends."

"I do not want to destroy your world, but . . . I will."

"I get it," I say. "Mutually assured destruction." It's the stalemate that has prevented World War III on multiple occasions. As bad as disagreements and hatred can be, no one wants to end all life on the planet. But the only way that works, is if both sides are actually willing to do it. If the matriarch feels its life—and all the Dread connected to it—is ending, it will, in turn, end humanity.

"I know it doesn't change anything," I say, "but I'm sorry. For what I did. For the colony I—"

"These are the harsh realities of the world we share. Conflict. Death. War. We will move beyond them eventually, but for now we must *both* accept what has happened and move forward."

"Forgiveness," I say.

"Yes."

I see my son. My parents and Hugh. I remember the way they made me feel, and the emptiness their departures left in my soul. But the matriarch shares this pain and more. Without either of us speaking a word, a weight lifts away.

"It is done," the matriarch says.

I glance at Maya. She's just watching, still lucid, almost hopeful. She's still gaunt and weak, but the look in her eyes . . . I see clarity.

"Are you okay?" I ask her.

She looks a little unsure, which, given her surroundings is understandable. "Better, I think."

"Do you remember?" I ask. I don't need to specify what I'm asking about. She knows. The sadness in her eyes says so.

"The memory is different now," she says. "Distant. Not me."

"It *wasn't* you." Maya's body might have thrust the glass downward, but she wasn't in control of it.

"I'm sorry I was lost," she says.

"We both were," I reply. While the Dread took her mind, Lyons took mine. Had both sides just left us alone, we wouldn't be here right now. I would have stopped Lyons before it got this far. "But we're back now, and I'm going to finish this, okay?"

She nods.

"I love you," I say, and look forward as tendrils wrap around my face. I've stepped into them before fully realizing I wanted to.

The past slams into my mind, but it's only vaguely recognizable, and slipping through my thoughts so fast that I can't get a clear image of any one moment. It's like all this information is pouring through a mental colander, leaving a residue and the occasional chunk of knowledge. A picture begins to form, and then a narrative.

The Dread are older than the human race, but not much older. They evolved in the mirror world, but as their senses took shape, they became aware of the world between, where they found evidence of the human race in the form of large inanimate structures—Stonehenge, the pyramids, the Great Wall of China— and eventually the world beyond. I see glimpses of now-extinct animals that predated humanity's rise. And then there are flashing images of Neanderthals and early Homo sapiens. Humanity was evolving, but so were the Dread. Most of the various species I'm familiar with hadn't fully developed yet. The Dread world was a chaotic place, sometimes spilling into the other worlds as wars and battles were fought *between* Dread.

In some ways, the mirror was an accurate reflection. While humanity fought for wealth and territory, the Dread did the same. Sometimes battles were fought in the same location, at the same time, amping the fear of men and more deeply instilling the hatred they had for each other. Mankind became more tuned in to the Dread, driven by increasing levels of fear, burying their dead in the earth around colonies, and sometimes offering sacrifices to the Dread, animal and human. The connection between frequencies became a strange, unknown codependency. Some cultures worshiped the Dread. Others demonized them. But as both sides slowly evolved, mankind began to sense the Dread more and more. What had been vague fear or a mere brush with the supernatural became actual sightings and rare physical encounters, especially when Dread, acting as disconnected angry individuals or bored youth, harassed humanity. The sensory ability to detect and later experience other frequencies that the Dread were born with began to emerge in the human race—it's how we feel their presence at all—and in a few thousand more years the Dread will have to share their world with humanity.

This realization led to a largely unified Dread world. While there were still small bands of Dread clinging to the old ways, pushing fear onto the human race, most Dread pulled back and formed a civilized society built around the matriarchs. Information was passed freely between all unified Dread. While the mirror world found peace in unity, the human race, long steeped in fear, continued to war. And they never truly forgot that there was another world just beyond their reach.

I see images of World War II. A word enters my thoughts: "Ahnenerbe," the title given to the group responsible for Nazi Germany's research into the occult. I see a laboratory. And a bell-shaped device. Two of them. The first . . . flew. The second opened a door. Exposed and frightened, the Dread made their first attempt at global manipulation, propelling powerful nations to unite against Germany. The technology was destroyed and forgotten.

Until recently. Technology, it seemed, would uncover the mirror dimension long before the human race's senses developed the natural ability. Enter Lyons and Neuro. Driven by his supernatural childhood torment and an impressive intellect, Lyons not only used technology to discover the mirror world but came to the partially correct conclusion that the Dread had, and were, influencing humanity. But without understanding why, he saw only evil, built up defenses, and set out to destroy the otherworldly enemy that terrified him. The following years were full of confusion for the Dread, not knowing how to communicate with Lyons without terrifying him and deepening his convictions.

Then came the first attack. The colony's burning was felt by all the matriarchs and broadcast to all connected Dread. Plans were set in motion, in both dimensions, resulting in the deaths of my loved ones. And then, I'm gone. No longer part of the story. Lyons became hidden, barricaded inside Neuro and a second location, which the Dread were able to infiltrate once—*two weeks ago*. One of the bats, which was attached to a Dread Squad soldier, made it inside the second location and overheard a conversation. A plan. Dread-day. It also saw a collection of devices every Dread could recognize after its image was broadcast by the matriarch Colby slew—microwave bombs. Hundreds of them. They would cook both worlds, but without radioactive fallout, the damage done to humanity's frequencies could be repaired.

The result of that intel is the current state of the world on the brink of destruction. Like humanity, the Dread have evolved, both physically and socially. A barbaric past has been replaced by a more logical present, and yet, like us, they are still capable of violence. Like most people, they would prefer alternatives and to be left alone in peace. But they're willing to burn the world if that's not possible. And they need my help, not because they're incapable of defending themselves, but because the actions I now take as the person who understands the truth will determine the fate of both worlds.

I open my eyes.

The tendrils pull back.

"What do you want me to do?" I ask.

"Choose," whispers the voice in my head.

I'm about to ask for clarification when an explosion rocks the archway entrance. Fifty heavily armed men, moving with the lethal efficiency of special ops soldiers, enter the chamber. They're followed by the last person I expected to see here. Lyons. My father-in-law. The man who would destroy the mirror world and, as a result, his own. But it only takes a quick look to see that he's no longer simply a man.

56.

Lyons strides into the colony's core, determination wafting from him. He's close to having his revenge for his childhood and the acts of violence against our family and to ending a war that he believes has been waged for generations but that, in truth, he began. But there's something else about him. Something different. A strange confidence, like he's already won. Given the amount of firepower the black-clad Dread Squad is packing, it would appear he's correct. If the Dread mole attempts to free itself from the earth, it will be cut down by RPGs, machine guns, and high-caliber weapons. Following the pack is Katzman, still carrying his backpack.

I don't know how many of these men are still outside. There could be hundreds of soldiers fighting out and around the colony, but that's not a concern at the moment. Aside from the microwave bomb strapped to Katzman's back, Lyons has all my attention. Not just because he's the architect of all this or because he's the one who stole my memory, but because I've gotten a better look at the man. He's changed. *Physically.*

The hunch is gone, as is the cane. Loose skin has been replaced by taut muscle. This is Lyons if he'd been a marine or a professional wrestler and twenty years younger. Maybe thirty. He's got a barrel chest, thick arms, and perfect posture. If not for the still-recognizable facial features and gray hair, I'm not sure I would have known him.

No one speaks or pushes fear or anything else. Both sides silently take stock of the other, forming strategies and picking targets.

Without a second thought, I do the one thing no one expects. "Lyons!" I try to look unruffled by his appearance and the knowledge of what he did to me and head toward my father-in-law.

Several of the Dread Squad members aim their weapons at me. They're hopped up on drugs, barely in control, and look confused by the appearance of a man. I hold out my empty hands so they can see I'm not armed, while simultaneously taking stock of the weapons I have in reach. The Dread left me with the two trench knives, the Desert Eagle, and Faithful. They took a big risk trusting me. I hope it wasn't misplaced.

"Stephen," I say, getting Lyons's attention.

Confusion fills his eyes, quickly replaced by surprise. "Crazy?" He steps closer to me, fearless despite knowing what I can do. And it's not without reason. He's nearly a foot taller than me now.

"Josef," I say.

"You . . . remember?"

"Everything . . . Dad," letting him know that our previous relationship is no longer a secret. I only called him Dad to rib him. He's always hated it. I hope the casualness of this old gag will lower his defenses. I wave my hand dismissively, even though I really just want to punch him in the face. But if I can get Lyons to listen, maybe back down, I am willing to delay the introduction of my knuckles to his nose, and to the rest of him. "You had to make tough choices. I understand that now."

He flexes his chest, watching me with predatory eyes. Dread eyes. "I know you better than that."

"Not anymore." I stop ten feet from him, within the reach of his men but not his meaty hands.

"Why are you here?" he asks.

"I came for Maya." I can see he's about to argue, so I point her out. She's two hundred feet away, between the two mammoths. "They took her to lure me in."

His surprise becomes suspicion as he seems to forget his own daughter. "Lure *you* in?" He turns those hungry eyes back on me. *"Why?"*

The Dread never said they were luring me in. It's entirely possible that she really is here as a human shield and to deter Lyons. When I was attacked earlier, I might have been seen as just another advance Dread Squad member. But when they caught me . . . the strategy changed. "To help me understand."

He turns away from me, casually looking at the Dread all around us. "And do you? Understand?"

"They're not what you think," I tell him. "They don't want a war. They—"

"Are monsters, Josef. Murderers. Of our family. Of countless others. They are little more than territorial bullies hiding in the shadows. They have nearly destroyed me. Twice."

I take a step closer. Weapons follow my movement, trained on my head. "It's more complicated than that."

"They got to you," he says.

"What?"

A smile forms on Lyons's lips. His teeth . . . they're black. "They got inside your head. Messed with your memories. Didn't they? Made you their puppet."

I say nothing because it could be true. Have I been manipulated? I suppose there is no real way to be sure. But Lyons quickly reinforces that he screwed with my mind first.

"You really are the perfect puppet, Josef. Your fearless nature made you quick to accept orders. You're not afraid to believe what you're told. You're quick to obey and slow to question. It's what made you the perfect assassin and the best man to handle the Dread. That's not the case anymore, as you can see." He motions to the men around us.

"The drugs will wear off."

"We have time."

Time . . . I look at my watch. "We have thirteen minutes." He says nothing so I fill in the blanks. "In thirteen minutes, the president is going to attack Russia's nuclear arsenal. When that happens, Russia will launch. We'll launch. And just to put a cherry on top, everyone else will launch."

"Then it's time we get started," he says. "Don't you think?"

"What's your goal, here? You kill the Dread, destroy a major colony, and then what? The Dread will—"

"Do nothing," he hisses. "I know what you think. That they'll push the president into some world-ending military action. That they've got their fingers on the button. And maybe they do, but there is a reason they haven't already hit that button. No one, not even the Dread, wants to cook the entire planet."

"They won't have any other choice."

"It's a bluff. They drew first blood, and now they're—"

"*We* drew first blood!" I shout. "*You* did. You destroyed their colony, cooked them alive. They have families, just like us. *Children.* And our family paid the—"

"You naive little boy." He looks down at me, hatred in his eyes. "They've been—"

"Evolving. Like us. Trying to understand. But mostly hiding from men like you. *And* me. We're as monstrous to them as they are to us."

He stares at me, one eyebrow cocked slightly higher than the other. "I am far more monstrous than you know."

A flicker of red illuminates his skin from the inside. He leans down so our faces are inches apart. "Everything you think you know is wrong. The Dread will not destroy both worlds. This will be a conventional war, and which side of the mirror do you think will win *that* fight?"

"You're wrong. I've seen it."

"When I destroy this colony, the control it exerts over the others will be severed. All of the Dread and colonies connected to this one will be lobotomized. You've seen it for yourself. How can the Dread hurt us then?"

"Preemptively," I say. "How long do you think it will take the Dread to push the world into nuclear war. Minutes? My bet is on seconds. You haven't seen what they can do. Not like I have."

Lyons shakes his head. "You're grasping. Weak. You shame yourself. The time for action has come."

"Is that why Katzman has a microwave bomb strapped to his back?"

He pauses to glare at Katzman, but the man doesn't notice. He's too busy looking at the silent Dread surrounding us. Lyons turns back to me, black smile returning. "If the big one doesn't come out to say hello, we're going to burn it out. We are not simply here to destroy, Josef. Today is our D-day. We are here to *invade*. And the best way to start an invasion is to kill the leadership. You know that. Then I'm going to wipe out the resistance, capture the weak, and turn the young against their own kind. They started a war with humanity, and now *they're* going to truly understand what that means. I'll destroy this place if it comes to that, but you and our enemy have underestimated my true intentions."

The full ramifications of the D-day name come clear. This isn't a simple assault, it's a beachhead into the Dread world, the first step of an invasion. "What about Maya? She'll be killed."

He glances toward Maya, his face softening a touch. "She has been dead for a long time. She is now as lost as you. I can see it in her eyes, just as I see it in yours. Death will be a mercy." He turns to his men. "Kill him."

I raise my hands as Lyons takes a step back. The men hold their fire for a moment. They probably didn't count on shooting a man with his hands up.

"Are you there?" I think, hoping the matriarch will hear my thoughts.

Whispering fills my head, much of it beyond my comprehension, but a single line is for me. "There is a natural cavern sharing this space."

"Get Maya out of here, please," I reply, and glance at my wife as though to say good-bye. "Thank you," I think to the matriarch as Maya is whisked away by a bull. It retreats toward the archway on the far end. She's safe. For now.

Me, on the other hand, not so much.

Lyons loses his patience. *"Kill him!"*

I slip into the real world and dive to the side, but it's unnecessary. The men and their weapons have shifted fully into the Dread frequency of reality. Their bullets can't reach me here.

And then, in a flash, they can. Five Dread Squad men wink into reality. I see them for a moment as they pop into the darkness, but then I'm blind. Rather than fight in the dark, I let my vision slip into the world between. Luminous veins, some as thick as a man, cover the walls. "You don't have to do this. You can still walk away." But then the five men, who must have also adjusted their vision, take aim and fire.

57.

The bullets pass through empty space. At least, I'm assuming they do. I'm no longer there. I've slipped back into the mirror world, taking a soldier by surprise.

I don't know who these men are or whether they have families or children who will miss them. But I do know they heard what I said: that peace is an option, that no one else needs to die. Maybe it's the drugs, or they've been brainwashed to not think, or they simply believe Lyons's Dread doctrine. I don't know. But I do know that they are still willing to threaten the safety of every man, woman, child, and Dread on this planet in service of my father-in-law. So when I act without hesitation, it's also without guilt.

The shock at my sudden appearance lasts just a fraction of a second. The soldier is already spinning his weapon toward me. But he's not quite fast enough, even pumped full of drugs. My fist finds his jaw, sprawling him back, directly into the path of a soldier pursuing me between dimensions. The falling man is nearly cleaved in two by the newly arrived soldier, who has shifted from the real world to the mirror world *inside* the other, destroying the matter that was the man's gut, cleaving a hole in his body just as I did the lab table back at Neuro. The falling soldier dies instantly and without a sound. The new arrival sees what has happened and screams. No one hears him, though. The chamber roils with the sounds of battle. Roaring, explosions, gunfire. Both sides have launched attacks.

I take a moment to look around, hoping to catch Lyons by surprise. But he's already moved beyond my reach, running—actually running—toward the Dread mole, which has yet to rise from the ground. A wedge of soldiers frames him, firing at everything that moves.

A second Dread Squad soldier shifts from the real world to the mirror right in front of me, spinning, assault rifle raised. Ready to put a bullet in my head. But he's too close for the assault rifle to be effective.

I grab hold of the still-hot rifle muzzle, pull the weapon out, twist it, and then slam it back into the surprised soldier's face. While he's stunned, I slip behind him and pull us both back to our home dimension, keeping my vision locked in the world between. The three remaining soldiers open fire, killing their comrade. While they continue the barrage, filling his oscillium armor with lead, I slip back into the mirror world and charge toward empty space. Hoping I've timed it right, I shift back, punching.

My fist connects with a man's face. I'm back in the cavern, and then I'm not. While the punched man falls, I dive and roll through the mirror dimension before shifting again, grabbing hold of one of the still-upright soldier's weapons, thrusting it up, and chopping him in the throat. While he starts to gag, I slip out of the real world once more, move to a new position, and return home again. I'm standing directly in front of the last soldier.

My strobelike assault, slipping in and out of view, slows the man, but the drugs keep him moving.

He discards his rifle and draws a blade, thrusting it at my throat. As the tip cuts a nick into my skin, I catch both of his hands in mine. We push against each other for a moment, maneuvering the knife away from and closer to my throat—that is, until I shift frequencies again, this time taking the man's hands and the knife with me. When I shift back, the now-handless man is screaming. I silence him by turning his own hands around and plunging the blade into his heart.

Taking a moment, I flicker in and out of the world between, leaving behind the blood on my hands, not because it's gross, but because it's slippery. I recover a Vector assault rifle and several spare clips from the fallen men. I then take the headgear from the man with a knife in his chest, clutched by his own severed hands. The black mask and round goggles make me look just like one of them. Just another Dread Squad. After a quick check of the rifle's chamber, I slip back into chaos.

The colony is a war zone.

More soldiers storm into the chamber, arriving in small groups. The Dread are being reinforced from the other side. Bulls thunder across the arena, taking streams of bullets before falling to the might of men. Men who are eventually going to run out of ammunition. Mothmen descend from above, tackling soldiers, tearing into them. Others simply carry the men up and release them, letting gravity do the rest. And still others are shot from the air. They're swift, but in the enclosed space, facing men who have trained to hit moving targets, they're dying more than they're killing.

A cloud of Dread bats swirls around the chamber. They're not attacking. They're panicking, swirling upward toward the ceiling and the many holes leading out. They're good for gathering intelligence, but I suspect they're closer to trained animals than to higher functioning Dread.

The two mammoths are making a mess of the human soldiers, kicking, stomping, and charging through the Dread Squad ranks. An RPG cuts across the open chamber, snaking a trail of smoke behind it. The projectile strikes one of the mammoth's flanks, detonating with a fiery explosion that sends a wash of gore over the men nearby. It also sends the remaining mammoth into a frenzy. Knowing what I do know about the Dread, I realize the two giants were probably friends. Maybe family.

An approaching buzz turns me around. A mothman descends toward me, clawed feet extended. I raise the Vector, but hold my fire and push a wave of fear at the thing while thinking, *It's me!* The thing swerves away, picking another target, but is shot down in a splatter of bright red.

Are my thoughts part of the whisper? The Dread whisper is now like a rushing wind. There are so many mental voices mixed together that I can't tell if there is any kind of actual communication getting through. The screaming on the human side of things isn't much different.

Until I receive a message loud and clear. A soldier punches my shoulder. "Weapons up, asshole!"

He rushes past me, firing. I shoot him in the back without a second thought. Then I turn on the rest of Dread Squad, pick a target, and fire.

Pick a target. Fire.

Pick a target. Fire.

I repeat the process five times before my treachery is seen by someone who doesn't receive a bullet to the head a moment later. Bullets chew up the chamber floor, then stop when I slip between frequencies, back to the natural cavern. I start running, slipping in and out of worlds, firing at soldiers as they try to adjust to my new position. It's an impossible task. Every time I leave the mirror world, I alter my pace and course.

The confusion caused by my interdimensional counterattack distracts at least a third of the Dread Squad in the chamber. It's just a moment, but it's enough for the Dread to attack anew. Charging forward, pushing a tidal wave of fear ahead of them, the mammoth and five large bulls slam into the enemy ranks, stomping, thrashing, and swiping with claws. Some men are trampled underfoot. Some find themselves crushed by massive bear-trap jaws. The rest are tossed about like juggling pins.

For a moment, the Dread have the upper hand.

But it's only a moment.

Two chain-fed M2 Browning machine guns, now resting on tripods, open fire from the far end of the chamber. The weapons unleash up to twelve hundred .50 caliber rounds per minute. That's like having rapid fire on the Desert Eagle and a nearly infinite amount of ammo. The thunderous roar of the two guns drowns out all the screaming, but the whispering in my head is still clear—and frantic.

As the mammoth and line of bulls are cut down and my presence is, for the moment, forgotten, I scan the chamber. Lyons is at the front line, his wedge of men now twice as long and two men thick. They're heading for the matriarch. I consider going for the machine guns, but the time it would take to reach them and take them out would mean leaving the matriarch at the mercy of Lyons. Were it any other Dread, I'd let it fend for itself, but the giant creature buried beneath this chamber is the key to life or death for our planet. If it dies, we all die.

Mind made up, I take aim at Lyons and fire a single shot, striking him in the back. He pitches forward but quickly stands upright. His armor absorbed the shot, but it should have knocked him to the ground and left him gasping for air. *I should have aimed for his head. Why didn't I aim for his head?*

For Maya. The man is still her father.

Lyons glares at me, oblivious to the danger around him, unflinching at the sound of gunfire, the closeness of Dread, and the fear they're pushing. Unlike the other Dread Squad members, who, despite the drugs, still flinch at the fear effect, Lyons appears to be impervious. He's fearless. And impossibly large. Powerful.

And . . . glowing. Radiating red from inside.

What has he done? Whatever it is, I'm going to undo it. And him.

I peel the mask from my head, let him know I'm still alive and kicking—and coming for him. And then I wink out of the mirror world and charge toward his position.

58.

I race through the cavern, alone except for the dead Dread Squad men behind me. The air is crisp, clean, and a welcome change from the tang of the mirror world. A distant roar reveals the underground river's outlet, which pours into the cavern, beyond my sight, no doubt flowing away, back into the earth.

Lyons had been a good hundred feet from me when I started running. If he's still pushing forward, he'll be within reach in just a few seconds. He'll be surrounded by his soldiers, too, but I really don't care.

At all.

Brief winks of light mark the arrival of the Dread Squad. Seven of them.

Not enough, I think. But then I remember what's happening in the mirror world. That he sent seven of his protectors says he realizes the danger I present. But he's still underestimating me. Had he really understood what I can do, he'd have sent everyone.

While the seven men take aim, I roar. Carried along with my voice, moving at roughly the same speed, is a whisper of fear the likes of which these men have yet to encounter. It's a gift, I realize, from the matriarch, and it's *painless*. The matriarch did a little more than return the last bits of my memory. While I can't feel the fear effect myself, I somehow know that it's on the level of what a Dread mole can produce. And I remember that feeling. It nearly broke me. No amount of drugs can overcome such raw, unfiltered terror.

I push it in waves, each invisible torrent crashing into and through the very souls of these men. I become their worst fears, in the flesh, rushing toward them. I'm so focused on generating this mind-numbing fear that I almost don't notice I'm also pulling the assault rifle's trigger, sending the last of my ammo into the seven men, ending their fear forever.

When the last of them drops in a heap, I stop, draw my Desert

Eagle, and slip back into the mirror world, intending to put a bullet in the back of Lyons's head.

Instead, I'm met by a thick fist, driven into my gut. I stumble back, pitched over, sucking air. The handgun drops from my grasp. Bent over, eyes shut, I can't see a thing, but I know everything has changed during my brief time in the cavern.

"I saw you coming." Lyons's voice is deeper than before. Stronger. So is his punch. "You always seem to find a way to surprise me, but not this time. It's your turn to be surprised. Your turn to feel fear."

When he says "fear," a ripple of energy flows through me. He's pushing fear at me, but not hard enough. I barely feel it. Still, he's adjusting to the change faster than I did. And in ways I didn't.

He's stronger, faster, all his previous ailments repaired, and then there's the glow radiating from under his skin like . . . veins of color.

Oh my God . . . The refinements he made to the Dread DNA that allow a human being to sense the world like a mirror-world resident were intensified, or perhaps lessened, with his own personal batch. *How long has he been changing? Did the alterations to his own DNA effect his mind? Is all of this a result of some kind of faulty rewiring? He wouldn't be the first person to have boosted aggression from a body-altering substance.*

"Look at me, son," Lyons says.

Catching my breath, I crane my head up. He stands above me, looking bigger and meaner than ever. He's nearly bursting out of his armor. Thick veins pulse with red light just beneath the skin of his neck. He's becoming more Dread with each passing second.

"I can see it in you. The fear." Lyons chuckles. "Look around, Josef. Your treachery has failed."

He's right about that. The only Dread left in the colony are dead or dying. That is, except for the matriarch, which still hasn't climbed out of its hole. Is it hiding? Knowledge surfaces, answering the question. *It's rooted.* The larger the colony, the older the matriarch. It's actually part of the colony, unable to rise up again, held in place by the colorful veins that feed everything in this world. If it leaves, it dies. And if that happens, the Earth dies on both sides of the mirror. The matriarch I killed in New Hampshire had been a youth, loosely rooted and inexperienced. It should have never left its colony. It would still be alive if it hadn't.

But staying hidden beneath the ground isn't going to help this subterranean behemoth at all. The Dread Squad numbers have been whittled down. A large number of the bodies littering the arena floor are human. But there are still forty of them, most uninjured, some aiming RPGs at the tendrils slowly warbling behind Lyons. Others are repositioning the machine guns on either side of the matriarch. If it rises, they'll cut it to pieces.

I am the last hope for both worlds now.

"You are not alone," says a whispering voice. The matriarch. She's still in my head. "Delay them."

I search the eyes of the Dread Squad soldiers, stopping on a familiar face kneeling down, opening a backpack. "If you set that thing off, you're killing the world."

Katzman pauses. Meets my gaze until Lyons's breaks it, saying, "Finish your job." The words propel Katzman back into action. He takes out a large black device with a black, domed top. The microwave bomb.

"We are liberating this world," Lyons says, "one colony at a time. And when they lose this colony, they'll lose control of colonies across the continent. They'll also lose control of the hundreds of millions of people they're affecting in North America alone. Don't you see what that means? Riots will end. The government will rein in control, easing tensions. We'll be *saving* the world. That you think otherwise is—"

"Educated," I say. "That's not how this works. The moment that bomb goes off, the matriarch will trigger nuclear Armageddon. You will destroy the world. And for what? Because you pissed your bed every night when you were a kid? Because the big, bad Dread made noise or moved things, made you feel a little screwy in the head?"

Lyons growls and flexes his fingers. The fingernails pop off, replaced by sharp, black talons. He's oblivious to the change.

"It doesn't matter what happened in the past," I say. "Genocide isn't an acceptable solution."

"*Genocide?*" He laughs. "They're not even human."

"I'm not sure any of us are really human anymore," I say, motioning to myself and the Dread Squad. "Have you looked in a mirror lately? Look at your hands."

He lifts his thick fingers up, inspecting them. He flinches upon seeing his sprouted claws. He looks confused, but it's just for a moment. Whatever discomfort he feels about his physical transformation is replaced by a wicked smile. The change has got to be altering his mind, too. This is no longer the Lyons I knew. No longer the man who was Maya's father. "I am becoming more than both races. I am . . . evolving."

"You're a monster," I tell him.

When he looks down at me, the sides of his head bulge, split with a slurp, and open, revealing a second set of eyes. "Monsters both."

"Sir," Katzman says. "It's ready."

"Start it," Lyons says.

"Don't!" I shout, but am quickly silenced by claws raking across my chest. The powerful and sharp-tipped hand tears the armor away from my chest, leaving faint, paper-cut-thin slices in my skin. Had I not been wearing the armor, I'd be missing my chest.

"Help is coming," the matriarch whispers in my head. "In the cavern."

Rippling energy courses through me. It's Lyons, pushing his fear, hammering it down on me like a weapon. I fall to my knees, clenching my fists, shaking and hissing through my teeth. A sob bursts from my mouth, embarrassingly loud.

"How does it feel? To experience fear after a lifetime of not knowing it?" Lyons steps closer, reaches out for me.

"They are ready and will follow your lead," the matriarch whispers.

"Actually," I say to Lyons, "I couldn't tell you." I turn my head up, not a trace of fear in my eyes, and smile. Turns out I'm a decent actor, though I have my short time as a fear-feeling person to thank for the authentic, trembling sob. Despite Lyons's inhuman appearance and increasing size, I feel nothing beyond the desire to beat him senseless. I didn't realize it at first, but then I picked up on the signs. Acting without thought. Disregard for bullets. A steady heartbeat. When the matriarch restored my mind, she didn't just return my memory but my fearless nature as well. "Surprise."

I slip out of the mirror world and into the real-world cavern. While I once again feel no fear, I have what might be the single largest "holy shit" moment of my life. And then I smile.

59.

The cavern is full of Dread crocs, all standing still, waiting.

For what?

For me, I realize. The matriarch has given me my own army.

There are at least thirty of them. Maybe more. The combined glow of their exposed yellow veins illuminates the space, allowing me to see the water-smoothed floor and craggy ceiling for the first time. The nearest of the crocs, a massive specimen, steps closer and leans its snout down. It's just a foot away. I can smell its warm, fishy breath. Had I still been able to feel fear, I might piss myself.

I reach out and put my hand on its head. "Let's go."

I push through frequencies, stretching the fabric that separates dimensions, and then, all at once, I pop through.

And I'm not alone.

In the time it takes to finger snap twice, the tide of the battle does a one-eighty. Back in their home world, the Dread crocs spring into action, lashing out, trampling and consuming the Dread Squad. There is resistance, of course. The drugged men fire their weapons, performing a mass "Hudson" killing of some of the crocs and each other in the confusion. But the battle is lost the moment we enter the mirror world.

I'm not sure if it's purposeful, but the Dread crocs leave Lyons alone—or rather, they leave him for me. While he's still recovering from the surprise attack, I draw both trench knives, leap forward, and drive the twin, foot-long blades into his chest.

He shouts in pain, staggers back, and falls to his knees. He seethes at me but doesn't say a word. Instead, he looks to his left, where a machine gun rattles away, the barrage holding back the wave of Dread crocs. The moment those bullets run out, the men holding that position are dead. But only one of them is the true danger. Katzman. He's leaning over the microwave bomb. I can't see what he's doing, but I suspect he's adjusting the timer. There's no getting out of here, and he knows it. They're going to kill us all, and maybe the rest of the world along with us.

And this is why you don't give bombs to men on drugs.

I pick up the dropped Desert Eagle and squeeze off a round. My aim is true, but the bullet strikes a passing Dread croc instead. My next shot strikes a soldier as he's tossed into the air, a human skeet. And then it's too late. Katzman is standing again, raising his weapon and adding it to the barrage holding the crocs at bay.

I run toward a croc, and when it sees me I mentally whisper what I want it to do. I have no idea if it is "hearing" me or under-standing me, but I need to close the distance between myself and Katzman, and I need to do it fast. When I was a kid, we had a dog named Kenobi. For fun, I would place treats on his nose and laugh as he snapped at it, launching the treat up and away. I called it a Kenobipult. What I want is the Dread version.

I leap at the croc and its head lowers down. When both feet land atop its broad snout, its head snaps up, either from reflex or un-derstanding what I wanted. Either way, the result is the same. I'm sent soaring toward Katzman . . . and the machine gun, which is now tracking upward toward my position. Before the first shot can be fired, I shift between frequencies, back into the real-world cav-ern, sailing through the calm, cool air.

This part is tricky. If I'm not as far as I think, I could take a bul-let the moment I return. I could end up inside solid stone or the jaws of a croc. So I try something new, adjusting the vision of a single eye. It's not like seeing the world between, where I experi-ence a little of both dimensions but neither fully. I'm actually see-ing *both* worlds simultaneously and separately, one with a human eye, one with a Dread eye. My shifting double vision is nauseating for a moment as my brain suddenly has two different visual feeds to process, but then the images unify and I see both worlds at once. Objects in the Dread reality take on a slight different hue, almost a glow.

I slip back into the mirror world just above the three Dread Squad men and Katzman. The first to fall is the machine gunner, when I shoot him and then collide with him. His body helps break my fall, but my body is also stronger, more solid, a point that is proved when the struck man doesn't get back up. The other two nameless soldiers spin to face me. One takes a bullet to his chest before he fully registers my appearance. The other is quick and manages to slam the butt of his rifle into my chest. The strike is hard, and painful, but the man has made a crucial error. As the blow shoves me back, I reach out, loop my finger around the trigger, and shoot the man, point-blank, with his own weapon.

Before I recover from the dead man's strike, Katzman is on me, kicking my hand and knocking the Desert Eagle away. In the brief moment when Katzman draws his leg back, I think of a dozen ways to kill the man, but I don't employ any of them. I need him alive to deactivate the bomb. Better yet, I need him on my side.

He strikes with an impressive two-punch combo. I block the strikes with my forearms and try to talk past the drugs, both synthetic and natural, pumping through his system. "You need to stop this."

"You said you were here for Maya," he counters. "I should have killed you."

His mention of Maya reminds me that I have no idea where the bull took her. *Is she still safe?* The distraction leads to Katzman clipping my chin. I block and dodge three more blows. "I saved your life."

Backed against the wall, I counter for the first time, striking his shoulder. He stumbles back, not noticing the ease with which my first and only blow found its mark. He's like a puppy harassing a mountain lion. As good at Katzman is, I was trained to kill men like him with a lethal efficiency he doesn't understand.

So I help him.

A quick series of strikes stumbles Katzman back, humiliating him more than harming him. He's defenseless against my speed, experience, and fearless nature, not to mention my increased strength and stamina. I bring the lesson to a close with a revelation. "I'm trying to save your life again."

He stands his ground but doesn't attack. Nor does he speak. He's waiting for me to make my point, or maybe he's just trying to figure out a way to beat me.

"The creature beneath this colony is called a matriarch, like the one I killed. Like the one Colby killed. But it is the oldest of them all and is connected to every colony around the world. If we kill it, we kill them all."

He starts to look hopeful. Like this is good news. I change his mind.

"Katzman, if it thinks it's going to die, that we're going to destroy their entire civilization, what's to stop it from killing ours? The microwave bomb will take time to kill it. It's massive. And underground. Plenty of time for the Dread around the world to instigate a massive nuclear launch. Is that what you want? To destroy *two* worlds? Is there no one in the world you want to protect?"

He blinks through the mania. "I—I'm married."

"Then let me paint a picture for you," I say. And, feeling a little bit like a news anchor, I begin. "Living in New Hampshire, your wife won't be one of the lucky ones. When the nukes drop down, she's not going to be killed right away. She's going to survive. For weeks. Maybe months. In a postapocalyptic, radioactive hellscape. She'll die slowly. Painfully. And alone. The human race, your wife included, *will* die horribly if you let this colony get cooked."

The image sobers him a bit.

He glances at the battle around us. It's winding down. The screams of men are fading. Somewhere in the distance, I hear the sounds of a struggle, but it will be over soon. The fate of the human race really does rest squarely on this drug-addled man's shoulders.

He glances left and right, a bit of fear in his eyes.

"Lyons is dead," I tell him.

The fear is replaced by surprise, but there is a trace of lingering doubt. "I don't know . . . He's—"

"I killed him."

His shoulders drop, signifying his compliance.

"How much time is left?" I ask.

"Ten minutes."

"Can you shut it off?"

"I think so." He crouches over the device. "And if not, I can just extend the countdown so there is time to dispose of it. Any metal container can absorb the microwaves if it's grounded, but—"

As his hands reach out, his body suddenly snaps rigid. Two long, black talons burst through his chest. A whispering squeal escapes his mouth, and then he's dead, face locked in a permanent expression of surprise. He's lifted up, dangling limply. Then, with a wet tearing, he's torn apart and discarded, falling in two directions, revealing his killer.

Lyons.

60.

He stands above me, even taller than before, the microwave bomb just behind him. He's shed most of his clothing, revealing tight coils of muscle stretching across his chest, twitching veins that look like worms under the skin, and sinister grin. The two blades I stabbed into his chest are still there, twin needles in a pin cushion. There's no blood.

His skin is thin, crisscrossed with severe stretch marks. He's growing faster than his human skin can handle. The thin white fabric of his flesh is nearly translucent, revealing the thick red veins just beneath the surface, twitching like ravenous, burrowing leeches.

I realize that Lyons's hungry glare and ongoing transformation should horrify me, but I'm just curious. *What has he done to himself? How can he claim to be fighting for humanity when he is no longer human himself?* Then again, the look in his eyes says he's operating on instinct now. The human intellect and all its machinations and misguided planning are either gone or sitting in the backseat.

Beep, beep, beep. A high-pitched digital chime cuts through the air. It's coming from my watch. The president's deadline has passed. "I need more time!" I shout, looking past Lyons to the slowly undulating matriarch tendrils.

The reply comes as a whisper. "We will wait—on you."

The message is clear. The Dread will stand down until the outcome of this battle is clear, meaning the president will stand down as well. But if I fail . . . if the matriarch and this colony fall, freeing Lyons to wipe out the Dread . . . the world will burn. All of us together, united at last, in the end.

Lyons reaches out for me, and I see his hands for what they've become—long, hooked claws pressed together to form one large curved blade, like a Dread mole's. There are no knuckles remaining, and the red-vein-covered black flesh of a Dread has burst out of the limb, his old skin dangling like that of a molting snake.

I'm about to dive out of the way when he stops short, arcs his back, and screams in pain. A sound like tearing paper fills the air. His chest splits open. Stretch marks give way. The monster inside is emerging.

"What have you done?" I ask, not really expecting an answer.

"To defeat the enemy," Lyons growls, "you must first become them."

It's a butchery of a Sun Tzu quote but reveals that this was, in fact, part of his plan all along. That's how he intended to turn the Dread against themselves. The DNA coursing through his body must have come from a Dread mole. And his plan could work. The Dread crocs aren't attacking him. Whether it's because they see him as one of their own or because he's radiating fear like a melting-down nuclear reactor emits radiation, I don't know. But if he can bend the Dread to his will . . . Fear or not, I *know* that's a scary idea.

But then there's the bomb. He's going to kill himself, too, un-less . . . I glance at the two archways leading out of the chamber. With the countdown surely moving below nine minutes, he might be able to escape. The circular trip back to the surface would take me far too long, but Lyons, with a Dread body, might just make it, especially if he can climb straight out the way I came in.

"I need help," I think, willing the matriarch to hear the words.

But it's Lyons who replies. "I'll be . . . with you . . . in a moment."

I don't know if the matriarch has heard me or not, but it remains silent. Could he already be controlling it, too?

Lyons lets out a roar, turning his head to the ceiling.

Skin explodes away from his body, bursting balloonlike. Gore splatters at his feet. Limbs thicken, claws extend, bright red light pulses hard. The remains of his body splits and falls away, his shed chest carrying away the two trench knives. But the cherry on top of this juicy hemoglobin sundae is what happens to his head.

His roar becomes garbled, and then muffled.

For a moment, I think he's choking, but then small, jointless fin-gers reach out of his mouth. Tendrils. Ten of them. The digits wrap around his face, clinging to his cheeks, digging into the meat. His head bulges. The skull cracks. The tendrils pull. What remains of his voice turns high-pitched as the last of his humanity is torn away and dropped to the floor like yesterday's slop.

When he turns his gaze back toward me, he's transformed. His body is like a bull's: dark, armored, and covered in veins but upright. His face resembles a matriarch's with an arc of five black eyes rising up and over two more and a mass of tendrils, but there is also a mouth beneath all those squirming digits, wide and toothed like a croc's. And that's when I notice the tail now sliding back and forth behind him, a line of short tendrils wriggling over the top of the tail and tracing a line up his back. He didn't just take DNA from *one* Dread, he took bits and pieces of them *all*.

He tries to speak, but it's just a garbled mess.

While he attempts to figure out whether or not he's still got vocal cords, I weigh my two choices. One, stand and fight, maybe win, but get cooked like a bug in a microwave along with the rest of the Dread. Two, snatch and grab the bomb, which is resting atop the unzipped pack Katzman carried it in; run like hell; and see if I can't get it far enough away to spare the colony, knowing that part of New Orleans is still going to cook. Either way, I die. While I would really like to kill Lyons, or die trying, that's not really a viable choice.

I dive forward, straight for Lyons, which is apparently the last thing he expected me to do. And to be honest, I'd barely registered the idea by the time I put it into action. He's tall enough now, perhaps fifteen feet in height, that I am able to duck down and roll between his legs. I come up in a kneeling position next to the bomb, fling the unzipped top over it, yank the zippers up, and leap into a sprint while reaching back for the handle like a relay racer grasping for a baton.

I grip the strap, jerking as the weight of it lifts off the ground. But it's over my shoulder and then on my back by the time I've hit my fifth stride. That also happens to be the moment Lyons figures out where I went and what I'm doing.

I feel the impact of his feet hitting the chamber floor as he gives chase. He's still pushing waves of fear, the energy quivering through me but having no effect. The Dread crocs, however, are scattering, whatever control the matriarch had over them now severed. Even the matriarch is retreating, the long tendrils snaking back, sliding into the earth.

A quick glance over my shoulder reveals that I'm not even going to make it out of the arena before Lyons has pounced on my back. His stride is clumsy as he adjusts to running on all fours, but he's already faster than me, and if he manages to get coordinated . . .

I'm not about to let him escape and destroy the colony, so I decide to turn and face him.

"Keep going," says a whisper.

I nearly respond, but if Lyons can hear me now, any information is too much.

So, against my better judgment and my desire to fight, I run. I can feel him gaining faster now, the impacts of his large, clawed feet echoing through the chamber, now devoid of everything but the dead and dying.

I leap over the corpse of a Dread Squad soldier, plotting a course through the field of bodies lying ahead of me.

But my feet never reach the ground. Sharp talons pierce the armored padding over my shoulders and lift me up. I reach back for Faithful, my only remaining weapon, but quickly realize it's not needed as I rise up far higher than Lyons could reach. I glance up, looking at the underside of a lone mothman, carrying me toward the ceiling, several hundred feet above.

A roar pursues us, but Lyons can't fly.

I watch him turn and charge for the archway. Wherever the mothman takes me, I don't think Lyons will be far behind.

We rise up toward the domed ceiling, which looks honeycombed. There are alcoves, like those belonging to the bulls, but these encircle the ceiling. Several of the alcoves lead outside. We rise up, our ascent slowing, until we've passed through an exit to the outside, near the top of the massive colony. Our descent begins smoothly, but the mothman is tiring—and now I see the wound, a bullet hole in its muscular chest. Two more in its gut. Glowing red plasma pumps steadily from the wounds. This mothman is dying. Pulling me from the colony will likely be its final act.

Twenty feet from the colony roof, the mothman breathes its last. We drop together, striking the roof and rolling down over the edge, landing in the thick sludgy earth separating the structure from the swamp.

I'm out, but Lyons is on his way, and—I unzip the backpack and look at the timer—I have six minutes to get this thing someplace where it won't do any damage. And that's not going to happen in the mirror dimension. Time to go home.

I slip through the world between and back to New Orleans in a blink. I'm in the middle of a road. Tires screech on the pavement as the bumper and grill of a pickup truck stop inches from my face.

"Get out of the road, asshole!" The truck speeds up, forcing me to dive to the side. A second car speeds past. Both are full of people, armed with baseball bats and fire pokers. I see at least two guns and am lucky one of them didn't decide to shoot me or run me over. A third vehicle, one I recognize, speeds up and screeches to a halt.

The SUV's door opens. Cobb runs around to the front of the vehicle, seeing that it's me. "Crazy," he says, using the name he first knew me by, "sorry I left my position, but I saw these people head into the park and—" That's when he *really* sees me. "Damn, man, what happened? Are you okay?"

I get to my feet. "We only have a few minutes."

"Until what?"

I show him the backpack. "This is a microwave bomb."

Cobb's skin goes pale so quickly that I think God must use Photoshop.

"But we have maybe a minute before Lyons shows up."

"Lyons?" Cobb says. "But he's old and—"

"Not anymore."

A distant roar punctuates my statement. Lyons has already reached the top of the colony and is now searching for me, probably moving back and forth between frequencies. I hurry around Cobb. "We need to move!"

A second roar, closer this time. Lyons is closing in. A quick peek into the mirror world reveals as much. He's spotted us in the real world and is charging through the Dread swamp, a quarter mile off, planning on taking us by surprise. We have thirty seconds until his gruesome arrival and another few minutes until the water molecules in our bodies are sped up so fast that we cook from the inside out.

61.

When Lyons arrives, I'm still outside the SUV. Cobb starts to scream, but I shove him inside the vehicle and slam the door. A long-clawed arm swooshes down toward my head. I duck while shifting back into the mirror world. It's just a momentary visit to confuse Lyons. When he pursues me between frequencies, I've already left. Back in the real world, the SUV peels away, Cobb swerving as he fights the wheel and the powerful fear instilled in him by Lyons.

Backpack slung over my shoulder, I run in the opposite direction, heading south. I glance back, expecting to see Lyons right behind me, but he's not there. I switch to double vision, viewing both worlds fully. My mind once again reels from the dual input. I'm seeing and feeling the solid ground beneath my feet, but I'm also seeing four feet of swamp water. My brain is telling me that there should be resistance, but I only see the water and can't feel it. As a headache catches fire behind my eyes, I see Lyons.

The monstrous form of my father-in-law is locked in combat with a Dread croc, that is perhaps just defending its territory or was sent by the matriarch—I don't know. But its interference has bought me time. I don't indulge the hope that the croc will stop Lyons. He's too powerful and wields fear in a way few Dread can match. I don't bother watching the results. Instead, I turn away from the fight and the mirror world, pouring on the speed.

Now that I remember myself, I'm aware of what I can do and the training I've received. I'm a little soft from my time in Safe-Haven, but I know how to push myself to the limit, and I don't worry about pushing myself right on past it. So when I pace myself, it's at a sprint, aiming for the southern end of the park, where a bevy of tourist attractions will help delay what I think could be a losing fight.

My feet slap over pavement, crunch through dirt, and squelch through soggy earth as I make my way through the park. And when an immovable object blocks my path—a tree, fence, or wall—I leap into the mirror world, pass through the obstacle, and land in the real world in time to continue running, undaunted.

A minute later, I feel the first signs of Lyons's pursuit as a ripple of energy. He's broadcasting fear like a radio station, pumping it into the airwaves. The park, aside from the people who nearly ran me over, appears to be empty. But they were just passing through. People are either hiding in their homes or part of a mob, but if anyone is unlucky enough to be in the park, they're going to feel him coming, no doubt spurring future reports of park hauntings. That is, if we're not all cooked in the meantime. The heavy weight of the backpack over my shoulders is a constant reminder of what's at stake.

The second sign of Lyons's closing distance is a constant whispering. It fills my mind, but unlike the incomprehensible Dread language, it's all in English. Despite recognizing the language, I still have trouble making sense of it as words and sentences overlap. What I do know is that it's getting louder and is hard to ignore.

I take a look back into the mirror world, but all I can see is swamp.

The path ahead is thickly wooded in both worlds, so I plow straight through the real world, dodging trees and careening through brush. I nearly plow headlong into a chain-link fence but manage to leap up and pass through it in the mirror world. Upon my return to the real world, I immediately dive forward, soaring over the supine form of Snow White, awaiting her prince. I roll back to my feet, but the concrete walkway I've landed on is unforgiving and reminds me of the punishment my body has endured.

Three sets of wild-looking eyes catch my attention. I spin toward them, expecting an attack, but come face-to-face with human-sized Three Little Pigs. They're dancing gleefully next to their house of brick, the wolf clawing its way out of the chimney. Strangely, stories like this, about hungry stalking wolves, were probably inspired by the Dread. How many fairy tales of trolls, ogres, and spirits were inspired by encounters with the mirror world?

Lyons shimmers into view behind the jolly pigs, swiping two aside and biting the eldest in half. Lyons overtook me and lay in wait, playing the part of the Big Bad Wolf.

"Really?" I say, "You want to do this in Storyland?"

Lyons roars and tosses the oldest pig's eviscerated lower half, striking an oversize Humpty Dumpty. The egg-man's bolts snap;

his hooked cane, which is embedded in the concrete walkway, breaks; and he topples off the wall. But, I'll be damned, he doesn't break. I take it as a good omen, and then run. I'm not ready to face Lyons yet.

The clear walkway and smooth surface allow me to hit my top speed in just a few strides. Lyons is quick to pursue but opts to barrel through the brick house, buying me a few seconds and a fifty-foot head start. Running through a stand of weeping willows, I cut through the thick curtain of Spanish moss and make a hard left.

Lyons dives after me, mole claws outstretched to impale my back, but he can't see me through the moss. He explodes out of the trees, covered in long coils of vegetation. Momentarily blinded, he clips the short stone wall of a fountain and spills forward, sending up a wave of coin-filled water. He tumbles through the water, crushing the fountain and far wall, sending a fresh river over the dry concrete. Then he's up again, shedding moss and lunging after me.

Lyons has the clear physical advantage, but he's not using his human mind to its full potential. He's acting ravenous. Uncontrolled. He's going to catch me eventually, but he's going to destroy all of Storyland first.

I make like Jiminy Cricket, leaping a short fence into the Pinocchio exhibit. Lyons has gained again and is just a few strides away. I charge into the waiting open jaws of a large bright-blue whale, atop which Pinocchio is seated, and leap through its backside by sliding into and out of the mirror world. I continue my flight on the far side of the display's tail, unhindered by the exhibit. A moment later, the whale explodes as Lyons charges into the mouth and out the backside, never shifting frequencies.

The four-foot-tall Pinocchio statue spins through the sky, flipping past me like Mary Lou Retton on fast-forward, and crashes into Little Bo Peep's white sheep. I nearly laugh at the frozen, wide-eyed expression on her painted face. I suspect it had never been appropriate until that very moment.

As I round a carousel and consider running through it, a sharp beeping sound fills the air.

The microwave bomb.

It's time to face Lyons.

I stop and turn around so quickly that it catches Lyons off guard. He flinches and slides to a standstill, fifteen feet between us. We're framed by a unicorn-themed carousel and a pirate ship. Not the most epic of battlegrounds, but I enjoy the juxtaposition.

I hold my wrist up, revealing the beeping watch that I synced with the bomb's timer when I was with Cobb. I reach up and push a button to stop it. "Do you know what that means?"

Dread Lyons's seven black eyes squint. He's still in there somewhere. "It means you've lost." I take the backpack off, unzip it, and dump a tire-repair kit onto the ground. I don't need to tell him that Cobb took the bomb, that he was going to find someplace to contain it or dump it in the ocean, which would reduce the weapon's impact. Either way, the colony would survive. The war he longed for and the vengeance he craved—for the deaths *he* caused—would never come to pass.

Not against the Dread, anyway. The cold gaze in his seven eyes says he'll be satisfied, to some extent, by reducing my body to pulp. The only question remaining is which one of us will take action first? The answer is never really in question. I make my move before the thought finishes.

62.

The handgun hidden among the tire iron, jack, flares, and orange cones is a 9 mm recovered from the SUV. It lacks the punch I'd need to kill Lyons, which is unfortunate, but it's a good start. The weapon comes up in an unflinching two-hand grip.

I pull the trigger. Just once. The black orb on the side of Lyons's head erupts, spewing a mixture of oily white and glowing red fluids.

His head snaps back, his jaw drops open, and tendrils whip the air. A roar warbles over the quiet Storyland walkways. When he's done, he turns the remaining six eyes toward me. I can feel his loathing for me. Like the Dread whispering, it's in my head, wordless, but clear.

And without effect.

My second shot bursts the Dread eye on the left side of his head. He shrieks again, and this time charges blindly, head turned away to protect his remaining eyes. This is it. I can end him right here.

I slip into the mirror world intending to reenter the real world, inside Lyons, just long enough to create a me-sized hole in his chest. Storyland disappears, replaced by a dark, green-veined swamp. With an eye still tuned to the real world, I watch Lyons charge. I visualize my attack, picturing the few simple steps. Eyes closed and breath held, I'll arrive inside his body. Just for a second. Then I'll slip back into the mirror world. Carried by his forward motion, I'll be flung into the swamp, the landing buffered by a foot of water. Simple.

But that's not exactly how it works out. Not even close.

Lyons turns his ugly head forward at that last second, slips fully into the mirror world, and swipes out with one of his big clawed hands. I manage to squeeze off three more rounds before I'm struck, but they just get lodged in the thick armor that is now his forehead.

The one bit of luck is that the curved tip of his long, mole claw misses me. While I'm not impaled or severed in two, the result is close to being lifted off the ground and flung by a rock-solid, over-size lacrosse stick. The impact catches me below the arm. I feel my ribs flex and then break. Three of them. *Snap, snap, snap.* And then I'm doing a repeat performance of Pinocchio's acrobatics, soaring through the air. As I reach the apex of my arc, I've got to make a few choices. Lyons is already chasing after me, so there won't be time to think once I land. He might just kill me, but I suspect he's going to toy with me. I'm a mouse to him now, and, like a cat, he's going to play with me until my body simply gives up.

Luckily for me, I'm a mouse with world-class military training, a killer instinct, and fearless nature. Mind made up, I finish my fall in the Dread world, letting the water soften my landing. I take the hit on my left side, protecting my freshly broken ribs, and waste no time getting to my feet. I've still got one more challenge to over-come before avoiding this immediate danger. Injured and soaked through, I need to jump at least three feet up.

I bend my knees and shove hard, three seconds until Lyons's arrival. The wet earth squishes beneath my feet, absorbing some of my energy. The water clings to my legs, not wanting to let me go. But then I'm free and rising. Two seconds to go. I lift my legs like a frog and, with no time left, return to the real world. Lyons follows and reaches for me but grabs a large plastic horse in-stead.

I land on the carousel floor between a unicorn and Cinder-ella's pumpkin chariot. Lyons is in a slightly more precarious situation. While his right arm is free to move, the rest of him is em-bedded within metal bars, a double set of Pegasus, and the floor of the ride. He wrenches the interfering horse out of the floor and tosses it aside. His free arm swings out, gouging a trough through the floor where I'd been a moment before. Even with my quick backward roll, he nearly catches me.

But now I'm on my feet and he's trapped.

"This could have gone differently," I tell him, reaching over my shoulder. "You were naive when you destroyed the first colony. I can look past that. And we lost nearly everything, you and I." Lyons stops struggling against the carousel. Actually appears to be listen-ing. "But it could have stopped there. It *should* have stopped there. Both sides drew blood, but if we're honest, you and I, and the rest of humanity, have done far more damage. I didn't know fear until a few days ago, but in that short amount of time, I learned that it can be conquered, like any other emotion."

I draw Faithful, feeling stronger with the blade in my hand.

Lyons eyes the weapon but doesn't move. Could he actually be considering what I'm saying? Was there ever a time when he listened—really listened—to me? I'm not sure. But I'm going to give him a chance. For Maya, whose fate is still a mystery, and who is the reason I need to end this.

"I'm going to ask you this only once," I say, stepping closer but still out of reach. "Can you let it go? Can you move past your childhood and loss, forgive your enemy, and move on? Show the Dread that we are better than them. Show them that humanity is more than war and destruction. Show them how to forgive."

I grip the machete tightly, anticipating his reply.

Unfortunately, I don't anticipate exactly how the response will be delivered.

Lyons disappears. It's a blink. A fraction of a second. And when he returns, he's a step closer, driving a hook-clawed hand into my gut like a giant fist. I pitch forward and fall back, gasping for air, but am thankful it wasn't the claws' sharp tip that had made contact.

The carousel spins as Lyons tries to reach me again. But he's locked up once more. Problem is, he already knows how to overcome that problem. When he disappears again, I throw myself away from him, injured but mobile and still wielding Faithful.

When Lyons returns, he's no longer trapped. He's still inside the carousel, but he's standing *on* the floor, not in it. With a savage roar, he follows my path through the ride, destroying unicorns, horses, and fairy-tale creatures with brutal efficiency.

The ride, it seems, is over. One lap around the slowly spinning carousel is all I'm going to get. After that, I'll be slowed by the ruins and he can continue plowing his way through.

I've got no tricks left that he can't match.

So we'll do it the old-fashioned way. Part man to used-to-be man. I step off the carousel, walking calmly, my back to Lyons. When I hear him smash free of the now-ruined ride, I turn around to face him, left hand clutching my side, right hand holding Faithful.

"C'mon then," I say. "Let's get this over with."

He stalks toward me, pausing to shake his head, throwing streams of glowing red from his ruined eyes. I take a quick look around for the pistol. It's gone.

Standing almost casually, I wait for the charge.

When it comes, I'm almost surprised by its quickness.

Almost.

Lyons's primary attack has been swiping at me with those big claws. He repeats the same tactic, or perhaps instinct, once again. I duck beneath the strike, step to the side, and hack down as the lumbering monster that was my father-in-law rumbles past. The chiseled blade tip cuts a gouge in Lyons's flank. It's hardly a mortal blow, but I've severed several of the thick, external veins covering his body. Blood loss will eventually slow him. Emphasis on eventually.

Reacting to the pain of the cut, Lyons brings his rear limb up and kicks out like a horse. Quick reflexes and Lyons's broad foot dispersing the force of the blow over a wider area save me. But the kick is still solid enough to send me sprawling toward my broken ribs. Fear or no fear, the impact will nearly blind me with pain.

I slip into the mirror world. The swamp buffers my landing, sparing my ribs. I'm about to slip back when I realize I'm no longer alone. And it's not Lyons. *Holy shit*, I think as I turn my head in a slow arc. The swampy clearing is surrounded by towering trees, sagging low with twisting black coils. But standing among the trees are hundreds of Dread. Bulls, pugs, mothmen, mammoths, Medusa-hands, and crocs. There are even two of those massive winged centipedes and a cloud of small bats circling the area.

They've come to watch the end of the two men who nearly destroyed their world. We're probably infamous characters to the Dread. Destroyers of colonies. Invaders. I suppose watching the two of us fight—the fearless man versus the Dread man—would be a little bit like watching Osama bin Laden and Hitler go at it.

Not quite, I remind myself. I *did* help save this colony and prevent a war between worlds. So maybe they're just here to cheer me on? Given the way they're all lingering at the clearing's fringe, they're clearly not here to help, though I suspect they might also be here to deal with the winner.

Lyons unknowingly takes advantage of the distraction. He explodes into the mirror world, slams a hooked claw into my shoulder and another into my side. I shout in pain as I'm lifted out of the swamp and slammed back down. Water surges into my mouth as the air is knocked from my lungs. I can't even scream when the hooked claws are yanked free.

I clear my head from the water, coughing and gasping, but am pinned. Lyons is above me, leaning closer. At first I think he's going to simply bite my face off with those snapping jaws, but then I note the tendrils writhing on his face. With those, he can enter my mind.

He can make me afraid.

He can erase my memory again.

It's a fate worse than death.

I'm about to use my last seconds to cuss him out when a voice shouts out, bold and strong. "Father!"

Lyons pauses. Glances up.

I follow his gaze, seeing Maya upside down. She's a mess and physically afraid, but I haven't seen this stern look in her eyes since before Simon died. She wades through the muck and water. Raises a finger at the monster she knows is her father. "You let my husband go."

For a moment, Lyons appears to consider her demand, but then his eyes squint. He roars at Maya in a way that says, *you're next*. It's all the motivation I need.

I slip into the real world, somersault forward, and stand.

It takes just a second, but I'm now in a race. If Lyons chases me and enters this world while I'm still here, he'll erase me. But if I move first . . . I shift back into the mirror world and miss my mark. I had intended to emerge inside Lyons, to replace his insides with myself. But he's stepped forward, and I've come up behind him, weaponless.

Technically, I've been trained to be a weapon, but that was against people, not . . . whatever Lyons has become. My best chance of stopping him was punching a hole in his body by slipping through dimensions. But now . . .

My eyes widen. I still have one weapon—the assassin's best friend, hidden in a pocket all this time, waiting for its deadly potential to be released.

Lyons swipes at me with his tail, but I'm already leaping for his back. The appendage sweeps beneath my feet. I land on his hard back, grunting as my ribs are bent inward. I manage to cling to the protective plates covering him and use my newfound strength to hoist myself higher. Lyons reaches for me, twisting his arms back, but his bulky muscles lack the flexibility. He spins and roars, reaching, clawing. I climb over his back, sliding up over the line of mammoth tendrils covering his spine, and stop at his plated shoulder blades.

In range of my target, I prepare myself for what will be one of the most basic, while at the same time complex, attacks I have ever performed. Step 1 is old-school, and I handle it with practiced fluidity. Holding on to Lyons's back with one hand, I reach into my pocket with the other, gripping the oscillium handle of the coiled garrote. I pull the line from my pocket, leap higher, and swing the line downward. As my jump reaches its pinnacle, the second handle swings down and around Lyons's neck. I pluck it from the air with my free hand—and drop. Pulling the line tight with all of my weight and strength around Lyons's neck.

Now comes the hard part.

While oscillium can reside in one frequency of reality, or all frequencies simultaneously, biological creatures—human and Dread—reside in one dimension at a time. And right now, the garrote resides in whichever frequency I am in, coming along for the ride. While I've been able to look into both dimensions at once, I simply changed the perception of one eye. What I need to do now is different, because in a second Lyons is going to slip back into the real world, and I need to keep my weight on the line. So I shift part of me and then all of me, not between frequencies, but into *all* frequencies: A, B, and B flat. The garrote matches my multifrequency state.

White-hot agony tears through my body and mind, but I never relinquish my grip. Lyons's roar becomes a choked gurgle, and he shifts back to the real world.

But I'm already there, pulling on him.

He goes back to the Dread world, where I still exist, having never left. I physically and mentally experience all frequencies of human and Dread realities. The sensation is nearly overwhelming, but there is also a kind of energy in the place, painful but powerful, and it sees me through until Lyons's body quivers and buckles.

He falls to his knees, landing in the Dread swamp. Still, I cling and pull. The oscillium wire slips through Lyons's flesh, cutting through veins, sinews, vocal cords, and larynx. The life goes out of him and the monster tumbles back, falling toward the water with me on his back.

I leave the mirror world behind and am flung back onto the concrete walkway, eyes still trained on all frequencies. I watch as Lyons topples over, falling through me to land, with a splash, in the Dread swamp. Glowing red blood seeps from his ruined neck, pluming out into the dark water. I get to my feet, watching both worlds as Maya falls to her knees, hand to her mouth, weeping for the monster that raised her.

I walk over the solid Storyland pavement, finding Faithful, which I stop to pick up and sheath on my back. Then I step up to Maya, the woman I forgot, betrayed, remembered, and never really stopped loving, and fall to my knees. When I slip back into the mirror world, she flinches back in surprise, but I don't see fear in her eyes. Is that what they did to her? Did they make her like me?

"You're not afraid?" I ask.

"Of you? Never." She falls forward, wrapping her arms around me. We stay there, immersed in the swamp of a mirror dimension, holding each other for several minutes.

"It wasn't your fault," I say, jumping straight to the crux of that matter that took her from me.

"I know," she says, squeezing me harder, which still isn't very hard. Suddenly aware of her fragile state, not to mention the fact that I'm probably bleeding out, I take one last look around.

The Dread watch us with quiet fascination.

"Are we done?" I ask, the question as much about me and Maya as the rest of the world on the brink of annihilation.

When I get no response or even a quizzical look, I shout the words, sending a burst of fear in all directions—except Maya's. "Are we done!"

The reply comes as a whisper in my mind. "It is finished."

I sag in Maya's arms. "Love you."

By the time she replies, we're kneeling on the concrete walkway of Storyland, breathing ammonia-free air in a world freed from dread.

EPILOGUE

Cobb found us ten minutes later. He'd managed to get the mircro-wave bomb to a bank. Once he revealed he was carrying a bomb that would cook everyone and everything within a mile unless it was contained inside something metal and grounded, the manager let him put it inside the vault. Under normal circumstances, I doubt the manager would have believed the story, but the whole world was hopped up on fear. Cobb saved the city and helped save the world without ever setting foot in the mirror world, which is fine by him. We've remained friends, but he wanted no part in what I'm up to today.

Maya, on the other hand, stands by my side, hidden in the woods of New Hampshire. She's been eating well over the past month. Recovering, body and soul. My body is recovering, too. I required a blood transfusion, which nearly didn't come in time, thanks to all the violence ravaging supplies. But there was an outpouring of goodwill following the cease-fire of Dread fear, and I pulled through. And now I'm not even sore. Whatever part of me is Dread still heals fast. At least physically. Despite the return of my memory and fearless nature, there are things I would like to forget. Things I've done and that I've endured.

Mostly things I've done. I can justify them, sure. I was one of the good guys, preventing terrorism or international organized crime. But the truth is that I don't know. Being fearless means not being afraid to carry out orders. There's no way to know if someone took advantage of that. I take solace in the knowledge that I saved the world.

Two worlds.

Things have been good between Maya and me. Rough, but good. A lot of the rough has to do with my unfettered honesty. I say what I think. But it also leaves no doubt about my honesty, and when I tell her I love her, she believes me. We've talked a lot. About Simon's death. About her father's quest for vengeance. About Winters. To my surprise, she understood and forgave me. Life will never be in short supply of painful memories, but we're moving forward. Together. And that's a gift. I thought I'd lost her forever.

And we're not the only ones healing. The heavy blanket of fear driving people to the streets and nations to the brink of war has lifted worldwide. I've gone over the timing and, as best as I can figure it, the Dread removed its influence from humanity, worldwide, when the matriarch spoke the words, "It is finished."

While I'm sure people are still getting the chills when they pass a Dread, I don't think the mirror world will be poking the human race anytime soon. We might not have the natural ability to move between worlds yet, but humanity is no longer a slave to the slow machinations of evolution. Technology allows us to do things we're not quite ready for and don't fully understand. Maybe we'll be ready to play nice with the Dread someday—they'll need a different name—but until then, I'm going to do what I can to slow the process.

"They're everywhere," Maya says, lowering the binoculars.

We're looking at the outside of the Neuro building. The branch of the CIA that supported Lyons's quiet war has descended on the facility. Where there was once a collection of black and gray vehicles in the parking lot, they're all just black now. I look for a splash of orange, remembering Winters's sacrifice, and a little bit more.

I take the binoculars from Maya and scan the area. There's plenty of security. Far more than before. But the building is still being repaired. There are chinks in the armor. All I really need to do is get beyond the damn electrified fence, which still exists in both worlds.

I stand from my crouched position, ready to make my move.

"Are you sure you need to do this?" Maya asks.

"Everything is in there," I say. "I don't think the Dread will be so merciful a second time around."

"Let the boy go," Allenby says from my other side. Her poofy hair is tied back. The look in her eyes says she'd like to do this herself. She's been by our side since we returned to the airport, bloodied but alive. We've been staying in the home she'd lived in with Hugh, the home she couldn't bring herself to sell, just fifteen minutes from Neuro. "He might not be able to stop the demons haunting our souls, but he can at least remove them from this world."

Allenby, like me, was more deeply involved in Neuro. She feels the weight of what happened and is determined to prevent it from happening again. Today was her idea. I only hope I can do what she's asked.

Maya sighs, gives me a sheepish smile, and kisses my cheek. "Be careful."

"Have no fear," I say and slip into the mirror world. Hand on Faithful, which is sheathed on my back, I scour the surrounding area. Not a living Dread in sight. There are plenty of dead, though, corpses from my encounter with the local matriarch. Her flesh has fallen away, leaving a large skeleton rising up the side of the oscillium building.

Thanks to the mirror world's disregard for the landscaping of men, I quickly find a tree with long, sweeping branches. I climb up slowly, trying not to break the veins covering the tree, but failing. I'm still not sure how this world works, but my best guess is that the Dread and this world are interconnected: all part of one big ecosystem, driven by fluid veins rather than the cycle of decay and rebirth that governs what I still think of as the real world, despite all frequencies of reality being equally real.

I slide down the branch. It bends under my weight but keeps me above the buzzing fence and deposits me gently on the other side. I lie on the ground, facing the woods, and slip out of the mirror world long enough to give Maya and Allenby a wave and let them know I am past the fence.

Free of interference, I run through the mirror-world swamp toward Neuro's oscillium shell. I pause at the bottom, considering what I'm about to do. It's a desecration of the dead, but maybe the Dread won't see it that way? I have no way to find out, and I don't think any of them are around to see this anyway. Stepping inside the matriarch's remains, I scale the side of the building, using her ribs and spine for hand and footholds. At the top, I turn toward the monster's massive skull. The tendrils are gone. The eye sockets empty. But the holes in its skull, created by the 20 mm rounds I fired, remain. I say my apologies and head on my way.

The ruined elevator shaft grants me entrance beyond the oscillium shield, and I quickly make my way inside the building, moving through the interior while in the world between. With my memory returned, I have no trouble locating the nearest security room. There's one on every floor. Looking into both worlds, I keep watch on the security guard seated in front of a group of monitors. The screens are alive with movement. Rooms are crowded as scientists, analysts, and men in black suits comb through and inventory everything. It's possible some of it has already been moved off-site, especially the data. There's nothing I can do about that, but I can stop them from getting any further.

Standing behind the guard, I send a pulse of fear into him. He twitches, looks around the small room, and writes it off. I give him a second, more powerful dose. He gets to his feet. Reaches for his gun—standard-issue. No oscillium. These guys have no idea what they're up against yet.

I slip between worlds just long enough to brush my fingers against the back of his neck. He shouts out, spins around, and aims his gun. Nearly fires the thing at the empty wall. I send a wave of fear into him so strong that he nearly pisses himself.

That gets him moving. As soon as he's out the door and no doubt headed to the bathroom, I materialize inside the security room and access the computer. Memory intact, I have no trouble finding my way through the protocols until I find what I'm looking for. There are a number of different alarms that can go off in this building. Fire. Intruder. Chemical accident. I choose the alarm that should get everyone moving. Biohazard. All levels.

The blaring siren sends people running for the doors. In two minutes flat, the building disgorges its living contents into the parking lot. I head out through the roof and take the express route down, sliding over the smooth surface. This is the last time I'll make that descent.

While the military guards round everyone up, I overhear some of the suits confirming that the building is empty and the arrival of a biohazard team imminent. But they're not going to have time to discover the false alarm. I stare at the parking lot full of people and send out a wave of fear. They step back as one, no doubt thinking about the possibility of biocontamination. I give them a second dose until they're thirty feet back and so afraid that I'm positive no one is going to suddenly get the urge to run back inside.

Then I put my hands on the outside of the building and give them the show of their lives.

The building is big. Massive. But it's partly constructed of oscillium, and I throw myself into the task without fear of failing. I can feel the oscillium, eager to obey, and then I feel the physical matter of this frequency, less willing but unable to resist. I've grown stronger over the past month and have been experimenting with my abilities. I am fully human. Fully Dread. And I can do more than either race can separately. I shift between frequencies, and the building, along with everything in it, follows me into the mirror world. One moment it's in the real world; the next, it's gone, disappeared, and all of Lyons's legacy with it. I turn around, still viewing both worlds, and smile at the astonished faces staring openmouthed at the large, empty foundation.

"Boo," I whisper, and give them a push that sends them running.

Sending a building between worlds and then making a crowd of government employees collectively shit themselves is bound to draw attention. But without Lyons's knowledge, they're going to be grasping at straws until this becomes just another unexplained mystery. It's a little much, I know, but I'm still a little bit Crazy with a capital *C*. Always have been.

While the crowd retreats from empty space, I turn back to the now-empty Neuro building. It's a pock on this world and will probably be an unwelcome remembrance of the time humanity almost destroyed them. Lyons's legacy shouldn't be remembered in either dimension.

I place my hand on the oscillium surface and focus my mind beyond reality, beyond the Dread, to a place among places that even the Dread do not know. I'm not sure if Lyons ever thought beyond the mirror world and truly considered the big picture of string theory. The mirror isn't a flat surface. It's a prism, duplicating and bending frequencies of reality like a reflection in a fun house.

I slip between variations of frequencies, enjoying the show of flickering realities and the strange beings and civilizations that populate our world. I find one that's devoid of life, barren and cold. I remove my hand from the oscillium surface as something like snow begins to collect on its surface. I wait and watch as the surface is quickly concealed, just another white peak among a thousand others, hidden forever from humanity—and whatever other intelligences might lurk just beyond the perceptions of man.

Allenby's analogy to musical notes was accurate, but limited. A, B, and B flat are just the beginning, or perhaps the middle, of a range of frequencies as vast as the cosmos, all peacefully coexisting on our small shared planet. When I listen, really listen, to all the frequencies, it's like music. There's melody in the quantum strings. I imagine the barely avoided war between human and Dread frequencies as a sour note, one that could have sent shock waves through other frequencies. So now I'm on guard, listening and watching to frequencies only I can experience. And if some-one—or something—disrupts the harmony again, I'll have no fear of being Crazy.